Praise for *What T*

"Morrissey stands out for her descriptive powers, her wonderful turns of phrase and the inner complexities of her characters ... she writes of the Newfoundland landscape with the lyricism of a poet ... Sometimes a reviewer wants to tell readers everything about a book, about all the layers of complexity, all the beauties and grace, all the revelations, but I'll restrain my enthusiasm in this case and conclude by saying: Read this book."
—Lewis DeSoto, *The Globe and Mail*

"A compassionate, insightful and gripping look at a family dragged through changing times ... grief is so movingly presented that readers will feel it as their own."
—*Winnipeg Free Press*

"As the plot ratchets up, a harrowing midway ride that has us strapped in our seats, Morrissey reveals the beauty and the terror of two economic realities, worlds apart from us and from each other."
—*Toronto Star*

"Morrissey's sentences always surprise and, like salted food, keep you wanting more ... At once a sparkling gift from Newfoundland."
—*Alberta Views*

"Told with [Morrissey's] familiar firecracker prose and gift for drenching her readers in the sights, sounds, and textures of her settings."
—*Quill & Quire*

"*What They Wanted* is Morrissey's wisest, strongest, and most assured novel to date and it is classic Morrissey. She creates words and images that are dazzling in their originality. The novel pounds with the sound of the sea and the incessant noise of the machines and jimmies that suck the oil out of the depths of Alberta. The last third of the novel is transcendent."

—*The Chronicle Herald* (Halifax)

novel reinforces Donna Morrissey's reputation as a gifted writer and storyteller. It is rich with descriptive metaphors and dialogue and it is as heartwarming as it is heartbreaking."

—*Atlantic Books Today*

"Morrissey is also an unapologetically emotional writer, and she succeeds at conveying the moods of men and women caught in a heartbreaking bind between what they want and what they need … Like [Thomas] Hardy, Morrissey writes with an intimate knowledge of the punishing rawness of her setting as well as her characters' dreams and disappointments."

—*The Gazette* (Montreal)

"[Morrissey] brings a passionate intelligence to the Canadian literary scene."

—*The Vancouver Sun*

"*What They Wanted* is a moving portrayal of a family and a way of life in crisis. Its poignancy in both story and expression will be remembered long after the last page is turned."

—*Edmonton Journal*

"Morrissey's depiction of Sylvie's agony when tragedy descends is the most moving description of shocked grief I have ever encountered. Equally wrenching is Adelaide's act of confession, by which she delivers her daughter from that dark night. I leave this novel caring about these characters as if they had entered my own life, and hoping—as the last pages hint—to meet them again. Morrissey has an authentic gift not only for creating characters who live off the page, but also for bringing alive the sweep of time and fortune that is bigger than any of us. These forces are not only history and material circumstance, but also the human bonds that, in a tangled and imperfect way, shape our spiritual destiny."

—*Literary Review of Canada*

"The action on the rig is brutal, complex, highly informed, and utterly compelling and it resolves itself in a finely written piece of industrial nightmare and something of a family reconciliation … A heartfelt picture of one family's loss and the few gains such sacrifices attain."

—*The StarPhoenix* (Saskatoon)

"With rich lyrical language and her distinct voice, Donna Morrissey draws us once again into the beauty, pain, loves, and wrenching losses of her characters. *What They Wanted* is both an extended poem and a gripping tale of a brother and a sister and their journey from their beloved Newfoundland shores into the chaotic and threatening oil fields of Alberta. The world to which we are given entry here was entirely unfamiliar to me before I read Donna Morrissey's fiction; now it is a part of me."

—Edeet Ravel, author of
Your Sad Eyes and Unforgettable Mouth

Praise for Donna Morrissey

"Donna Morrissey is terrific, an absolute original."
—David Adams Richards, author of *The Lost Highway*
and *The Friends of Meager Fortune*

"There's a sense in Morrissey's writing that William Faulkner has met Annie Proulx … If her first novel [*Kit's Law*] is anything to go by, Morrissey is almost certain to set new boundaries in fiction in Canada."

—*Atlantic Books Today*

"Morrissey's voice, innocent, wise, funny and boisterous, and so expertly tuned to the music of the Newfoundland dialect, is simply irresistible."

—*Books in Canada*

"Donna Morrissey is a wonderfully gifted writer. The setting of her books is Newfoundland, but their appeal is universal. She unashamedly cares for her characters and sees them as real people with real lives worth caring and reading about. To read one of her books is to wind up laughing or crying or somehow doing both at once."
—Wayne Johnston, author of *The Custodian of Paradise*

"A Newfoundland Thomas Hardy."
—*The Globe and Mail*

"Dazzlingly authentic. Both physical and emotional landscapes are charted with exquisite care."
—Alistair MacLeod, author of *No Great Mischief*

"Morrissey knows of what she writes."
—*Toronto Star*

"Comparisons to Annie Proulx are inevitable, but *Kit's Law* exists in a valley of its own saying, and in the directness of its tone, establishes its own authority."
—Thomas Keneally, author of *Schindler's List*

"Perhaps Morrissey's greatest asset as a writer is that ring of truth. From the verisimilitude with which she depicts life in the outports to the note-perfect dialogue to the rich and colloquial narrative voice, Morrissey rarely falters."
—*Quill & Quire*

PENGUIN CANADA

WHAT THEY WANTED

DONNA MORRISSEY is the award-winning author of four novels, *Kit's Law, Downhill Chance, Sylvanus Now*, and *What They Wanted*, all set in Newfoundland and all subsequently translated into several languages. *Kit's Law* won the CBA Libris Award, the Winifred Holtby Prize, and the American Library Association's Alex Award. Both *Downhill Chance* and *Sylvanus Now* won the Thomas Head Raddall Atlantic Fiction Prize, and *Sylvanus Now* was the winner of the Atlantic Independent Booksellers Choice Award. Her screenplay, *Clothesline Patch*, won a Gemini Award. Morrissey grew up in The Beaches, a small fishing outport in Newfoundland, and now lives in Halifax.

ALSO BY DONNA MORRISSEY

Kit's Law

Downhill Chance

Sylvanus Now

DONNA MORRISSEY

What They Wanted

CHAMPLAIN COLLEGE

PENGUIN
CANADA

PENGUIN CANADA

Published by the Penguin Group

Penguin Group (Canada), 90 Eglinton Avenue East, Suite 700, Toronto, Ontario, Canada M4P 2Y3
(a division of Pearson Canada Inc.)

Penguin Group (USA) Inc., 375 Hudson Street, New York, New York 10014, U.S.A.
Penguin Books Ltd, 80 Strand, London WC2R 0RL, England
Penguin Ireland, 25 St Stephen's Green, Dublin 2, Ireland (a division of Penguin Books Ltd)
Penguin Group (Australia), 250 Camberwell Road, Camberwell, Victoria 3124, Australia
(a division of Pearson Australia Group Pty Ltd)
Penguin Books India Pvt Ltd, 11 Community Centre, Panchsheel Park, New Delhi – 110 017, India
Penguin Group (NZ), 67 Apollo Drive, Rosedale, North Shore 0745, Auckland, New Zealand
(a division of Pearson New Zealand Ltd)
Penguin Books (South Africa) (Pty) Ltd, 24 Sturdee Avenue, Rosebank, Johannesburg 2196, South Africa

Penguin Books Ltd, Registered Offices: 80 Strand, London WC2R 0RL, England

First published in Viking Canada hardcover by Penguin Group (Canada),
a division of Pearson Canada Inc., 2008
Published in this edition, 2009

1 2 3 4 5 6 7 8 9 10 (WEB)

Manufactured in Canada.

LIBRARY AND ARCHIVES CANADA CATALOGUING IN PUBLICATION

Morrissey, Donna, 1956–
What they wanted / Donna Morrissey.

ISBN 978-0-14-301427-0

I. Title.

PS8576.O74164W43 2009   C813'.54   C2009-903398-4

Visit the Penguin Group (Canada) website at **www.penguin.ca**

Special and corporate bulk purchase rates available; please see
www.penguin.ca/corporatesales or call 1-800-810-3104, ext. 477 or 474

For our beloved brother, Ford

THE HOPE OF HEAVEN
DEVASTATES EARTH
AND YET
LIKE CATS
WE CARRY WITHIN US
KNOWLEDGE
OF THE WAY HOME.

———————

David Weale

PROLOGUE

I REMEMBER CLEAR AS YESTERDAY those last days in Cooney Arm, the sea dying around us and taking Father's spirit with it. And my, but he had fought. Long after his brothers and the others left he'd stayed, netting cod, netting salmon, spearing flatfish, hauling crab-pots, trapping eels and rabbits, hunting seals and turrs and bull birds, and landing capelin and squid and all else the sea hove at him.

Then the ocean gave no more.

For months we all watched him—me, Mother, Chris, Kyle, Gran. We watched as he sat at the table looking out to sea, his head turned from Mother's hands as she fussed with his tea and biscuits and scolded him about distressing his poor old mother, Gran, who was forever standing on her stoop watching over him as he rotted within himself, along with his stage and his flakes and his boat. But it wasn't just Gran who Mother was worrying about. It was always Mother's job to worry the most, and for months she'd been lamenting Father's fate, lamenting her own need of wanting him out of this darkness, this terrible, terrible darkness he was sinking into, wanting him back in his boat with the sun colouring his face and the wind brimming his eyes and that awful, awful smell of sickness washed off him. But the fish were gone, sucked into the bowels of a thousand foreign factory ships, leaving Father, and a few other struggling inshore fishermen, sitting weighted at their kitchen tables, staring out the window at their languishing boats.

Finally the morning came when Mother threw down her dishcloth, clasped his chin in her hand and lifted it, the stark blue of her eyes staring into the pits of his, and spoke.

"You done your best and now it's time to go. It's for the children now, not us. We've beggared enough from the land, and we can't pawn bones." Leaving him staring after her, she marched across the footbridge spanning the brook, stopped to pluck a handful of daisies from the meadow, and went straight-away to her three little dears sleeping in the graveyard. After spreading the daisies on top of their beds she sat for a moment, brushing away bits of broken seashells dropped by the gulls and tracing a finger across the names scrolled across the centre of each of their crosses. I had trailed behind her, watched her lips move in silent prayer. She left the graves after a short while and went to Gran, who was standing on her stoop, worrying. Putting her arms around Gran's bony, shrunken shoulders, Mother spoke softly, pressed her cheek against the old woman's, and then started back towards her house.

She didn't seem to notice me trailing behind her. Most times she hated my trailing behind, and would chase me off. She didn't seem to notice anything now as she walked briskly towards the house, her step filled with purpose. Once inside, and without a glance at any of us watching, she stood on her rocker and stripped the curtains off her beloved window overlooking the cliffs and the sea pounding through the neck. She faltered then, as though she'd bared herself in public, and held the curtains to her breasts, tears running down the round of her cheek.

I remember Chris pressing against me, his body trembling. I remember trembling too at this sight of Mother, as well as

Father, faltering, for in that moment I saw how that which contained me could be broken.

The following three days were the most unsettling I'd ever gone through. Taking care of Kyle, who was just a toddler, I watched as Mother packed—first her own house, and then Gran's. On the fourth day, when all was battened and bundled, Father came in from his woodshed with a chainsaw.

I'd never felt so frightened as in that moment when he pulled the rip cord and the thing screamed to life there in the small confines of the kitchen. Instantly he shut it off, seeing the fear in my eyes.

"It has to be halved," he explained. "We're leaving, see, and we're taking our house with us. The house has to be sawed in half so's it'll float through the channel of the neck. See? The neck's too narrow to float a house through. That's all. We'll put her back together fast as anything. Go on outside now, take your brothers outside."

We all fell back, choking the doorway, as he hauled on the cord again and started the chainsaw roaring. With a fire burning in his eyes he squinted through the blue gas filling the room, gunned the trigger, and stuck the blade against the outside of his bedroom wall, cringing as it ripped through plaster and splintering wood.

Chris started crying. Mother picked up Kyle and herded us outside. From across the footbridge and through the leaky windows inside Gran's house we sat through the day, watching as he sawed. Periodically he'd shut off the saw and come outside, dragging eight-foot logs that he'd cut for firewood back inside the house.

"He's shoring up the roof," Mother told us, "shoring up the roof so's the house won't fold in on itself."

Well into the evening Father worked. I scarcely moved from the window, watching the flickering white light of the lantern following him through the house. Come morning the house was perfectly halved and he'd gone in boat to Ragged Rock, where Mother was from. Mid-noon he was back with two thirty-foot skiffs, a dozen men, and two dozen steel drums to use as floaters. For two more days we watched as the men jacked up each half of the house, hooked a block and tackle to a dead man, and launched each section of the halved house over a series of wet logs laid out side by side and down to the water. Once both halves were standing on the beach the men roped them each to a ring of oil drums, then to the motor boats, and started floating them across the short distance of the arm, through the narrow channel of the neck, and out into the open waters of the bay.

The moment the two halves of the house hit the water I raced back to Gran's house, for, due to an illness of Mother's, it was Gran who mostly raised me, and her house I lived in till the day we moved from Cooney Arm. I stood sickened inside the doorway, looking wildly around the kitchen, at the warm old couch by the stove, my fingerprints smeared onto every conceivable surface looking back at me. Gran crept to my side and I held on to her hand, sickened further by Gran's face looking more greyish and grained than the weather-beaten door we were leaning against. We wouldn't be needing any of Gran's things now, our things. We'd be living with Mother, in Mother's house. I broke down crying. Never had the old couch and creaky table felt so dear. Never had Mother looked so tall and far removed from me as she stood on the shore helping Chris and Kyle into the boat.

"Be sure it holds tight," cried Gran as Father closed her front door, latching it securely against the wind. Father cradled Gran's shoulders, for he knew that her joy in her house matched the joy he felt in his own, that they had both built and moulded their homes around themselves, each nail hammered and puttied with pride.

"You'll be back. Soon as the ground thaws, you'll be back for your gardening," he promised as he walked her to the boat.

"But they'll have burnt it," cried Gran, "like they done the houses in Little Trite, the government will burn it."

"Nay, we're no longer sure about that. Might've been the Trapps that burned their own houses. Hard to tell what's truth these days. Besides that, we took no money. We're no part of their gawd-damned resettlement bullshit. This will always be ours to come back to. Hey, Doll?" he said to me, and capped his big hand around the crown of my head in a comforting gesture. "You sit with Gran now, we're gonna have a fine time of it tonight putting our house back together." He smiled, rubbing my head and knotting my hair, then lifted me into the boat where Mother and Chris and Kyle were already waiting. Lastly he lifted in Gran, and leaning his shoulder to the bow, shoved off the boat and leapt aboard himself.

Gran collapsed beside me on the thwart as we bobbed offshore, her eyes mired onto her house, its windows shuttered with dirty, broken pickets from her yard—excepting the window by her rocker in the kitchen. That window remained unshuttered, the curtain pulled aside as though she were still sitting there, in her rocker, looking out. She leaned against me, whimpering, "Least he can still sit and watch when he comes agin," and dabbed her eyes with a crumpled bit of cotton as she wept for her man whose soul was still restless in the sea that took him near on fifty years before, and who sometimes came ashore when winter storms riled the ocean, stirring him from his watery grave. Silent, a waft of air, he'd drift through the door and sit in her rocker, creaking his way through the

night, leaving naught but a few drops of water on her floor
come morning to mark his coming and goings.

I wept too. Not over poor old Grandfather Now who I'd
never known, but over my father and his silent cries as he
stood at the bow of his boat, looking back over the meadow
where a fortnight ago his own house had been and where now
was gouged earth and a spattering of black stumps like
tombstones over a fresh-dug grave.

Once we'd motored out through the neck we turned
towards the open waters, watching quietly as the two halves of
the house floated before us. Forty miles up and the bay ended
in a wide basin with a small outport, Hampden, sloping from
its centre. To the right of the outport was a cliff jutting into the
water, and it was to the other side of this cliff that Father steered
us and our split-apart house. Nothing stood there except an
abandoned, salt-bitten wharf and a large sandbar a little farther
up from a river piling into the sea. A crane from a nearby log
boom stood waiting on the wharf, and within a relatively short
time the two halves of the house were hoisted off the steel
drums and sitting on top of the wharf looking like one again.

Then, surprisingly, in a moment I shall never forget, Father
looked to Mother, his dark thatch of brows curling over his
eyes, and grunted, "This is as far as she goes. By jeezes, if I can't
work on the sea, I'll sleep on it. No gawd-damned mortal
telling me where I sleeps."

Mother blinked with astonishment. But then, when she
understood what he meant, that he intended for the house
to remain there, its back squished against the cliff and
wooded hillside behind it and her front step to be the wharf
itself, she wagged a finger of warning in his face and hissed,
"If a youngster falls over and drowns it'll be on your soul,
not mine."

They looked away from each other then, but I looked to them both, a knowing stirring deep within me that the morsels for my well-being were stowed within my mother's larder, and the key to its lock was in my father's hand.

ONE

T HE WHITE OF THE ICE-CHINKED BAY glimpsed through
breaches in the trees, the coldness of its breath already on
my face. The road veered to the left and then the bay opened
wide before me, miles of pan ice glaring white beneath the sun
and so tightly pummelled into the basin that it buckled
upward, forming ridges some ten, twenty feet high in places.
Hummocks they called these ridges, and scattered amongst
them were the loftier heights of trapped icebergs, their wind-
polished peaks sparkling like opals.

I fumbled for the handle on the rented car and tightened
the window, hating the harsh coldness of the ice, hating how
it crunched up over the beach, wedging against the roadside
and near cramming the car against the black wall of rock to the
right of the road. After a year on the gently contouring lands
of Alberta, the Newfoundland coastline felt more rugged,
harsh. Cutting around a sharp turn, I geared down, straining
across the seat for a closer look at Father's woodshed, the plaid
bush jacket belonging to my younger brother Chris left lying
on a pile of unsplit wood, the axe flung aside as though a call
had sounded.

The car almost stalled, then jolted ahead the last few yards,
rolling to a stop as the road ended on a sagging grey wharf that
jutted thirty or forty feet to its left, into the sea. Encumbering
the right side of the wharf, and wedged into the cliff behind
it, was the house Father had floated forty miles up the bay

from our old homestead in Cooney Arm. Sitting in his favourite spot, slouched against the side of the house with his feet dangling over the wharf, was Chris. He wasn't sketching seals or humpbacks on this day, or paring birds out of wood, lips pursed in a melodic whistle as he plied and coaxed his knife around the curve of a wing or a beak; instead he was staring moodily out over the ice, his slumped shoulders carrying the forlorn look of a forgotten child.

I knew that look. Had seen it all through our growing up years, each springtime when Gran would take me back to Cooney Arm and leave Chris bawling on the wharf, reaching after us. For he too yearned for that old homestead where he would cling to my hand as I dragged him amongst the barred-up houses and wooden shacks of the small abandoned outport, answering his growing stream of questions of why God, why fish, why rain. Since the day Father gave in to the emptied fishing grounds and wrenched his house from those blessed shores we had often stood, staring back the way we'd come, longing for those huge fat days of summer with the wind sweeping sweetly over the finches and the meadow and the three little dears sleeping in the graveyard. And too, there were worlds in those barred-up houses in Cooney Arm, worlds hidden amongst the emptied bedrooms and drawers, whose voices remained locked into the wood as though awaiting the souls that once were to come back and reclaim them.

"Bloody governments," Father told us, "is why the people were forced to move, gawd-damned arse-up governments, screwing up the fishery and forcing people to move in search of work."

Yet, despite Chris's thirst to return to Cooney Arm, he balked that first summer when Gran and I were readying ourselves in the boat, going back to plant Gran's garden. One hand clinging to Mother's, the other reaching for mine, he stood, his mouth quivering with both want and fear. Mother's skirts he chose, and his tears wet his face as he peered out from behind them, watching the boat leaving without him. Come fall, day before school when Gran and I returned, the boat brimming to the gunnels with spuds, turnips, carrots, and cabbages, he was sitting on that very spot, back to the wall, legs dangling over the wharf. Piles of shavings from his carvings floated towards us on the water as he held out long, slender arms to Gran, sobbing as he told her of his many dreams, one in which the moon swallowed her house whilst she turned to water inside.

"Poor boy," said Gran, holding him to her. "Poor, poor boy." Tears crept from her eyes as he proudly presented her with three small drawings, astonishing her with his flair of lines. The first depicted her crouching in her garden, snipping turnip greens, her knees embedded in the earth. The second showed her with a broom made of cabbage leaves, sweeping her garden free of caterpillars. The third had her kneeling beside a potato bed, her knees again embedded in the earth, her hands curled in prayer, her hair loosened and swept into a cloud of wind. "My, my," she kept saying, "my, my" as she gazed at her broom made of leaves, her hair swept into a cloud, "my, my." And yet it was his manner of drawing that so touched her, his faint, wispy lines so effectively capturing her likeness yet barely discernible on the paper in places, and so easily erased by the slightest smudge of a thumbprint that she held her breath whilst others examined them for fear of being erased herself.

As he grew so did his drawings, his lines lengthening with his limbs and enveloping his pages, his images becoming more and more dreamlike as he sprawled across the table, the wharf, beach rocks, the woodpile, sketching the abandoned houses of Cooney Arm and their spirits swarming through their windows, Father's decrepit stage sitting before two moons, me floating laughingly in the curl of a hurtling wave, Mother billowing out sheets that fluttered into clouds. Always his images appeared wispy, airy, as though seen through a mesh, a veil of light. And always there was no beginning or ending, each image arising from nowhere and fading into nothing, and all in between a swirl of lines appearing to be one, as in a spool of thread unravelling itself into thought.

He rose now as I stepped out of the car, softly calling his name. He was two years younger than me, yet taller, his eyes the same glistening brown as Father's, his hair the same thickness and coarseness, but fair and full of light whereas Father's hung darker than peat across his brow. I ran to him and was engulfed in his arms, my face smothered in the myrrhy smell of Father still clinging to the corduroy.

"Why are you here?" I cried. "Why aren't you with them?"

His voice was strained. "Did you go? Did you see him?"

I shook my head, wiping my eyes on his sleeve. "I called from the airport. I— Mom says he's fine. His heart's badly damaged—but she says he'll get better. Why aren't you with her, Chris—you know she wants you there."

My voice faded. I knew why he wasn't there. We were one and the same, Chris and I. During those times when outside forces threatened our world—like when Gran fell to the floor with a dizzy spell, or our youngest brother, Kyle, was choking on a marble, or Father chopped his hand with the axe—we'd fled, Chris crouching into my back as I crouched behind the house, the both of us hiding from what was probably a far simpler incident than what we were conjuring up with our frightened thoughts.

"But why didn't you drive straight there—from the airport?" he asked.

"Mother said to come get you."

"What—she didn't think you'd be crazy to see him?"

I circled my arms around his waist, resting against him. "I needed to see you," I whispered. "Mom says you're taking it hard. Ohh, Chris, it must've been horrible." I buried my face in his shirt, needing a stronger smell of him, of Father. His arms tightened around me, a soft moan catching in his throat. The shrill *chewk chewk chewk* of a fish hawk warned off a predator. Over his shoulder I watched the bird of prey flapping out of the woods, the white underside of its wings fanning out against the sky.

"Kyle. And Gran," I said, looking to the house. "They're at the hospital? I forgot to ask Mom."

"Kyle's driving the truck—"

"Ky's what?"

"He's seventeen, Sis."

"Lord. And driving Dad's new truck? That should get him on his feet soon enough—Kyle driving his brand-new truck." I stood at the edge of the wharf, looking down onto the second of Father's brand-new purchases that year—a sleek, fourteen-foot rowboat that had cost three years' savings. Its stem looked straight as an arrow, its flared bow extending upwards and outwards, lending an air of lengthiness and grace to its rounded sides. Meticulously painted the deepest of greens, it now sat motionless on the ice, Father's heavy winter coat laid neatly across a thwart, his gun and lunch bag tucked inside the cuddy. I raised my eyes, staring out over the sea packed tight with pan ice. Its surface was rugged but so white and pristine that it echoed silence into the vastness above it. And yet an insidious groaning sounded from beneath as it continually crushed against itself, grinding and gouging itself to bits. It made me shiver, thinking about Father, seeing him as I'd seen him a hundred times, holding on to the gunnels of his punt, shoving it over that shifting, heaving mass, jumping from ice pan to ice pan across loosely opened channels, and whenever a lead presented itself, leaping aboard his boat and paddling across it.

"Hunting them damn old seals," I muttered. "No wonder he's tore up, heaving his boat over that, year after year. Couldn't he wait? Couldn't he wait for the ice to break?"

"He was excited," said Chris. "About his boat. Couldn't wait to try her."

"Well, how come he was by himself, then? Didn't he have nobody going with him? You can't launch a boat over ice by yourself."

Chris's face twisted with self-reproach.

"What's wrong?" I asked. "You were supposed to go with him? How come you didn't, then?"

He looked at me, his honeyed hair and face warm as summer. But it was his eyes that always held me, their cherry brownness so soft, so momentous with emotion that even when they were glimmering with laughter I hurt for them. "Why, what's the matter? Chris, what's the matter?"

He looked away from me, his lips so tightly compressed they quivered. He swiped at them with his fist, an act that lent a hardening to his mouth. I fell quiet, watching self-dislike take hold of him like a cancer.

"Chris. Chris, you don't think it's your fault, do you?"

He beckoned me towards the house. "Go. Get washed or something, I sees to the gear. Then we'll go see him." He hoisted himself off the wharf onto the ice, grabbing hold of the boat as the ice swelled and ebbed with the sea beneath, crunching against the wharf.

"What're you doing?" I asked as he took a box of gun shells out of his pocket and opened them for a quick count. I threw up my arms with a quick show of temper. "Ohh, for gawd's sake!"

"I got someone going with me."

"Right, sure you do. When? When are you going—aren't you coming with me to the hospital?"

"Tomorrow morning. Tomorrow morning I'm going."

"And who's going with you? Who?" I demanded as he didn't answer. "Ohh, for gawd's sake, what's the big deal about a bloody old seal. We don't even like seal, Mother hates the stench of seal—it's only Father, and you think he's thinking about seal right now?"

"Just—go get ready."

I stared at him, seeing his face tighten with guilt. "You got yourself thinking something now then, you do," I said softly. "And how's Dad going to feel, you blaming yourself—never mind Mother. She'll be hooked up alongside of him she hears you're out on that ice. Chris, you can hardly keep up with Dad—how are you going to do this on your own?"

His face darkened and he made to speak, but the shifting pan of ice beneath him suddenly hove upon a swell, sending him grabbing awkwardly for the gunnels. "Go," he yelled. "Else you'll leave without me."

He turned his back, stowing the shells in the cuddy along with Father's lunch bag, his shoulders tensed with that old stubbornness that sometimes arose within him and that was always a reassurance to Gran. "Bit of backbone does him good," I heard her say to Mother once after Chris wore them both down in one of his rare upsets.

I marched in a huff to the house, then stood looking back. Chris was slumped over the boat, motionless, staring out to sea. He could slump for hours like that, without moving. Like he had no bones, as I'd often thought of him as a youngster, finding comfort in whatever seat he happened upon, whether it was a rock, a pillow, or once even a bottomless bucket turned upside down that he'd slowly sunk further and further into till his knees were flush with his chin and I had to yank him out of it. 'Course it wasn't a comfortable seat he'd been sinking into; he simply hadn't realized he was sinking, his attention snared by a fly caught in a web etched between two pickets and buzzing furiously as a spider worked its way around it.

"Flies don't feel nothing," I'd said after he'd been pulled from his reverie as well as the bucket and was besieged with sorrow for the fly. It was always his way to be so absorbed by a thing that his eyes would fill with the hugeness of it and he'd forget a simple thing like hooking the fly from the web if he wanted to save it—as though he felt totally removed from the thing, or that he was the thing itself. And in those moments when his mind was called to something, like why he didn't hook the fly from the web, his eyes would so fill with self-reproach that I'd quickly divert his thought and then stand back watching as he almost immediately dissolved into something else. Always I marvelled at his absorption in the ordinary. Always I marvelled at his unordinary presentation of it later with his pencils.

Where are you now, I wanted to call out as he continued gazing out over the ice. As if hearing my thoughts, he flashed me an impatient look.

"Right then," I muttered. Pulling open the door, I stood for a moment, my crossness with Chris colliding with the acidic smell of Mother's bleached floors, of lemon-tinged wax and pine-smelling cleansers. Above all was the poignant smell of lavender, Mom's favourite scent, infiltrating the room from its bundles hanging from the kitchen ceiling and growing in planters along the window benches, its feathery purple blooms prettying the window since the first I could remember, whilst its oils permeated the dryness of Mother's winter skin. I leaned against the door, breathing deeply for a moment, allowing the scent to embrace me. As a youngster I thought the scent was Mother's, and the lavender a pretty plant that smelled like her.

I stepped deeper into the house. It had been a bit more than a year since I'd been home, and my eyes flitted anxiously over the wide, open space of the kitchen and living room, the windows flushed with light, the dark wooden table and chairs spruced to a shine, the black polished woodstove, cold today, but so eternally cracking out heat in memory that I hovered unconsciously towards it, holding out my hands, and shivering in the stillness of the emptied house. My eyes lingered on the warped wooden legs of an old rocker, so utterly Mom's as it faced a window looking away from the water, her faded blue shawl draped around its back, a pile of well-marked books sitting on an end table beside it.

Across the room, near the window overlooking the water, was Gran's rocker, her woollen shawl hanging from it should she find a draft, a basket for her knitting beside it, her oil lamp from Cooney Arm sitting nearby so's to give her the soft yellow light she was used to. A breeze tinkled at the kitchen window. I turned, half expecting to see Dad leaning one arm onto the window bench, the other on the table as he gulped back tea, staring out the same window as Gran, searching for fish, seals, birds, boats, and whatever else the sea flung towards him. Echoing through the rooms were Chris and Kyle's shouts as they rode the humpty between Mother's and Gran's rockers or cushioned themselves amongst pillows bright as wildflowers springing from the sofa.

A nice house. Mother kept a nice house. But it was Gran's house where I'd spent the first seven years of life. And ever since the move from Cooney Arm sixteen years ago, when me and Gran moved in with the rest of the family, I'd never felt quite right. Like a sprout from a different seed, suited, yet with a scent unlike the rest. Backing out of the house, I quietly closed the door.

———————

IT WAS AN HOUR'S DRIVE to Corner Brook, a small city that had grown out of a paper mill. I recalled how much Mother loved it—the paved highway rolling out before her, curving around the sandy shores of Deer Lake; the cragged grey cliffs climbing out of the thick blackish waters of the Humber River, the snowy heights of the far distant mountains, purplish on a hazy day. "So beautiful," she exclaimed to Gran once, upon return, "the houses so nicely painted, and the trees all in a row, and the grass perfectly green and trimmed, and, oh, what flowers!" Once, a taxi driver drove her through High Station where the rich people lived and she hardly spoke for a week, so filled was her mind by the grandeur of things.

Father made the trip once. "Hurts me teeth," he said when Mom tried persuading him back. "Driving on pavement hurts me teeth."

"Ahh, you poor fool," she said, "your mind's still anchored with your boat."

"And that's where it'll stay, clear of the stink of mill rot," he returned.

"Listen to him, just listen to him; forgets the fish guts he sniffed for thirty years," said Mother, and huffed out of the room, leaving him telling Gran how he'd been sitting in his truck near the mill when the sea hove up a burp from the heavy sludge of bark rotting on its floor, the stench worse than farts from a horse's arse.

I smiled at the memory. "He's gonna be fine," I said now with sudden certitude. "He's gonna be fine. But you—" Chris was shifting about worse than a crampy youngster in the passenger seat. "Why are you doing this—blaming yourself? How foolish is that? Well, then?"

"Watch the road," he growled. "Christ, for gawd's sakes!" He jolted upright as a truck blasted past, leaving the car shaking in a gust of wind. "Jeezes, keep your eyes on the road. How's Ben?"

"Ohh, who knows about Ben."

"There she goes."

"There *you* goes! It's complicated stuff having a heart attack, never the one thing causing it—was probably building for months."

"I said how's Ben!"

"And I said I never sees him."

"Never?"

"No. Never. Few times."

"He's still working the rigs?"

"Yes."

"With Trapp?"

"No doubt."

"He's still drawing?"

"Who knows. What about you?"

He shrugged.

"Well, are you drawing?"

"Sure. Most times."

"Thought maybe that when I start my grad studies—year from now—you'd come stay with me for a while," I offered.

"What—you're going back to school?"

"'Course. Do my master's. Perhaps a doctorate. Why stop till it's done?"

He shook his head. "Envy you that. Fixing your mind on something and keeping it there. Chore for me to read a comic—and I love comics."

I looked at him in disbelief. "Says he who crawls inside a pencil for hours and don't blink. What's that if not discipline? Christ almighty, how come you're always ranting on about Ben's drawing but never your own? You're better than him. Yeah, you are," I said to his snort. "Pours from you like life. Ben draws a boat, it's just that—a boat. You draw a boat, and it's every boat that ever was."

"Jeezes let's not start that agin—"

"You never allow for your talent—"

"Here she goes."

"Thinks I'm talking through my hat, don't you. Well, I'm not talking through my hat. Been to enough art showings these past five years to know something when I sees it, and you got something, brother, you really do. I think you're a visionary, a true visionary. Privileged. And here you are groping and fumbling about with nets and chainsaws! Jeezes. Them days are passed when you gotta hide your paints and jig fish. You can do anything you want now, school's in! Did you get those brochures I sent you?"

"What brochures?"

"Art school in Halifax." I held my breath. I'd done far more than send him brochures. I'd actually filled out an application into the art program on his behalf and signed his name to it, submitted it to the art college along with a portfolio I'd made up with the drawings he'd given me through the years and an essay explaining why "I" wanted to pursue that course of study. "It's where I'm doing my master's. Gorgeous city—no more than a big town, really, and quite close to home, can hop the ferry in the morning and be home before Mother turns out the light. Did you—well, did you get them—the brochures?"

He was gazing out his side window, scarcely listening.

"Chris, did you get the damn brochures or not?"

"No." He glanced at me irritably.

"Well, you should've, you should've had them by now. It's a well-recognized program and I thought you'd find some of the material interesting. Nice old artsy building, cobblestones out front, great bar right alongside with live music and juicy burgers. Lotsa people our own age milling about, most of them from Newfoundland," I added. "Always somebody hitching a ride back home for the weekend, or driving and wanting somebody along for company."

"Yeah, you'll like it there," he said vaguely.

"I'm thinking about you, brother."

"Yeah, well, you just think about yourself, enough to think about yourself. See that little pine tree over there, next to the tall birches? Father got it tagged for this year's Christmas tree. Don't mention it, no cutting allowed. We'll get it late some evening, when it's dark."

"You're ignoring me."

"Think you'll be home for Christmas?"

"Don't want to listen to talk about university art programs. Afraid you might have to do something. Like make a plan, leave home someday."

"Will you just watch the gawd-damned road."

"I'm watching the gawd-damned road, and I'm telling you that's half your gawd-damned problem right there, don't want to leave home. How come? That's what I can't figure—how come you don't wanna leave home, because you don't, do you?"

I looked over at him, trying to see what was behind his eyes, what was in his head, what he was thinking. It was always like that; any time I ever spoke to him about leaving he'd scoff it off, turn to something else, make jokes out of it. Surprisingly, he was holding himself back this time, his chest tensed and his mouth working as though he were struggling with some feeling he couldn't put words to. Kinda reminded me of those times when we used to hide behind the house in fear of some unknown fate.

But it was no youngster sitting beside me on this day. I could see thick cords jumping in his neck as he strained away from me. I could see the veins roping his wrists as he nervously flexed and re-flexed his hands into fists. He bit his lip as though to quell whatever thought he was struggling with and my fingers itched to touch him, to do away with whatever strain I was putting him under.

"It's not such a big deal, you know," I blundered, "leaving a dead-end logging town built around a post office."

He snorted. "There goes her nose agin. Haughty, by cripes—"

"I'm not haughty."

"Hell you're not. Anything outside the outports is a step up for you. A bog."

"Oh, foolishness."

"Foolish, hell. You ranks everything over the outport. The whole island's a outport to you, and now you've left that— rather waitress in some oil town—"

"Grande Prairie, Alberta, and it's a pretty city with bars that quadruple the pay offered by any bar in St. John's or Corner Brook. That's why I'm there, to make fast money."

"Sure you're not chasing Ben?"

I near drove us off the road.

"Ohh, Christ, is that what you think? That I'm chasing Ben Bonehead Rice?"

Catching his grin, I sucker-punched his leg. Glad to have a smile back on his face, I decided to keep the application into the art program for another time, the return trip, maybe, after we visited with Father and made sure he was going to be all right.

As though ensuring silence for the rest of the drive, he switched on the radio, cranking it loud. For the rest of the drive we sat mired within our own thoughts.

INSIDE THE HOSPITAL PARKING LOT, Chris was the first out of the car, looking up at the sprawling, red-brick structure. I followed him across the lot, starting to feel apprehensive. The warming spring sun and heartening smell of fresh earth gave way to the emptied white light of long hospital corridors and the acrid odour of sickness and antiseptic. Inside the heavy doors of the intensive care unit, cowed by the silence of pending death, Chris faltered. I took his hand then and we crept like two frightened youngsters past the hushed, uniformed figures and their whitish faces hovering over blue-screened monitors that charted failing hearts in curtained-off beds. Through an opening in one of the curtains I saw Mother's coat draped over a chair.

Chris hung back, pulling on my hand. "Say nothing about my going sealing," he said lowly.

I shook my head and then held my breath as he lifted aside the drape, nudging me forward. I expected to see them both, but there was just Dad. I near cried. So big and dark in memory, his hair fanned by the wind, his black brows shading his eyes as he stood in his boat, he now lay still beneath a white sheet, his hair without sheen, his face with the pallor of an aged tombstone. His breathing, aided by rubbery oxygen tubes pronged and taped to his nostrils, sounded long, deep, and raspy.

I bit into my fist, watching as Chris approached the bedside, his eyes fastened to Father's hand, brown as bark against the white of the sheets and pierced with needles and tubing. Carefully he touched a finger to Dad's and stared into the dulled, dark orbs of his eyes, their faint glimmer of life.

"Looks better," Chris said thickly.

Father blinked in response.

"Best not to talk."

Father nodded, staring a steady stream into Chris's eyes, flooding them with the confusion of his weakness. Chris, as though his heart were too full to hold more, stood back, saying gruffly, "Brought someone to see you. Sylvie—your Dolly," he added lamely. Pushing away from the bedside, he bolted outside the curtains.

I gripped the bed railing so's not to run myself. Father lifted his hand weakly. I tried to speak, but couldn't. Taking his hand, I forced a smile at the needles. "A pin cushion," I said with a shaky laugh, "one of Gran's pin cushions." I leaned over him and pressed my mouth against the warmth of his brow.

"The boat," he whispered.

"The boat." I forced a laugh. "Is that what you're thinking about now, your boat? Chris got it tied to the wharf."

He nodded. "Next week. Home next week."

"No doubt. Be snowshoeing on the downs soon enough."

He tried to smile.

"Seriously," I whispered, my eyes filling with persuasion as he searched them out.

Satisfied—else overcome with fatigue—his breathing deepened and he lapsed into sleep. Laying my palm against his cheek, I felt its roughness, almost tasting the salt from the days he straddled his boat in the stiff morning gales, hand-jigging codfish in the ways of old, face bared to the wind, legs anchored to the sea. How tall he'd stood those early mornings in Cooney Arm when he tossed me and sometimes Chris aboard with him. We'd squat in the stern, white-knuckled to the gunnels, as he rose against the sky, all big and black in his sou'wester and oilskins, doing his dance with the sea as he jigged: one hand up, one hand down, one hand up, one hand down, his hips swaying with the swell, his boat bucking with the lop. How strange his face looked now, all still and pale on that stark white pillow, his squinty eyes bereft of weather and so looking like death it was as if they knew what death was.

And in a sense he did know what death was—or a form of death. From the moment he picked up his chainsaw and started his first summer in the woods he cursed over the sweltering heat away from the sea, and the flies, the gawd-damn flies—blackflies, sandflies, mosquitoes—all swarming inside his nostrils, his ears, his eyes, and gawd-damn deer ticks gouging and breeding in his flesh. Many times I'd be hanging about the wharf when Father got home from the woods, and I'd listen to his cursing, and then Mother chiding him for his cursing, for his being wimpy over flies, for going straightaway out in boat with his nets when he'd already worked all day and hadn't had supper yet, hadn't washed, hadn't fixed the latch on Gran's door, hadn't rested.

"I gotta breathe," he'd shoot over his shoulder, already pulling away from the wharf, "the heat, the heat, there's no getting from the gawd-damn heat; can't breathe, no wind, no air, no gawd-damn air."

"Give up the nets, give up the nets, Sylvanus, working yourself in the grave with them damn, bloody nets."

And on and on they would argue about his working the woods, his nets, and the handfuls of fish that were hardly worth his while. Till now. Till now, as usual, when Mother proved herself right.

Chris reappeared from behind the curtain.

"He's sleeping," I whispered.

"Is he okay?"

"I don't know. You find Mom?"

"I—no. I think I knows, though."

We fell silent, looking into the grey of our father's face.

Chris nudged me. "You want to go find her?"

I nodded, but was unable to leave. "Hardly looks like him, do it?"

"He looked worse yesterday."

"Imagine if he'd died."

He abruptly took my arm and led me back out through those heavy doors. I followed, sniffling quietly as he led us through a series of corridors. Mother was sitting in the front pew of a small chapel. She looked shrunken, her shoulders tiny like a girl's. She was bent before a crucifix, her face the pallor of Father's.

Chris spoke her name. She rose, rushing towards him as she always did, as though he were a font from which she must drink. Unlike me, who she'd held aloof from birth. Small wonder. Three dead babies and me the fourth one born, small wonder she held me aloof. And then that "dark spell," as Gran called it, the weeks and weeks of darkness that Mother succumbed to after my birth, so dark a spell that it bruised her skin in places and blocked her nipples from milking, I once heard her old friend Suze say.

But I hadn't fared bad. Gran brought me across the brook to her own house and fed me goat's milk from a bottle, and such great comfort I was to that dear woman that when Mother started getting well, Gran pleaded to keep me. Which served them both, as Mother was soon pregnant again, and suffered morning sickness straight through to the last day of her pregnancy.

Given that their houses were a stone's throw apart, and that Gran and Mother were tighter than blood, Mother was as much a daily fixture in my life as Gran was. And I grew happy and warm, never knowing but that Mother was happy and warm too. Till I saw her coddling Chris that first time. The way she smiled into his eyes as he suckled her breast. Such a change, such an incredible change came upon her, a glow that touched her eyes, her skin, dissipating a form of darkness from her face that I hadn't before noted.

Naturally I can't recall these things. But some part of me did. It watched now as Mother clung to Chris in the small chapel, caressing his cheek. It remembered how she used to smooch him with kisses when he was a baby, how she used to squat beside him on the shoreline, watching and smiling as he scooped up wriggly-tails from amongst the rocks, but then one day when I scooped up a worm and brought it home she brushed it from my hand, squished it on the stoop, and then scrubbed my hands, gently but firmly, with a bar of soap, chiding me about dirt.

Mother put Chris aside, reaching for me. "You've seen him?" she asked, putting her arms around my neck. I nodded, and clung to that familiar scent of lavender, all warmed and fused into my mother's skin. "You'll not let him see that," she said as I started to cry. She pulled back, the sharp blue of her eyes piercing through the tears in my own. "He thinks he's getting better, and that's what we'll let him think—he's getting better …" She faltered, turning towards the altar.

"Isn't he, then—isn't he getting better?" I choked.

Mother looked at me, then at Chris who was paling visibly. "Yes, oh, my yes, he's getting better, of course he's getting better," she cried, both hands reaching for Chris. "But—oh," she said, her voice dropping with a sudden realization, "you don't know, you never talked to Gran, or, or Kyle. 'Course you didn't, how could you," she added with a silly laugh, "when they only just left—"

Chris broke in. "Don't know what? What is it?"

"He'll not work again. Your father will not work again." She spoke with such conviction it was as though she herself were commanding his fate.

"The doctors—?" I asked. "Is that what the doctors are saying?"

"Yes. No. They don't rightly know yet, but he'll never be the same, they said he can never work in the woods again."

"There's other things, he'll work at other things," I said, infusing my tone with hope.

"Sure, other things," said Mother. "What other things, Sylvie? There's the woods and fishing on the trawlers. Your father won't do that, he'll never fish offshore on them trawlers." She looked around emptily. "Might as well have killed him, he can't work the woods. No, no, don't take it like that," she pleaded as Chris sank onto a chair, hanging his head. She sat beside him, her tiny, pale hands cupped around his like a clamshell. "He's alive, thank god he's alive. Be grateful for that. And we'll keep him alive, keep him home, resting. There now," she soothed, drawing Chris's head to her shoulder, "there now."

I sat next to her, speaking in the same soothing tones as Chris leaned forward, hanging his head again. "He's strong, Father is. Chris, he'll get past this. He'll find his strength again, and he'll find other things to do."

"Sure. Sure," Mother repeated, her tone becoming lifeless. "He'll get past this. Live another twenty years if he don't go dragging about chainsaws." She rose, wrapping her arms around herself and crossing the room in short, quick steps. "How are we going to do that," she demanded of the air around her, "how are we going to keep him from the woods? He gave up fishing, it'll kill him to give up the woods, too. Damn old fishing— that's what done it to him—working the woods all day long, then coming home to them damn old nets. And if he wasn't dragging about nets and chainsaws he was traipsing through the bogs, dragging a gun. Never stopped, he never. Never stopped for a minute in the day—whatever he thought he was made of. Even the blessed Maker took his one day of rest. And dragging that old boat over that ice by himself. No wonder he's near dead, dragging that boat across the ice by himself."

"We can't say that," I cut in, noting the pained look on Chris's face. "Others fish and log and live long, healthy lives."

"Others," snorted Mother. "We're not talking about others, Sylvie, we're talking about your father—and how he slaved at two jobs for twenty years. Others didn't do that—two jobs for twenty years."

"He was never working when he was fishing," I argued. "Would've killed him in a worse way if he couldn't fish."

"Well, it has now, hasn't it—it's killed him in all ways."

"He's not dead—cripes, you talk as if he's dead. He'll find his way through this. He'll start doing things differently, is all. Perhaps a bit of fishing, with his rod—or his jiggers. He always loved jigging, no strain there."

"Providing he's sitting in an armchair on the wharf, there'll be no strain," said Mother dryly. "That what we're going to do—keep him in an armchair on the wharf?"

"I'll haul his boat," said Chris. He was still hunched over, elbows on his knees, head hanging like a weight from his shoulders. He raised his eyes to Mother's. "I'll haul his nets, too. The fish are making a comeback. So might Father. Maybe he can just go back to the way he used to be."

"The way he used to be?" Mother stopped her pacing and sat between me and Chris, laying an arm around Chris's shoulder. "Was there a time he wasn't slaving his self to death?" she asked with a glimmer of a smile. "But you're right. Least with fishing he's not cursing his soul to hell like he is in the woods. God, he hates the woods. No wonder he's near dead, always working against himself."

Her hands fell onto her lap. So helpless they looked, lying there palms up as though waiting for something. I touched one, then folded my hand around it. "What else did the doctors say?" I asked quietly.

She rose in a huff, my hands falling away like the discarded hands of a toy doll. "What else is there to say?" she answered absently. "Chris, did he speak to you—did your father speak?"

Chris stared at my discarded hands as I held them oddly in my lap. "Sylvie," he said softly. "He spoke to Sylvie."

"A few days—is that all you can stay?" Mother asked me, her tone softening. "You should be with him, then. Go. Go sit with him, he don't like being alone, not in this place. Did you see Gran? No. No, course you didn't, I already asked. That's another worry, Kyle driving your father's new truck—you know your father bought a new truck, do you, Sylvie? First time he ever went to a bank—pray Kyle don't have an

accident—god forbid, not just for the truck's sake. Are you
sure you can only stay a few days?"

"I—well, if you need me. Or if Dad needs me here, I can
stay—"

"Rest is all he needs," said Mother. She wrung her hands
and started pacing again. "Rest and making sure he stays in that
bed once we gets him home."

"I can come back from Alberta. Maybe I'll move back."

She looked at me in wonderment. "My, you don't mind
flying across the country like that? You makes it sound like a
trip across town. Certainly, you were never one for sitting still.
Always on your feet, running here and there." Her blue eyes
shimmered for a second, as though gazing through a veil of
tears onto a beloved memory. "You've done so well," she near
whispered. "Making the dean's list—my, you should've heard
Gran—poor Gran." Just as quickly the blue eyes darkened and
she was wringing her hands and pacing again. "She's too old
for this, too old and worn out. God forbid she sees another of
her boys die. She'll be glad now that you're here, Sylvie, she's
been watching planes, wondering if that's the one you're on—
will you go, sit with your father—Chris, perhaps we can have
tea, did you have supper?"

"I'll sit with Dad—" Chris began, but I silenced him with a
sharp look. After waving him back to his seat, I gave Mother a
quick hug and left the room.

A series of wrong turns and I found my way back to the
unit. Quietly I stepped behind the curtain draping Father's
bed. He was sleeping, his face grey upon his pillow, and with
his eyes shuttered behind thin, crinkly lids, he looked like an
old weathered house without light. I laid my hand on his
heart, feeling its faint pulse beneath the rise and fall of his
chest. His mouth twitched.

"Dolly," he mouthed, without opening his eyes, and in the quiet of his love my heart broadened. I sat, folded my arms onto the cool white sheet covering him, and cushioned my head, my cheek touching the warmth of his hand. Through the oxygen tubes his breathing sounded loud and deep. I slowed my breathing to match his and must've fallen asleep, for I awakened to slobber on my arm and Mother talking lowly to Chris about the long flight from the prairies, how tired I must be.

———————

"YOU LOOK NICE," said Mother at the hospital doors as Chris and I were leaving. "Your face is nice." She touched a hand to my cheek. "Must be that prairie air—nice and dry. No salt chafing your skin," she ended with a smile.

"Perhaps you can visit sometime," I offered. "You always talked about travel."

"Talked lots of foolishness when I was young." She looked at Chris, who was pushing out through the doors. "Be sure you drives, Chris—your sister's tired. You let him drive now," she called after me, and followed as far as the curb. "Chris, you drive now. Watch for moose—be careful."

I stood beside the car, raising my face to the darkening evening sky. A faint drizzle dampened my brow and I closed my eyes, grateful for its coolness.

"You all right? I can drive," said Chris.

But I motioned him towards the passenger seat and slipped behind the wheel, lowering the window. I drove slowly past the hospital doors, and Mother was still standing outside, her eyes wearing the same wariness as when I used to trot from Gran's house to hers, clamouring for Chris to come play. "Take his hand, take his hand," she'd call. And me, just two years older than Chris, guarding his every step as we mucked about the

meadow, forever steering him away from the cliffs, from rotting
jelly fish, rotting capelin, dead birds, dead anything that might
hurt him, forever mindful of Mother's eye watching after us.

"Worse thing ever happened, she got pregnant with Kyle,"
I said sulkily.

I felt Chris's look of surprise. "What's that suppose to
mean?"

"She got sick and I had to care for you, is what it means.
Like she was jealous every time she seen me walking off with
you. Like I was taking you from her."

"Whoa, Sis, now how foolish is that?"

"Not foolish at all. I can still hear her singing after me every
time I led you along shore, *Don't go too far, don't go too far*—it
was Cooney Arm, for gawd's sake! Six boarded-up houses.
Where'd she think I was taking you?" I lapsed into silence,
hating the sulkiness of my voice, hating even more that I'd
spoken out loud and Chris was staring questioningly at me.
Not at my sulkiness, though, for he understood that, and was
always apologetic in the face of it, as though a part of him also
remembered our mother's breasts milking for him but not
for me.

"Jealous!" he exclaimed. "Now, how'd you come up with
that—jealous of who, of what?"

"Of me, you—that it wasn't her out running about with
you."

"Cripes, Sylvie, now *that's* foolish."

"What would you know—you were lots younger, and
always looking at your feet."

"Nerves, Sis. She had bad nerves, she always got bad nerves."

"Right, bad nerves. Chase down a grizzly, Mother would."

"So she'd chase a grizzly—don't mean she wasn't scared of
it. She was scared of something."

"Yeah. She read too many books. The old always said too much reading drives you mental."

"Oh, come on," chided Chris, and I had the grace to flush at my own silliness. "In the hospital, after they wheeled Dad away, first person she said to call was you," he said. "Always talking about you—how hard you works, graduating university with honours, how you'll travel the world—she's always saying that, you'll travel the world someday. And—*and*," he repeated for emphasis, "when you're coming home next! She's always wondering when you're coming home next."

"And when I'm here she never knows what to do with me."

"You're always arguing with her, that's why—the both of you, always arguing. Why don't you come home more often? She don't like you staying away. True," he added as I drove in silence, "she's always talking about you. And Dad—jeezes, Dad—he looks bad, don't he—gawd, he looks bad ..." His words trailed off.

I steered us onto the grey, darkening highway, rubbing my brow tiredly, seeing our father's face, all worn and ashen on his pillow. Aside from the yellow line shooting rhythmically beneath the car, that was how the whole world appeared to me this evening—the hills, the trees, all limp and grey against a pewter sky.

Till I neared home. Till I turned off the highway and finally onto the rutted side road leading to our house on the wharf. Then the rocks themselves burst into colour, the trees and sky and all else around me dissolving into a thousand pictures of Father: walking wearily from his stage after a day's fishing back in Cooney Arm, sitting at Gran's supper table, falling back on the daybed after he'd eaten, cuddling me on his great, heaving chest, his snores rattling my bones, hugging me tight against his itchy, worsted sweater, hugging me tight against his wet, scaly oilskins, trundling about his stage, shouting for me to come help lay out the fish, laughing at Mother's complaints that he had me smelling like himself, a pickled capelin.

I didn't care about his smell. I loved sniffing pickled capelin. I loved it that Mother, Chris, Kyle—all of them—squirmed against his itchy, worsted hugs and his scaly wet oilskins; that nobody else liked going into his stage as I did, helping him lay out his fish in the puncheons; that only I worked the flakes alongside him, laying out his fish to cure in the sun; that only I accompanied him in boat sometimes, crouching anxiously in the stern as he leaned easily over the gunnels hauling his nets, grunting and cussing if the catch was poor, whistling and singing if the fish were thick and he was piling them at my feet.

More pictures came before me—pictures of me sitting at Mother's table, being home-schooled along with Chris, and Dad winking at me across the room; Dad looking innocently away should Mom, all prim, proper, and teacher-like, turn her attention towards him; Dad sitting beside me at the table, learning from Mother how to read and write and laughing at his clumsiness with a pencil; Dad walking me home after lessons—staying for a while during those cold, bitter nights, running the heated flat-iron over my bedsheets before tucking me in—as Gran always did—and heating dinner plates in the oven, wrapping them in towels and placing them beneath my cold feet before bundling the blankets around me. It felt like he was mine then, when he sat on the side of my bed, his head so close to mine as I said my prayers that I could smell his sour, pickled breath and feel the scattered strands of his hair, all soapy and vinegarish, tickling my face and making me squirm through the amens.

Abruptly the pictures changed. We were no longer in Cooney Arm. The soft darkness of Gran's firelit corners was

blasted by garish electrical lights that lit Mother's house on the
wharf, leaving me—along with Gran, Father, the boys, and
sometimes even Mother—blinking like nocturnal creatures,
flitting about the house like bats searching for a rayless niche
in which to roost. How disoriented I'd felt those first months
in Mother's crowded household, with all the attention
constantly heaped upon me by Mother, the boys. Times I'd
run, looking for Father and finding him equally disoriented,
hunched over the wharf, looking back to Cooney Arm, gutted
by the loss of his stage, his flakes. Home from a day's work in
the woods, he'd sit carefully amongst Mother's new, brightly
patterned cushions on the sofa and watch, confused by my
resistance to Chris and Kyle's overzealous attention to my
every move, confused by my defiance with Mother over some
small thing, confused by my new math and the queer gawd-
damned way of mixing letters and numbers.

My most favoured imprint was the day of my first birthday
living in Mother's house. Father had bought a watch from the
store in Hampden and hung it on the outside knob of my
room door because he was too shy to give it to me and wanted
to make a joke out of it. It hung there all day—nobody else
saw it, and I refused to see it, fearful of its not being mine and
that he'd see the want in my eyes. Gran finally spotted it, and
brought it to the supper table and gave it to me, chiding him
for his foolishness. I felt too shy beneath his gaze to properly
hook it around my wrist. And so Mother, looking a mite shy
herself in her new dress that she was wearing just for my
birthday, leaned close, helping me hook the watch strap, she
too chiding Father for his foolishness—all of us hiding our
shyness behind his foolishness.

So why had Mother looked shy, I pondered now, but then
pushed the thought away as I drove past Father's woodshed

and pulled up to the wharf. Turning off the headlights, I sat for a minute, staring at the house, at the smoke pouring from the chimney, the windows yet unlit in the growing dusk. A wooden cubbyhole was built to the side of the house, Father's chainsaw, his bucksaw, his handsaw laid inside, along with a box full of jiggers and bits of fishing gear. Other stuff, his barrels, puncheons, nets, was stored in the woodshed or rotting into the ground in Cooney Arm.

Wrapped in canvas at the end of the wharf lay an anchor, an old motor, some boat parts. Poor Father. He hadn't the heart to build another stage here on the wharf. Why bother when fishing had become more of a fun thing than a mainstay? And now everything he owned was all scattered about—like Father himself, his soul wandering the emptied fishing grounds of Cooney Arm, his heart fighting for resurgence in some hospital room in the city.

TWO

"**W**HERE'S THE NEW TRUCK?" I asked Chris.

"You passed it, back by the woodshed. Tucked a bit behind." He got out of the car and headed towards the boat tied to the wharf. I climbed out behind him, a stout breeze gusting my hair across my face.

"I don't want you going," I called out, then cursed as his step didn't falter.

The house door flung open and Gran appeared, clutching the front of her woolly green sweater and clinging to the doorjamb like a withering old vine.

I ran to her, wrapping my arms tight about her shrinking, knobby shoulders, scolding her for being out in the cold.

"Much odds, this old bag of bones," said Gran, her voice quavering. "Did you see him?"

I nodded, kissing her soft, powdery cheek. "Yes. Yes, I seen him." We held each other tighter in the face of this new thing. Taking my hand, Gran led me inside, her grip not as strong as I remembered, her voice more brittle, shaky as she asked about Mother.

"She's fine, worrying more about you than herself."

"Ahh, she worries for nothing. Sit. Tell me about your father, I makes tea."

I sat in Gran's rocker, speaking assuredly of Father's recovery. Fire snapped inside the stove, and I relished its heat. I relished, too, Gran's wiry frame, her hair all white now and caught at her nape, her darkish brows lending strength to her fading green eyes as she moved about the kitchen in her odd, faltering manner—from bending over in her garden, plucking weeds at every turn, we always teased her.

"She got a fright, my Dolly, your mother got a bad fright," said Gran, "seeing him crumple across his boat like that. She was watering her plants when she seen him through the window. Did she tell you?"

"No. Did you? Did you see him, too?"

"I was in the room. She never called out at first—didn't want to frighten me. Poor thing. Wonder she didn't drown, running over the pan ice like that." Gran's mouth quivered—whether from emotion or age I couldn't rightly say—as she continued telling the horrible story of Mother dragging Father off the boat and onto his back on the ice, screaming out for Chris to run, run, for the doctor. He was conscious by the time the doctor got there, his eyes moving, his breathing short and quick, but he was making no sound, no movement. Pain, he told Mother after he woke up in the hospital, he was locked so hard into pain he thought it was crushing his chest, and he could do nothing but breathe—seen an angel, he said, but then the angel cursed and he saw it was his Addie instead.

Gran smiled and sat a cup of tea and plate of scones before me, kissing the top of my head. "Lord bless them both. Sugar your tea, I gets some milk."

The door opened and Chris came in, his nose watering from the cold, and Kyle behind him. No matter his seventeen years, Kyle looked a boy with his stout, pudgy frame—still carrying his baby fat, we always teased him. His face was rounded, not comely like Chris's, yet his cheeky grin had always been an instant draw. He looked at me now and I half thought he'd come lumbering over as when he'd been a youngster, pulling his ears or plugging his nostrils with his fingers to garner a laugh. Instead he offered me the saddest of smiles, crossing the room to sit stiffly on the arm of Mother's rocker.

Mom won't like that, loosening the arms of her rocker, I wanted to say, to tease him, to lighten his worry. Instead I dumped two spoonfuls of sugar into the cup of tea Gran laid before me and took it to him.

"Suppose you still got your sweet tooth," I said, and ruffled his hair. He smiled a tiny, frightened smile. Keeping his eyes from mine, he took the cup, nervously jiggling his foot. "Hey." I touched his shoulder. "Dad's gonna be fine. Truly."

"Come on, Kyle, my love, come have tea with Gran." Gran scraped back a chair beside where Chris was sitting at the table, brooding out the window. I went to the kitchen cupboard, plunged my hand into the cookie canister, thankful it was filled with our favourite ginger snaps, and took a fistful to Kyle. "Here, stuff your face with that," I said, shoving them at him. I laughed along with him at his clumsy effort to catch them from spilling onto the floor.

"What're you brooding out the window for?" I chided Chris, sitting back down in the rocker. "Or is it your face you're looking at—is that what he's doing, Gran—admiring himself?"

Chris shot me a dubious look and turned back to the window, wondering out loud about whether it was wind or rain overtaking the evening.

"Wind, you silly thing," said Gran. "Sky's too thick for rain. Haul back your chair. Stop fretting, as your sister says. You'll be having bad dreams agin tonight. Kyle, turn on the lights—or light Gran's lamp instead. Feels warmer with the lamp lit, don't you think, my Dolly? Where you going—not fit to be out," she said as Chris scrooped back his chair, heading for the door. She grumbled as he said something about the boat. "Be sick with the flu before the week's out, watch and see if you're not," she called out as the door closed behind him. "Kyle, you lighting the lamp for Gran?"

Kyle struck a match to the wick. His face was pale despite the buttery glaze of light flaring through the chimney. Raising the wick, he placed the lamp on the table and sat beside Gran.

"What were you doing, you and Chris," I asked, "when Dad took sick—what were ye both doing?"

He shrugged, his face glum.

"Oh, come on—you were doing something."

"Nothing. We were doing nothing."

"Nothing!"

"Drawing. Chris was drawing. On pieces of birch rind." He shrugged again, his eyes, big and blue like Mother's, flickering around the room. "Dad!" he said accusingly. "He was supposed to call out when he was ready. We didn't know he was leaving."

"No, he didn't call out," said Gran. "I would've heard him if he had."

"Chris was ready—all dressed to go," said Kyle. "Never heard him call is all."

"Because he never, I tell you," said Gran. "I would've heard him if he had. Blaming himself now, is that what Chris is doing?" She looked crossly at the door. "Go after him, Kyle— tell him to come in from the cold, and make sure he ties on his father's boat—I don't like that wind this evening." She peered across the table through the window. The night beyond was charred black by heavy cloud, the wind hitting stiff against the pane. "Loosen up the pack, keeps blowing like this."

My stomach tensed at Gran's words. Last thing Chris needed in the morning was loose pack ice with its trenches and leads and slush holes that could swallow a man more quickly than a swamp hole. I looked at Kyle. He was chewing the side of his thumbnail, foot jiggling, as he stared out the window.

He knew. He knew what Chris was doing. "Hey." I kicked his foot and forced a smile. "Pour Gran more tea. I'll go get Chris."

I let myself outside, the wind, dampish and with a touch of warmth, swaddling my face. A southerly. It had turned. I looked over the wharf onto the ice, greyish beneath the thick night sky, and to where Chris was standing, a dark shape against the darker, larger shape of the boat. I knelt beside a grump on the wharf and watched as he rifled through the bundles of clothing and gear he'd stored in the boat earlier that day. The ice was heaving fretfully beneath him and crunching against the wharf. Keeping hold of the gunnels for balance, he lifted a length of rope that was ringed through the bow and tossed the looped end up onto the wharf where I sat.

I fingered the cold, soggy thing resignedly. There was no arguing. The set look on his face, the determined manner in which he moved about the gear, the gun, the shells already stowed in the cuddy—it did away with any protests I might've made. And aside from Mother and Father and Gran—and perhaps Kyle, too—there wasn't a soul in the whole of White Bay that wouldn't have him doing this very thing at such a time. Helping his father. In fact, they'd be more surprised— perhaps accusing—if he didn't.

"Remember how we used to sneak into those boarded-up houses in Cooney Arm?" I asked quietly. "Well, do you?" I said again, irritably now, as he hadn't spoken, hadn't even glanced my way.

He shrugged. "Not lately."

"And how we sometimes spooked ourselves, thinking we heard voices in the wood? That's how I see you, full of voices and all boarded up. Yeah, I do, I really do," I said to his tired look. "Full of things you can never fully say. I can see you now, sitting for hours, when we were youngsters, staring at a mud hole. Or a rock. Or just sitting and staring, and thinking so hard you'd either burst out bawling or burst out laughing, or both, scaring the bejeezes out of me sometimes." I smiled. "Always remember the time you dozed off at the supper table with a crust of bread across your face. Had Mother worried to death. *Like he goes into a trance*, she was always saying."

"Yeah, well, she still thinks that."

"Daydreaming, I think she calls it now." I caught a duffle bag he threw up onto the wharf and propped it next to myself, watching him climb inside the boat, sorting through some canned food in Father's lunch bag.

"I never worried," I said. "I always knew you were seeing the newness of something."

"The newness of something."

"Yeah. The newness of something. I remember once, you drawing a finch. You started with a claw gripping a twig when I would've had you starting with its head, its beak. And then when you'd done, there was no head or beak. The page held no place for it, not even the other foot. Just one tiny, wiry claw clutching a limb. And I never saw a bird again without seeing its claws first—I told you, you takes the ordinary out of everything. Do you remember that—drawing that claw? No, you don't," I said to his blank look.

"Sylvie—"

"Let me tell you why you don't remember that claw. You've never been outside of it to see it. Like Dad, once, trying to tell me how grand Cooney Arm was when I'd never been anywhere but Cooney Arm. But I remember *feeling* its grandness, the way we used to be half scared, half excited climbing over them cold, wet cliffs. And feeling the falls thundering through the rock—like it was thundering through me, too. Sometimes, when I used to get up and walk away, my legs would be rubbery—remember that, the power of it? And then racing along the beach and them big sounders rolling up on shore—remember that? How cold they were, smashing about our feet? Gawd, they were cold. And the wind, near lifting me with it sometimes.

"I can't remember feeling anything that strong since I was a youngster," I said nostalgically. "But you"—I leaned towards him, unable to keep my tone from becoming urgent—"you always feel like that, don't you? You don't need the wind or the cliffs. You feel it inside. I see it every time I look at you—always fidgeting and squirming—never quiet unless you got a pencil in your hands, or a knife. Or going into one of your *daydreams*, as Mom calls it. Yes, it's true," I said at his skeptical look. "You know you do. Just sitting on a wharf you feels it. Like something inside of you, never at rest, always drumming through your bones, stirring your blood—it must pummel at your fingertips, do it, trying to get out?

"I'm not talking crazy," I said as he rolled his eyes. "I'm not. I'm talking your talk, you don't even know your talk—that's why you've got to leave here. What frightens you, Chrissy—what keeps you on this stupid, friggin wharf? No, don't go, listen to me—oh, there he goes," I said with resignation as he leaped upon the wharf, walking away from me. "Why can't you leave—why can't you ever leave?" I yelled, and got up to chase him. But he was swinging around to face me.

"So's you can go," he said evenly. "I stays so's you can go. Somebody's got to be here. Somebody's got to help him—tar his roof, his shed, lug wood, split wood, stack wood, mend the wharf and all the rest of it. He don't stop, he's always at it— hunting, fishing, fixing this, fixing that, and a hundred other gawd-damned things that got nothing to do with wages."

"But—"

"But nothing. Jeezes, Sylvie, he'd be dead by now if not for the bit of help I gives him. It's not much, because, yeah, you're right—surprise, surprise—I'm not cut from his stock; I'm not good at any fuckin' thing. But!" And here he drew himself upright. "I'm helping a bit. Yes, that's right, I do help him a bit. Till the other day," he added bitterly, his face dropping, "drawing *birds* when I was suppose to be launching the boat alongside of him."

"Ohh, don't think like that—"

"And you'd still have me go, would you?" he asked, his eyes challenging mine. "Him on his sick bed, and you'd still have me go?"

"'Course not. I mean when he's better. You can't always do this—live his life for him. He wouldn't want that. He just don't think of it, is all, you wanting to go off; else he'd have you in art school if he thought of it, he'd love it if you went to art school."

"Sure! He'd love it," said Chris dryly. "Drawing birds—he can hang them around his bed and shoot at them while he's getting better."

"So he would shoot at them, why wouldn't he—that's what he does, isn't it, shoot birds? And yes he would love it, he'd feel it right to his bones, shooting them birds. And that's what he'd have for you—doing something you feels straight through to your bones. Besides, there's other ways of helping," I cajoled as he started away from me once more. "Can always send money home."

"That right? And how much they paying art students these days?" He walked off towards the woodshed, leaving me staring hopelessly after him.

I jammed my hands in my pockets, facing the sea, the wind hard on my back. A clump of ice thudded against the wharf and I looked down sourly, as if it were a surly dog growling up at me. "Dirty stuff," I muttered. "Dirty, filthy old stuff."

That night I eased into the bed I shared with Gran and lay restless, listening to the ice creaking and groaning outside the window, the wind rattling at the panes like phantoms. One of the boys—Chris? Kyle?—was equally restless, for I could hear the scrooping of their bedsprings through the joining wall. Sighing for the thousandth time, I curled into Gran's back, resting my cheek on her pillow, all scented with face powder. The wind fell off at some point during the night, and a heavy quiet descended.

———————

COME MORNING, I awakened to an eerie silence. Gran was just up, her side of the bed still warm. Flicking apart the curtain, I blinked in surprise. Blue. The bay was bereft of pan ice, the sea a choppy brilliant blue beneath a full sun and with scattered bits of slob ice floating atop its surface like fettered clouds.

Heaving aside the bedclothes, I wrapped a housecoat around my pyjamas and padded barefoot down the hall into an empty kitchen. Muffled voices from outside. I bared the window onto Gran, her shawl wrapped around her nightdress, and Chris, readied for sealing in heavy, dark clothing, standing near the grump, looking down to where the boat had been with a stunned look on his face.

"The boat's gone," Gran greeted me as I ran outside, her voice shrill in the sharp morning air.

"Gone. Gone where?"

"With the ice, it went out with the ice. And just as well— Chris was going sealing, he was, and not letting on to nobody." Her gnarled hands grasped the sleeves of my housecoat. "You tell him—tell him we don't need no bloody old seal meat, Dolly. Enough his father's in the hospital, all we needs is him drowning himself this morning, all we needs."

Chris came towards us, his face taut. "The rope," he said to me. "I threw you up the rope—did you tie it on, did I tell you to tie it on?" He stared at me beseechingly, his eyes near black on a blanched face. And had I thought for a second—had I known what he needed—I would've replied differently. As it was, twas the truth I told.

"No. No, I never tied it on, you never said to tie it on—oh, but wait. Oh, shit, wait, I should've known—I should've known to tie it on."

His shoulders slumped. So filled was he with the fault of his own doing, he could only shake his head helplessly.

"Phone around," said Gran. "Someone might've found her. Perhaps she run aground—on Big Island, somewhere— Chris!"

Chris was walking off, his ears filled with his own denouncement. Kyle appeared by the side of the house. Slipping his hands into his pockets, he followed behind Chris, carrying the same dejected slump to his shoulders.

"Leave them here today," said Gran as they vanished inside the woodshed. "I'll stay with them. You go by yourself, Dolly, spend some time with your father, let your mother get some rest."

"No— Oh, Gran, I can't leave him—"

"He'll not listen yet. And your mother's needing you, she's worn out, poor thing. Say nothing about the boat—your father's heart will stop he hears his boat's gone. Go on now, go be with your mother. You'll spend the night with her? She'll need that, you spending the night with her in that room."

Gran walked stiffly to the house, the wind cutting her nightdress to her legs. The sun was just slanting across the shed door as Kyle peered outside. Seeing me looking towards him, he gave an apologetic nod and then hauled the door shut—Chris's instruction, no doubt.

"Some good doing that now," I muttered, "when it's himself he needs protecting from." Receiving nothing but a gust of wind for my words, I followed after Gran, readying for the drive to the hospital.

———

MOTHER WAS SLEEPING in an armchair in a windowless waiting room, her face wearing the same pallor as yesterday despite the yellowish light from a heavily shaded lamp falling across her brow. She stirred as I neared, her straight dark hair falling away from her face, baring strong cheekbones tauting her skin, a defiant chin, and a fine, fine brow. A striking, strong face, I thought with a second's pride, for, aside from Father's brown eyes, I knew I carried my mother's likeness.

I pressed closer, drawn to her mouth which was softened by sleep and curving into a natural smile. How quiet she looked without her glittering blue eyes cutting through the light. They had intrigued and frightened me as a youngster, sitting at the table with Chris during home-schooling times, she standing tall before us, no longer the mother sounding out warnings and ordering us about, but like a beautiful teacher-aunt of sorts, speaking richly and clearly about foreign places and people. I can still remember how those eyes sharpened with intent as she queried our learning, snapped impatiently if we failed an answer, then bore through us as she lectured about thinking deep and thinking far so's someday we might travel past the outports, past the island itself, and on to bigger worlds.

Once, in the middle of a lesson, I fell into daydreaming about owning such eyes, thinking how much prettier I would look with deep, glittering blues instead of the dulled browns I'd been given.

"What're you thinking?" Mother had said sharply, and I dug my eyes into the book laid out before me, scarcely breathing as she came to the table. Putting a finger beneath my chin, she tipped my face upward and smiled, her eyes sparkling like a sunlit sea. "Well then?" she repeated more softly.

"I'm going to go everywhere," I answered breathlessly, then delighted in her proud look.

"Heavens, that's a good plan. And what're you going to be—a teacher? A nurse?"

"I'm going to be a captain."

She laughed. "Now, there's lofty," she replied, and I hugged into the moment, spending the rest of the lesson and many more after that imagining myself getting off ships and airplanes, Mother waiting on the ground while I ran towards her holding out bags of presents with fancy glass jewellery boxes inside, and watches and rings and strings of necklaces.

Why, I wondered now, touching a finger to Mother's hand resting on the arm of the chair, had I always been coming from a distance towards my mother? Gran's house was no farther than a bedroom away, and Mother was more of a fixture than Dad—coming twice, thrice, a dozen times a day sometimes, when either me or Gran was feeling poorly. Always she was traipsing through the door, bringing soup, bringing stews, bringing buns or whatever she was cooking for her own dinner. She came most evenings, too, no matter that Father was still there, lying back on the sofa with me on his chest and snoring. Jostling him awake, she'd send him home with the boys and sit, sipping a hot toddy with Gran, stretching good beside the bustling hot stove and helping ready me for bed.

She never bothered with ironing sheets and heating plates as Gran and Dad always done, but she always listened to my prayers, and then hovered for a second, gazing down onto my face before kissing me and tucking me in. Sometimes she rested her cheek, cool and sweet with lavender, against mine, and I could still feel its imprint minutes later as she dawdled about the room, straightening the bedding, tidying the clothing strewn about the floor.

"Say good night to Mommy," Gran always said in the doorway as Mother was about to leave.

"Good night, Mommy," I would say, my mouth lingering over the word *Mommy*, trying to feel its warmth in my heart as when I said the word *Gran*, or *Dad*, but I never could really feel it. I couldn't see it much either, in those cool blue eyes as she leaned down a second time to kiss me. Mostly I saw that sense of wariness I always felt when my mother stared at me closely, as though it were a spectre, not her child, that lay upon the pillow. I don't remember when I first noted that guarded look, and yet I always felt it, veiled, exposing itself in those most private moments when she thought I wasn't watching.

It was the lie that grew between us, that we knew only in our hearts; a lie that rendered me a nervous, fidgety child with a silly, shrill laugh that was always too loud and lasted too long whenever Mother was about. I took to standing quietly whenever she wasn't paying attention, fixing dark, searching eyes onto her face. Those times she looked up unexpectedly, we'd both be startled and I'd run off. I took to hiding—in the nook of a tree, a rock, a gatepost, scuttling behind doorways and corners. And in that great expanse of air, of open beach and meadow comprising the tiny inlet of Cooney Arm, where there existed only birds and passing clouds to cast an unexpected shadow around one's feet, it was always startling for Mother each time a movement of air or shadow signalled an unseen presence.

It got so she started searching about before laying down a laundry basket or picking up the hoe, as though she felt unsafe till my whereabouts were established.

"Like the ghost," she complained to Gran in the garden once, "appears out of nowhere," and she pursed her lips irritably as I stared up into her face with a shrill set of giggles.

I never meant to spy on my mother, or startle her. I simply wanted to be near her, to watch her, examine her, yet safely at a distance, as though it were some wild creature I scouted, whose mannerisms I was intrigued by and uncertain of. Like her sudden cries of fright or fun over some small thing with the boys, her spurts of laughter or anger at Father, her manner of sinking to her knees near a drill of cabbage and holding handfuls of dirt before her as though sifting through it for something lost, those hours of quiet she spent sitting on a white-speckled rock by the brook, watching the water flowing past. "Shh, quiet, now, Sylvie," Gran whispered those times we spied her kneeling by the graves of her three little dears sleeping in the graveyard, "same as sitting in church when you're sitting in prayer."

Once, while Gran was puttering at the bin and I was polishing windows, I spotted Mom kneeling besides the graves. "Are the three little dears ghosts?" I asked, for I knew about ghosts, heard them all the time in the boarded-up houses. Plus I'd woken up several times from a deep, deep sleep and heard the rocker creaking in the kitchen, knowing it was Grandfather Now's ghost coming to keep watch through the window.

"No, Dolly, they're not ghosts," Gran had replied, "little angels is what they are."

"So why're they buried?"

"They're not in the ground, Dolly. Graves are marking places, is all, marking where they last slept."

I'd been struck by that. "They slept? They were real like me?"

"Goodness mercy, yes, they were as real as you, and now they're pretty angels. Take down them curtains, we'll wash them too."

"Are ghosts angels?"

"I don't think so."

"But will they be sometime?"

"I suppose so."

"When?"

"When they finds their way home."

"Where's their home?"

"Goodness mercy, Sylvie, bide your tongue and bring me the curtains—mind now you don't trip over them."

"Their home's in heaven, right," I said, "where all the animals go, and where they plays with children and don't bite them?" This last was spoken with conviction, for ever since I'd found the ribcage of our old cat, Boots, who never came home one day, and I sat crying over his bones, Gran had explained to me about how all animals went to heaven, moose and bears too, and played with the children on huge fields of flowers.

I dropped the curtains, clasping my hands tight to my heart. "Oh, Gran, I can't wait to die," I busted out with an excitement akin to the time Father took me to my first show at the theatre in Ragged Rock.

With a gasp of fright Gran stepped over her curtains and sat me on a chair, telling me another side of the story of death, about how it's only God who chooses when one goes to heaven, and how, if somebody does something silly, like walk out in the water over their head or roll off a cliff so's to die, God met them at the Heavenly Gates and sent them back to their mothers and grandmothers in shame, for thinking they could take on the role of God, and the rest of their lives would be spent washing dishes and ironing clothes for punishment.

I took particular care skirting the water's edge the following days, and stayed away from all cliff tops. Yet each time I snuck inside one of the abandoned houses, hearing ghosts creaking the walls, a huge curiosity grew within me. I carried on plaguing Gran with questions about ghosts and how come they got lost, and do they never find their way home, and where's home anyway, and can they see us, and how long are you in the ground before you becomes an angel, or before you becomes a ghost, or do ghosts become angels?

When my questions outgrew Gran's patience and started causing her worry, I made up my own answers and told them to Chris. "Close your eyes now," I'd say, laying him out on an old weed-choked grave in the graveyard where the three little dears slept, "it's how we become angels—we die first, get laid out in a grave, and then comes up through the dirt like a ghost, only with wings, and flies to heaven. And if you don't keep your eyes closed, you don't grow wings, you don't go to heaven, just rots in the ground or drifts around the shore in wet clothes like poor Grandfather Now, or gets trapped in the walls of old, boarded-up houses, waiting to find your way home."

It was the one game Chris liked. Spread out on the grave, covered in leaves and grass, and sometimes with a white crocheted cloth over his face that I snuck from Gran's drawer, he would lie still forever—long as he could see through that bit of cloth. One day I covered his face with a scrap of flannel, and after a couple of minutes he flung it aside and started to bawl because it was too dark. I calmed him, then raced back inside the house, found the crocheted one from the drawer, and raced back out, starting the game again. It was a sunny autumn day, with a full wind and lots of leaves gusting about. Laying Chris back down on the grave, I covered his face with the crocheted cloth and buried his body in withered leaves.

Then, kneeling beside him, I stuck my finger into my eyes to make real tears and started moaning and swaying as my mother's sisters and brothers had done over fat Nanny Ralph's burying in Ragged Rock. When Chris was deathly still I laid myself out on the grave nearest him, still moaning, and covered myself with handfuls of leaves and grass, then covered my face with the scrap of flannel and shut my eyes against the diffused blue of the sky coming through. For the next while we both lay there, perfectly still.

With the sea smashing upon the rocks and the wind rustling the trees and swishing through the tall timothy grass overgrowing the graveyard, neither of us saw or heard Mother coming through the gate and making her way to kneel beside her three little dears. Nor had she seen us. When I, hearing a sound, popped up from my grave, and Chris sat up from his, the cloth falling from our faces, dead leaves falling from our heads and shoulders, Mother's eyes constricted in fright. Her face went pale, paler than the dead grandmother's. She clenched her fists before her face and let out a ragged scream, shaking so hard it appeared she was falling over.

Frightened of a wrongdoing, I clambered to my feet, yelling at Chris to come, and flew out of the cemetery. Chris made to follow but Mother called after him in a sharp, tinny voice. She called after us both, but I kept running, past Gran's and down amongst the abandoned houses. I pushed open the door to one of them, Uncle Jake's, where Father sometimes stored his nets, and crept over to a partially boarded-up window, looking back towards the graveyard. Mother was still sitting there, holding Chris in her arms and kissing the top of his head and rocking him like a baby. She looked up once and, afraid of being seen, I crept away, hiding inside an emptied, darkish closet near the porch.

I'd often hidden there with Chris, hoping to see or hear one of the ghosts in the walls. Sometimes I came without Chris, crouching in the dusky light, pretending to be one of the ghosts. Once, I became so intently fixed on the silence singing through the house that I felt myself becoming lightheaded, and it started to feel like I was fading, drifting, fusing into the singing somehow, and a quiver of pure joyousness shot through me. So strong was that feeling, so strong the sense of losing myself, that I was immediately gripped by a shiver of fright and snapped open my eyes, grasping hold of the walls. Scrabbling out of the closet, I raced off to Gran's with a terrified heart and a need to be seen.

It was the fear of a youngster having done wrong that I was feeling on this day, crouching in the closet, hiding from Mother. A prickling went down my back and I felt my heart-beat quicken. It started beating faster in that cramped corner, and suddenly I could hear it—*thump thump thump*. My stomach was cramping with fear and I thought to flee. But then something creaked somewhere, and I froze. The walls started up with their singing. My breathing grew raspy and I wanted to scream. Another creak sounded, and blood sluiced like cold brook water through my veins. Then the sound of Mother's voice uttering a curse as her foot must've gone through a rotted step.

"Sylvie, Sylvie, where you hiding—Sylvie."

I pressed both hands to my mouth. The door pushed open, letting in a stream of silver light across the greyish room.

"Sylvie!"

My name echoed through the emptied house. Through a partial opening in the closet doorway I watched Mother stepping inside. I watched her treading cautiously past the closet into the dimly lit room. I watched her standing still for a moment, then moving her hand to her heart as though she, too, heard the singing. Quietly, she moved towards the window, her hands clutched before her as if frightened of touching the walls. It was my moment. She'd left the door open and it stood just a few steps away. Sucking in a good breath, I took a stealthy step outside the closet, cringing from the rustling of my clothes. I hesitated, then lifted my foot for another step. Mother was peering out through the window. Bursting to breathe, I crept forward another step. The floor creaked and then my lungs caved, making a dreadful hissing sound. Mother spun about, her hand flying to her heart as I, red-faced and with bulging eyes, stood in the silver stream of light, breathing raggedly.

"Sweet jeezes!" groaned Mother, and staggered back against the windowsill. Tearing out the door, I never looked back.

Nothing was ever said about it. Not by Gran, Dad, or Mom. But Mother didn't come the next day to sip tea or hot toddies with Gran. And when she did come, that wariness was foremost in her eyes when she looked at me, and her lips barely touched my cheek after she listened to my prayers that evening and kissed me good night.

"I'm going to be a traveller," I kept offering from my pillow by way of atonement. Getting nothing of the usual smiles of encouragement, I strained to touch her hand, wanting to avow my innocence, that I hadn't been trying to spook her in the graveyard; had simply been playing dead, was all, and likewise, hadn't meant to frighten her in the abandoned house. But Mother's ghastly reaction when Chris and I rose from the grave like that, and then her staggering with fright at the sight of me inside the haunted house, and then never yelling at me for what I'd done or speaking a word of it to Gran or Dad, and her staying away from Gran's like that—she'd never stayed away from Gran's before, not even when Chris was sick or the baby was sick did she stay away from Gran's—well, all these things measured so big somehow that my voice felt like a whisper in a windstorm, my innocence a matter of no consequence next to Mother's fright.

Now, seating myself on the edge of the hospital sofa, I touched my mother's slender white hand resting on her lap, wondering how much I had contributed to its pallor. For it hadn't been an easy fit, the coming together of me and Gran in Mother's house. Wonderful, Father promised that last day in Cooney Arm as I reluctantly packed my bag, it would be wonderful—all of us eating and sleeping beneath the one roof finally, being a real family. And there would be a real school with real friends other than my brothers, and everything would be nice, he promised, smoothing my hair and kissing my face. But I felt his weightiness in the manner in which he held me so tight, as though I were a pillow for his own fears. And so's not to burden him more I let him believe that I believed him, and started packing my room.

Despite my wretchedness over leaving Gran's house, it did feel like a real family that first day, pushing off from the shores of Cooney Arm, huddling towards each other, watching the beach, the meadow, falling away from us. And it was a moment that gave a good start to our all living together, for we'd been kind to each other those first few weeks, everyone helping the other unpack, and touching and speaking to each other gently as though we'd each been bruised by the one falling rock. And it suited me fine in the days to come that Mother was always hovering over Chris, fixing his hair, fixing his collar—mostly for the love of touching him, I always felt—for it was Father I coveted. Many times in Cooney Arm I pretended that Father belonged to me and Mother belonged to Chris, and that we all watched over Gran and Kyle, making for the perfect halves of the one family.

Perhaps—as when Dad had halved his house in order to launch it from Cooney Arm—if the house had remained divided, allowing for each unit of this perfect family to remain on its own shelving, it might not have fallen in on itself—at least where me and Mother were concerned. But the house was already formed when I entered it, with Mother its crossbar, and Dad and the boys—and now me and Gran, too—forming her framework. In Gran's house it was me who'd been foremost and centre, polishing its floors and windows since I'd been big enough to drag around a broom. And from the time I could swing an axe I was chopping kindling, lugging wood, and stogging that old stove so full that it singed the air with heat whenever Gran needed to bake bread, make soup, or chase off them cold winter days when her old bones creaked more than the rafters in a squally wind.

Yet in Mother's house I was shooed to the sidelines with the boys, watching as she swept, mopped, and dusted right down to the farthest corner in every room, including the one I shared with Gran. I'd stand resentfully beside my bed, protesting as she polished my bureau or decorated it with doilies and dried flowers, tucking my things—rocks, a bird's nest, Boots's tiny, polished skull—into drawers, or worse, into boxes and suitcases that she'd push under the beds or into the closets along with the other things from my old room in Cooney Arm.

"Take it out when you needs it," she'd respond to my yelps of protest, and carry right on with her cleaning and tidying. Except those times when she strolled determinedly towards me with a ribbon or clips or some article of clothing. She didn't shoo me away on those days, but would stand arguing till the sun went down over my refusal to have my hair combed and fixed. During those times, I actually ran outdoors, or to my room, barring myself inside for fear of becoming no more than a thing myself, all prettily polished and tidied and tucked inside a fold of Mother's house.

I got no sympathy from Gran. Back in Cooney Arm, Gran had always lauded my swiftness with a dishcloth or a scrubbing rag. Now she sided with Mother and was forever directing my attention—as Mother did—towards homework, or out to the wharf, watching that the boys didn't fall overboard. Neither was Father much of a consolation. A brooding figure he'd been, those first years in Hampden, hunched over the wharf and looking back towards Cooney Arm, gutted by the loss of the fish, his stage. And instead of lazing back on the sofa when evening came, snoring out the strains of the day with me on his chest, he was now going off to bed, into that room he shared with my mother, whose door was always closed, emitting tiny gasps of cool air whenever it opened as I walked by. When he did settle on the sofa, throwing his feet upon the humpty, it was always Kyle clambering over him, and sometimes Chris. Never me, for under Mother's critical eye I suddenly felt too big for anything I used to do, all my cozy comforts replaced by big-girl dresses, big-girl ponytails, big-girl ways of sitting in a chair with my knees beneath the table and not comfortably tucked beneath my chin.

Tricked. I felt like I'd been tricked out of my nice, warm home with Gran and staged in Mother's, which held nothing of its comforts. All the things I'd brought from my life in Cooney Arm, tucked now into boxes beneath the bed, felt no more than souvenirs of a home that once was. And worse, every time I crept around the house—hoping to escape attention, homework, the boys—and accidentally scared Mother by appearing silently in a doorway, she'd accuse me of sneaking about.

"Just like when you were small, always spying," she cried out once.

"I'm not spying," I protested.

"Yes, you are, nobody walks that quietly without they're up to something."

"Perhaps I'd like to be alone for once," I shouted, and seeing the disbelieving look on Mother's face, flounced to my room in a fit of frustration. In an effort to prove my innocence, I started walking more quietly at all times, keeping a preoccupied look on my face and pretending I was looking for something, should Mother look up from her cooking or cleaning or reading with a start. Times I feigned a start myself upon a sudden gasp from her. Mostly it was during those quietest of moments—when the boys and Father were outside somewhere, and Gran dozing in her rocker, and the house humming along with Mother as she tidied her kitchen or living room—that I tended to appear. Always, during this silly, repeated exercise, I wore a preoccupied look, then bafflement each time Mother jumped or shrieked in fright. Once, she was so startled she dropped and shattered her prized candy dish she'd been about to wash.

"Nobody walks that quietly, Sylvie, without they're trying to," she cried, looking piteously at the glass scattered around her feet.

"Gawd, you always says that."

"Then why you doing it—always trying to frighten me?"

"I don't. I'm not—lord, everybody else always hears me."

"Everybody else—you only does it around me, whatever kind of game you're playing."

"Well, you knows I'm in the house," I kept going as Mother fell to her knees, picking up bits of glass, "what's so strange about me walking down the hall—you rather I stayed in my room all day?" Getting nothing more than a painful yelp from Mother as she pricked a finger with a sliver of glass, I gave a righteous huff and went outside, muttering loudly about the unfairness of her accusations when I was simply walking down the hallway, was all, simply minding my own business like the day in the graveyard, like the abandoned house thing—just minding my own business when suddenly, poof—there's Mother, all in a jitters and frightening her own self with her own jittery nerves.

"Jumpin's, why's everybody so rabbity," I complained a few days after the broken dish, when I appeared out of the hallway, startling Gran this time.

"You'll give us all heart attacks," warned Gran as I glided to the sofa, picking up the catalogue I'd been flipping through earlier. I sat with my back to them both, hearing Gran tsk. A

sideways glance at Mother showed her pursed mouth as she
kept silent, stirring the meat and onions she was frying up on
the stove. Gran, letting out a small groan over the ache in her
legs from the foggy, drizzly day outside, shuffled to where I was
sitting and poked at my back with a gnarled finger.

"I tell you, you're making your mother sick," she said
irritably.

"Jumpin's, I didn't do nothing."

"You're making your mother sick, I tell you."

"How's I making her sick—I don't do nothing to make her
sick."

"You just frightened Gran," said Mother firmly. "So I'm not
imagining things when you frightened Gran as well. It's how
you've always been, sneaking about."

I jumped to my feet, swinging around to face her. "I don't!
I don't sneak about, you always says that, and I don't. Well, I
don't," I yelled as Mother went, tight-lipped, back to her
stirring.

I threw the catalogue on the sofa. "You always believes her,"
I charged Gran. "Ever since we moved in here you always
believes her."

Gran tsked again, sitting back down in her rocker.

"Well, it's true!" I yelled. Hurt by Gran's not listening, and
with a surge of brazenness, I looked to Mother, saying in a
loud, prim voice, "Not my fault you're always thinking I'm a
ghost. Well, that's what you thinks, isn't it, that I'm a ghost? You
always looks afraid of me, like I was walking around dead or
something. I believe you wishes I was dead, anyway."

I fell silent for a moment, Mother's face going all white
again. "And perhaps I wishes I *was* dead," I yelled, my voice
turning into a whine. "I wouldn't have to live here then, she
only likes Chris anyway," and felt the cut of my words in

Mother's flinch. "Leaving here anyway," I shouted, half bawling now, and fled down the hall, "soon's I finishes school, I'm leaving, I won't be living around here."

I slammed the door of my room and fell across the bed, heart pounding, ears ringing, no different from that moment when I'd sat hidden in the closet of the boarded-up house. Only this time I wasn't holding my breath. I'd just blown it out like a tempest, releasing a tension in my chest that I hadn't realized was there till now, with the sudden release of its being gone.

But, like any rutted container in a storm, it remained empty only for as long as it takes the elements to fill it again, and instantly my chest tightened with another thought: that my carelessly flung words had hurt Mother, a hurt I couldn't fathom, given how foolish and of little meaning I felt the words to be. For sure I had yelled worse than those before, cussed even, and gotten scarcely a backhanded glance.

I pulled the blankets over me, but then hearing Gran's voice rising in the kitchen, I snuck off the bed and eased open the door, listening.

"Start ignoring her, maid," Gran was saying, "long as you keeps it in your head, she'll keep doing it, she'll keep carrying it out."

"Carrying it out—carrying what out?" asked Mother, but then kept on talking, scarcely able to keep her voice down as she rattled on about the ridiculousness of my words, the silly things I was getting on with, my foolishness. "For goodness sakes, you seen her, Gran, how you suppose to ignore someone traipsing like a ghost through the house?"

Gran's voice fell, and straining to hear, I leaned harder against the door, creaking it. Both voices stopped for a second, and then carried on in normal tones about Father working too hard in the woods. I threw myself back across the bed, balling up the pillow and winging it at the wall. Even Gran was blaming me for Mother's bad nerves. To show them I didn't care, I bounced off the bed, opened the door with a quick soundless movement, and glided down the hallway more quietly than a swan crossing a summer's pond. Snatching up the catalogue that I'd thrown on the sofa and looking to neither of them, I glided back to my room, closing the door in the same quick, soundless motion.

For the rest of that week and the following I glided through the house. I glided about the wharf, too, as silent in my rubber boots as I was in stocking feet, taking no apparent notice of anyone, most especially Mother and Gran. Neither did they seem to notice me, except in the usual way of a parent—how's school, got your homework done, are you hungry. Always I shook or nodded my head, as silent with words as I was with my footstep, spending most of the days in my room, needing nothing from nobody. I did notice, however, that Mother was no longer gasping out loud those times I appeared unexpectedly before her. Not that she wasn't startled, for I saw in the way she pursed her mouth or whipped her hand to her heart that she was. But nothing was ever said, and after a short while it all faded into nothing, Mother's frights, my emanations. The rowing might've stopped too, if not for a comment I overheard Mother making to Gran a few months later, on Christmas morning.

I had ripped the wrapping paper off a pair of shiny black shoes that had rhinestones across the toes and soles that clicked loudly against the vinyl floors as I excitedly pulled them on and tap-danced down the hall.

"Could've saved myself a few grey hairs," Mother said to Gran, and vexed by the quiet laugh they shared, I threw Mother a dark look and tapped extra loud coming back up the hall.

Another series of rows started, this time over my noisy step. But now Mother kept a smile on her face and paid me no more attention than she did Chris and Kyle roughhousing about the sofa. Within a short time I gave up—or forgot—my tap-dancing routine, and found other things to bicker over with Mother.

That was one thing that never changed, me and Mother bickering—much to the anguish of everyone else, most especially Father. Times when I'd fling out through the door and hunch beside him on the wharf, taking up his sullen stare out the bay, and he'd ply me with soft talk, trying to get at the reason for my apparent anger with Mother. But I could never say, for I never knew, beyond the trivialities of the moment. Going beyond that took me back into the graveyard, the house of haunts, or some look in Mother's eye—conscious moments that capped some deeper thing I was never able to properly see or give expression to. Yet, for all its elusiveness, it bubbled along just below the surface in my relationship with Mother, obscured in its brackish waters but requiring only the slightest slackening of the tides for that black edge of a dorsal fin to jut between us.

"Going to university anyway," I'd say loudly to Father whenever Mother was lurking within earshot. "And after that I'm moving to Rome."

"Learn to navigate Hampden first," said Mother, patting my head in passing, "or are we just a stepping stone now? Stop pouting, get your boots on, you're late for school."

I sniffed hard at that one and dragged my heels out the door, miffed that my travel aspirations, having once garnered such looks of delight from Mother, had somehow become the family joke.

Worse, I hated the overstuffed school in Hampden. They made fun of the way I talked. Plus, coming from the quiet of Cooney Arm with simply Chris and Kyle for company, the number of kids I met that first day in a real school felt like a mob, stoning me with words. I got used to it quickly enough, though. The kids even started being friendly, inviting me to birthday parties, bonfires, soccer games in the field behind the school. Sometimes I went, but it was never fun. I simply wasn't the type to make close friends. And there were always so many of them, and so highly charged and caught up in each other's lives that they felt like one large family. As with Mother's house, they were fully formed before I arrived; I never felt a comfortable fit. Besides, I'd already made up my mind sitting at Mother's table in Cooney Arm that I'd be travelling far and wide the minute I finished school. So why bother planting feet on a stepping stone, I kept asking myself, casting surly looks at Mother.

———————

ONE WEEK IN EARLY JUNE, about five years after we left Cooney Arm, I got so homesick for the life I'd once had in my own little house with Gran that Father took me for a walk up the road to where the river emptied into the sea. It had been so long since we'd been alone that I almost felt shy walking beside him. The tide was out, the sandbar shimmering wet beneath the sun and spreading about a quarter mile out, almost flush with our house on the wharf. Hundreds of gulls cried and strutted about, their feathers white against the browns of the sandbar as they snatched hold of clams with their beaks and took flight, dropping and cracking the hard shells on the rocks below.

"Nice way of making supper, hey," said Father, skirting one of the smashed clams as a burly gull swooped down, suckling the wet, slimy muscle out of the broken bits of shell.

"Yuh," I said, and noted his hand swinging by his side as he walked. Somewhere in the past few years I'd grown too big to naturally grasp hold of his hand. I trailed behind as he followed the river deeper into the estuary through little crooked paths amongst the immense alder bed, bringing us to a meadow not too unlike the one in Cooney Arm.

"Pretty, hey?" Father said, gazing upon the hills to the far side of the river. They rose tall, steep, forming a wall of patch-worked greens. Growing tired, he sat on a rock near where a strong current gutted itself over the rocks, drowning out most other sounds but its own gurgling. I sat beside him, watching as he listened quietly to the song of the river. His thick, dark hair was longish, past his usual cutting point, and there was an ease about him that I hadn't felt since before the fish went, before the hated move from Cooney Arm.

"Thought I might build agin, here—near the river—your mother's getting crippled up, arthritis," he said to my surprised look. "Needs to get away from the water. Think this might be a nice place?"

"Is she going to be crippled?"

"Noo, just aches and pains is all. She'd like it here, away from the wind, have a garden."

My twinge of alarm faded, and I looked about disinterestedly. "What about you, you like living near the water."

He gave an offhand shrug. A brown-feathered sparrow with a grey crown flitted onto a shrub nearby, letting out a series of short, incessant chirps to which Father quickly responded with a low, trilling whistle. I noted again how he wasn't looking as glum as he used to. "Long as the family's all right I can live anywhere," he said and leaned back on his hands, watching as the sparrow took flight, flittering into the thicket.

"But you hates it here."

"Gets silly after a while, don't it, hating something because you're mad at something else, you think? Time we had a bigger house—you needs your own room."

I scoffed. "I don't need my own room, I'd rather sleep with Gran, and I wouldn't like living here in the woods, too many flies. Besides, there's no road, how're we going to get places?" I got up, bored with sitting and scratching flies off my neck. "Can we go back now? I don't like it here."

He kept gazing into the thicket where the little bird had flown, then slowly got up, brushing off the seat of his pants. "Tomorrow," he said, starting back along the river, "we'll go to Cooney Arm, camp over for the night, you want that?"

I eagerly agreed, and the following morning glided through the house in ghost slippers again so's not to wake the boys, not wanting them along on this coveted trip with Father to the place of my heart. Gran had given up her garden, and it had been a few years now since I'd been back.

The one-hour boat trip took forever, and then finally we were motoring through the rock-choked channel of the neck.

Father shut off the motor, letting in the roar of Bear Falls as it foamed an angry white whilst crashing down the centre of the tree-draped hills. The few abandoned houses on the flat, grassy land beneath looked small and weathered, sagging heavily inwards. I turned to Gran's house, its yellow paint all blistery and cracked, the weathering beneath encroaching like a grey fungus over whatever yellow was left. And the gouged-out earth where Father's house had been was grassed over now; with its thick spattering of dandelions it looked little more than a sunken grave marking where the house had once stood.

I shivered. The sky was cloudy and a brisk wind chopped the water, cooling the air. Father lifted me out of the boat and

I stood for a moment, looking about. It felt eerily quiet in a sudden lull of the wind. Everything looked so small.

"It's because you've grown," said Father.

I wandered over to his old stage, its floorboards no longer trustworthy to stand upon, then trailed along the beach, stepping over anchors left behind by the uncles and now bleeding red onto the rocks. Farther up on the bank were bundles of netting that looked like clumps of rotting seaweed. The ribbed skeleton of a boat, tossed inland by the sea, lay beside the abandoned house where I'd crouched with the spirits.

I walked slowly through Gran's broken-down gate and untied her front door. I nudged it open, the hinges squeaky and stiff, and made to push my way inside but suddenly pulled back, unable to stand the smell of mould, of decay. Rot. The whole place—Gran's house, everything—felt like death.

Father was in the graveyard, ripping handfuls of last year's dead grass off the three graves and clearing away space around the crosses. He'd brought a bucket of white paint. I retreated to the falls, grateful for the bounteous rush of air from the cascading water. Something caught my eye near the back step in Gran's backyard. My breath caught in my throat and then slowly released itself. On a nail beside Gran's back door was one of her aprons, the kind that looped around her neck and tied around her waist, hanging past her knees. It used to be blue and was nearly white now from the sun and snow, and hung in tatters. For a second I thought it was Gran, stooped, as she always was, over a bucket of scrubbing water or a dustpan or some such thing.

I huddled on Mother's white-speckled rock near the brook, hugging my knees, the vapour from the falls settling like a wintry mist on my face. After Father had painted the three crosses and tidied up the graves, he came and stood beside me, watching the gulls squawking and swooping over mussel shells they'd dropped and shattered on the rocks.

His dark eyes beneath their brush of brows looked sadly at the decaying wooden structures and then back to the gulls again, the water lopping against the shore, the sun just breaking through the cloud, perking open the dandelions that had claimed the spot where his house had stood.

"Wanna go?" he asked.

"Thought we were spending the night."

"If you want to."

I shook my head.

"Let's go then."

For the first time in the years since we'd left Cooney Arm, I relished hopping into the boat. And for the first time ever I didn't look back as we motored through the neck.

THREE

I SAT FORWARD on the springy sofa in the hospital waiting room, watching while Mother stirred, as intrigued as I'd been as a child by those thickly fringed eyes fluttering alive.

"What's wrong, my, what's wrong?" she cried upon seeing me sitting so close and looking so pensive.

"Nothing. Nothing," I said. "I—everything's fine. I just saw Dad; he's looking better. Sit back," I coaxed as she made to rise, "sit back, it's early."

She shook her head. "Lord, if I lives through this."

"You will. And he's doing great." I watched as she rubbed her temples, rubbed her eyes, noting the tired lines on her face. "Gran's worried about you."

"She shouldn't worry, then. Enough on her mind." Mother broke into a yawn. "My!" she exclaimed, shaking it off. "Feels like I haven't slept in days."

"Why don't you go home for a day? I'll stay with Dad. Why not, you should, you should go home."

"No. No, I'll not leave him. I'm fine—you've been in? You've seen him?"

"Yes. Yes, I told you. They're bathing him."

"I told them I'd bathe him."

"They're doing other stuff too. Oh, just sit back, Mom."

She sat back, unable to stop yawning. "My," she said again, and rubbed some more at her eyes. "Chris!" she exclaimed, glancing about the room, "Where's Chris—and Kyle?"

"Doing stuff around the house."

"Stuff—what stuff?"

"Cleaving wood. Are you eating?"

"Cleaving wood?" She eyed me suspiciously. "They got lots of time for cleaving wood. How come they're not here?"

"Tomorrow. They're coming tomorrow. You need some breakfast—seriously, why don't you go home for the day, let Gran feed you. I can sit with Dad—will you take a day?" I pleaded as she rose with a brisk shake of her head.

"I'll not leave, Sylvie, don't start with that again. The boys should be here, too—where's my purse, lord, search by the sofa—he'll not like it the boys aren't here, does him good to see the boys."

"I told them to stay with Gran. I'm leaving in a couple of days, I want to spend some time with him."

"He likes seeing everybody here, your father does. First time he's ever been sick."

"He'll be fine with me. Gawd, Mom, there," I said, exasperated by her inattentive searching for her purse. "I told you, I want to sit by him all day. Besides, the boys are looking after Gran, she's tired."

"Where, Sylvie, I can't see no purse."

"By the chair leg—there." I darted forward, rescuing the purse from behind the chair. She took it gratefully and sat back, pulling out a compact. "Quite the fright, I know," she said, eyeing herself in the dusty little mirror.

"You look like a girl," I said.

"I looks like the hag." She slipped the compact inside her purse and shut her eyes, clasping her hands in her lap. "My," she began, and as though too fatigued to speak, lapsed into silence, laying back her head.

"What? What're you thinking?"

She blew out a deep breath. "Gawd knows what I'm thinking. Thinking about everything. What about Gran, how's she holding up through all this? She looked so tiny in this place, thought she was going to vanish."

"Just fine, I told you. She sent you some bread, worried you're not eating enough. You want me to get tea?"

"No, not yet. I can't drink tea this early. Bless her, she's worrying herself to death, I knows she is."

"She said you're not to think about her. It's good the boys are there, though."

"Bless them, too," she murmured. "Such good boys. We were blessed there."

"Oh? Was I the curse?" The words kind of slipped out and I smiled to take away their abruptness.

Surprisingly, Mother smiled too. "Lord knows you tried to be," she said, fighting back another yawn. "Like your father, stubborn as cowhide."

"That right, now. Gran says I'm like you."

"God help you. Like neither of us," she said quietly. "Like neither of us. Your grandmother, that's who you're like; steady like your grandmother—guess I've got lots to be thankful for." She held out a pale, slender hand, and I took it like a gawky youngster unexpectedly handed a delicate piece of china and not knowing where to put it.

"You always worry, Mom," I said, my voice but a whisper.

Her hand slipped like a cool breeze from my grasp. "Always them nights I sits worrying, my girl. Nights I sit by the window and pray, like I'm holding up the world—my own world, at least," she added dryly. "Gran always says she's praying for them who can't. I envy her that. All about myself I've been."

I blinked at this bit of divulgence. "I've never thought that about you."

"It was back before you could think. It was always your father—back in Cooney Arm—who kept things together. Even with the fishing all but gone, he held things. Never knew my comforts." She rose, pacing the small room, wringing her hands, pausing before a small framed portrait of the darkly bearded Jesus. "Everything changed after we left the arm. Mostly me holding things together—even when he's working straight through winters and summers and keeping the house warm, feels like it's me holding it. Is there retribution in that?" she asked the framed portrait, her tone turning persuasive. "Make up for all them years I spent worrying about me?

"Well"—she turned back to me, more silent now than Christ before my mother's bartering—"we'll soon see how good I do."

"But he got used to everything," I said. "Working in the woods, and he kinda enjoys living on the wharf—like living in a boathouse, he often says. You can't say he let himself go."

"Ohh, I don't know, I don't know anything anymore. He's not able to work in the woods again, that I knows. How's he going to deal with that? And money—not like we can live on Gran's spuds. We'll have to give the truck back, unless he sells his boat—kill him to sell his boat." She started pacing anew, wringing her hands.

Shaken by her words, I stepped impulsively before her. "I've got money saved. I'll take over the truck payments."

Her face took on a scandalized look. "My lord, no. We're not that poor we'd take your money. Good god, your father would have a fit."

"Why? No different than Chris helping."

"All the difference in the world, you way out in Alberta, scrimping and paying your way through university."

"Mom, I've graduated."

"You'll be going back to university, I knows that about you, Sylvie. And besides, your father wouldn't stand for it—he'd jump overboard before taking your money. Now go sit with him." She gathered her purse and sweater and some change sitting beneath the lamp on a coffee table. "All this way for just a few days—you couldn't get more time?"

"I'll stay if you want."

"No. No, you go and work. That's the most you can do, take care of yourself. You'll come back for Christmas though, won't you? For sure you'll be home for Christmas, your father's foolish over Christmas. My, such a long ways to travel for just a few days—"

"The boss wants my job for his niece," I cut in. "He'll boot me first chance, but I don't care about that, I'll stay longer if you want."

"Thought there were jobs galore in Alberta."

"There are. But this one makes big dollars—seriously," I said to her dubious look, "it's a bar in town, and the tips are huge. I make as much as a roughneck—which is why I can send money home—"

"Don't start that again—and for the love of god, say nothing to your father—he'd die on the spot." She gave me a quick hug. "And I'm well aware you graduated, didn't have to remind me of that." She pressed her cheek against mine, then kissed it. "Now, go sit with your father while I finds a washroom."

As I watched her slight frame scurry away I lifted my hand to my cheek, feeling an absurd notion to cry. Emptied from thought, I wandered through corridors, finding, finally, the heavy glass doors of the intensive care unit. I pulled back the curtains surrounding Father's bed and stood for a moment looking down upon his ashen face, the darkened hollows of his eyes.

"Looking lots better," I said reassuringly, stroking his hand.

He nodded, his smile wan, and I leaned my face next to his, longing for that great, heaving chest and loud healthy snores.

"Your mother?" he whispered.

"She's getting washed. She'll be here in a minute." I felt him relax, his breathing easier, more natural than yesterday. "Such a short time, already seeing a difference," I said lowly, wondering if perhaps the doctor was wrong and he'd soon be his old, strong self. "Everybody's well—Chris, Kyle, Gran. All wishing you home soon. And you'll be fine too, soon enough—snaring rabbits and snowshoeing over the downs. You'll like that, won't you, back in the woods again—fist fighting with the hornets?" I smiled, touching a small, dotlike scar on the side of his neck with my fingertips.

He grimaced and I drew back, examining a few more faint, darkish dots on his throat. He'd stepped on a hornet's nest once—the size of a football, he said later—that had been concealed amongst the deadwood, and had gotten swarmed by hundreds of them, buzzing around his head, searing his face, his neck, his hands as he tore through the brambles, beating and clawing at himself. He tripped, hit his head on a rock and near stunned himself, then went mad, he said, as one of the dirty little bastards burrowed inside his ear. He drove it in deeper with his finger, trying to hook it back out, and with a black cloud of angry, stinging wasps buzzing about his head he tore through the woods, screaming like a banshee. When finally he broke through the trees and came out onto the road his throat was raw, his face and neck a red, swollen mass, his fingers puffed out like sausages.

"Remember well that day," I said, fingering his lobe.

He pulled another face.

"The molasses," I said, pulling forth the memory of Mother forcing his head sideways on the table and holding it still whilst

Gran poured thick blackstrap molasses into his ear. I remembered too, without saying now, the table shaking with his fear
as he gripped it, feeling the molasses creep coldly into his ear.
And then Mother turned his head to the other side, near
fainting when the molasses started trickling back out of his ear,
bringing with it the black, shiny hornet with its sticky, black
legs.

"Ooh, jeezes, what a horrible thing that was—good then,
there'll be no more woods." Immediately I cursed my tongue
as his smile faded. "For a while anyway," I quickly added. "Till
you gets better again."

He tugged at my hand, his breathing growing agitated. "The
doctors," he said as I stepped back, hearing Mother's voice
outside the curtain. "Tell me, Dolly. The doctors. What're they
saying?"

I was spared a reply by Mother slipping in through the
curtain, smelling fresh as soap, her hair pulled back with
combs. "He's worried about not getting back in the woods
again," I said.

"No more you're not." She looked him up and down.
"Laying you out in boat like a babe in a cradle when I gets you
home, and mooring you off the kitchen window. Let the water
rock you for a bit—you likes that, don't you, being rocked?"

"The doctors," said Father, wrestling for her eyes.

"The doctors," she snorted. "The doctors got no say in how
you're going to be treated. Did you have breakfast? How come
they haven't fixed your hair—Sylvie, find me a comb, he looks
a bigger fright than me. And when you goes home, tell Chris
to burn his paddles, and his saws, too. See if that don't trim
your tail," she said, fussing with his sheets as she kept on
scolding him about his worrying, his overworking, his driving
her to the brink.

She would've been banished by the nurses had they heard her speaking so to one so sick. But I saw how he was unable to keep from grinning as she continued threatening him with a floating bed moored at the kitchen window. I saw, too, how he kept turning to her hands fussing with his blankets, his pillow, recognizing in them a strength, a decisiveness that tolerated no fussing in return, a decisiveness he was gratefully accepting of—most times—I thought, watching a faint shine grow in his eyes. But god help them both when the showdown came over his paddles.

———————

SUZE, BEN'S MOTHER and Mom's old friend from when they were girls drying fish on the flakes down Ragged Rock, came later that evening for a visit. She was a big woman, her springy dark curls and quick smile so like Ben's it tripped my heart. A squall of wind, Mother called her, as she blew in through the quiet of the waiting room, her flushed cheeks like those of an overly excited youngster, her big grey eyes snapping as she dragged me and Mom to the cafeteria for a late supper. Afterwards she accompanied us back to the room, determined to spend the night with us. She stuffed herself into one of the armchairs and pushed down the back, sprawling her legs across the coffee table in front of her.

"I balls my coat into a pillow and won't feel a thing," she assured us, settling into the chair like a duck into its feathers.

Tilting back her armchair, Mother too settled in, directing me to the sofa. "I didn't sleep there the past two nights," she argued against my protests, "so why would I tonight? I couldn't breathe if I had to lie down in a place like this—and the chair's comfortable, and I'm up and down all night long anyway checking on your father. Besides, the size of this chair," she said, nestling into the yawning mouth of the wingback. "Now, tell me, Suze, did you check on Gran on your way down?"

"Ye-es, spinning like the top, she is. My, the go she got. And there's my own mother then, crooped up on the couch like an accordion; couldn't sit herself up if the cushions caught fire. And Benji called—worried as anything about Sylvanus he is. That Benji—got me worried sick, he do—way out there in Alberta, working them rigs. I curses them rigs and his going off like that."

"My, Suze, Ben left home for university, not the rigs," said Mother.

"Still, he never comes home—would've tied him to the door if I knew he'd just go off like that—whatever he found so grand in St. John's. Could hardly get home for Christmas after he left—still wonders how he hardly ever comes home."

"Not much here for him, I suppose," said Mother.

"Holidays, Addie—he can come home for holidays—got to beg him every time. And now that he's way out there—do you see him much, Sylvie?"

"Ben's good." I was shaking out the flannel sheet Mother had tossed me, fitting it around myself as she and Suze were doing. After plumping up a small lumpy cushion, I laid back, stifling a yawn.

"And that Trapp fellow?" said Suze. "You see him? Brr, gives me the shivers he do—that's who lured Benji off, I knows that to my bones. Curses the day Benji started bringing that fellow around. Weird bunch, they are, hey Addie. You don't like them either, do you? No, maid, didn't think so. Don't know anybody who does—do you, Sylvie? You like that Trapp—whatever his name is—I only ever heard him called Trapp."

"Don't see him much." I squirmed deeper into the sofa so's to deter Suze's attention. Through half-closed eyes I watched as she and Mother fussed with their sheets and cushions. I watched Mother dim the lamp, and the shadows softening their faces as they leaned towards each other, lowering their voices as one does during late-night conversations. The weight of the past sleepless nights settled around me like a thick blanket. With a growing contentment I listened to Mother's voice, and Suze's, discussing Father's condition, his strong-mindedness, his ability to turn around a river if he so desired, and how perhaps he'd be on his feet in no time, going against the odds like his brother Jake, who'd had two heart attacks by now and was supposed to be dead three years ago and was still lugging wood and traipsing through the woods with a gun.

"Yes, he'll be fine, I'm starting to think it," Mother was soon saying, her tone strengthening, gathering conviction with each hopeful word. And with Suze pushing her onward she was soon past worrying and was chiding him now, as though it were he sitting before her and not Suze, for his foolishness the past few years, working himself to death, not listening, not resting.

"And sure, putting his house on the wharf like that," said Suze. "Lord, before his eyes opened in the mornings he was already out in boat—never took a break at all. First sight of a bird and he was motoring towards it with his gun. Oh my, I laughs now, thinking about that—him putting the house on the wharf, knowing how much you hates the water."

"If he couldn't sit on it during the day, he was bloody well going to sleep on it at night," said Mother.

"And worries nothing about getting washed out to sea in a storm. And him telling me then, he was only thinking of you. Yes, yes he did, that's what he told me—he was only thinking of you, that you'd never have to climb a ladder agin to wash a window, the sea would wash them for you—silly fool. He forgets how you always liked it outdoors—always in the garden you were. My, you were one for the outdoors, I can see you now, sneaking off up the woods, wanting to be alone on the cliffs. Never sees you outdoors anymore, not since you left Cooney Arm."

"Used to love that meadow in Cooney Arm," said Mother. "And the falls. Never did get used to living on a wharf." She tossed her head as though the notion was still unthinkable. "Sylvanus—he always talked of building a new house up by the river. But," she shrugged, "I don't know. It's like we went into hibernation after we moved to Hampden. Never did wake up to the place. Think I always blamed it for our having to move there—silly as that sounds."

"Well, it must agree with you then, for you haven't been sick a day since you left the arm. My lord, when I thinks of all that sickness you used to have."

"Cursed," said Mother with a tight laugh.

"Silly thing."

"Who wouldn't think it, losing three babies like that." She lowered her voice, her tone taking on an anxious timbre. "I thinks back on those days—Ohh! All those nights I worried, waiting for little Sylvie to be taken. Always thought I was going to be punished again, that she'd be taken. Was always waiting for more punishment. Truly, I never felt like a mother till Chris was born and took to my breast."

My lashes fluttered open during those last words. I'd been partly listening, as I always listened to my mother and Gran talking—gathering bits of their past like a jeweller gathering gems, hoarding them in my pocket so's to refit and solder them later into that one great stone. And this piece stuck like a shard in my palm. Was there never a time when I'd been first in my mother's thoughts? That even during those first days—first *moments*—of life, I was viewed as some kind of check mark, some pending sign, some outcropping from an ongoing struggle between her and God? Small wonder her breasts wouldn't milk—not out of fear for the poor suckling babe, but out of fear for herself.

"And then all that sickness leaving you after Chris was born," said Suze. "Strange how that happened, hey? And you never had nothing with Kyle either. Yes, my maid, good—good it never come back, especially after all that happened, having to move and everything. And now with Sylvanus sick like this ..." Suze's voice trailed off.

"I was thinking earlier how it feels like me holding things together now," said Mother. "Thank god for Chris. Least I got him to fall back on, keep things going about the house." Her face brightened at the mentioning of Chris like the moon drawing light from the sun.

"Yes, thank god for Chris, he's a man now," said Suze, "and I hope he stays around for you, not like Ben—no help to his father at all, Ben's not—his first pair of boots and he was racing out the door. Like I said, I would've tied him on if I knew he was hardly ever coming home again. All I does is worry."

"Chris asked for two suitcases for Christmas last year," said Mother with a quiet laugh, "for him and Kyle, teasing me they'd both be leaving soon as Kyle graduates. I told him he'd be buying his own suitcase then, and he'd better hide it from me, else it'll be used to pack wood in, not his clothes."

I made a disgruntled sound and Mother looked at me with sudden unease, both of us remembering my sixteenth birthday and her surprise gift of a suitcase—three of them, dark red, each fitting snugly into the other. "What, you can't wait till I finishes high school?" I'd said jokingly but with a tinge of sharpness in my tone. For no matter that I'd grown into my teenage years and made peace—sort of—with living in

Mother's house; we'd never made peace with each other and had bickered and chaffed each other till the day I packed those three matching suitcases and eagerly left home for university in St. John's three months before enrolment started. For months afterwards Father had been ill tempered towards Mother, believing I'd seen those suitcases as an invitation to leave home and not, as she claimed, as merely support for my university dreams.

Pulling myself up from the lumpy cushions, I leaned towards her. "And do you think a child begotten is a mother's to keep?" I asked, unable to keep the crossness out of my voice. "Shouldn't *all* of one's offspring be encouraged to go off and make lives of their own?"

"Well sir, I thought she was sound asleep," said Suze in that hushed whisper that carries loudly at night. "Sure you can't all fly away from home, silly. Somebody's got to stay back and care for the old, hey, Addie maid."

Mother opened her mouth to speak, but lapsed into silence as I held on to her stare with the same round-eyed boldness as when I'd been a girl challenging her over a sum at the kitchen table. "Goodness, she still got that brazen look," said Mother, and broke into an affectionate grin. "See how lucky you are," she added, gesturing towards Suze, "she'd have you anchored home from your travels, caring for your contrary old mother."

"That I would, and you knows I would," said Suze, "and besides all that, what's the sense of having a family and getting attached anyway if you all goes off someday? Might as well put us old out with the horses, we got no young left to fill our time with. What do you say, Addie?"

Mother's smile of agreement waned before my accusing stare. "What is it, what're you thinking now?" she asked, fighting for clarity through the dimness of the room, keen for the thought behind my words. Then, equally eager to leave them, she looked at Suze again. "I think we got her frightened—she'll be stuck home someday, making soup and hot toddies for the old."

"Don't know how lucky they are," said Suze. "That's what I'm always saying to Ben, he can go off and not worry about a thing. And when something goes wrong he always got a place to come back to. Because for sure things don't always go right out there, always times you got to come home."

"Isn't that something we do naturally, come home to care for our sick?" I asked impatiently. "You're making it sound like an apprenticeship—something we readies ourselves for at our father's table."

"That such a bad thing, learning from your father's table?" asked Mother.

"Suppose not, but suppose none of us ever left—how would we ever create new ways if we're held back in the old?"

Mother balked. "And what do you think happens to us who never leaves home, Sylvie—you think we grows stagnant like bog water? Sir, the things she says."

"I didn't meant it like that—"

"Praise the lord, I hope not, for there's not a minute in a day when the water's not changing its colour or the wind don't touch me differently. You don't have to go off to find newness, if that's what you're saying. Newness grows out of every day—no matter where you're standing, for them with eyes to see it."

"I'm not haughty enough to think you bog water, Mother. I'm saying we need to feed off others, not just our fathers. And to do that, we gotta venture off the stoop sometimes."

"Oops, there they goes, popping off like firecrackers agin," said Suze, looking from me to Mother with a knowing look. "You're both haughty if you ask me, hardly ever comes for a visit, neither of you. Especially you, Sylvie—don't think you've ever stepped a foot inside my door. And all your mother's saying is that not all things can be learned from books, that's all she's saying, and I agrees with that."

"And all I'm saying is, I was taught at a very early age to think deep and to think further than the world I was born into," I said steadily. "Do you renege on that, teacher-mother? Or was it something you wanted just for me?"

The words kind of slipped out, and I held myself taut before Mother's look of discomfort, then sudden anger.

"You wanted to," she said deeply. "You always talked of leaving, and yes I encouraged you, for god help the youngster whose mother lacks the passion of dreams. And good that you did leave—for you learned how to think and how to work, and that's all the learning you needs right there. But we don't all have to leave home to learn that, so you don't have to worry about Chris. He's learning that right here with his father."

"Chris?"

"Yes, Chris, that's who we're talking about, isn't it—well, I am then," she replied to my baffled look, "and all those letters you write him about some art school in Nova Scotia. What's that all about, if you're not trying to lure him from home?"

"Lure him. My gawd, Mom, you makes me sound like some kind of predator."

"I just don't know why you're always at him, is all."

"I'm not always at him, I just write letters is all, they're about everything, about me and what I'm doing. Gawd, do you read his mail?" I said with a guilty flush. "Anyway, what if

I do encourage him towards university? He's got such a great talent, wouldn't you like to see him developing it?"

"He is, he is developing his talent, he's always at his drawing. Paper a house with the stack of drawings under his bed. And for all that, he likes getting away from it, too. He likes being with his father." A cajoling tone entered Mother's voice, then hardened at my look of impatience. "Fine then, it's not just for his father I'd like to keep him home, but for me, too. I'm never comfortable with how he keeps going off—like he's having a spell. I don't trust him working far from home, amongst them who don't know his ways."

"His ways? What're you talking about, his ways?"

"The way he keeps going off, you knows what I'm talking about."

"Jeezes, Mother, you still think there's something wrong with Chris—"

"I do then."

"Ohh, for gawd's sakes—"

"My, they're right back at it!" exclaimed Suze. "I'll cover up my head if ye keeps it up—swear to gawd, I'll cover up my head." She held up her blanket threateningly.

Mother drew back into her chair, her mouth tightly pursed. I remained tense, looking from her to Suze, then back to Mother as Suze asked, "Why, what's Chris at these days—he's got you worrying agin, don't he."

"No. No, nothing different, just the same old thing, really. The way he goes off sometimes, wouldn't hear a train bearing down on him. And he could very well have some sort of epilepsy," she said with emphasis to my disbelieving look. "I took him to doctors, they found nothing, and—ohh, I don't pay that much attention to it anymore, it's not a thing that threatens him—I watches him come to himself when the kettle starts whistling, or if he's out walking in water and his feet starts getting wet. But I don't think he should be working at just anything either. It's good he's with his father, someone watching over him."

"Mother, Chris *don't* have epilepsy. He's just going off in daydreams, is all." I tossed aside my blanket impatiently. "Gawd, I can't believe you still think that. He just needs something to keep his attention, is all—something challenging and disciplined. Perhaps then he'll pay more attention to what's going on around him, not to mention taking his talents further than doodling at the kitchen table. How's he going to find his own way if he's not nudged out of the nest?"

"Oh, and that's what you're planning on doing, is it—nudging him out of the nest?" Mother sat forward, a cross look on her face. "Why, who are you to point his way?"

"Who am I? I'm his sister, I sit at the same table as he, remember? Or do you forget that I, too, lived?"

The words were out, the look of surprise registering on my face the same as on Mother's. I quickly opened my mouth to say something else, to cover the awful thing I'd just said, but nothing came to me. I had laid open my wound and now shivered from the rush of cold air encircling the exposed flesh.

The quiet of the room was jarred by the sound of voices in the corridor. A man's voice, a woman's, speaking lowly, carefully, and then the muffled cry of an outraged child. A door closed, the child's cry muffled, then silence again.

Mother's face saddened. She looked at me imploringly, sinking back into the cavernous shadow of the chair. I fidgeted with the flannel sheet, feeling its roughness against my cheek. Rather the proud-standing teacher-mother tolerating no interruption to her words than this tiny-shouldered woman being swallowed by the thick, rounded arms of her chair and looking at me with such guardedness.

Suze pumped herself forward, looking curiously to me, a protective hand touching Mother's arm. "My, the strange way she got of putting things," she said to Mother. "And what's you even talking about, we started off with the old, taking care of the old, and mercy knows where you've carried it. Sure, it's not something I ever thinks about, who's giving what to who. We all looks after the other—that's only right, isn't it—especially with the old. Sure, they took care of us. And besides that, they might end up taking care of us agin, yet. We don't know the future, do we?"

Mother was pleating and unpleating the tail of her skirt, her eyes cast down. She brushed at the fabric, making away with the pleats. She looked at me, my rounded eyes slowly withdrawing from hers.

"The future," she said with a scornful laugh. "Hard thing to see, isn't it, the future? Cripes, I hardly know my past. Gran always says it's in later years we start looking back and seeing the rights and wrongs of ourselves." She grimaced. "I keeps looking back, but nothing's come to me yet that's making me any smarter."

I felt sickened by the ill look on her face. I forced a smile and struggled for some thought of agreement between us. "No doubt most prayers are changed by hindsight," I said lowly. "Still, we keep making them, eh?"

Suze looked from me to Mother, unsure of whether twas a laugh or a lecture we were both needing. Her eyes on Mother, she gave a deep chuckle. "I laughs at what you just said, Addie, about looking backwards. I can hear Ben now, every time I harps about his forgetting everything I done for him while he was growing up—he turns and says, 'How far

ahead can you walk, Mother, with your head turned
backwards?' Silly fool, I always tells him, you thinks with your
heart, silly fool, not your eyes."

Both Mother and I smiled, grateful for the relief Suze's
words brought us, grateful for her laughter, her distracting us
from ourselves, from each other. For neither of us could probe
that other thing my outburst had let into the room, the wound
that was once solely Mother's but through the years had
migrated from her maternal walls into me and was shared now
between us.

Mother looked at Suze, her smile tinged with a sadness. "I
don't know about that," she said, "thinking through the heart.
That's when I gets muddled, when I think through the heart.
It becomes more of a feeling than a thinking thing, and I've
always been one to sink with feeling. And Chris, too ..." She
trailed off, looking towards me, her pursed mouth showing her
tiredness from the past few days. "But I've never worried about
you, my girl," she said sadly, as though speaking a truth she'd
just now discovered within herself. "You've been thinking
with your head since the day you were born, you've been.
Never worried about you taking the wrong step.

"Anyway, time for sleep," she said with resolution. "We'll be
talking all night if we let ourselves. Now, tuck into that
blanket, Sylvie. You too, Suze. Time we all tucked in, else we'll
be dead to the world come morning, and Sylvanus will be
washing his own hair, wondering what happened to us."

———

I BEGGED OFF BREAKFAST with Mother and Suze come
morning, and walked for a long hour through the hilly, tree-
lined streets of Corner Brook. Many things came to me, most
of them about Mother, prompted by that ill look on her face

the night before. She'd been quiet that morning, letting Suze
do most of the talking. Even with Father she'd been quiet, her
drawn expression a carryover from last evening's conversation
no doubt, for she kept looking at me, silently appraising me as
one might an unread book, attempting to deduce its most
hidden secrets from the few lines scratched across its cover. As
I was trying to read her.

At one point she'd turned quickly from Father's pale face
and croaky voice, her eyes welling up with sudden tears, and I
quietly passed her a tissue, unobtrusively taking up Father's
attention with a glass of orange juice. She touched my
shoulder gently, almost shy like. It triggered for me the
occasion when Gran found the watch Father had given me for
my birthday, back when I was a girl, and I'd been too shy to
properly hook it around my wrist and Mother had done so for
me. Her eyes had momentarily brushed mine as she bent
towards me, hooking the strap, and I'd glimpsed her shyness,
recognizing it immediately, for it was the same meekness that
was guarding my own heart during that moment. I remembered too how she'd been wearing her new red dress, and how
special it made the moment feel, that she was wearing it for my
birthday. And how, when I'd impulsively told her how pretty it
was, she bent down and nuzzled her forehead against mine.

It broadened my heart, that nuzzling of brows. And yet, how
fleeting the moment had been. Within a heartbeat Mother was
fussing over the teapot having cooled, ushering Gran back to
her chair to finish her dinner, scolding me gently for getting
jam on my dress—rendering the nuzzling one of those things
that mothers do without thinking, like patting a loaf of bread
before slicing it.

I wondered now if Mother remembered that moment, and
if so, how her account of it might differ from mine, and if so,

which of us had knowingly or unknowingly played editor, rewriting a more desirable ending for a more palatable self. Where, then, does truth go?

An illness crept into my stomach. What of memory is truth? It was a staggering thought, and for a moment I felt a great fear, like those split seconds sometimes upon awakening when all sense of self is still caught back in the nether world of sleep and the eyes alone are opened onto the blankness of a room without memory. I clutched my arms around myself, needing to feel the solidity of flesh and bone, like the ghosts from Cooney Arm whose lives have been vanquished into time, leaving behind fragments of soul clinging to wood, no longer knowing what, if anything, is real, and frightened of their invisibility.

The air was becoming cool, my legs tiring from the long walk. I started back to the hospital, quivering a little, as though the bones that had formed within me were transmuting back to the pliability of youth, faltering beneath the rigidity I'd been sculpting upon them during the past years.

———————

WHEN I RETURNED Mother and Suze had gone for lunch and it was Chris visiting with Father, who sat stiffly now in a chair beside his bed. With his crop of black hair somewhat fashioned into place and his hospital johnny-coat replaced by the blue-striped pyjamas he wore at home during cold nights, Father was looking less like a corpse and even sounding a bit like himself as he asked in a rough, wheezy voice about his boat, the wind, the ice, groaning his displeasure as I scolded him about his worrying.

"You'll need your moaning for when you gets out and can't find your paddles," I said, my fingers combing his hair affectionately. "Mom told him she's burning them," I said to Chris. "Said she's gonna lay Father out in his boat like it was a cradle, and moor it off the kitchen window."

Chris smiled stiffly, his colour resembling the morning's porridge.

"Have to sell the boat," said Father.

I jolted, as surprised by the urgency in his tone as by the statement itself.

"She thinks I don't know," he went on, his voice falling into a whisper. "I heard them. Outside the curtain. Not allowed back in the woods." He shook his head over our splutters of protest.

"You don't worry about nothing," blurted Chris, "I'll take care of the truck till you gets on your feet—" He stopped, silenced by a silvery bead of water swelling out of the corner of Father's eye.

I hand-scrubbed Father's head. "Turned down," I sniffed. "You'll be back on your feet and working in no time, you know it. You don't listen to them, Dad. And I got money enough saved—stop looking like that," I cried as Father cringed beneath my words, his shame burning through his skin. "You've done for us all these years, it's our turn now to do something for you, will you let us?"

He shook his head weakly and I fell silent, feeling like a tyrant youngster trampling over his sick heart, and he too weak to lift me off.

Chris leaned forward in his chair, then back, grasping at his knees while he stared at Father, as though resisting the urge to touch him. He raised his eyes to mine, sharing the wretched secret he was carrying in his heart. But this father who had borne our growing years with gentleness, who had put aside his own passions and hurt for our own well-being, was not about to be abandoned. I felt the conflict in my brother's heart, I saw the resolve in his eyes.

———————

"I'LL SEE YOU TOMORROW," Chris said as I walked him to the parking lot around noon. He dug out the keys to Father's truck, a brand-new 1980 Chevy Silverado, and unlocked the door, letting out that newish smell of vinyl and leather as he swung it open. "Tomorrow," he repeated, hushing my need to talk, "we'll see about things tomorrow."

He drove off, a sense of urgency to the tilt of his head as he leaned over the wheel, shading his eyes with the visor, pulling abruptly onto the city street. A gleam of sunshine from the roof of the cab and he was lost from sight amidst the city traffic, leaving me with a pounding headache and a sudden desire to be sitting beside him rather than facing another long day with Mother.

I turned wearily back to the hospital. I'd be flying back to Alberta the next morning and wanted to spend as much time as possible with Father. Thankfully, Suze was still about, although she spent the greater part of the day shopping, leaving Mother and me to ourselves.

"Ben never did come much—after he left," I said to Mother. "How come—Suze sure dotes on him."

"Doted too much," said Mother.

"How so?" I asked.

Mother was tidying the sitting room from where we had spent the night. She shook her head to my questioning, passing me the flannel sheets to fold.

"Well, then?" I pushed, unable to curb my curiosity about Ben.

"Well, then, nothing," said Mother. "She was just too *smothering* is all."

"Too *smothering*?"

Mother tried to brush aside her words. "I don't know, Sylvie. She was always at him, hovering—always trying to nurse him. He was a big youngster, and she still kept trying to force the breast on him. I remembers him now, gagging. Yes, she was silly like that," Mother replied to my growing look of distaste. "Almost four—near school age—when she finally stopped trying to force the breast on him. Shh." Mother looked to the door as if Suze might be standing there, and lowered her voice. "Now, don't you go talking about this."

"I won't. Gawd, no wonder Ben never wants to talk to her."

"Not that she done it regularly," said Mother. "When he was sick, that's how she used to try and comfort him. He was always sickish with asthma, and went to sleep on a snowbank once. That's how she found him, sleeping in the snowbank, his face starting to cover over with snow. She thought he was dead and she never got over it."

"Gawd," I repeated, unable to get past the wretched image of Ben being smothered against his mother's breasts, gagging against her nipples.

"He was handled too much," Mother whispered, and then moved away as a nurse came into the room.

I meant to ask Mother more about Ben and Suze but was kept busy after that, with Father being moved from emergency to a room on the ward. For the rest of the day our attention was focused on him—bathing him, shaving him, trimming his dark, shaggy brows, stuffing minty breath fresheners into his mouth (he hated them), doing his toenails, his fingernails. No doubt our conversation from the night before dogged our steps, but there were moments when we moved as one around Father's bed. It felt nice. It was the first time I'd known Mother and me to stand side by side, working together. Always there'd been Gran, the boys, Father, and always Mother's daunting fortitude as she held things together, as she might see it. Easy enough when all things concerned were within her arm's reach. But here, now, was a different kettle of fish. Father's near death had forced her to stretch further than the confines of her own doorstep, and I felt her unease about what tomorrow would bring, about the uncertainty of this road newly laid out before her.

And I felt the silent look of appeal in her eyes as she walked me to the parking lot and hugged me goodbye. She complained about my going back to Alberta in the morning, looking so vulnerable that I felt the same resolve well up inside of me as Chris had felt earlier with Father—to make sure that things would be okay, that I would make them okay.

Giving her one final, cheery wave, I started towards the car. Already I was impatient to begin tomorrow's journey back to Alberta, to the extra hours of work I'd take on and the pocket-loads of tips I'd be counting out and sending home.

———

"AND SO HE'S GETTING ON. Good, and so should we, then," said Gran over a late supper that evening. Chris, I noted, was unnaturally chatty, his shoulders no longer slumped as they'd been yesterday, the same burning fever in his eyes as when he'd left Father at the hospital. Wolfing down his potatoes and sopping up the gravy with bread, he chided Kyle, "Come on, come on, eat up."

"There's a band playing at the club tonight and we're going," he said to me, sucking on a chicken bone.

He balked as I slapped his hand from his mouth, ordering him to go wipe the grease off his chin. "And I'm not going to no club," I declared, getting up and scraping my plate onto Gran's.

"Yeah, we're going," he said. "Least you can do on your last night home, go out and see some people."

"Go—ready yourself," said Gran. "I can manage a few dishes."

"Ohh, I can't stand crowds, Gran, you know that." I dropped a handful of cutlery into the sink, turned on the taps, and squeezed dish detergent into the running water. "Pass me your fork," I ordered Chris. "Ky, you finished? Sit down, Gran, let me pour you some tea, you still like it cold?"

I poured Gran's tea into a tumbler part filled with cold water and then started rinsing the glasses, half reassured, half worried by Chris's frenetic mood change as he kept yakking about the dance. We hadn't had an opportunity to speak alone yet, to plan for the days ahead, and so despite my reluctance, after the kitchen was cleared away and Gran tucked into her rocker with her knitting and her lamp lit, I allowed him to persuade me into my coat and boots and out the door.

The sky was still bright outside, the trees gathering darkness. My foot slipped on the muddied trail—a shortcut to Hampden leading up through the woods behind the house. "I don't wanna go to the damn bar, Chris. Let's just go for a walk, we need to talk."

"For an hour," he said, "and then we'll talk. Come on," he coaxed, "and watch the stairs—they're slippery, too."

I grunted, scraping the mud off my boots on the half-rotted bottom step. They were a series—about three or four sets—of little stairways that Father had built over the steepest part of the trail so's to shorten our walk to the school up Hampden. With crooked hand railings made from stripped juniper and pieces of plank bridging the muddied, levelled spots, those stairs were always the best part of coming or going to school, whether it was fear or excitement edging my step. I paused beside a brook all throaty with roots, choking its way through the underbrush down the hillside, and stood for a moment, the air minty cool upon my skin. I looked down at the sea. It was bluish black in the half light of evening, fretting amongst the rocks on shore, with the steeply wooded hills appearing as darkened humps against the sky—like shoulders, I thought, great mammoth shoulders of the earth settling into sleep. What I ought to be doing.

"Lose your way?" called Chris from above.

"Oh, just keep going," I muttered, and paused again at a rustling from below. Kyle's head popped through the brush.

"Thought you were staying with Gran," I said.

"She likes sitting by herself." He brushed past me, his breathing heavy from his upward climb. Chris sprang from the bushes, barrelling him almost to the ground.

"It's he, Paunchy, who's scared to be alone," he taunted, knuckling Kyle's midriff. He grunted as Kyle managed a punch to his gut. I skirted them impatiently as they tackled and yelped like pups, just as they'd been doing since they were youngsters, and wondered again at Chris's mood swing. Breaking through a canopy of branches, I came upon mounds of rotting sawdust and the long, low structure of the old sawmill sagging in its midst, its clapboard roof and walls blackened by weather. I cringed from the memory of that screaming, monstrous saw and how it had curdled my blood in those first years here.

Two of the Trapps from Ragged Rock owned it. They'd had a falling out with the other half of their clan and moved to Hampden a few years before Father floated us from Cooney Arm. I'd never seen a Trapp up close, except for one of the older ones, years ago, motoring from Ragged Rock to Cooney Arm, buying salt fish from Father. But I'd certainly heard the stories about their queerness, how they clanned together, taking nothing from nobody and bringing home wives from the far side of the island so's to have nobody visiting them. And they certainly looked clannish, I'd thought, that first time seeing a bunch of them in the store in Hampden, the women and girls wearing dark, drab dresses down past their knees, their eyes both shifty and shy, and the men all bearded and bald, with something akin to scorn curling their lips.

Undoubtedly, the people of Hampden were relieved that the Trapps stuck to themselves, minding their own business in their cliquish way. And I learned to ignore the Trapps too, given the manner in which they'd treated Father.

It was during that very first month we'd moved from Cooney Arm, still settling ourselves. The Trapps didn't like it that Father had started cutting a path through the woods bordering their sawmill. They said nothing, owing to its being public property. Just stood there, was all, when Father first came in sight of their mill, their heads tilted back in a haughty manner, as though daring him to step one foot over their boundary line. Father just kept swinging his axe through the brush, his eyes darker than I'd ever known them, seeing nothing but his own madness. For he was mad those first few months, prowling the house like a cut bear, and would've probably thrived on a fist fight, wanting something to put his spite upon.

And the Trapps lured him good one morning. It was before Gran, Mother, or the boys were awake, only me, trailing behind him up the path the way I used to trail behind him to his stage in Cooney Arm. There had been no sound from the sawmill that morning, the air quiet as church on Sundays. But the second we came into its sights it screamed into life, near shocking me out of my shoes. I bolted after Father and stood still as stone, as did he, staring at a pile of logs thrown across his half-forged path, blocking him from going any further. He looked towards the mill. Aside from the timbers rattling from the screaming taking place within it, the only thing moving was a steady stream of sawdust flowing from beneath its rotted flooring like yellow pus. Throwing aside his axe, Father started towards the mill.

"Stay there, Dolly," he said as I started after him. "I said stay," he ordered as I kept following, as incensed as he over this deliberate blockade. Turning back, Father lodged heavy hands on my shoulders, steering me towards home. I walked as far as a pile of brush then ducked behind it, watching him. A tremor of fear shot through me as he neared the darkened doorway, and I called out. He couldn't hear over the noise of the saw, and my fear heightened as he marched through the doorway without breaking stride.

I thought to run back down the hill and tell somebody, but there was no one, only Gran and Mother and the boys. I thought I heard Father's voice but knew I couldn't possibly over the whine of the saw. I tried to stand but was riveted to that darkened doorway and the shrillness of the saw growing louder. I turned sharply towards a pile of lumber stacked partways between me and the mill. There was nothing there, yet my nape tingled. Something moving at the side of the lumber pile caught my eye and I bit back a scream. A young fellow, about twelve or thirteen, with a small, pointy face and thick reddish brows, crouched quiet as a cat, staring at me.

My stomach cramped. I bent over, my skin prickling as though foreknowing of that cold day to come when fate would factor this creature's footstep into mine. He pounced towards me with a flat hahaha laugh, his thin, pinkish lips scarcely moving. He hissed as though shooing me away, but I stood unmoving, snared by the glassy green eyes now upon me.

Just as quickly he stepped back with a laugh, his eyes softening, as though tiring of some game we'd been playing. "What's your name?" he asked, his tone a touch nasal. "What's the matter, cat got your tongue?" I didn't move, my eyes fixed on his face.

At that moment Father's voice broke through the shrill cry of the mill. "Batter to jeezes," he roared upon seeing the young fellow, and marched towards him with a handpick held threateningly in each hand.

Springing backwards, the catlike figure vanished into the woods.

Father started back towards the woodpile. His mouth curling as contemptuously as the Trapps', he plunged the tips of each handpick into a log—one onto the end and the other midway down the length of it—and yanked on it with such force that his face and neck contorted. After hauling the log free from the path he came back and plunged the handpicks into the next log, dragging it to the side in turn. An hour later the path was cleared. Flinging the picks towards the mill, he took his axe from my outstretched hands and resumed his slashing through the woods.

I hung close by him for the rest of the day, my eyes scanning the nearby woods as he finished the path, my stomach still churning from that flat hahaha laugh and those glassy green eyes. Towards evening, sitting around the supper table with the boys bickering with each other, Mother talking over their squabbling to Gran, and the kettle whistling off steam, I soon forgot about my fear. Yet that night, half asleep on my pillow, it blew back on me like a bad wind. I bolted upright, a pair of luminous green eyes flashing at me through the dark.

There were no more barricades after that. Father said nothing of it to Mom or Gran, so I hadn't either. I wondered if Father even remembered my being there, till several weeks later when Chris and I, sporting new clothes, our hair spruced to a shine—mine hanging down my back in two wet, skinny braids, Chris's brush-cut standing straight up on his head—stood on the wharf, readying to take the path for the first time to school. I hadn't seen Father watching through the window, else I might not have quailed from taking that first step.

Immediately he pounded on the window, his eyes fierce beneath their black thatch of brows. "No one going to bother you up there," he shouted through the pane. "You go on, now. Take your sister's hand," he prompted Chris. "Stay on the path."

I nodded, trying to swallow my fear, but he'd seen it anyway, and flung open the door, coming towards me.

"I'm going, I'm fine," I said hurriedly, but he was grasping my shoulders so hard he near lifted me off my feet.

"You got nothing to fear from that crowd," he said, his eyes black as peat, his voice fighting for calm. "You seen what they're like: stand timid and they'll roll you in shit; stand straight and they'll walk off—they don't like the bother. Besides, they likes bigger game than you, so go now. Be scared of nothing. That scruffed, weasel face," he added, as I kept staring at him, "is he what's scaring you?" His voice softened. "Go on now, he belongs down Ragged Rock. Was just visiting his uncles, is all, he's gone back down."

Clutching my books, I started up the first of the little wooden steps, Chris plodding behind. The shrill scream of the saw grew louder as I approached. Against my will my step slowed. My eyes darted towards the lumber pile, expecting that reddish pointy face to lunge before me. Then suddenly the saw whined into a silence. Something—perhaps the thud of a footstep on the path or the flapping of a warbler's wings flittering through the bush—caused me to tighten my grip on Chris's hand. But then, as a cock knows the first rays of the sun, I suddenly knew my father was on the path behind me. And that the Trapps weren't going to hurt me. And that Father had learned that, else he never would've sent me past the mill alone. It was my fear he was watching over, not his. Releasing Chris's hand and pulling his attention away from the tracks his new sneakers were making in the mud, I walked steadily up the rest of the path onto the Hampden road.

Less than a fortnight later Mother received word that her father was ill, and I found myself wandering along the dusty, cratered road through Ragged Rock. Since then I'd heard plenty about the Trapp fellow from Suze, who lived in Ragged Rock and was frequently visiting Mother. His name was Vernon, but he'd been nicknamed Trapp by the outporters because he embodied all the ills of the entire clan, people said. There was no one thing to condemn him, merely a series of things that rendered him bad stuff, like how in grade school he'd pinned youngsters smaller than himself to the ground and blown air incessantly into their nostrils till he near smothered them. And how he snuck up behind girls, pressing the pads of his thumbs against their eyes till they saw flashes of white, and then how he'd run off laughing as they cried out in fright and pain. And how the only thing he got along with was a half-surly dog that was always trotting at his heels.

It was this last bit of information that came to mind the day I wandered along the road in Ragged Rock and saw Trapp sitting on the beach, wrestling a stick out of the mouth of a tan-coloured mutt with four white paws and a white-tipped tail. Barking and whining, the dog dropped the stick and laid its two front paws upon Trapp's knees, licking at Trapp's face,

its tail wagging excitedly. Trapp kept stretching his neck
sideways, upwards, backwards, trying to escape the sloppy pink
tongue, laughing—nothing of that flat hahaha I'd heard from
up besides the sawmill that day, but the same mirthful laugh I'd
hear from Chris or Kyle whenever Father dug his fingers into
their ribs, tickling them hard.

Suddenly the dog's head snapped up and Trapp was on his
knees, watching two girls and a dark, curly-haired young
fellow—all of them about the same age as Trapp—striding
purposefully onto the beach. It was Suze's son, Ben. Tons of
times I'd seen Suze's photos of her favoured boy, heard her
stories of how grand he was with his curly dark hair, his
penchant for drawing, and how he charmed the old ladies,
taking tea with them and drawing pictures of their cats. The
two girls halted near the top of the landwash, cross looks
marring their faces as they pointed accusingly at Trapp. Ben,
ignoring the dog now leaping and barking about his feet,
strolled up to Trapp, and without warning, punched him in the
face. Trapp staggered backwards from the blow then sprung at
Ben, the both of them going down in a tussle. The dog's barks
turned to snarls. It drew back on its haunches, its ears perked
forward, its tail no longer wagging, its hackles rising. A loud
groan from Trapp and the dog leapt at one of Ben's flailing
legs, sinking its teeth into his calf.

I closed my eyes at the scream from Ben, and opened them
to the bedlam of Ben hobbling about with blood running
down his leg, Trapp coaxing the barking dog to his side, Suze
running down over the landwash, shrieking like a gull. An old
man who must've been Trapp's father or grandfather, with his
reddish scraps of hair and brows garnishing his thin face, was
also running towards the fracas, a rifle slung over his shoulder
and a brace of rabbits flung to the side.

"Shoot it! Shoot that gawd-damned dawg or I'll be shooting it for you!" Suze was screaming at the old man.

"What did he do to that dog—what did he do?" snarled the old man.

"Matters not what he done," cried Suze, "you don't have dogs chewing up youngsters—put that gun to its head, or by cripes I'll call the cops, you won't get away with it then, I calls the cops."

"I said what did he do to that dog?" the old man growled at Trapp.

Trapp, his mouth a tightened, crooked line, was squatting beside his dog, refusing to look up. Ben was holding on to his bitten calf, his mouth tightened as much from pain as from a reluctance to speak, I thought. Suze swooped beside him, hurtling further threats at the old man and the dog. In a fit of rage the old man grabbed Trapp by the scruff, twisted him towards where their home must've been. The dog scampered after Trapp, and at another shriek of indignation from Suze, the old man raised the gun, took aim, and fired. The dog let out a surprised yelp, leapt into the air, and fell to the ground.

"You stay the jeezes away from my property," the old man roared at Ben, and walked off without a glance at Trapp, who at the sound of the gunshot and the yelp from his dog stood frozen. He turned to where the tan-coloured heap of fur was shuddering through its last breath. From a distance of thirty, forty feet, I could see the rapid heaving of its chest. Running to the dog, his shoulders loosened, and Trapp crumpled to its side.

Ben was staring in horror at the dying dog, at Trapp. He remained impassive to his mother's cajoling sounds as she wrapped her arms around him, trying to steer him towards the road. With a choked cry he pushed her aside, watching as

Trapp, his hands clenched into fists, shoved them beneath the lifeless clump of fur and hoisted the dog into his arms. His slight frame staggering beneath the weight, and four white paws dangling about his knees, Trapp started up the shore.

From where I sat I could see the wet on Ben's face, hear his sniffles as his mouth screwed up and it looked as if he would cry. Suze caught hold of him, and after a slight scuffle between the two, she dragged him along by the arm, cursing the Trapps and their damned surly dogs and threatening Ben with a month in bed if the bite got infected and he came down with rabies. A last backward look at Trapp, who was vanishing now behind a bend in the beach, and Ben shoved away from his mother, bolting, with a slight limp, towards home.

It was another seven years before I saw either Trapp or Ben again. It was the beginning of summer and I'd been to the post office for Mother. Instead of the road, I'd taken the shoreline back home, climbing around the outcropping of rock that separated Hampden from our house on the other side. The base of the outcropping could be navigated only during low tide, and was chancy even then, with wet kelp and rioting waters that licked coldly at my ankles each time my foot slipped into a crevice. With the surf and a relentless wind pummelling past my ears I didn't hear their voices till I was nearly upon them.

They were in a slight inlet, sitting in a dory that was bobbing on the water and tied to a rock with a short rope. Trapp sat the closest to me, wearing the same straw-coloured mane, but with ruffs of chin hair and sideburns that gleamed like copper in the strong summer sun. He was slight like a girl, yet his arms were long and ropy as he hung them outside the boat, paddling his hands through the water.

Sprawled in the stern of the boat, absorbed by something he was drawing or writing on a notepad, was Ben, all knees and elbows, the slight edge of a moustache lining his upper lip and tight, dark curls capping his head.

I'd heard bits and pieces about them both through the years from Suze during her visits with Mother. Trapp—even his kinfolk called him by his last name—had shown himself to be the smartest of the clan, and according to Ben, Suze reluctantly reported, he was the smartest student from that part of the bay, and amongst the smartest in Memorial University of Newfoundland, where he'd been on the dean's list.

And Ben, Suze was always quick to say, was the nicest, sweetest boy, whose dark, shiny curls were a draw for women and girls alike, and who, despite his having grown up, was still taking tea with old ladies after church and drawing them pictures of their cats. The fact that Ben and Trapp had become like brothers made for a bad taste in Suze's mouth, one she was always spitting out in disparaging Trapp's *cagey* look or his *sly* look or his *shifty*-eyed look. Equally incensing for Suze was that ever since that old man shot Trapp's dog, Ben was always dragging the bugger home for supper, for Sundays, for sleeping over—and on and on Suze would rhyme off the ways Trapp unnerved her when he was in her house, watching her, watching the youngsters, watching Ben, watching everything that moved, as though he'd never seen the insides of a house before, or them that lived there, having a chat and busying about.

Crouching behind a slate of rock, I watched them, just as I had all those years ago on the beach in Ragged Rock. Their dubious fit was never more apparent than in this moment, Ben sitting studious over his notepad and Trapp sitting restless, rocking the boat, his lips skimmed back into a grin as he flicked droplets of water into the air, hunching his shoulders skittishly as they rained back onto him and Ben.

"Bugger off," Ben muttered, brushing the water off his hair. Trapp gave his flat hahaha laugh that after all these years still prickled my skin like needles. He flicked another handful of water into the air, then crouched back with the skulking look of a banned pet as Ben leapt to his feet and grabbed a paddle, darting it threateningly at Trapp.

"Out!" yelled Ben. "Out, out," and raised the paddle as though readying to strike. Trapp, with another hahaha, leapt out of the boat. Slipping on a sliver of kelp, he fell to his knees.

Laughing, Ben slapped the water with the broad side of his paddle, sousing Trapp's backside and sending him skittering over the rock towards the slate ridge beyond which I crouched. I ducked down, but within the second Trapp was leaning across the ridge, his pointy face sniffing at me, his green eyes ignited by the sharp sunlight.

"Boo," he said lightly.

I scuttled backwards, slipped, fell hard on my backside. I got quickly back on my feet, ignoring the hand Trapp offered, as unnerved as Suze by his cagey look, his skulking grin, and that long ago memory of panic he'd set off inside of me. Tossing back his head, he leapt over the rocks towards Hampden, his form lithe, his limbs fluid, his crazy ha ha ha's caterwauling out like a rutting cat.

Ben, oblivious of my presence, was settled back into the stern of the boat, his notebook positioned on his knee, his head held back, gazing up at the sky. Curious, and disarmed by the softened contours of his face, I crept towards him, my movements muffled by the sea grappling with the rocks. I drew within an arm's reach of his dark, curly head. From my slightly elevated vantage point I saw over his shoulder to his fingers cramped around a pencil, posed motionless over what I now saw to be a sketch pad. Centred on the page in thick heavy lines was the fat, fluffy cloud hanging overhead.

"Clouds should be shaded," I said after a moment's watching.

"Oh? How's that now?" I flushed to my roots as he leaned back his head, seeing me upside down through eyes the clear grey of a winter's sea. "Well, then?" he challenged.

"Clouds are always shifting," I replied.

"That's why I nail 'em to a page. Else it's the shape of the wind I'm sketching, not clouds—you think?" he asked with a grin.

I grinned in return.

"What's your name?" he asked.

"Sylvia. Sylvie. Called after my father, Sylvanus."

"Ahh—well now, haven't you grown." He gave me the once-over, then, with an appreciative nod, toed the thwart before him with the tip of his boot. "Climb in," he coaxed. "Sure you can," he said to my reluctant look. "I'll draw your face. Or your hands. You can lay them on the gunnel, or clutch a paddle. Wonk me if I moves the wrong way. You have a brother, don't you?"

"Two," I said.

"Right, two. And one of them draws strange stuff. So says Mother."

"What do you draw?"

"Stick-dogs is all. And clouds sometimes. Coming aboard? I won't hurt you. Aren't you our god-girl, god-baby, or something?"

"Your mother's my godmother. And my mother's your sister's godmother."

"Egads. I think I got it. So, how old are you?"

"Fifteen."

"Fifteen." He eyed me again. "You look older. All right, you can still sit aboard. He won't be back," he said as I looked back along the shore where Trapp had gone. "He don't like being chased off."

"Why are you here?"

"Visiting my aunts. And working the sawmill with Trapp and his uncles."

"For the summer?" I asked.

"Yup. For the summer. What do you think?" he held up the cloud, thickly edged and caught in a moment's stillness. "Think I nailed it? What about that hand of yours—gonna model it for me? Fine, then. I'll sever me own—will you strap it around the paddle after I'm done? Can't do much with one hand."

I laughed and climbed into his boat, thinking later how easy it had been to sit chatting with him as he sketched my hand resting on the paddle, sharing with him stories of Chris, and his long, slender fingers, at the age of three, drawing ant's tracks across his room walls, and now at the age of thirteen, drawing blue clouds on a red sky with a blazing purple sun and no fear of its right or wrongness.

"This I got to see," said Ben, and in that creaky, leaking boat kept afloat by a mother's prayers he rowed us around the outcropping and up to the house, where Chris was slouched, his legs dangling over the side of the wharf.

Scoffing at Chris's shyness, I ran inside and was back out in a second toting a stack of his drawings. Like a proud mother, Ben said of me as I stood flashing them before him, all loving and admiring, pronouncing, "See, he can draw, can't he—and look, all dream stuff—even when he was three he was drawing dream stuff."

"Nooo, ohhh, shut up—give them back," Chris kept inter-jecting, face flushed as he snatched at the papers I was passing to Ben.

"Hold on now, buddy, let's see," said Ben. Holding Chris back, he peered intently at the mesh of lines on each page, their half-formed images of eyes fading through hazy skies, rain splattering into weeds amongst rocks, women raising their hands to walls of fire, and, his latest, the vein-ridden throat of a horse stretching off the page.

"Where the hell do you get this stuff?" asked Ben. He lowered the drawings, looking to Chris, staring, as I often did myself, at his wide-mouth smile, his shimmering brown eyes, his quick little shrugs. "Pablo," Ben said quietly, "we've our own little Pabs."

Given that he worked just up the hill at the sawmill, he was to return quite a number of times during the rest of that summer, loitering during his lunch hour, having a quick chat with Mother, Gran. But mostly he lazed about the wharf, eating thick ham sandwiches his mother made for him and sitting with Chris, their backs resting against a grump, sketch pads on their knees, and Ben, awed by Chris's quick manner of sketching, making games so's to quicken his own crude hand.

"Okay, the window by the door," Ben would call out, pointing to the house, or "the gull on the grump" or "the can by the kelp," and they'd hunch over their pencils and paper, drawing till I sounded a whistle, upon which they passed their sketches, without glancing at the other's, for my judgment. Always Ben lost for his attempts at exactness, always Chris won for his embellishment.

"You favour Pabs," Ben continually protested.

"Perhaps I'd rather the shape of the wind than a boring old cloud," I taunted him once, after I'd given him another low grade for a particularly good likeness of Father's boat.

"Is that right, now?" His sooty grey eyes appraised my face, and it felt like a bird fluttered to life in my chest. "Well, you listen to me, Mother Picasso, the wind's a fine thing. But I like a clear line—everything nice and defined. Now then," he pointed to the grump, "if you'd just sit over there and turn sideways, perhaps I could get a better look at your crooked nose. Chris, buddy, see your sister's crooked nose? Let's draw your sister's crooked nose."

I pulled a miffed look and sat on the grump, holding up my nose in an exaggerated profile. Afterwards I quickly denounced Chris's hooklike portrayal, declaring Ben's subtle tilt the winner.

"Proud," snorted Chris, shunning the X drawn across his portrait, "she's proud, Ben, that's what she is, proud."

"Yeah, that's the way of women, buddy, proud," said Ben. And then, ruffling my hair as though I were a youngster, he was off, strolling back to his summer job bundling up slab wood for the Trapps. I stared after him, the length of his stride, his tight jeans, the snug fit of his T-shirt across his shoulders, and the bird in my chest took flight.

One afternoon, after Ben had sauntered down from the mill chewing on a ham sandwich for lunch and commenting on my skinny knees, I yanked on his curls and was instantly deluged by the warm, springy feel of them. I darted inside the house with a sharp sense of embarrassment shooting through me, as though I had committed an act of intimacy against him, had touched his private self. Kyle was whimpering and snotting by the window, his face scabbed with chicken pox. I pulled him aside, taking his place.

Ben was dropping his lanky frame alongside Chris, who was slouched beneath the window, his legs dangling over the wharf, his mind no doubt engaged by his inner realm of wingless birds and feathered frogs. Disappointed that Ben hadn't chased after me, I kept spying through the curtain, listening as he chatted with Chris, his voice rising and falling with the charm of a flute streamed by a summer's breeze. When next I sauntered out the door, thinking of some inane thing to say, I stood before him mute, the words stuck in my throat like a river choked by weeds. Scarcely noticing my presence, Ben brushed the breadcrumbs off his mouth and took his lanky self back up the path to work.

———————

THE MEMORIES OF BEN broke off as I cleared the path past the sawmill and emerged onto a dirt road. Chris and Kyle were still behind me, their yelps having given way to a deep quiet. Slightly out of breath, I wandered to the tip of the brow and looked down at the tiny outport of Hampden, its houses rising tidily up the side of the hill, windows glowing into the softly darkening evening.

"Nice, hey," said Chris, coming up behind me.

"Yeah, it's nice," I said.

"Miss it?" he asked.

I hesitated. "Yeah, I miss it. Although it's never felt like home. Did it to you?"

He gave his quick little shrug. "Never thought about it."

"What *do* you think about?"

"Not much. Either I'm sleeping, or like Mother says, gone off in a trance. Which feels like sleeping."

"You don't *really* go off in trances, do you?"

"Don't know. Don't remember. See this?" He flashed a big-faced wristwatch. "Got it set to beep every hour—just to check the time." He grinned. "Hates missing supper. Mother's always at me for missing supper."

I kicked at his boot. "Big youngster, still letting Mother cook your supper."

"Hey, growing boy," he replied, patting his belly. "So, what feels like home to you—Cooney Arm, still?"

I looked pensively about the outport. For sure I never felt this place was home. Never wanted to be back in Cooney Arm, either—leastways, not after that last trip with Father. "Don't know if I've ever really felt at home," I replied. "In Gran's house I was always looking to Mother's, and then in Mother's I was always looking to Gran's. No matter whose table I was sitting at, or how sweet the jam, it always felt like I was just halfways home."

Chris looked at me with a raised eyebrow, and I was struck for a moment by his likeness to Father and the maturation of his boyish face. "That's a queer thing to say," he said deeply. "Can't imagine you feeling that way."

"Yeah, well, I still feel that way. Most times."

He shook his head. "Can't figure it, Sis. You always acted like you knew exactly where you stood, where you were going, how you were getting there—graduating high school, university—gonna be a captain or something, weren't you? And travel the world?"

"Well, that kind of stuff I've always had clear. It's the other stuff, I guess. The inside stuff that bothers me—always feeling haunted about something. Perhaps I crouched with the ghosts in Cooney Arm too many times. Got myself a haunt."

"Aah," he said knowingly, "now you're making sense—least, the halfways home bit. Gran's always saying haunts are them caught between two worlds."

"So why're they caught—she tell you that?"

"Nope." He gazed up at the evening star, its eternal setting brightened by an invisible moon, and shook his head. "Perhaps there's just one home for haunts, and they're scared of going there."

I followed his gaze. "Sometimes when I'm feeling homesick, or just missing all of you, I look up at that sky and tell myself it's the same sky looking down on all of you. Makes me feel better."

"Me too," he exclaimed. "Really. I think the very same thing when I wonders about you—that we're all standing beneath that evening star. I calls it Sylvie. Yeah, I do," he said to my skeptical look. Reaching one arm towards the heavens, he intoned dramatically, "'Proud Evening Star, in thy glory afar.'"

"My lord, he's quoting Yeats," I said in astonishment.

"Allan Poe," he corrected. "Come on, be no beers left."

"Chris, we need to talk."

"Later. Somebody's about to make a surprise attack." He tugged me along, looking guardedly for Kyle through the alder bed crowding the roadside.

"So what does Al Poe say about the moon?"

"That it's me—pale beside your tiniest starlight."

"Yeah, right." I struck his arm. "Nothing pale about you, Chrissy, you're brighter than all of us—just haven't started shining yet. Proud virgin moon is what you are, on the cusp of everything."

"Christ, here she goes, always—" He broke off midsentence, sniffing the air. "Little bastard's sneaking up. Stay here, Sis, keep talking, grunt a bit so's he'll think it's me."

As Chris stole off into the alder bed I took a last look at the outport, at the orange-painted house where Ben's aunt lived and where he stayed that summer he worked the sawmill with Trapp. He'd left for university a few weeks after that day of my self-afflicted muteness. And until he left I stayed mostly in the house when he'd visit, venturing outside long enough to beat a mat for Mother, hang out a tea towel, a pudding bag, or some such thing—staying long enough to evoke some silly utterance from him, whereupon I sped back inside. Through the white gauze curtains I'd watch when he strolled back to work, or rowed around the outcropping in his leaky boat en route to the swimming hole at the mouth of the river or to the mud flats to dig for clams. Each time I saw anew the strength of his arms as he plied his paddles and the clear evening light in his eyes, heard the lilt of his voice and his flutish laugh as he called out silly things to Chris who'd run up to the river or the mud flats to join him. Longingly I'd watch after Chris, frustrated by my self-imposed exile. Eagerly I'd await their return trip, lying on my bed, ears tuned to the window, listening for the squeaking of Ben's tholepins, the swishing of his paddles breaking through the water. And every time I heard them I'd curl my knees to my stomach, sickened by the sweetness of my pain.

And then he was gone. Back to university, leaving a desire that rooted itself through me like a rhizome, sprouting fantasies of springy black curls and sooty grey eyes at each turn in my day. And no matter he never came back the following summer or the next, working the oilfields out on the prairies somewhere, in the heat of my thoughts he felt a heartbeat away.

A rustling of the alders and Chris tore out, startling me.

"Shh, where is that little bastard," he whispered, eyeing the bushes. Kyle popped out of the alder bed some distance ahead, whipping back a fistful of rocks. Chris danced as they struck around his feet, and dove back inside the alders with a war whoop. All up and down the roadside the bushes shook and snapped as Chris and Kyle beat and fought their way through like grouse fleeing a hunter's gun. A scream from Kyle, and there was Chris dragging him from the brush by the neck and dumping him onto the grass, sitting astride his back and smooshing his face into the turf.

I resigned myself to the ruckus and walked past them, wondering again at how Chris could shift so quickly from self-contained, manlike mannerisms one moment to boyish clowning around the next.

FOUR

VOICES SOUNDED as I neared the club: a group of young fellows huddled around a parked truck and a couple of girls sitting on its dropped tailgate. Chris was suddenly trundling beside me, Kyle quick behind, both of them shaking twigs from their pant legs and smoothing back their hair. Tucking his hands into his back pockets, Kyle walked with a more measured step towards the parked truck then veered towards a couple of guffawing younger teens just appearing from behind the club, bottles of beer bulging through their jackets.

"Pop. Pop bottles," said Chris, nudging me ahead as I was about to call after Kyle.

"He's too young to drink."

"It's pop, I told you, go—go."

He nudged me up the steps to the club door then drew me inside. It was crowded, and darkish. Elbowing aside a few drunken patrons, Chris cleared a spot for us at the bar and then signalled to the bartender. I squinted through the smoke, recognizing none of the people either moving about or sitting around the tables. A three-piece band on an elevated stage against the back wall struck up a heavy-metal number and a swarm of bodies started for the dance floor. I shook my head to Chris's prodding for a shot of rum, settling for a glass of red wine poured from a two-gallon box that was perched on a shelf beside a strong yellow light.

"Too warm," I complained to the bartender, but he was already hollering at someone farther down the bar, leaving me staring morosely at Chris, who was downing a shot of rum with one hand and cradling a beer in the other.

"Throat on fire?" I asked.

He flashed a grin, his cherry-brown eyes dark as Father's in the dim light. Leaning with his back against the bar, he looked around. "See anybody you know?"

"No. No, and I don't want to, I can't hear in this racket—Chris, I'm not staying long—"

"Them fellows over there, that's your school buddies, isn't it? You sure?" he asked as I shook my head.

"No, there's nobody here I hung with—what're you doing?" I asked, watching as he downed another drink. "Christ, do you always drink like this?"

"Hard week, Sis. By jeezes if it weren't."

"Yeah. Guess it was. Frigging hard week."

"I'm leaving with you," he said.

"Good, finish your beer. What'd you bring us here for, anyway?"

He set his glass down heavily on the bar. "In the morning. I'm going with you to the prairies."

"How nice."

"Already packed. Suitcase is stogged full and sitting on the bed, ready to go." He stared at me, his eyes so earnest that even in the smoky light I could see his fear and determination. I stood wordless for a moment, then doubly shocked as he pulled out a plane ticket, folded and refolded yet crisp as lettuce.

"Talked with manpower this morning. That's where I went after I left you. Tons of work on the rigs. Hang out in a bar, get hired." He called out to the bartender, raising an emptied glass.

"You can't be serious."

"Told you. Already packed."

"Chris, be serious, you can't leave *now*—not with Dad sick."

"So much for 'Leavin' the gawd-damned wharf and sharin' a place.'" He faced me with that old stubborn look of his and downed another shot of rum.

"Stop that—stop that drinking. Chris—oh, jeezes, Chris, they'll be hooking Mother up next to Dad—you can't possibly leave, they all need you now, more than ever."

"Wood's all split and stacked, deep freeze is full. Kyle can do whatever else needs doing."

"Wait, no—Mother will think this is me." I hung on to his arm pleadingly. "Look, I know what you're feeling, about the boat. I have some money. We'll buy another boat. And I'll help with the truck payments, too. And then when Dad's back on his feet again—then you come. Will you just friggin' listen—"

He shook off my arm, then leaned his forehead onto mine, staring into my eyes.

"Ticket's already booked. Sitting right next to Sis."

A couple of girls bumped up against us, grabbing Chris's arm, pulling him onto the dance floor, laughing at his awkwardness. I called after him and they beckoned me over, but I shook my head, shooting desperate glances at Chris. One of my old schoolmates got up from his table and made his way to the bar, or perhaps me. Not wanting to talk, I plopped down my wine glass and hurried outside, looking for Kyle.

The night was swarming with young people, shouting and laughing and flaring matches to cigarettes clamped between teeth, their faces lighting up in the dark like yellow moons. Kyle was off to himself, leaning against the side of a parked car with his hands jammed into his front pockets, doodling the ground with the toe of his boot. I watched for a minute, feeling a sense of loneliness about him that didn't bode well given the number of friends traipsing about. No doubt he was fully aware of the ticket in Chris's pocket. I leaned back beside him against the car, trying to see his face through the dark.

"Well, then?" I asked. "What're we going to do about it."

He shrugged, digging harder at the ground with his boot.

"He's told you, hasn't he?" I said. "That he's going to Alberta? I never asked him. You don't think that, do you—that I asked him to go?"

He shook his head.

"Well, what's he saying, then?"

"Nothing. Just going, is all," said Kyle.

"Yeah. Well, I'm not letting him come. Gawd." I kicked at the ground. "Can't believe he thinks he's doing this. Where the hell did he come up with it?"

"Just says he's going."

"Yeah. Right." I scoffed at the thought. "What can I say, then—you know, to get his mind off this?"

Kyle gave a short laugh. "Nothing. He's going. That's the way he's thinking."

"Ohh, he's being so foolish. Well, I'm going home. Gran—does Gran know?"

He shook his head.

"Something else to worry her. All right, then, I'm going—you coming?"

"I'll wait."

'Course he'd wait. He hadn't been a minute from Chris's side since the day he started walking. I strode away, feeling through the dark Kyle's watching after me. A light snapped on over the clubhouse door and I looked back, catching his face in the light, all still and pale. Another reason for Chris to stay home, I found myself thinking, to take care of Kyle, and then

"Well then, he's choosing to leave, isn't he?" I cried triumphantly. "So why don't we just leave him alone and let him go, then? And who's to say he wouldn't be more content sitting in a room somewhere all by himself, making art? If that's what life fitted him for, he should be doing it—lord knows we're not all fitted for happiness, are we?"

Mother's eyes fixed upon mine, as though searching for something she might've missed.

"Not just the one thing that makes a person happy," said Gran, looking to us both. "Your mother's right on that, Dolly. And we can trick ourselves too," she said, looking to Mother. "There's many a sad soul out there that thinks they're happy simply because they picked their own path."

"My, Gran, is that what you thinks of me," asked Mother, "that I'm fickle, that I tricked myself into thinking I'm happy?"

"No, my maid, I don't think you fickle—wouldn't easy, is all, making a fancied path in our day. Talk to the boy, Addie, I hears him outside."

I turned to the window, catching Chris peering through the curtains. He peered closer upon seeing Mother, and frightened he would run off, I ran to the door. "Tell her," I said, latching onto his arm and dragging him inside, "tell her it's not me putting ideas in your head."

"For sure I needs *some*body putting them there," he said with a grin, "not like things grow there all by themselves." He staggered backwards and leaned on the doorjamb, the smell of rum filling up the house. "No sir, not like things grow there—whoa, where we going?"

Mother had latched onto his other arm and was dragging him towards his suitcase and pointing at it as though it were the cause of his leaving. "You unpack it. You unpack it right now and put your stuff away."

chided myself for thinking the same as Gran, as Mother, as Father, and almost everybody else in these outports—everybody wanting everybody home. Not for worries about the one leaving, but for them left behind, as though a house couldn't properly shore itself without all hands abide.

I hurried along the road, then down the path, stumbling over tree roots, feeling the damp of the sea seeping through my skin. Stars glinted coldly above the blackened treetops, casting bits of silver onto the last of my father's knotty, hand-hewn railings. I slipped off a wooden step and cursed, squelching ankle-deep through wet moss and thinking, for a second, I heard my mother's voice through the water lapping against the pilings.

No, Chris, you can't leave just yet, I thought as I neared the house. But soon. You'll leave soon, for you're too big for this meagre scrap of life in the outports.

Perhaps it was this last thought passing through my mind that, upon opening the door and seeing Mother standing in the kitchen, brought such a look of guilt to my face. I looked guiltier still as my glance fell upon the opened suitcase sitting on the chair and a pile of clothes spilling out of it. Chris's clothes—Mother had found his suitcase. Gran, wrapped in her long, thick nightdress, her hair loose and fluffed about her shoulders, was hunched alongside, gathering a couple of tea things off the table and looking confused as to where to put them.

"You've done this!" said Mother, her lowered voice adding to its intensity.

"No," I said, unnerved by the pallor of her face. I stepped inside, quietly closing the door. "No. I—he just told me—"

"You did, yes you did," said Mother. She held up her hands, warding off any further protest. "It's why you went on the way you did at the hospital, you knew he'd be leaving. No use arguing, my lady—he wouldn't leave his father, not like this; you've talked him over."

"No—why do you say that—I've not talked him over."

"Not outright, maybe, but there's ways of bringing about what you wants without saying nothing, and you've always been good at that, my lady, getting what you wants—then why would he think to do this?" she demanded as I stared at her confusedly. "He's never wanting to go away—especially now with his father sick." Her voice turned cold. "It's all them letters you wrote him—telling him about the oilfields, and the money to be made—that's what got him thinking like this. All them letters—*proud you got no water slopping at your window*, that's the kind of thing you tells him, and gawd knows what else." A torrent of anger coursed its way through her, finding a well-worn path. "Well what do you say now that it's come to this?" she cried, charging along recklessly. "You think now you haven't persuaded him when he's packed his bags, leaving his poor father on his sickbed?"

I darted towards Gran, speaking in the hurt tones of a child. "You don't think that, do you, Gran? That I talked him over."

Gran was still holding on to the tea things. "You can't fault her for the boy's doing, Addie. He's too much himself to be ordered about."

Mother shifted her eyes from mine, her face taking on a discomfited look. The opened mouth of the suitcase with its overflowing clothes gaped up at her with such impudence that she marched towards it, pushing down its lid. "He'll not be leaving this house then, I can promise you that," she directed at me. "He's not himself these days—he's too upset over his father to be thinking clearly."

"That's what I'm telling you," I pleaded. "The boat—did you tell her about the boat, Gran?"

"She knows about the boat. Addie, you tell don't fault her for his leaving." Gran's hands q laid the tea things back onto the table. Stretchi wrist from the sleeve of her nightdress, she lowere her rocker. "Fighting over nothing," she grumble you, always fighting over nothing."

"She's always thinking the worst of me," I said

"Are you saying you don't want this?" Mothe "After all you said in the hospital last night abo leaving home?"

"University. That's what I was talking about— wrong with that?" I flashed as Mother's face fl scorn. "You think he's gonna be fishing and loggi life? You think he's fit for no more than that?"

Mother's eyes burned. "I told you before, my la is your father or your grandfathers. And they fishe all their lives. As long as you can't tell me why the in the field, there's learning enough right here."

My eyes went without bidding to the pile books beside her rocking chair. I lowered my he thought of Chris fumbling awkwardly with the bo footing on the pan ice. "One thing I know," I repli as I did so, "Chris is no more cut out for hunting than I am."

"What do you know about that," said Mother. " been here. He sings like the lark all morning long helping his father with his fishing and work stuff. gift—we all know his gift, and how he loves it. Bu like it as much if he wasn't helping his father, too? I content in other ways? Least he's choosing what he c what makes him happiest right there, choosing his and he should be left to it."

"Aw, cripes, Mother."

"You're not leaving this house in no morning, it'll finish your father you takes off like this."

"Aha, now, don't go doing this." He gave a silly grin, draping his arms around her, forcing her to his side.

"You'll kill your father, you'll kill him," she threatened, pushing him away, "and Gran, too—she can't sleep a wink when you're not in the house. Speak to him, Gran—and what about Kyle—he's too used to having you about, how's he going to be without you?"

"He'll be fine, just fine, won't you Kyle—Ky? Oops, where's Ky?"

"Oh, you'll laugh, you'll laugh all right," cried Mother as he lurched to his suitcase, shoving his clothes back in. "Bet Kyle's not laughing, though—call him, go out and call him." She marched to the door, swinging it open. "Kyle! Ky!" She stepped outside, her voice fading into the night.

"Go, get her back," said Gran as the wind nudged the door shut behind Mother. "She'll be sick come morning—Sylvie, go get your mother." She hunched over, picking a shirt off the floor. "Here," she said to Chris, "before it's trod on."

"Nay, I don't need that," said Chris. "Show, let's see—what is it—nay I don't need that. Thanks, Gran. Thanks." He flashed her a grateful smile, then cocked his ear to the sound of his brother's voice arguing with our mother. "Ky's the one needing help. Go get him, Sis."

I shook my head. "Come on Gran, they'll fight it out, let's go to bed. My, you're all worked up," I exclaimed as she stood there, the shirt dangling from her hands. She let it fall back to the floor and sat down in her rocker. I went to her, rubbing the thin, bony shoulders the way I used to those first days in Mother's house when Gran would shuffle about, not knowing what to do or think without the comfort of her own floors beneath her feet.

Chris belched loudly. He snapped the locks to his suitcase and lifted it off the chair, thumping it to the floor beside Gran's rocker. Then he knelt before her, a silly grin on his face as she patted his cheek. "I'll be back before Christmas, all right?" he said, then hung his head tiredly as Mother came back inside, a sharp draft cutting across the room. She held the door open for a minute, calling out to Kyle.

"He won't come in—Chris, go get him. Kyle!" she called.

Chris looked at me, his eyes suddenly wearied. A twinge of pity struck me, and without will I gave him a bit of a smile. Instantly his grin was back, and so poignant with relief were his eyes that I shook my head with warning, thinking he would lunge towards me, kissing my face as when we were youngsters and I brought him pretty rocks from the beach.

"Little bugger," cried Mother, closing the door. "He's been drinking, too—I think he's getting sick out there. Where you going? Sylvie, where you going?"

"To bed."

"Wait, don't go yet."

"Can't stay awake, Mom. I'm dead." I paused, saddened by the anxious look brittling her eyes. As with the night before, I searched for the brilliant blues of that teacher-mother who'd stood before me in the smallest of rooms in Cooney Arm, invoking thought and intrigue. But those eyes were lost to us both now, darkened by her fears. And her voice, as she carried on with her pleading—"Talk to your brother, Sylvie, tell him he can't leave, talk to your brother"—was full of the common-place, the shrunken sphere of her own secluded world.

"I can't argue it, Mom. I just—I'm just too tired right now." I tried to pull away, but was held in place by the urgency gathering in her eyes. With a feeling akin to pity, I kissed her cheek and then trudged down the hall to my room.

———————

I WAS SLEEPING when Gran slipped into bed, but awakened immediately. "It's like she don't like me sometimes," I mumbled into Gran's back.

Gran's voice was full of strain. "What brought her home, then? She come to see you off. Took courage to leave Sylvanus, sick like that."

"But you seen how fast she turned."

"Fright's what you seen. She's frightened of Chris's leaving."

I fumbled beneath the blankets, reaching my arm around Gran, no bigger than a wrinkle amidst the flannel of her night-dress. "Swear to gawd, you're shrinking," I said.

"Dare say I am. It's in the mind the old lives, Dolly, and that takes more and more room all the time. Be better off yourself, if that's where you done your rambling."

"Ooh, here we go agin." I found her hand, so tiny and warm, and trembling, like holding the breast of a frightened bird. "Are you cold?"

"Go to sleep, now."

"But why are you shaking?"

"Been shaking for years."

"Gran."

"Can't withstand things like I used to, is all. No strength left."

Mother's words came to me, about caring for the old. "You want me to stay longer?" I asked. "I can quit my silly old job— I already offered to for Mom."

"Not washing a dish that takes strength, Dolly. It's other things now—watching ye go off. But you got to go. Your

mother once cherished that notion. And your poor uncle
Elikum. He always wanted to go places but never found the
courage. Might still be alive if he followed his heart. You go on
now, tomorrow, and let Chris follow. No love's harder than a
mother's. Remember that tomorrow. Remember that when
you thinks on your mother."

"I'll make Chris stay."

"Nonsense. His mind's set."

"But she's so upset. And you, too. It's always like that around
the bay—everybody hating somebody's leaving. Why? Why
does everybody get so upset?"

"From the way we used to live, I suppose. All by ourselves,
getting what we wants from the other. When somebody leaves
then, we feels crippled. Go to sleep, now—don't have a
nervous stomach, do you, getting back on that plane?"

"No, Gran."

"Go to sleep, then."

IN WHAT FELT like minutes I opened my eyes to a gentle
shaking of my shoulder, a tinge of light diffusing the dark, and
Chris leaning over me. Like phantoms we glided through the
greyish light of dawn, gathering belongings, pulling on
sweaters, boots, fumbling only at the door when Kyle appeared
from his room. They stood close for a moment, the two
brothers, unsure of how to say goodbye.

"Later, buddy," said Chris, "we got it figured, hey?"

Kyle nodded.

"Right, then. So—you'll drive Mother about and keep the
woodbox filled." He clapped Kyle's shoulder and they gave
each other a clumsy hug. Their arms fell apart, and Chris
hurried out the door, Kyle standing there watching after him.

I put down my suitcase and threw my arms around Kyle.

"Don't be lonesome, now—he'll soon be back," I whispered.

He dug his chin into my shoulder and I hugged him hard, feeling the smallness of his shoulders beneath his shirt. "You'll take care of things?"

He nodded, his fine hair brushing my cheek. "Make him call Mom, won't you?" he asked, his voice rough.

"I will. You know I will. And we'll call you, too." Kissing his face hard, I let myself outside and leaned against the door. The air was cool, salty, and I breathed deep as I looked out to sea. The hills, the water, the sky were the same ashy black, and the air so still I heard the flutter of a gull's wing. Other sounds came to me in the amphitheatre of early morning: water lapping against the pilings, the timbre of wavelets upon rocks, the far-off drumming of sounders—surely they must've been my first sounds, for I was suddenly soused with loneliness, a longing for that lullaby of long ago. An impulse struck me to rush back inside and bury my face in the warmth of Gran's pillow. Instead I walked slowly towards Chris, who was jamming his suitcase plus a sleeping bag into the back seat of the car, motioning me to hurry.

FIVE

THE SPEED OF THE JET ENGINES flying me back across the country felt much slower than the flight home a few days before. Tightening my stomach through a bout of turbulence, I thought back over those early hours of morning. As in a dream, I carried before me the ghastly image of Mother's face peering through the darkness of her window as I slipped behind the wheel and pulled away from the wharf. And now, strapped inside the plane with Chris holding his head painfully in the window seat beside me, staring down at the boreal forest beneath us, it felt like a dream that kept going deeper.

I looked at him, his shoulders heavy with our mother's fear, our father's sickness, and yet his eyes, fastened to the earth below, were still awed by the grandeur of the Newfoundland spruce forest that had filled his window during takeoff, the distant, long-range mountains grazing the sky, their teeth rounded by time.

The forest had settled beneath us now like a cloak of mosaic greens, its festoon of ponds glistening like scattered pearls. The plane lurched and I instinctively reached for his hand, hating lurches, hating flying, although I'd never say so to him, being the eldest and all. He patted my hand reassuringly, his gaze never leaving that outer scaleless void where even fear is overwhelmed.

Folding my coat and tucking it against his shoulder, I prepared for a long sleep, shaking my head to the attendant rattling past with a food cart and wishing I could be more awake, more enthused about our first trip together since the boat ride from Cooney Arm to the Hampden shoreline. And Chris would love the prairies, I knew he would. I'd shared with him in letters my feelings of ease upon that endless flat land with the big blue sky reaching down around me like a bell jar, fat clouds floating overhead. And I loved too the ease of the wind over the land, so fine and gentle and playing itself to the indulgence of thought—the perfect place for you and your dazes, Chris, for a day rolls on forever and you can track the sun from dawn till night, and with no dirty old water slopping at your window.

I felt a pang. The letter Mother must've read. But I'd been joking. I loved the water slopping at the window. I'd written further down on the page how I missed the damn old water slopping at the window, and my pillow with Gran, and my place at the table, sipping tea with Father—even missed groaning with Mother about the slob ice filling the bay and seagulls shitting on the wharf. Had she not read that far? I shifted in my seat. Perhaps she had read that far. Perhaps she remembered only what best served her conviction: that I, Sylvie, was stealing her boy from home. The weasel making off with the prize chick.

I opened my eyes onto his soft yellow hair, his face smooth yet pained as he tried tucking his head onto his shoulder for comfort. He stiffened, trying to stretch out his legs beneath the seat in front of him, his eyes clinging to the window and the endless green belt of forest with nary a track nor feature to hold him.

"The real prairies are Saskatchewan, not Alberta," I said quietly, wishing we'd hurry and cross into those flat lands all squared and circled by plows and grass so's he'd feel more easy, more grounded again, at least in the familiarity of man's markings, if not the land itself. "We'll drive there some weekend."

"Is it as flat as you say?" he asked.

"Watch your dog run away for three days."

He laughed. "I knows the wind don't gallop over that."

"Grit in holes you didn't know you had."

"Make for good hunting, eh? Ben doing much hunting?"

"Don't know, don't see him, sleepy time now."

I plumped up my coat and tried for sleep. I felt more than heard Chris grin, a hint of mischief finding its way back, and I leaned into its comfort. Maybe it was going to be fine, I consoled myself. I'd find him work, perhaps in the construction site just down the road, the big new hotel going up— good crew, always in the bar for a beer after lunch, most of them from the Maritimes—they'd take care of him. After work he could meet me at the bar and we'd drive home in my old but nice red car. Home. Mmmm. Yeah, better warn him about that, I thought; but hell, that would be fine too—perhaps it would all be fine, we'd make lots of money and send it home to the family. Plus, I could send back what I'd saved for grad school if I had to. Mother couldn't argue if I tossed my money in with Chris's and we both sent it home.

I squirmed about for comfort, thinking it was good in other ways that Chris was finally leaving home. Perhaps he'd be open to art school—if Dad recovered well enough. Once he got a taste of living on his own, of being immersed in his drawings and amongst others like himself, he'd want more than a room in his father's house. For he was like me in some respects—we both needed a larger world to draw upon than a rocky cove, no matter the sweetness of its shores. And despite her resistance, surely Mother understood. Had she not pined for that something other once? And perhaps life had planed away that unrest inside of her, but surely she remembered her want for some one thing that was just out of sight down the road, the key to some heavenly room perhaps, if she could just walk far enough to reach it. For what is life if not that vitality of spirit, if not the tension between what is and what could be if one were to walk a little farther down that road? And in that, perhaps, Mother had failed herself, or had given over to a different want. Surely she would come to see that, and be glad of Chris's having left. She would nurture the bright, shining colours in his young eyes before they muted to those softer shades, and worry lest everything slip into shades of grey as they had for Father.

"Sis."

"Mmm."

"I think you likes him."

"Ohh!" Pulling my coat off his shoulder, I bunched it to my other side and buried my face. Mercifully, the attendant passed out little pillows and blankets, and I was able to cover up. Sleep, however, curled as I was like the letter C, was impossible.

And keeping Ben out of my head was impossible, too. Against my most ardent wishes I saw him striding across the noisy, crowded student centre at Memorial University in St. John's. I remembered how my insides quickened, how my cheeks flushed foolishly. I was three weeks into my first semester and feeling quite at ease amongst the throngs swarming through the corridors and classrooms, yet as I approached Ben Rice it felt as though I'd just discovered my feet. 'Course, I wasn't sure at first it was him, given the curls rioting about his head, the bottom half of his face partly bearded, and his eyes hidden behind rimless, stylish shades. And he was taller than I remembered, and looked kinda older.

Clutching my armload of books, I continued after him as he vanished inside the campus bar. I searched through the dark-red lighting, spotted him and called his name, hurrying towards him, proud of the hardcover philosophy books I was toting, holding them higher so's not to escape attention. He turned towards me and I managed a casual smile. Then, removing his shades, he walked straight past without seeing me, the smell of pot lingering in his wake, and took a seat amongst a lethargic crew of hennaed redheads and bearded guru types, all seeming to meld together in their T-shirts and jeans. Relics from the early seventies, I thought, bemused. Along with a few metalheads in ripped leather jackets sitting on the sidelines, they were keeping a wary distance from the spike-haired punk rockers with studded chokers and chains holding court a few tables away.

Ben looked about, trying to signal a waitress, then got up again and strolled towards the bar. Eagerly, and more than a bit nervous, I moved into his path.

"Hey, buddy, I like your hair," I said, and stood back with a saucy tilt to my head, examining him. I burst into giggles as he stared at me through enlarged pupils, for it frightened me seeing them all dilated and glazed, with only vaguest sign of recognition. And I'd suddenly realized that, aside from a few hours played out upon a summer's green some three years before, I knew nothing of Ben Rice.

Ben's eyes cleared and his face relaxed into that old enthusiastic manner I so remembered. Grinning, he grasped my shoulders, and with a loud "Well, whaddya know," drew me against him in a bear hug, kissing my cheek.

I pushed him away, so exulted I thought I'd burst.

"What's that, what's that?" He pulled me back, sniffing my hair, my neck. "Is that Hampden dust? Man, I crave Hampden dust," and he gave me another tight hug.

I pushed him away. "You drunk or what?"

"Drunk!" he snorted, highly offended, and reeled back a step, studying me anew. "Naw. Never. Well, whaddya know! Listen, sweetheart—ah—" His eyes clouded and he swayed on his feet. "Oh, yeah, right—just a sec—little boys' room. You wait—see over there—way over there," he pointed to his seat amongst the longhairs, "go sit by crazy Trapp—hey, Nutcase," he yelled, "look who's here. So how's our little Pablo, eh, and how are you? Hold that thought—wait till I gets back." He paused, steadying himself on his feet for a second, and stared at me. "Hey, Sis, whew—you've grown. Mother said to look for you—" He swayed again, and thinking he might fall, I held on to his arm.

He laughed. "Go—sit with Trappy—wait for me—you'll wait for me?" He gripped my hand, and then, without waiting for an answer, moved off with such a tremulous step it seemed the slightest breeze would topple him.

I looked back to his group, seeing Trapp for the first time. He was leaning back in a chair, more focused on the blue puffs of cigarette smoke emitting from his mouth than on the longhairs nodding about him. He'd grown more catlike, his reddish blond hair matting his forehead and his seventies sideburns and tuft of chin hair framing his pointy face. He squinted through the smoke at Ben's receding back, then at me. Taking another drag of his cigarette, he blew a smoke ring towards me as one might a kiss.

I gave an uncertain smile, but then laid my books on the nearest table and sat facing the doorway Ben had drifted through. I opened a book, pretending to read, thinking of thoughts to share with him. I'd received a letter from Chris that morning, and took it now from one of my books along with a small sketch of the bay depicting fog swirling over the water, faces and hands barely discernible through the mist, reaching longingly towards something off the page. Sliding a comb out of my purse, I swept it through my longish fine hair then finger-fluffed my bangs. Five minutes passed, then ten. I dug out a lipstick, glossing my lips, smiling back critically into a little hand-held mirror. A few bits of gossip from home flitted through my mind, and I made note to mention them.

Fifteen, twenty minutes later, when I finally realized Ben wasn't returning, my thoughts fell into emptiness. Gathering my things, I left the bar.

A group of history students I'd been spending time with were sprawled around a table in the nearby student centre. They were much more conservative than Ben's crew—the fellows with shorn hair and ball caps, the girls sporting ponytails and sweatpants, our most adventurous evening thus far featuring little more than cold beer and cigarettes. A comfortable crew no doubt, and yet throughout the next few days I wore my eyes out searching through the packed cafeteria and bar looking for Ben. It had surprised me how quickly I'd adapted to university life with its hordes of students, the constant rumble of chatter, the air clouded with smoke and fairly ringing with the clanging of cutlery and dishes and serving trays. But in my daily searches for Ben all that became a huge irritant.

I was sitting beneath an oak tree on the campus grounds, trying to find a moment's quiet, when Ben happened upon me.

Calling out my name, he came loping through brown puddles of autumn leaves and sprawled beside me, his tangled hair looking more like dreadlocks than curls.

"Hey, hey, so I didn't dream it," he said, a bit winded, his eyes wearing the same wasted look they'd had in the bar. "Sylvie. Sylvia Now." He laughed and tugged my hair so hard it hurt.

I touched his hand, smiling, feeling shy and intensely aware of the passage of time between us, the unfamiliarity of his presence. "You stood me up. In the bar," I blurted. "You were supposed to come back, you didn't."

He sobered, his eyes searching mine. "Sorry about that. I was kinda ... under the influence."

I shrugged. "It's okay." Striving to find some commonality, I started on about his mother. "She made me promise to find you, she's worried sick, says you never call home or visit her— and the number you gave her don't work."

"Cuz she wore it out," he said, falling onto his back. "Jeezes, she was calling ten times a day." He gave a mock shiver then rose onto his elbow, studying me. "So, how're you doing— damn, you're pretty."

"Thank you, thank you muchly," I said, flushing, "but, anyway, that's the message from your mother—you missed her birthday, she wants you to call her."

He pushed aside a look of irritation. "When I get another phone—damn, keep forgetting," he said unconvincingly. "Soo, what courses you doing—how's Pabs? I don't remember this long hair," and he tugged it again, drawing a yelp of protest from me. He laughed, and I didn't care that his eyes were wasted and his pot-fuelled laugh didn't have the trueness in it that I remembered from those lingering days on the wharf. It was just so good to be sitting with him again, to be teased by him again, and in a very short time I was sitting comfortably, chatting away. I pulled out Chris's swirling fog faces, holding it before him, pleased by the studious manner in which he examined the sketch.

"Are you still drawing?" I asked.

"Naw. I can't draw—play around a bit, is all."

"What's that, then?" I pulled a sketch pad from the open mouth of a canvas bag he'd dropped beside him. There was a brick hastily sketched on its cover. Putting on my old taunting look, I scrutinized it carefully. "Muddy it up," I intoned. "Soften it with petals—metal petals, infuse it with time."

He laughed, his eyes softening on my face. "Still the same strife-breeder. A brick's a brick, silly girl. Yeah, you're a strange one; straight as a flute, yet riddled with thought."

"How do you know I'm straight—what's straight—is that a bad thing?"

"That's a good thing." He tossed a pile of leaves onto my head and lay back laughing as I brushed them aside, pitching a handful back in his face.

It became our favoured place to meet, beneath that disrobing oak tree. Then the chilly October wind drove us into the cafeteria or the bar, where we indulged in our old silly ways of arguing, of me bedevilling the realism he loved in art, his belief that today's world is tomorrow's history, catch it if you can. And me with my staunch belief that history is as contingent upon tomorrow as it is on today; that art, like time, isn't a thing to be caught, but pours through us like dreams through sleep.

"And here we have a trunk," I said, coming up behind him in the student centre one evening, watching over his shoulder as he doodled a rough wooden trunk on a scrap of paper. "So, now, what kinda trunk is that?" I asked, sitting down beside him.

"A nothing trunk." He tapped my fingers with his pencil, smiling. "You're looking nice. Here, have a sip." He pushed me his paper coffee cup, its steam reeking of whisky.

I took a gulp and near choked, yet despite my watering eyes managed to keep a calm face and a steady voice. "So, when's a trunk just a trunk?"

He took back the cup and touched a finger to one of the fat whisky tears rolling down my cheek. "All the time. It's always only a trunk. Your mother," he said. "You look like your mother, same eyes, only brown."

Mesmerized by his attention, I stared at the trunk with mock contemplation. "A trunk's always a trunk? Noo, not so— shh, listen." I held a silencing finger to my lips, peering closer at the sketch, thinking back on those boarded-up houses in Cooney Arm. "There's voices in there," I whispered. "Oh—but the lid's closed—can't hear them too well. Let's pry it open a crack, let them out—a memory, a piece of clothing, maybe, trailing from its insides."

He shook his head solemnly. "Nope. Sorry. My trunks are all neatly packed."

"Hey, don't leave," I blurted as he shoved his book inside his bag, "just cuz I pack more into a trunk than you do."

He stared at me with bemusement. "You old enough to have dinner with a man?"

"Uh?"

"Dinner. You old enough to have dinner with a man?"

"I—uh, actually own my own booster seat."

He ruffled my hair, pulling me to my feet. "C'mon, dinner, grab your books." Wrapping an arm around my shoulders, he led me through the student centre, my heart near bursting. He hailed a cab and scrunched in beside me, the smell of liquored coffee from his breath beguiling each breath of mine during that glorious ride downtown, corrupting any thoughts of study, essays, due dates, and all else remotely connecting the world outside to the back seat of that cab.

The harbour wind whipped at our backs as we climbed out on Water Street, chasing us deep inside an overpacked bar with low, heavily beamed ceilings and lights so dim I could scarcely see across the room. A folk singer stood in a corner before a microphone, fingerpicking a medley on an acoustic guitar. Digging out a bar stool from beneath a pile of coats, Ben bolstered me onto the seat, leaning against my back as he sought the bartender's attention. After ordering beers and fish and chips he managed to secure a stool next to mine, and we spent the next hour munching chips, drinking beer, and talking over the music—Ben talking mostly, and me trying to hear over the drummer and electric guitarist who'd joined the folk singer. Most times I read his lips or simply nodded and smiled, caring nothing for what he was saying, only that he was sitting so close. I'd kissed a few guys, made out some, but nothing drew me like those wintry grey eyes of Ben Rice.

A clap on his shoulder and Ben hastily swallowed a mouthful of beer. Trapp. And a fistful of the big-haired reds and bearded gurus from the campus bar. They jammed around Ben, lighting up smokes and shouting at the scrambling bartender for beer, for wine, for bags of chips and pretzels, hollering at each other—and then, the unforgivable—nudging Ben off his stool so's one of the reds—who apparently was having a rough night—could sit.

Clamping my resentment with a smile, I nodded to the faces Ben introduced me to, smiled at Trapp, all the time wishing Ben would take my arm and lead us away from this densely packed bar, the stench of pot floating off his friends. But Ben huddled eagerly into them, puffing smoke and talking into their faces, chortling and thigh-slapping and occasionally tweaking the locks of the reds as he'd done mine. A few times he gripped my shoulder, giving me a shake, asking, "You all right? Like the music?" and before I had a chance to answer he'd be jostled aside by the stream of bodies making their way through or the big-haired reds nuzzling around him or the gurus hip-butting their way into the action, all of them swaying and singing, guffawing, cigarette ash falling onto my clothes as they bumped or stretched past me for beer or ashtrays or wine glasses, the smell of pot like burnt rope on my tongue.

Midnight saw us squishing inside a couple of cabs with the same hooting and hollering, and motoring back to campus. Being crushed against Ben brought some measure of comfort, but it ended quickly when, upon Ben's orders, the cabbie pulled up before the first-year residence.

"Sleep good," he whispered into my ear, and fell backwards out of the car as he opened the door from behind him. Standing on the curb, I watched as he bundled himself back into the cab, which peeled off with the door half shut. Disappointed, I walked to my matchbox room inside the dorm.

Couple of days went by before I saw him again. He was sauntering through the cafeteria looking like a shaggy dog with his unkempt curls and bearded face. Slouching on a chair beside me, he took a sip of coffee then offered me his cup, the steam once more pungent with whisky.

"Morning specialty?" I asked, wrinkling my nose, unable to suppress my excitement at seeing him.

"Hair of the dawg," he replied. "Wanna play? Come on, let's get outta here—great band playing tonight, gonna be a party."

It was only Tuesday. I had an exam in the morning. "I can't be late," I said.

That became the way of it during the passing weeks—Ben stumbling across me in the cafeteria, where I just happened to be sitting. And then the two of us heading downtown to the same loud, congested bar, occasionally dropping by the basement apartment he shared with Trapp and one other guy for an intense hour of smoking pot and chugging beers so's to save money once we got to the bar. Despite the faded jeans and lacy tops I bought at the Salvation Army store, the two-inch cowboy boots and floppy earrings, I received little more than polite smiles from Ben's pals before vanishing from their sight like a pricked bubble. No doubt it was the age difference—I was five or six years younger than most of them; I was Ben's "little sis" from the outports—which, much to my chagrin, was how he introduced me. And how he saw me, I was starting to realize with a sinking heart, for several times I'd caught a quick exchange between him and his friends wherein he'd warn them away from passing me anything more than a joint. Sometimes I caught him looking my way with a guilty expression—the brother thing, no doubt, leading his younger sis astray.

"Stick to the beer," he ordered me one evening as they all popped pills and snorted coke around me. A command easily followed, given how nauseated I was suddenly becoming—and I'd taken only a few puffs of pot. Most times I didn't smoke at all, preferring wine.

"Babysitting, babysitting," Ben grumbled in good humour, walking me around the block for air.

"Drugs—is that all you and your friends do?"

"In between breathing."

"God, how come you does so much drugs?"

"Just what I need—another mother," he said dryly.

"Some might think so." And then I held my sick stomach and hobbled to a park bench. "Can we sit for a while—I just need to sit for a while."

"You didn't do anything, did you—pills?"

"No."

"You certain?" His tone had become tight with worry. "Perhaps you shouldn't be here—be with your own crowd."

"I don't have a crowd."

He was quiet for a moment. "That's not a good thing back there," he said, gesturing to his apartment, "the drugs. Pot. Stay away from that shit."

"Why don't you?"

"I will. Graduating soon—gonna be a big boy."

"Soon? When?"

He was still looking back towards his apartment, and missed the startled look on my face.

"Yeah, gotta do some cleanup soon—real soon," he ended on a quiet note, then turned back to me. "I have something to do. I have something to do over the next week. And then, then I'm gonna clean up. C'mon, I'll call you a cab."

"But when are you graduating?"

"Next semester. How you feeling?"

Next semester. I grappled with the thought of Ben not being on campus. Swallowing back the bile that was still welling up in my throat, I stood and started down the road.

"Hey, Sis, you're going the wrong way."

"Meet you at the bar."

"Hold on, I'm calling you a cab."

"I'll save you a seat." Stiffening my shoulders, I carried on walking. He followed, muttering loudly. So's to deter him from that *Sis* business and *You're nothing but a child* business, I put on a gay face for the rest of the evening, shouting over the music into the faces of the big-haired reds, the bearded gurus, grinning at their jokes, listening with feigned looks of interest to their sporadic expulsions of personal observation and insight into the Stones' influence over the skinny-legged singer prancing about the tiny stage and the drummer's flamboyant Peter Criss drum rolls. I kept checking to see if Ben was looking my way, but aside from his periodic big-brother glances, he spent the rest of the night deeply engaged in conversation with some burly reddish-haired guy I'd never met.

Trapp, like the solitary cat he resembled, hovered in the background as he always did, and yet was seldom farther than a foot from Ben's side. Times I caught him looking at Ben's friends with the same look of detachment as I did. At one point one of the big-haired reds had been crushed up beside him and made some apologetic remark, to which Trapp saluted her with that Cheshire smile of his. She turned her back to him, linking her arm through Ben's, oblivious of the long tunnel of smoke Trapp was now blowing into her back-combed, beehived hair. Catching me watching him, he flashed a conspiratorial wink and grinned, stunning me with the charm of a genuine smile, and started tunnelling more smoke through big red's beehive. I gave my first honest grin of the evening and settled into a feeling of inclusion felt heretofore only with Ben.

It was a feeling short-lived. I didn't see Ben the following day, or the next. Towards the end of the week I had it figured he was distancing himself. I kept hearing his worried tone when I'd gotten sick, kept seeing his big-brother guilty look. And most disturbing was the knowledge that he'd be gradu-ating the following semester.

Friday evening came and suddenly, amongst the crowds on campus, I never felt more alone. Ben's face, his laugh, his rioting black curls haunted the corridors, the cafeteria, the campus bar. A fantasy was what he'd been during those summer days back on the wharf, a mesh of unformed lines like one of Chris's drawings. But now that I'd touched his flesh he was more firmly fixed before me than any of those deeply entrenched portraits from his sketchbook of yesteryear.

After handing in a big research paper I headed for the downtown bar, feeling sickishly obsessive yet unable to dissuade my step. Ben happened to be standing outside the bar as though waiting for someone. He looked uncertain upon seeing me, then grinned, and taking my arm, led me down a couple of streets to a tavern where he said he sometimes hung out.

Maybe it was that genuine smile I'd exchanged with Trapp that made me so carelessly invoke his name as we neared the tavern. Or maybe I was so overwhelmed by Ben's taking me somewhere other than the usual bar that I needed to say something extra interesting so's to reward his attention. Whatever the case, ever since that charming, co-conspiratorial smile with Trapp I'd been plagued by the notion that he was as obsessed as I was over Ben.

"So, is Trapp gay?" I blurted.

Ben near tripped over the stoop of the tavern. He gaped at me as though accused of some heinous crime. I walked inside, regretting the impulsive question. "Where did you get that?" he demanded. He jerked on my arm, turning me to face him, then shushed me as a waiter hurried past, calling out a greeting to Ben. "Where the fuck—" Ben started again, but I drew away from him and into the dingy dive with its odour of stale beer and vinegar, butt-seared carpets, and thick smoke from hand-rolled cigarettes drifting like fog into my face. Harsh coughs and raspy voices filled the air and laughter wheezed from faces that crinkled like dried mud as I walked past them.

"Over here," Ben ordered.

I followed him to a table where more waiters, bearing trays of wings and french fries, busily swung back and forth through saloon-style kitchen doors, creating a draft and the illusion of air.

"What kind of place is this?" I began, then sat back as a waiter materialized out of the haze.

"Kinda place Paul McCartney hangs out in," said Ben. "Couple of Black Horse," he said to the bartender.

"Paul McCartney!"

"Yuh, inspires him." Ben leaned in urgently. "Now, what the hell's this about Trapp being gay!"

"I didn't *say* he was gay, I *asked* if he was gay."

"Why the fuck would you ask that? Hold on a second." He got up, his attention snared by the burly, reddish-haired guy he'd been talking to in the bar a week ago. "Just a sec, be right back," he said and went over to the guy. They exchanged words. They exchanged something else, too, from Red's pocket into Ben's.

I dragged a thumbnail down the centre of the beer label, drenched in disappointment. Obviously I wasn't the reason for Ben's being in this bar. I watched as he continued talking with Red, growing warm beneath my jean jacket. I rolled up the sleeves so's to show off the plaid lining inside the cuffs, then impatiently pulled the jacket off and slung it over the back of my chair.

Clapping Red's shoulder, Ben finally took his leave. "Sorry about that," he said, sitting back down. "Had to work something out. Now then." He landed his beer bottle on the table with sudden consternation. "So what were you saying—" he glanced about, lowering his voice, "why the hell did you think Trapp's gay?"

I shook my head, wanting to do away with the subject. "It was stupid, I shouldn't have said it."

"You got it from somewhere—where the fuck did you hear that?"

"Ohh, relax, Ben, cripes, it's not contagious, nothing's out to get your penis."

He sat back with a look of surprise. My arms prickled with fright. I had invoked his penis. My head started shaking and I forced it to shake sideways so's to make it look like an extension of speech as I quickly exclaimed, "Nothing, nothing, just the way he looks at you is all, like he's jealous."

"Jealous! Jeezes."

"No, I didn't mean that he was—only that—" I trawled for words, my neck growing hot. "It's just that he doesn't look at women," I blurted.

A look of relief swept Ben's face. "Jeezes, that's cuz he's a ditz, I told you he was a ditz, a social ditz. Jeezes"—he took a swig of beer—"you had me going. How do you know he don't look at women? He looks at women."

"Well—he doesn't look at me, and I'm a woman." I wrapped my arms behind the back of my chair. Inadvertently Ben looked at the smallish but nicely rounded front of my T-shirt, its two puckered points.

"Can see, perhaps, why you think that," he said, and laughed a little too hard.

"Oh, you're not sure? You like to check the merchandise?"

The words had come out fast. They hung like bits of my clothing around him, leaving me bared.

Ben was gripped in silence. I flushed. I started pulling on my jacket, an excuse to twist my face from view. I fisted through a twisted sleeve, hooking the cuff on my watch strap as I did, tearing at the stitching. "See that," I muttered, examining the cuff, "should always check your merchandise—just never know what you're getting, eh." I smiled flippantly.

Ben raised his eyes to mine, holding them, but then they fell. "That's why I like 'em twice but nice, from the second-hand stores," he said lowly. "Wear 'em when I want, chuck 'em when I don't." He touched the back of my hand, and then stroked it with an unbearable gentleness. "You wouldn't do that to something nice, would you—something new and nice?"

Trapp appeared by the table, a jarring release from the awkwardness of the moment. The relief in Ben's voice as he greeted him was painful to bear. "Grab one for me," he called as Trapp trekked to the bar. "What about you—hey, where you going—?"

"Ohh, another jaunt through the cleaners," I said with a feigned tiredness. "Gotta keep things at least *looking* fresh and nice. You know." Flicking my hair over the collar of my jacket, I swaggered on my two-inch heels towards the exit. Trapp looked up as I sauntered past.

"*Waarm* evening," he drawled in the broad, flat brogue of the old-timers around the bay, flattening out "warm" to rhyme with "arm."

"Yeah, sure, *waarm* day," I said irritably, and caught what might've been another real smile abort itself on Trapp's mouth.

For days I burrowed into my room, hurrying through campus so's not to encounter Ben, eating in the smaller, more obscure cafeterias. I became a slob, and wondered how Mother would react to the humps of clothing mounding my floors, bed, chairs. Myrah, my skinny, outport roomie, who'd become my first bosom pal and who was going through a real breakup, became equally a slob, and rather quickly our tiny room descended into beer haven squalor, with rows of empties lining our windowsills and coffee table like abandoned, beheaded soldiers. Shredded beer labels fell like confetti onto our laps, our beds, into our boots, our morning cereal. I took up smoking, fighting my way through nausea till I could finally hold a cigarette with grace, and bags of pot started taking up residence in a concealed portion of the junk drawer.

"Holy christ, Sylvie," said Myrah after she found me painfully twisted around a wooden chair one morning, staring at a cold cup of tea, "is it still that bad?"

"Worse," I whimpered.

"Ahh, come on, let's get out, go for a beer—what time's it—almost noon, come on, they're not worth all this." And for the tenth or twelfth time that week I trailed a step behind Myrah as we traversed the university grounds, listening to her tirade about men's stupidity. I hung on to her every word, hoping to find a salve for my hurting, fool heart. If I'd just kept my mouth shut I'd at least still be hanging with him and sharing laughs. Most times I was content with simply his company, anyway—ohh, I cringed a thousand times rethinking that wretched moment of Ben's rejection, his discomfort, his gentleness.

It was during one of Myrah's rants, marching beside her through a crowded corridor, that I literally crashed into Ben. Too late I saw him and Trapp pushing against the flow of bodies and coming towards us. Deliberately Ben sidestepped in front of me, offering an unconvincing apology as I collided against him, my books bruising my ribs.

Muttering something unintelligible, I flushed hard and bent down as much to hide my face as to gather the papers that had slipped from my binder and scattered at my feet. He bent beside me, his leather jacket buckling upward, exposing an airline ticket in his inside pocket. "Where you going?" I asked, so's to divert his attention.

Instantly he was on his feet, zipping his jacket. "Going home for the weekend," he said with a wry look at Trapp. He clapped Trapp's shoulder, nodding. "Yuh—weekend off."

Trapp was rapidly chewing the corners of his mouth, his eyes squirrelling from me to Myrah as though we were about to discover his secret stash of acorns.

"Soo," said Ben, bringing his attention back to me, "how you been doing—haven't see you around."

I stood beside him, fitting my papers back inside the binder. "Fine. Just fine. And you?" I looked him boldly in the eyes. He was smiling. I smelt his whisky coffee breath. Myrah clicked her tongue.

"Me?" He drew a look of concern. "Geesh, I've been studying, actually." He lifted a finger to his throat, feeling for a pulse. "Must be something going around." He gave an affectionate smile, and I thought for a moment he was gonna chuck me beneath the chin in some fatherlike gesture for having said something cute. I made to dart around him and he caught my arm, pulling me sideways against a row of lockers. "Where you running off to? Why did you run off the other night?"

"I, uh, I have a class, I have to go—"

"Settle down, you're like a dog with burr—what's the matter with you anyhow, cripes, you're like a dog with burr."

"You just said that."

"So I did, you got me circling like a dog." He fell silent, then gave a self-conscious laugh. "What're you doing Monday night—I'll take you to dinner, would you like to go to dinner?"

"Where?" I asked.

"Where—I don't know where, we'll find a where. Whatsa matter now," he asked as I hesitated, "you gotta think about it?"

"Yeah, I gotta think about it. I have a class on Monday night."

"After class then. I'll meet you in the cafeteria. Around nine—half-past nine?"

Myrah clicked her tongue, more sharply this time.

Ben shot her a crude look.

"Half-past nine," I said.

He gave a quick nod, a tentative smile, and then, with a curious look at the stone-faced Myrah, followed after Trapp who had since lost himself amidst the river of bodies flowing through the corridor.

Monday evening I was sitting in the cafeteria, waiting. I was wearing a crinkly-textured T-shirt I'd bought for the occasion and a new pair of skin-tight jeans. My hair was loosely curled and heavily hair-sprayed so's to hold the curls in place. I was wearing an underwire bra that penned me in like a whalebone corset yet pushed my breasts upward in an alluring manner. I was wearing blush and gloss and eye shadow. And huge hoop earrings that stroked coolly across my cheek each time I bent my head to look at my watch.

An hour passed. No Ben. The cafeteria started emptying. Janitors scraped aside chairs and tables, sweeping the floors, slopping them with heavy, wet mops. The last few bodies left. I'd never heard the cafeteria so quiet. Gathering my books, heart weighted more with disappointment than anger, I left.

Next evening I was back again, wearing the same earrings and jeans and crinkly-textured T-shirt, thinking I might've gotten the time wrong. On the third day I forced my step away from the cafeteria, away from the campus bar or any of those places where I might run into Ben. Keeping my thoughts from obsessively returning to him, however, was like trying to forget the rock in one's shoe.

It was Mother who told me. Ben had dropped out of university with Trapp and gone to Alberta to work in the oilfields. Poor Suze was crazed with worry, Mother said, and couldn't figure it because he'd only a semester left before graduating with his engineering degree, and his marks—while low—were passable, and he had money in the bank. And Trapp, too, had just a semester left towards an engineering degree. Why in the name of gawd would either of them quit now, the distraught Suze beseeched me each time I came home after that.

"Because that's what lots of students do," I lied to her that first time she came to Mother's house to see me. "They suddenly get tired and take time out, works for a bit, then goes back to school and finishes. Not a thing to worry about."

It was not an answer that comforted Suze. She wheezed for breath, her padded cheeks exuding a rashlike redness as she flapped her arms and wrung her hands and paced the small confines of the kitchen, worrying for her boy.

"He's not a boy, Suze," Mother said consolingly, but still she carried on with her flapping and wringing and pacing. I kept my comments to myself, relieved the poor woman knew nothing of her "boy's" wasted eyes and whisky breath.

For the longest time university life without Ben felt about as exciting as a Sunday sermon. But time smoothes the sharpest of stones, and thankfully, after a few months of ardent study and good grades, I was once more traipsing lightheart-edly through campus, this time with Myrah and a keen group of philosophy students I'd taken to studying with.

———————

IT WAS DARK when the plane rattled down the runway outside Grande Prairie, the sky racked with thunder and lightning. I found my car in the parking lot and drove us through the night, straining to see through the sheets of rain and shushing Chris, who kept swearing at the rutted road and exclaiming over the lightning forking across the uninterrupted sky.

SIX

I DROVE for fifteen, twenty minutes through the worsening storm, then pulled onto a side road, lurching through potholes, the high beams funnelling a faint yellow through the woods pressing in on each side.

"Where the hell you taking us? Where's the city?"

"Something I been meaning to tell you," I replied, slowing to a crawl through a washed-out section of road. "Well, easier to simply show you now." I cut sharply to the side and braked, the headlights striking a row of darkened tents huddling near a river, some lit from the inside with candles and flashlights, others with the whiter, brighter light of lanterns.

"Welcome home. Ninth one down is ours."

"What—?"

"It's a boom town, brother. No room at the inn. Don't worry," I said to his shocked look, "it's a nice, big tent—can sleep eight men, long as they stretches out nice and straight."

"You're living in a tent—smothering jeezes, wait till Mother hears this."

"Mother won't," I said hotly, reaching around to the back seat. "You don't tattle from school. Now, help me get my bag. Chris!" He was staring aghast at the huddle of tents, the river sloughing blackly beside them. "Look, there's no place to rent, is all. People sleeping in cars, everywhere. We're lucky. And beside, it's just for the summer; why waste money on high rent? Cripes, a thousand bucks for a porch is what they're charging."

"What about winter—you never slept outside all winter."

"'Course not, stayed with a girl from work. She got married and I got the boot. Will you stop looking like that? You got it good—there's four to six people sleeping in most of them tents. And really, it's kinda cool," I added lightly. "All kinds of people, mostly French, and they're all great. If it wouldn't pissing right now, they'd be sitting around campfires, playing guitars and stuff."

"My sister's a freaking hippie."

"I'm not a freaking hippie—ohh, christ, the look on his face—"

"You do acid?"

"Yes, I sees everything green. Now, will you help me get my bag?"

Minutes later we were running and slipping on the wet grass, the rain zinging cold on our faces, and then crawling inside the tent, dragging our bags. Chris sat back on his ankles in the dark.

"It's flapping like hell—who pitched this?"

"I did. Works good when it's slack—more give to the wind."

"And more take, you nit! We'll be in the river by morning."

"Ohh, take off your boots, roll out your bag. I can't find the matches—you got matches?"

He flared a match. My sleeping bag was neatly laid out to one side of the tent, duffle bags lining the walls of the other, a little plastic table with candles and a lantern sitting near my bedding. "We'll save the oil," I said, lighting the candle. "Shove all that stuff aside and spread out your bag. What're you sitting like a dummy for? You slept in tents before."

"Not how I pictured city living, Sis. Cripes, if Gran knew this—"

"Yeah, well, she don't." Pulling off my boots, I dove into my sleeping bag with a loud chattering of teeth and skimmed out of my wet jeans and sweater. Then I zipped up the bag and burrowed deep inside, muffling through my pillow, "Blow out the candle when you're ready. You tired?"

He grunted, pulling off his boots, his jeans, muttering something about ventilation. Puffing out the candle, he zipped himself inside his bag and lay quietly.

"Well, good night, then," I said. "It'll be nice in the morning, you'll see."

"Hum mmmm."

"Sorry you came?"

"And miss this? Gawd, no."

I grinned. "You'll be fine. Really, it's a lovely park."

The wind thumped louder on the tent and the sound of the river grew nearer. Within a minute I heard him shuffling in his sleeping bag till he was lodged against my back.

"Sis," he whispered. "I'm skeered of hippies."

"Oh, *please* don't go saying hippie—we're *punk*, now—hardcore *punk*."

"They're French, Sis. Suppose they does acid and eats us for french fries?"

I kicked at his feet. "Get away—will you get away?"

He let out a moan and dug his head deeper into my back. I yelled, and the brunt of my elbow found his cheekbone. He yelled back and we both laughed, the tension from the past few days dissolving like salt in hot water.

"You nervous?" I asked.

"Who's not—freaking river's getting closer."

"I mean of being here—away from home. Still having them wild dreams? Well, then?"

"I'm thinking—let's see, there was the three-legged horse one. And the two-headed snake. And the bush of fire—"

"Burning bush? That's God, Chrissy—lord, you dreams about God?"

"And the other one, too. He was laid out on an altar, his body was all bunched out. Like, with food. And I was eating one of his ribs."

"You were eating the ribs of Christ? Jeezes, Chris—so what did he taste like?"

"Like that. Jesus. Tell me one of yours."

"I don't dream no more."

"You always dream."

"I just stopped—there's one I had—oh, gawd, it was stun."

"Tell me."

"I was in the jungle getting attacked by a tiger and was screaming *'Tarzan, Tarzan, come get me!'* and he yodels back, *'Not now, Jane, I'm on the phone.'* Yeah. There he was—Tarzan, with his spotted thingy around his waist, and talking on a tree phone. And then the tiger jumped me."

We broke into laughter. "So, tell me last night's," I coaxed, "what did you dream last night?"

"Gross."

"Tell it."

"I'm tired." He yawned.

"The dream."

"It was about lice."

"Head lice?"

"On my hand."

"And—?"

"There were three of them. And they were white. And big. And bloated with blood."

"Grandfather lice," I exclaimed. "Remember Gran talking about them? On the fishing schooners, and places like that, they'd be in your head for so long they grew big, fat, and old. But there was something else—something else she used to say about them—"

"Ugh, can we sleep now?"

"Least you weren't eating them. Wonder what the psychology books would say to that. Mmmm, the number three. The colour white. Yeah, I know what they'd say—they'd say you were either carting the holy trinity about on your palm—or," I added to his groan, "that you, me—we're all parasites, feeding off the face of the earth."

"Nice."

"Well then, what do you think it means?"

"Never thinks about it."

"Right. Forgot. Tell me then, what do you think about? When you're off in your dazes, are you thinking?" I nudged him as he faked a snore. "Come on, Chris. Is there nothing you ponder?"

"Once I asked the science teacher a question. Learned not to ask no more."

"What did you ask?"

"Can't remember."

"What did you ask?"

He shuffled onto his back. "Jeezes, once you gets onto a thing—"

"The question!"

"The question was," he said through another yawn, "how come there's so much order out there in space—you know, how the sun and moon and stars all have their own paths, never interfering with the others—and here on Earth we have the same thing with the trees and water and animals—everything with their own path, and everything sticking to it. And then we—the smart ones—people—we're the ones running amok?"

"Good question. What did the teacher say?"

"Same thing. Good question. Would I like to write an essay on the answer."

"Good answer. Did you write the essay?"

"Not yet. Tell me what you'd write. Talk quiet now—take your time," and he evened his breathing as we used to do as youngsters, trying to fool the other into believing we were sleeping.

"I'll tell you what I think," I said. "I think God's too huge to create small things. Like feelings. So, when we're all running amok, we're creating feelings—you know, love, joy, sadness and all else—and those feelings makes us think. Like, why. Or why not. Which makes us, little brother, makers of consciousness, the Earth's consciousness. As long as we continue to think, we continue to create. How's that for feeling a mite important. Eh?" I elbowed him.

"Yeah, mmm."

"Yeah, mmm, that's what I wonder about too—yeah, mmm. Tomorrow," I said abruptly, "I'm talking to this foreman about getting you work. There's this hotel going up—actually, there's three—but this one's just down the road from the bar. Be a good place for you to work. Good bunch of men there. You listening? Chris?" I kicked him. "Tell me something, you don't really go off in trances, do you? I mean, really, tell me. You can't be climbing scaffolds if you—well, got this thing."

"Thing?" He stirred awake.

"Well, then, I'm only checking. Mother got me half convinced there's something wrong with you."

"Mother," he groaned.

"What happens, then, when you goes off like that?"

"Happens? Nothing happens. For jeeze sakes, Sis, can't we just sleep. I wanna get clear of that fuckin' river out there."

"Do you lose time—when you're in your trances?"

"Who knows, hell!" he said in irritation, and carried on in loud, whiny tone, "One minute I'm up on a ladder, putting putty along a windowsill. And then a leaf floats by and I'm seeing its little veins, and the little veins become tiny bones, and the tiny bones turn into webbed duck feet, that then becomes the wings of a bat—and there you have it—next thing I knows I'm upside down in a tree. Whaddya think—am I still part maker of the Earth's brain? Tell me, Sis, what's all with you and Ben? Huh?"

"Go to sleep," I muttered.

"Perfect," he muttered back.

I fluffed up my pillow and kept trying for sleep, but was thwarted each time by fuzzy images of curly black hair and sooty eyes.

The first time he'd strolled into the bar in Grande Prairie and saw me prowling about slinging beer, he'd gotten quite the start—like he thought I was chasing him. I'd fretted about that very thing as I readied for the big move, but then put it aside. It was a grand opportunity Myrah had happened upon in the local newspaper—a bar in Grande Prairie, Alberta, looking for Newfoundland waitresses, paying triple the wages offered around town and quadruple the tips. With my degree filling one pocket and student loans depleting the other, I was soon flying into the sunset with Myrah.

I knew from Mother that Grande Prairie was where Ben and Trapp were both working, and no doubt I looked to see them each time I strapped on my change apron and faced the loud, crowded barroom. But it had been three years since I last saw Ben, a good stretch of time, and the sour memory of waiting in a cafeteria for a supper that was never dished served more to breach than bridge. The kick in my heart, then, upon first spotting him looming through the barroom door was as much a surprise to me as the sight of my lean figure toting a serving tray and slinging beer was to him.

His curls were cropped close to his head and his beard shorn, revealing a fixed jaw and a graven face. His eyes, I was relieved to note—for his mother's sake, not mine—weren't wasted and hidden behind shades, and were the same clear grey as when he'd slouched about the wharf, scrutinizing my knees and criticizing my crooked nose. His stunned look upon seeing me gave way to confusion as I approached. Then a kind of nervousness flushed his face and he backed away as though he might flee.

"Hey, look who's here," I said airily, wiping off a table and pulling out a chair. "Want a beer? You looks awfully sober."

"What're you doing here?" No smile, no greeting nod.

"Oh, change of scenery. Bit of shopping. How's your sidekick?" I moved to the next table, stacking empties on my tray, trying not to feel his eyes appraising me with such an odd look of fear, as though he wished me an apparition that might vanish upon touch.

"Was that a no—to the beer?" I asked. "Perhaps an Irish coffee?" Balancing the loaded tray on one hand and plugging two more empties onto my thumb and forefinger, I faced him in my old taunting manner.

He smiled a curious, sad smile and shook his head. "It's good to see you again," he said. "But—I gotta go. Looking for someone."

"Sure, next time." I walked away from him and laid the tray of empties on the bar, my arms trembling.

The next day he was back, sitting on a barstool with the same graven look.

"Myrah found this great ad in the paper in St. John's—just what I was looking for—a chance to pay off the loans, save some money for grad school," I offered, wiping down the bar before him.

"So, where's the roomie now?" he asked.

"Sinuses. Couldn't handle the bar—too smoky. She's working across town in a hotel restaurant—forgets the name— up on the main road coming through town."

"And you've found a place?"

"Basement apartment, one room—I lost the draw and got the sofa. Lucky to have it, I guess—everybody sleeping in trucks, what with the oil boom and housing shortage. Guess you know all that, eh?" I smiled and went off with my tray, picking up empties and taking orders.

I wasn't the silly, flighty schoolgirl anymore, but it unnerved me whenever Ben was in the bar. Brought back all those tender memories of girlhood love and the terrible hurt when he'd just taken off like that. It was his fourth or fifth time back, sitting on the barstool, that I realized there was something wrong with Ben's face; that he wasn't simply being reserved, or worried by my appearance on his turf, for even worry spirited a face. And Ben's face was without spirit—like Kyle's the night outside the bar when he'd known Chris was leaving for the oil rigs.

I noted too that he was staying for longer periods of time, yet always near the centre of the bar, which, amongst the constant parade of patrons assailing me for beer or whisky or change for the cigarette machine, reduced our conversations to snatches. And never did he speak of himself, diverting all talk to Chris, or home, or the dump of snow that had just whitened the streets of Grande Prairie.

Sometimes, as I swerved my way around the room and caught sight of him hunched over his beer, I felt a huge sense of loneliness about him—not the loneliness one feels for a friend, a lover, or family, but for himself, the laughing free spirit who drew cats for old women and gulped back spiked coffee and hung out in low-life bars that supposedly inspired Paul McCartney. I burned to plop my tray before him, demanding why—why the hell he was working the rigs with only five credits left for an engineering degree, why the hell he wasn't visiting his poor, bewildered mother, where was Trapp, why the graven image, and more important than all of that—why did he leave me waiting for a dinner that was never served?

But I couldn't do it. He felt too much like a bird that had clipped its own wings, and at the slightest questioning he'd be hopping to another perch. I didn't want that, for I felt it was me, and some sense of who he used to be, that he was needing, not the bar itself. And either injustices grow smaller with the passage of time or mine was a forgiving nature, but I no longer felt angry at Ben. And worse, as I declared to the tutting Myrah one morning over breakfast, I no longer *wanted* to feel angry at Ben.

Once, on a snappish winter's day, with the late-afternoon sun glitzing the snow-packed sidewalks, he came up to me as I was leaving the bar and invited me to dinner. His eyes, as we sat across from each other at a wooden booth in a steak house, were sheepish with guilt, and I knew he was remembering his last invitation, and the No-Show. Yet he said nothing. And it was this, his continuing silence about anything of the past few years and the sadness in his eyes, that stole across the table like a long shadow, touching me with a hint of foreboding.

So I was surprised when, after we'd washed down the last of our steak with beer, he asked about my graduation, ordered an expensive bottle of wine for a toast, and with his eyes crinkling a little into their old, taunting manner, ribbed me about the airiness of philosophers and how he'd have to put rocks in my pockets to keep me from floating with all them airy thoughts inflating my head.

Folding my arms onto the table, I lazed into this unexpected burst of warmth like a turtle on a sunny rock. "Let's hear some of your thoughts," I said boldly. "Loosen the lid on that trunk of yours. Show me something from the past few years."

It took a minute for him to remember that evening in the student centre when I'd taunted him about the trunk he'd doodled, its lid tightly shut and no telling clothes trailing outside to hint at the owner's story. When he did remember, his smile faded.

"Rocks," he said simply. "Full of rocks. Sink a boat." He drank the rest of his wine and laid down his glass, letting his hand rest on the table beside mine. I examined the broad, hairy width of it, ridged with veins, his knuckles chafed by weather, and resisted the urge to trace my finger along that wormy bluish vein. I looked up. He was smiling that sad smile again, his eyes filled with more uncertainty than when he'd drifted around campus with enlarged pupils, patting the rumps of dogs that weren't there. At least then I knew his hallucination. This new incertitude baffled me. And I hated that sad smile; it reminded me of Father's the last time he motored from the shores of Cooney Arm, looking back upon his stage, his flakes, and all those things reverent to his heart that he'd been forced to leave.

"Heard from Pabs? Still weaving with his pencil I hope?"

I smiled. "Yeah, he's always at it."

"Yeah, he's amazing."

"Thought you were good, too."

"I was just playing around."

"But still, you were good."

He raised an eyebrow. "Weren't you the one grading me bad? *Exact*. Too *exact*. Weren't they your words? Destroyed me, I think." He shook his head. "Man, he can draw. I remember studying him—those times we hung on that wharf, sketching. I was always trying to figure him out, how he saw things, drew things. It was like if I could figure it, I could have it too." His tone turned pensive. "Think my whole life's been like that, trailing behind others, taking on their ways."

I looked at him with surprise. "How do you get that? You were always the main attraction."

His face softened onto mine. "Only you saw it that way," he said gently. "Actually, it was the pot I kept feeding everyone— for a price—that was the main attraction. Helped pay the bills, but—" He pulled a face. "Let's stick with you, more inter- esting. Ran across you in the library once, going through Descartes's meditations like a miner with a pick. What got you onto philosophy, anyway?"

He was pulling bills out of his pocket and laying them on the table for the waitress. I picked up my gloves, reluctant for the evening to end. "Sorry about rushing," he said apologeti- cally, "but it's a two-hour drive to the rig."

"You're driving tonight?"

"Yep. Philosophy. You were telling me, why philosophy."

"I dunno. Curious to know where babies come from— before the womb and after death. What about your engineering—did you—did you ever finish? And what about Trapp—you never mention him."

"Trapp's been better. And I did finish the engineering. So— where babies come from—before the womb. What got you thinking about that?"

We'd left the restaurant and now he was taking my arm and leading me down the icy sidewalk. He was a head taller than me, but it felt like more than that as he crunched a path in his chunky, steel-toed boots through the banked snow towards my car. Holding on to his arm, I told the story I always told whenever I was asked: about Mother's three little dears sleeping in the graveyard, and how I'd thought them romantic creatures, like angels, but how that notion was dispelled when I played dead myself once, nearly frightening poor Mother to death.

Ben listened quietly, thin flakes of snow glinting on his dark curls as we paused within the umbrella of light thrown off by a street lamp.

"And that's it really," I ended. Then, prodded by his silence, I added a few other things, things I hadn't told anyone, about how I understood—in that moment of Mother's fright—what Gran's flowery language had tried to tell me: that the little dears had been real babies with fingers and eyes like mine, buried now beneath the ground in coffins that held nothing of the flowers and sunshine that covered them but were worm-ridden and dark and cold.

"Despite Gran's assurances," I went on, "that the dead rise from their graves and take on the wings of angels, I was never so sure. Why, then, was my mother still planting flowers and sitting by the graves if there was nothing down there? Truly, it was the deepest of mysteries," I concluded with a flourish of hands. "And it still is. Don't you think?"

He dug his hands in his pockets, a smile twisting his mouth. "And have you figured it?"

"Lord, no. It can never be figured—it's the *figuring* part itself that intrigues me, and the numerous other mysteries it leads me to. 'Course, you're the one who likes everything defined— didn't you say that once?"

We were standing quite close now, the snow thickening on his hair, melting on his mouth.

"Sylvie, I've gotten caught in something," he said abruptly.

"Oh lord, he's married." I was only half joking.

He shook his head. "That would be simple," he said dismally. "It's just not something I can talk about right now. Do you understand?"

I didn't, but nodded anyway. Moving past me, he used his forearm to swipe the mantle of snow off my windshield. Then he brushed the covering of snow off my shoulders and quickly, gently, pressed his mouth against my cheek. "I won't be around for a while," he said lowly. "Got some things to do. Perhaps we can have a drink after—a long drink, eh? Where's your keys—get inside. Start your car—make sure she starts."

He waited for a moment as I started the car, swiping snow from the back windshield, and then he was bounding back to the sidewalk, watching as I crunched away from the curb.

It was a few weeks later, late evening, before I saw him again. I was walking along the same sidewalk to my car. It was bitterly cold, the air white with ice crystals. Ben was walking towards a nightclub, his bared head hunched into his shoulders, the tips of his hair frosty grey. Clinging to his arm was Trapp, his feet slipping and sliding beneath him as he grinned like an irate child. Ben stopped upon seeing me, Trapp colliding against him. I stared at Trapp, a wool cap pulled down over his ears, his face bone-white beneath the neon lights of the club, ruffs of sideburns and chin hair patching his face. He slipped when he saw me, and was saved from a headlong flight by Ben holding tight to his arm, steadying him.

"Hey, how you doing?" I asked, looking at them both.

It was Trapp who responded. "Dandy, just gawd-damned dandy, and how's Miss Sylvie?" he leered, straining to keep going.

I was taken aback, his manner highly offensive, even for Trapp.

"It's his birthday," said Ben, giving me an apologetic smile. "Been working straight through for a while now. Might say he's broke out."

I watched as he gave Trapp a push, sending him staggering ahead, and tried not to show Ben that I knew his lie. Nobody worked the rigs with facial hair, given the threat of sour gas and the need for close-fitting oxygen masks.

"Where you off to?" asked Ben. "Wanna join us for a beer?"

"Think I'll pass," I replied, watching Trapp tumbling to the sidewalk. A couple came out of the nightclub, stepping distastefully around Trapp, who kept slipping onto his knees as he tried to get up. Ben was instantly beside him, helping him to his feet. He looked back to me with a quiet smile, his eyes appealing for some sort of understanding as Trapp remained leaning against him for support. To spare him further effort I called out good night and went in search of my car. I looked back once, peering closer to see Ben wiping spit or puke off Trapp's mouth with his coat sleeve, no different from a father wiping his youngster's mouth clean of ice cream.

Throughout the rest of the week I kept seeing them, Ben dragging the staggering Trapp up one street and down another, in and out of the dance bars and pool halls. I kept a clear path, and was more embarrassed for Ben when Trapp spotted me leaving a drugstore once and heckled, "Well, if it ain't little Miss Sylvie. How's she going, little Miss Sylvie?"

"His birthday," Ben mouthed apologetically, shoving Trapp's face into the sleeve of his coat. I walked past with a flash of irritation, wondering about the poor bitch of a mother whose youngster must've laid half in, half out of the womb for five days straight in order to command a five-day birthday.

Ben caught up with me, his hand tightening around my arm.

"He's—coming down hard. Sylvie—"

"What, off drugs?" I faced Ben. "What the hell's going on with him—with you? And why the hell is he so—so *disdainful*—of me?"

"He's not, he's just a bit screwed up right now, he'll get over it."

"Get over what?"

Ben stared at me, his face closed up like a clam shell. "I won't be around for a while," he said quietly. "Going to a different rig in the morning. Be back in a few weeks. Perhaps we can have that drink." He touched my arm and smiled, a deep, tender smile that would've sent my heart skipping beats like a faulty piston in days of yore.

"You keep in touch, buddy," I said, and patting his hand reassuringly, carried on down the street "like I hadn't a care in the world," I said to Myrah later, making up my bed on the sofa, "and no more I don't—he's never offered anything but friendship, and I'm always drooling at the mouth—god, I'm sick to death of mooning over Ben Rice—been mooning over him all my life, it feels like."

"He's a tease," cut in Myrah.

"Ohh, god, no, he's not—he's nothing, he's a friend—a friend who likes me a lot and deserves more than a mooning, foolish schoolgirl every time he tips his hat or tosses a smile— that's how he is with everybody, really friendly, and it's just this stupid part of me that keeps thinking, *Ahh, it's him, it's him, he's the one who's gonna save me*—eh, save me from *what*, you might ask, good question." I looked at Myrah, who was no longer listening, her curly head thrown back in the rickety armchair we'd found on the street, her eyes dazed into the shape of hearts.

"Well sir, she's mooning," I exclaimed.

And she was—she'd been in a state of bliss for weeks over some guy from back home who was part of a mud crew for the rigs and was spending his time off in the hotel. He swore Myrah was a Sandy Olsson lookalike, his favourite dancing girl from *Grease*. I suffered through that movie time and again whilst Myrah studied the facial tics and head tilts and hairstyles of the actress, adopting them for her own so's to enthrall the already smitten mud-man who was beginning to hint about engagement rings. Which started my heart skipping like a faulty piston again each time some dark, curly-headed fellow entered the bar, reminding me of Ben.

"Poor bastard, good thing he don't show up," I whispered to Myrah one night during a love scene between Sandy and Danny Zuko, "for I'd probably be at his ankles like a Chihuahua, yapping on and on about all the grand reasons why I study philosophy, hoping to impress him—gawd, why do I keep blistering over that poor bastard?"

"Ahh, he's just a fixture in your head is all," said Myrah, "a habit, kick it, and why *don't* you have a boyfriend? Never known you to have more than three or four dates with the one fellow."

"I dunno—after a few dates, everything just wears off."

"Then it can't be love."

"Whatever that is. Would probably wear off with Ben, too. Who knows. Perhaps it's only fantasy I like—gawd, there's a thought."

And indeed it was a troubling thought, for looking back, the
romantic prospects I'd met during the past years never felt
right—least not the way I'd imagined love, or even lust, might
feel. Mostly what I felt was a huge want in my heart that was
never satiated, no matter how cute or clever the man. And the
want was burning big these days, triggered no doubt by the
reappearance of the sooty-eyed Ben. And why not, I rational-
ized. As the first recipient of my misguided heart, it made
perfect sense that he'd always be a Pavlovian bell.

Armed with that understanding, I disallowed any further
thoughts of Ben Rice. And after a few months without any
sightings of either Ben or Trapp, I was once again free of those
obsessive desires—till the trip home, and Chris getting me all
stirred up in memory.

SEVEN

THE WIND DIED OUT and the rain stopped in the quiet hours of dawn. I woke up late into morning, and late for work. Cussing and marshalling Chris through the tent flaps, I squinted through the morning sun into the swollen brown waters of the Wapiti River sliding just a few feet past the tent, smelling of drowned earth.

"Ohh, just keep going," I muttered over Chris's grumbling about our near drowning. A quick look around and I was dashing through the campsite, flicking my hair into a ponytail and hauling on a jean jacket, cringing from the cold, wet grass soaking through my shoes. "Chris!" I looked back impatiently as he lagged behind, staring dazedly at the dozen sagging, rain-drenched tents, their reds, yellows, and blues a crescent of colour between the muddied riverbank and the green wall of trees rising behind them. A few campers were muddling about in jeans and T-shirts, longish, unkempt hair framing sleep-worn faces as some shuffled with towels and soap to the river and others tidied up their campsite from the night's storm. A breeze tinkled amongst the pots and pans dangling from tree hooks and bared limbs overhanging stone fireplaces, and I laughed as Chris walked into a fully strung clothesline between two trees, suffering a shower of last night's rain down the open neck of his shirt collar.

"A hippie camp," he exclaimed in wonder. He shook himself off like a half-drowned pup. "Look—look at buddy," he exclaimed, pointing to a young fellow sauntering from the woods with a roll of toilet paper in one hand, the other scratching at a mane of blond curls shimmering over his shoulders. "Jeezes, if it wouldn't for his tits, I'd take him for a girl."

"His name's Jordie, and he's gorgeous—hey, Jordie," I called, "meet my brother."

"Hey, man," said Jordie.

"Hey, b'y," replied Chris, and bolted for the car. "My sister's a freaking hippie," he kept repeating as we climbed inside, "my sister's a freaking hippie."

"Hippies retired years ago, brother. They're just happy campers with no rooms to rent. Will you stop gawking— cripes, they're just back-to-the-land kinda folks."

"Wouldn't be on my land. Chrissakes, you can't all camp this close on a river, where's they shitting?"

"Oh, for the love of gawd."

"Well, wouldn't be in my river if I owned it."

"Chris, it's me—I'm one of the campers. Would you run off your sister?"

"And what's they all crowding the one spot for—cripes, the river runs for miles—say no more." He threw up his hands in defence as I popped the clutch and faced him. "But I'll tell you this, I'll be hauling down that tent this evening and pitching it downriver—or upriver—wherever the frig up is around here."

"Yeah, gonna be fun." I backed the car along the muddied path, turning onto the highway. Least he's looking outside of himself, I thought with consolation.

"See that?" I asked after we'd driven a few miles down the highway. "That restaurant over there, and all them shiny new trucks parked beside it? You know how many new trucks they got in this town? Everybody got a new truck in this town.

Street bums got a new truck in this town. And you might too if you listens to your sister."

He grunted.

"And you know what else they got?" I asked. "They all got brand-new stereos bouncing around in the back of them trucks. Still packed in their boxes. No place to put them. But they got them. And perhaps you will too—if—?" I threw him a look. "If *what*?" I demanded as he kept to his glumness.

"If I listens to me sister."

I gave a stout nod. "Now, think how smart you'll look come fall—riding home in a shiny new truck with a galvanized boat in the back and your head tucked inside a cowboy hat, strutting spurs. Man. Saltwater Cowboy."

He smirked. "Saltwater cowboy. Yup, that'll be me. Me and Ben. Saltwater cowboys."

"Ben?"

"Oops. Forgot."

"Forgot what? What's Ben got to do with this?"

"Jeezes, can't mention his name."

"Ben's not around, I keep telling you, I haven't seen him in months—gawd, you'd think he was your best friend, the way you keep talking about him."

"Fine, fine, can't a fellow goof around—jeezes. So what else are they all buying with their money?"

"Nothing. They give what's left over to their sister. Then they asks what else they can do for her." I directed his gaze out the window. "Look about you, what do you think, pretty flat around here, huh?"

"Yeah, great place for marbles."

"And other things. Do you know that prairie boys don't get as seasick as Newfoundlanders travelling to the offshore oil rigs? Something to do with no horizons. Prairie boys are used to no horizons. Something else you'll be strutting about when you goes back home—motor for hours on stormy seas and no puking. Brother, the things that's gonna come to you—if," I paused, and we both repeated in unison, "if I listens to me sister."

I laughed, punching his shoulder, and he punched back, admiring the quickly greening fields cradling Grande Prairie, the smell of wet grass wafting through the car, and the huge sky, startling blue from last night's rain.

"See that church over there, and all those buildings around it?" I said as we got into town. "Used to be a big field last summer. The town quadrupled in size overnight, and you'll be hard pressed to find an old person strolling the sidewalks—or even a local. Throngs of young people is mostly what you see—all from back east. The only Albertans I've met are the bartender I work with and the guy who owns the corner store where I used to buy milk."

"What do they think of us all crowding in like this?"

"Bums and creeps, according to the politicians. Don't know about the common folk, can't say we're not good for business. Pretty town, eh? Nicely laid out, clean and quiet for the most part—if you look past the construction sites. Hotels and houses springing up like mushrooms. Been bit of a downturn lately. But it'll turn around."

He gazed at the storefronts and restaurants as I found parking in front of the saloon-style bar where I worked. Getting out of the car, I dug a handful of change from my purse and ladled it into his hand as he stood looking about. "Call Gran," I said. "There's a pay phone inside the bar—hey, where you going?" He'd pocketed the money and was starting up the sidewalk.

"Having a look around, see you in a bit."

"But, wait—call Gran first."

"I'll call up here—seen a pay phone."

"But I wanna talk too—Chris! Oh, bugger him," I grunted impatiently as he disappeared behind a feisty group of men bailing out of a truck and piling towards the bar. I followed them in, catching a last glimpse of Chris cutting across the street and heading between two buildings, looking for all the world as if he knew where he was going.

The air was already thick with smoke inside the bar, and with its crowded tables and babble of voices, not too unlike the one we'd left the night before in Hampden. Till you looked closer and saw that there weren't any women, only men: hard drinking, hard talking, darkly clad men with big rough hands and weathered faces. They were all wearing muddied, steel-toed boots and on their heads varied-coloured caps with their company logo barely discernible through ingrained dirt. Truckers, rig hands, service men—all ages. My eyes lingered on the younger ones like Chris. Some I knew from working the bar, but I felt I knew them all, their smooth, eager faces and soft hands masked behind false swaggers as they guzzled back beer, trying to keep stride with their elders. And with the amount of practice they were getting they were seasoning pretty fast. But it wasn't all for show. With the minus-forty winds freezing their faces the past winter, they'd been guzzling as much for warmth, especially those hellish evenings working past dark. Many nights they'd walked stiff as pickets into the bar, clawing ice off their mouths and eyebrows. I could still smell it now, like stale beer, the ice melting from their faces and dripping onto the radiators as they huddled over them for a blast of heat, lips too stiff to form words, swigging back whisky (when they thought I wasn't looking) from mickeys jammed in their back pockets.

After strapping on my change apron, I leaned across the bar and tapped my serving tray on a bald head partly bent beneath the cash register. A black-whiskered face growled up at me, eyes livid in the light pouring into them through the blood-red lampshade.

"Another five minutes and you'd have been filing for pogey," he rasped in a smoke-shredded voice.

"Yeah, I know, I know," I cut in, aborting Cork's well-rehearsed diatribe about last chances. "So, the nice little niece is still without a job?"

"Day's not out yet."

"Yeah, yeah, I hear you. Where's my float—get me my float."

"Your da make it?"

"Just fine, thanks, Cork. So, you missed me a bit, huh?"

Cork smirked. "Miss anything with tits in this gonad saloon."

"Charmed," I replied. Taking my tray to a nearby table, I stacked it with empties and then dragged a damp rag across the newly lacquered tabletop. I moved to another, noting as I always did the freshness of the butt burns—like the hardwood floor beneath my feet, untouched by time but scuffed and scarred by the sudden influx of heavy boots and their chain-smoking owners.

"Four whiskies and jug of draft, Cork." I boxed the empties and put my tray on the bar, stacking it with clean ashtrays. "Brought my brother back with me—to find work. Any of them contractors?" I asked, glancing about the room.

"Spin a bottle and pick one, Skinny." Cork landed a jug of draft on my tray and rang open his cash register, his bull-like face turning whimsical as he swept a pile of change off the bar. "Hear that—prairie gold," he drawled, rattling the coin into his till. "Love that prairie gold."

"Yeah, count it wisely—back home we could walk on water once, the fish was so thick."

"That's the nature of it, Skinny—nothing lives forever. Even stars burn out. Bring your brother around, we can use him in the club down the road."

"No bar work, thanks."

"Whoo—the lady's got airs. Listen to me, sweet madam," he said, hosing steaming hot water over the jumble of glasses filling the sink, "I got collars white as snow tucked away somewhere— that a smirk? Don't believe I got collars white as snow?"

"Yeah, 'course I do."

He slapped a steamed pink hand onto mine. "Mind your manners then. Go wriggle them hips. You're sitting on a fortune."

"Chrissakes, Cork."

"Just helping you along."

"Stuff it." I busied myself serving the men. As though spoiled from their week's hiatus, my eyes started watering from the smoke and my head ached from the loud hum of voices.

A different voice sounded amongst the babble and I turned towards it as might a new mother in a nursery full of bawling newborns. Chris was waving from the doorway. Beside him stood Ben, his curls scrunched beneath a ball cap, his face quirked by a hesitant grin as he held up a hand in greeting. I quelled the sudden leap in my heart, focusing on Chris as he thumped Ben's shoulder, mouthing "Look who I found" as though their discovery of each other was some miraculous feat. Marching to the bar, I set down my half loaded tray and called out to Cork, "That construction crew from back east— the ones building the new hotel down the street, they still coming around?"

"Like church on Sunday. Pansy-assed drinkers, not worth the spit polishing their glasses. That your brother?"

I looked at him in surprise. "How'd you know that?"

"Looks like you, only prettier. Here," he said, hefting a jug of draft onto my tray, "teach him the ways of men."

Ben and Chris were seating themselves at a corner table, talking intently. They pulled back as I approached, Chris's eyes, his smile, striving to appease.

"Ah, good call, Sis," he exclaimed as I laid the jug and two glasses before him. "Dryer than a rusty faucet."

"Good to see you," said Ben. He gave me a tight hug. "Mother's been updating me on your dad," he said quietly, "must've been a helluva time." He squeezed my hand and sat down. I noted the lines marking a jaw that had sat rigid too long, yet the haunted look in his eyes had eased since I last saw him, a hint of his old revelry showing through. My flesh still warmed from the touch of his hand squeezing mine, and I absently rubbed it against the side of my jeans.

"Dad's gonna be fine," I replied. "And so," I looked to them both, "what are the odds of this—the two of you *finding* each other?"

"Darndest thing," said Ben dryly. "So happens I'm in town for supplies—groceries and stuff." He looked to Chris, who was pouring the beer.

"Found this great art shop down the street, Sis," said Chris. He passed along a glass for Ben. "Thought I'd do some drawing—you know, between making money and buying trucks." He tipped his beer towards me as though his words were reimbursement for some ill deed, then clinked his glass against Ben's. "Cheers, buddy." He drank deeply, the froth gathering against his upper lip like milk, then thumped his glass on the table and grinned at Ben, at me, his face freed from worry for the first time in days.

I smiled despite myself. "Did you call Gran?"

His grin vanished. "Fine. They're fine. Mother phoned from the hospital already, Dad's doing lots better. He's up and walking some—believe that? Gran's making soup for supper, and Kyle's at the hospital, too." He stopped. "Gran said to say her shaking's stopped—what shaking? Never seen Gran shaking—did she mean her hands?"

I was kept from answering by a drunken voice hailing me from across the floor. "Back in a sec." I moved off, spending the next ten, fifteen minutes fetching beer, fetching rum, my fingers automatically sorting the cash, all the while feeling an unease about Ben's sudden appearance and his meeting up with Chris. And yet I kept warming to the sound of their voices rising and falling through the babble, sounding terse and heated at times, then jovial and soft with laughter. Such a familiar sound from my past it was that my step involuntarily slowed each time I passed their table, a part of me craving the music of their voices, the almost forgotten song of our last summer together, pulled from its dusty sleeve.

"That construction crew," I said to Chris, setting another jug of draft on their table, "they'll be here later today. Stick around, now."

Taking a deep gulp of his beer, Chris landed his glass onto the table in a combative manner. "Got a job, Sis. Working the rigs. With Ben and Trapp."

His words fell against my ear like a heavy drumbeat. His eyes, as he turned them onto me, were fraught with purpose and perhaps even a tinge of excitement.

"I knew it, I knew it!" I turned to Ben, who was throwing up his hands defensively.

"Wasn't my idea, thought you knew all about it."

"Anyway, nothing to argue about," said Chris, assuming a casual air. "Was gonna tell you—"

"When?" I cut in angrily. "From across town in a phone booth—"

"I came here, didn't I?"

"Hiding behind Ben."

"Think he got us both," said Ben. "But hey, listen, it's not that bad—rig work. I got him a peasy job."

"Four thousand, three hundred accidents in one year—out of a crew of seven thousand, five hundred," I snapped at Ben. "When? When did you fix this up?" I demanded, unable to keep from glaring accusingly at Ben.

"When you were at the hospital. Ben called to see about Dad— No!" Chris smacked the table with the flat of his hand. "This got nothing to do with Ben. It's got to do with me, understand?" His eyes hardened, his mouth compressing so tightly it twisted his jawline, and for one bizarre moment my brother appeared a stranger before me. "You're bad as Mother," he said deeply, "thinking others got to put thoughts in my head, that I got none of my own." He held my stare, his whole being so tightly strung across the moment that his top lip began to quiver.

"Why don't I come back later," said Ben.

"Finish your beer," said Chris. "We're leaving together. Not a big deal, Sis." He relaxed into his seat. "I came to work and I'm going to work—*and*, I'm figuring my own path. Look—buddy the bartender is glaring—you're getting fired."

"Why didn't you tell me—why didn't you tell me you had things planned—"

"Because I'd done enough fighting with Mother. Because some things can't be talked about with you." He motioned towards Ben with the slightest of nods, and I flushed, whisking away to tend to other tables. Yet my eyes kept darting to Chris, to Ben. They were sitting back from each other, casting sombre looks my way.

Emptying a tray of smutted ashtrays into a bin, I made my way back to their table. "Why didn't you tell Mother?" I asked accusingly. "How come you let her think I talked you into this?"

Chris shoved back his chair, snatching his jacket off the back. "Not arguing with you, Sis—same as arguing with Mother; neither one of you listens, you're just alike."

"Oh, bull."

"Look, you're gonna get fired, buddy the bartender is shooting daggers."

"Wait, you just wait," I ordered as he headed towards the door. "Chris! Ohh!" I turned on Ben as Chris vanished outside.

"Come with us," said Ben, abruptly. "To the rig. Really," he added to my blank look. "Cook's always needing a helper—the camp's a bit rough, they keep quitting. But—" he glanced around the bar, "handle this crowd, you can handle anything."

"Yeah sure, just give me a minute I changes aprons. Ben, go get him back, please."

"I'm serious. We've had two quit in the past six weeks, and Cook's desperate. You'll be hired in two seconds. Hell, you're hired now, if you want it. Think about it—when was the last time you up and done something spontaneous—think about it, will you think about it?" he asked.

He smiled that old tender smile.

My pulse remained flat, the blood pooling like still water in my veins. "What's he going to do, he's got no work clothes or nothing—he can't just go off to a camp." I moved away from him, straightening chairs, hustling tables, removing empties. Ben hopped by my side, tossing in a word when he could.

"I'll take him shopping, I'll take him with me to Peace River this evening, be back in the morning, think about the offer—Sylvie." He gripped my arm, facing me. "I won't take him if you're not agreeing. I'll bring him back here tomorrow, see how you feel. Got that?"

"Sure, I got that." I waved Ben aside, clearing a load of empties off the cigarette machine, dropping a handful of quarters inside for a pack of smokes for one of the patrons, silently muttering, "Bloody hell you'll talk him out of it, not when he's riding that stubborn streak of his."

I swerved around the tables, staring more openly now at the multitude of rig workers, their scarred hands and fingers missing, their bruised and scratched skin, their wearied, overworked eyes. The accident stat I'd thrown at Ben hadn't come from thin air; I'd read it in *Maclean's* whilst waiting on laundry a week ago—dated, perhaps, but only by two years, and from what I'd been reading in the papers, it still applied. Roughnecks, lean and tough, the equivalent of yesterday's cowboy (the article went on to say), were daily wrestling hundreds of tons of steel pipe miles into the earth in search of oil … death and mutilation are simply part of the risk … thirty-nine dead in the past three years, eleven dead in the past ten months … some crushed under tons of steel, others hit by whiffs of poison gas, food wolfed down in between one-minute pipe changes, lotsa money and lotsa cost of flesh and blood, inexperience, insufficient training, fatigue, twelve-hour shifts, fourteen days on, seven days off, work fast, make money, get out, safety issues resisted by governments and roughnecks alike—trying to force a roughneck into more respectable hours like telling a cowboy to trade in his horse for a Jeep.

The afternoon dragged on square wheels. Before going home that evening, I called Gran from the bar. She was just back from the hospital with Kyle and was having a cup of tea now before bed.

"Be another couple of days before he's home," said Gran. "He's done damage, but he was walking the hallways this evening."

"And Mom?"

Gran paused. "Your mother's fine, don't go worrying, Dolly. See to things out there, and she'll be fine."

"But how is she, Gran—do she still think I talked Chris into leaving?"

"She knows Chris well enough for that. And she's too busy with your father to worry about much else. Do he have a job yet, Dolly?"

My turn to pause. "Actually, yeah, he does, already. Guess what, Gran, he's going to start with Ben in the camps. Tomorrow morning. Tell her that, will you—that might make her feel better, that he's working with Ben. Ben will take good care of him."

"My, that is good, then. Yes, I'll tell her that, I'll tell her that this evening. For sure, she probably already knows—Suze is down with her tonight, and probably Suze knows."

"Yes, probably she does. You don't go worrying now, Gran."

"Nor you either. And so, you're getting on, then?"

"Your tea's cold by now, you still like it cold—"

"I'll add a drop of hot water. Kyle, put a drop of hot water in Gran's tea." Her voice faded as she spoke aside to Kyle, and I could hear the aged tremor in her tone.

"You got your lamp lit?" I asked, feeling a twinge of homesickness. "Let me talk to Kyle. Ky? How are you, got Gran's lamp lit for her?"

His voice was small, too young for the worries just now put onto him, but he spoke well. "He looks better by the day," he said of Father. "Mother's the one who's depressed, doctor said it's supposed to be Dad, but it's she instead."

"Don't go telling your sister that," I heard Gran grumbling in the background, "she'll be worrying for nothing, and stop chewing your fingers, you'll be down to stumps by morning."

"What're you chewing your fingers for," I chided Kyle, "stop that worrying, and now listen to me. I'm transferring money into Mother's bank account. I want you to talk with one of our uncles—Uncle Manny, perhaps—and tell him to start looking for a boat for Dad, like the one he lost. You don't tell Dad this, or Mother, not even Gran, just do it, all right? Tell Uncle Manny not to say nothing till he's got a boat. It'll be another couple of weeks before I get the rest of the money, but he can start looking."

I thrived on the relief in Kyle's voice. "I can do that, I can look too, I knows where to look, I'll stop by Deer Lake on the way to the hospital tomorrow, me and Gran, she'll like that."

"But hold on now, I don't have all the money yet, it's gonna take a few more weeks."

"Yes, I know, I'll just look." His voice grew eager, and I felt in him that sense of strength that comes with taking things back from fate. Leastways, some things. So much depended on Father's health now, and how much of it he'd get back. Reassuring Kyle had brought a lift to my heart too, and after assuring him and Gran for the thousandth time that things would be fine, I left work and hurried to catch the bank before closing time.

I thought of Chris, the sense of purpose, the excitement on his face when he had entered the bar, and felt a stab of guilt that I'd trodden over what must've felt a great accomplishment, securing a high-paying job overnight, working alongside his bud Ben. Worriers all of us, I chided myself, driving back to the camp. Probably a gift from God, Ben's calling home and Chris getting a job so fast. Five months down the road, and with both our wages plus overtime for Chris and tips for me, we could have a boat bought and ten or fifteen thousand dollars sent home—what Father probably made in a year in the woods. And perhaps by Christmas we could all be home, gathering around the table, gifts galore for everybody.

I'D NEARLY talked myself happy by the time I returned to the bar the following morning. It had felt like a fast night, jet lag from the trip across the country making for a deep pillow. A couple of circles around the bar, staring back into the wearied eyes of all those rig and service hands, and I was back to worrying again, looking expectantly to the door, watching for Chris and Ben.

"Well, how-dee-do, she said nothing about bringing back her sisters," said Cork. I glanced up as three assorted brunettes entered, rib-hugging tube tops clinging to their nipples and jeans tight as skin dipping beneath their bellies. They moved into the dimly lit bar, their flowery scents wafting behind like a meadow's breeze. Choosing a table closest to the men's washroom, they sat, bracelets and neck chains tinkling, and turned inviting smiles to the room.

"Know what I like about them sisters," said Cork, eyes digging inside their well-rounded tube tops, "everything's up front with them babes. And what's not is a billfold away—yeah, that's right, Skinny, everything's got a price. Go do your rounds," he cackled over my grunt of disgust. "Every cocksucker here is bulging to treat them ladies."

"No argument there," I muttered, scratching orders from the sudden rash of fingers snapping for my attention.

Swerving about the tables, I laid down jugs and glasses, counting out my pay from the mound of bills constantly being replenished in the centre of each and every table. One of the things that had astounded me my first day on the job was the pile of tens and twenties the men tossed indiscriminately on their tables, and how it never went down, no matter how many rounds I served. It was these piles of bills the three women were openly eyeing as they lit up cigarettes and casually chatted while surveying the room.

"Couple more whiskies, Cork." I rested my tray on the table, sorting through the handful of coin I'd just earned.

"See over there, you see over there," Cork commanded, pointing with a whisky bottle towards the hookers. A young fellow had seated himself at their table and was walking away now amidst jeers and laughter. Taking his place was an oldish fat man, his sleeves pushed up around massive arms, his cap stuck in his back pocket. "Know what you're seeing there? Proper ways of women is what you're seeing there—turning away young bucks for fat-ass piggy banks. Learn from them—always chuck what you want for what you need."

"Chrissakes!"

"Just helping you along—"

"Chuck it, Cork."

"Watch them knickers, Skinny, they're starting to knot."

———

AFTER ANOTHER HOUR there came a lull. "Can I make a quick call, Cork? Check on my father."

He rasped his consent, shoving a pile of coin from the bar

towards me, nodding towards the pay phone in the small
alcove by the washroom doors. I had the number to the
hospital in my jeans pocket and dialed it quickly, feeding coins
into the slot. Partway through the first ring Mother answered.
Her tone sounded tired upon saying hello, and then turned
crotchety as she recognized my voice asking how she was
doing. "My, I thought you were Suze at first," she said, trying
to cover her terseness, "she's calling every half hour, I don't
know what she thinks, that I'm suddenly going to up and die."

"She's—probably worrying more about you than Dad."

"Your father's doing just fine. Washed and dressed himself
this morning. He's sleeping now—tired him out talking with
Chris."

"Chris called?"

Slight pause. "So it's true, then—he's with Ben?" A subtle
tone of relief in her voice.

"Does that make you feel better?" I asked with a kick of
anger.

"I'm just asking, Sylvie, what do I know what you've got
cooked up—especially now the two of you are together."

"What do you mean, cooked up?"

"Suze brought down the mail," she replied. "All them
brochures for Chris. Should I keep them here, or perhaps—"
I could hear her striving to keep the edge out of her tone—
"perhaps he won't be coming home before he moves to
Halifax?"

I rested my head against the cool metal of the phone. "Next
time he calls, ask him," I said quietly.

"Your father's awake. Here, he wants to speak to you."

His voice sounded groggy and confused in my ear. "It's
Sylvie," I heard Mother say, and hated that she'd put the phone
to his ear, that he was straining to wake his self up.

"No need to say nothing," I cut in, "just checking on you, is all."

He spluttered for a bit, and then started sounding stronger, asking me about the trip back, when I was coming home again. There was nothing of resentment in his tone, and I breathed a bit easier knowing that.

"You keep a watch for Chris, Dolly," he croaked. "Headstrong, he is—like your mother," he added, mischief creeping into his tone. "Should see her, more white in the face than me, I think she rather herself lying in bed, getting the attention."

I heard Mother chiding him in the background, and the clatter of trays—his lunch, he said, they were serving him lunch, and what a poor fare supper was last night. Spuds with no salt or butter.

It bolstered my feelings, hearing Father joking like that, and if not for Mother, I'd have been feeling rather chirpy by the time Ben came swinging in through the doors. He shook his head as I looked past him for Chris.

"Out in the truck," said Ben. "Bull-headed like his old man. Not budging from his decision to work the rigs, and he's not budging from the truck because he don't want to fight with you. So." Ben looked at me questioningly. "I meant it yesterday—about you coming to work with us." He looked past my shoulder, making a face. "I better get outta here, you're boss don't look happy. Listen, change your mind, gimme a call." He pulled a card from his back pocket and tossed it on the tray. "Here comes your boss, you're gonna get fired, you makes a lousy waitress anyway."

He quickly left the bar, leaving me facing a snarling Cork. An effusion of apologies and I was back to cleaning tables. Through the window I caught sight of Ben crossing the street. I saw Chris sitting in a huge, godawful truck that was encrusted with dried mud and with a rusted wheel-wench soldered to its front grille, and its flatbed loaded with sacks of spuds and bagged groceries. Ben climbed into the driver's seat, settling beside Chris. Lowering their caps to the sun, they gave each other a high five. The engine jolted into life and they rattled down the road, leaving me with a pang of sudden loneliness, of having become the dissonant chord in the song of camaraderie that had once been ours.

I picked up my tray and turned back to the room, back to those roughened hands and wearied eyes of the men, cigarette smoke coiling around their heads like phantom nooses.

A cheer rose from the bar. The hookers were rising from their table with three older men. One of the girls turned at the door, blowing kisses around the room. The rejected young fellow from earlier staggered to his feet with a loud howl, ducking kisses as a gunslinger might dodge bullets, drawing louder cheers from his pals. I looked back out the window, mechanically taking orders. The godawful truck was heading west, towards the campsite. Dumping dirty ashtrays into a sink, I slapped them about, hosing them with hot water. Cork snatched the hose from my hand, waving his cloth crossly before my face, threatening me with firing.

"Know what, Cork—you got a real bony butt." I took off my apron, chucked it on the bar, and followed the hookers and their fat-assed piggy banks out the door.

I plucked a parking ticket from beneath my car wipers, flung it onto the dash, strapped myself in, and started down the street. The sun was burning through the windshield and I lowered my window to a warm wind, shoving a Jim Morrison into the tape deck. Cranking the volume, I turned onto the highway, thinking oddly of Mother again, sympathizing with that unrealized desire of hers to travel abroad when I was but a girl. And I thought of Chris, those feelings of unrest pummelling through him. Good then. Good for him. He was taking that extra step away from our father's door, the one I'd already taken, the one our mother had failed to take. I felt the first sense of peace since leaving home, for as Chris said, I had no right to decide his path.

Or had I already forged the twist that had taken him thus far?

It was a question I would return to many times during the few short days to come.

EIGHT

THE MUD-CRUSTED TRUCK sat near the campsite looking like something dredged out of the river. I pulled up beside it and started across the campground, the multicoloured tents like enormous kites resting on the grass, gaily strung clotheslines stretching between them like tails. Along the riverbank lazed some of the motley-haired campers with their guitars, their bared skin already browner than the river running alongside them as they hummed and played popular folk songs of the day. A dog yapped after a squirrel scampering up the trunk of a tree. Two crows clutched the limbs of a birch, staring beady-eyed at a shiny pot of water heating on the fire pit below as two young girls scraped and sliced a bundle of carrots and spuds. Chris stood outside my tent, heavily dressed in dark clothing, the beak of his cap turned backwards, his face wearing the dazed look of a missionary happening upon his first tribe in some unmapped land.

"Baywop!" I muttered with a scant trace of affection. I glanced at Ben squatting beside a trio of girls near the river, their laughter tinkling over his words like spring water over ice crystals. Chris watched me coming with a pained expression.

"Already told you, not arguing with you," he said, and ducked inside the tent. I ducked in behind him, falling to my knees, rolling up my sleeping bag just as he was. He sat back on his ankles, watching. "What're you doing?"

"Ben didn't tell you? My, but he likes a secret. I'm coming, too. Uh huh. Got a job. Cook's helper."

His mouth gaped open. "What—wait a minute, you can't come—you can't cook—"

"Give back," I said as he pulled the sleeping bag from my hands. "Unless you comes to your senses and stays home, too."

"Home!" he scoffed, punching at the side of the tent. "Freaking la la land—look, you can't come—you're nuts, you can't follow me to the rigs, smothering jeezes—" He looked appealingly to Ben, who was pulling back the flap, staring in at us. "Will you talk to her—she's gone nuts! She's cracked! She thinks she's coming to the rig!"

"Can't be fighting on the rig," Ben said and dropped the flap back in place.

Chris stared after him in astonishment. "She's not coming—Ben! Jeezes, look at her, like the cat," he cried as I clawed my sleeping bag out of his hand. I ducked out of the tent, Chris ducking out behind me.

"She's not coming," he said to Ben. "Jeezes, man, I can't have her on the rigs with me."

"*Man!*" I mocked him. "Well, *man*, guess you're just gonna have to." I stood bemused as Chris fixed his eyes on a tangled-haired youth climbing out of the tent next door, a white cloud of smoke puffing out behind him.

"What's they doing now, smoking themselves?" he asked with a snort. "Thinks they're capelin or salmon or something?"

Ben busted out a laugh.

"Go hide your ignorance," I muttered to Chris, and crossed over to the fellow for a quiet word. Minutes later I was back. Ignoring Ben's retreat to the girls by the river, I stared calmly at my brother. "Tent's rented, the car's looked after."

Chris was staring at me like a disenchanted monk. "Fine, then, fine," he snapped. "You'll love it in the woods, especially when you gets a grizzly on your tail."

"Be you up in the tree, little bugger—you wouldn't hear a train coming, you goes into a trance. Out of the way, I have some packing to do."

––––––––––––

A SHORT TIME LATER and we were heading down the highway, bouncing and jolting on the springy seat: me in the middle, Chris clinging to the door handle, Ben hunched over the wheel and complaining about the frost-pocked pavement as he drove us straight south.

"Ribcage. Riding a ribcage," said Chris for the hundredth time as Ben plied the gears with relish, both of them leaning into the cab's heaving and jolting as might riders on cranky horses. "So, tell me about the rigs, *man*," urged Chris, elbowing me, "like, what I needs to know, *man*. Did you know, Ben's giving up his job for me," he said to my testy look. "What do you think of that—moving himself up to roughneck and giving me his greasing and scrubbing job."

Ben mustered a smile. "Not something I'm bloody happy about, bud. Moving up on the rigs is a backwards step to me."

"Right, so what's that agin—what's my new job—rousty. Roustabout. Like it, Sis?" He kept elbowing me, making me laugh. "So, what else do I gotta know?" he asked Ben.

"Keep the hell outta the way."

"Keep the hell outta the way," repeated Chris.

"Else they'll have you running around looking for bird cages."

"Bird cages."

"Bird cages. For their seed."

"Their seed—ahh, their *seed*," said Chris, inadvertently scratching his groin, chuckling softly. "How about I bring them fresh socks instead?"

"See, he's getting it," said Ben.

"I don't get it," I said.

"Heh heh, hope not," said Chris. "So, all right. So, how do you know what's gotta be done?"

"See, he's getting it," Ben whispered to me, "told you he'd get it. Now, then, here's how you know what's gotta be done: if it moves, grease it, if it don't, scrub it. And that's it, Pablo, that's the life of a roustabout—have a grease gun or a bucket of diesel dangling from your wrist at *all* times, and be going somewhere at *all* times. The best place is behind the mud tank. Warm as toast when it's cold, shady when it's warm. Thought out lots of stuff curled up behind that mud tank—see that pine?" He pointed through his side window. "Ever see pine like that?"

"Big, hey. Jeezes, never seen pine that big," said Chris. He leaned within an inch of the windshield, the beak of his cap shading his eyes as he took in the jack pine and balsams flanking the roadside, the mossy forest floor, and the multitude of meadows patchworked with the deepest and tenderest of spring greens. "A garden, a frigging garden, what do you say, Sis? What's the matter, not saying much—changing your mind, aren't you. Told you not to come. Want us to take you back—not getting sick, are you?"

I waved him off.

"Sure you're not getting sick? We can stop if you're getting sick."

"I'm not getting sick."

"You getting sick?" asked Ben.

"She always gets sick on bumpy roads. Couldn't take her nowhere when we first left Cooney Arm. First sight of a car and she was carsick."

"Oh, Chrissy, *please*."

"Just saying—every time we drove to Ragged Rock, first thing we had to do was put buckets and wet rags aboard the back seat—used to get sick myself, just watching. Ooh, man, look at that," and he was leaning into the windshield, pointing at a bald eagle gliding overhead.

"Two—two of them," said Ben, "see that, buddy—two of them."

"Them heads ... whoo, man, look at them white heads— and that wingspan—see them, Sylvie?"

"Yuh, I see." I gazed along with him at the snow-white heads of the eagles gliding through the blue. I pulled back, laughing as he craned his neck further, near busting through the windshield with excitement, like when we were young-sters combing the beach and he'd burst ahead in his eagerness to see what new thing lay just ahead—a sunfish, a dead shark, a pretty bottle cast ashore during the night.

"Look at that tree over there—cripes, the size of it." He clutched the dash as Ben hit a rut, exclaiming, "Jeezes, what pine, what pine. Wouldn't Father love this."

His face shadowed. He sat back, resting his elbow on the window and leaning his cheek against the ridge of his knuckles.

"Hey," I nudged him, "so we'll take a picture and send it to him. Think he won't like that—nice picture of a pine tree to look at?"

He half smiled. "Six weeks' burning is what he'd see."

"Yep, that's our da. And them birds would make a damn fine gravy."

"Hey." Ben tossed us both a glance. "Your father's got some rounds left in him yet. Tough as hide them old fellows are. Cripes, the old man's been smoking and dragging about boats and houses since he was nine. Nine! I was still wrapped in me blankie when I was nine."

The truck hit a deep rut, throwing me against Ben, my bare arm pressing against his. I felt its heat, smelled it. His ratty white T-shirt was stretched so tight across his chest I could see the padding of chest hair beneath, pressing spongelike against the thin fabric. He rubbed his jaw, making a scratchy sound with his day-old stubble, and I saw a nick where he'd shaved too close. Could he smell me, I wondered, and tried to remember whether I'd dabbed my collar that morning with a bit of lavender from the vial Mother had given me and that I always kept in my purse. I hadn't. Cigarette smoke. Cigarette smoke from the bar is what he smelled. I shifted sideways towards Chris.

"Who's who, that's what you needs to know about the rigs," Ben was saying. "Who's who, so you know who you're talking to, so you don't tell the wrong man to bugger off. And the first man you pays homage to is the fellow who gave up his cushy job for you, got that? You got that, buddy?"

"Yuh, got that."

"Good. Now then, here's how you keeps your main man happy. You brings him his coffee. Important you understand that—you're always bringing your main man coffee."

"Right, got it. What's the other workers like?"

"Babies," said Ben. "Pretty as babies."

"Babies."

"And Push is the prettiest. Push is the boss—the tool push, biggest job on the rig. Lovely man, Push—hemorrhoids hanging down to his knees. Gets a bit mean sometimes. And that's where you learns love for your fellow man, when he got hemorrhoids hanging like cloudberries down to his knees, because, buddy, that's a bit painful, so you expects the man to be always firing off his mouth. It's when he starts firing you, as in *Get the fuck off my rig*, that's when you punches the sonofabitch, because a bad case of hemorrhoids is no cause to be firing a man. Hey, just giving him the facts," he added after a grunt from me.

"Getting like your mother, Ben; running on like a brook."

He laughed. "Tongue like a machete." Crossing his arms atop the steering wheel, he looked back at me.

I flushed, the sun burning through the windshield making me hotter, heady with the smell of heated vinyl coming from the dash. Ben settled back, one hand loosely sitting on the steering wheel, his other falling onto his thigh, his arm lazily grazing mine with each sway of the truck.

"The babies," said Chris. "Tell me more about the babies."

"Just do what you're told," said Ben. "And if anybody gives you trouble, sic Sis onto them."

"So, Push—you call him Push because he's a pushover?"

Ben turned to me with a disparaging look. "Greener than a spring pasture," he said with a groan.

"Told you," I said. "Should've left him in the tent."

"Left him in the tent," muttered Chris. "Good thing I got confidence." Baring his teeth, he nipped my shoulder. "So, let's see now," he said over my yelp, "Push is the tool push, biggest job on the rig, and you call him Push and he's a prick—"

"*Pious* prick," corrected Ben. "And he owns the rig. He's the manager, top hand, in charge of everything—crew, equipment, overall drilling operation. He sees to everything and everyone and he wants no screw-ups. He wants to drag that rig to the next hole, and the next, and he wants nothing left behind

when he leaves but a hole, and it got to be straight. The rig's
his life and he don't want it getting blown to hell. That's what
happens if you're not doing your job, not watching them
gauges, she can blow. One thing you always keeps in mind,
there's a whole fucking forest buried beneath us, and it's been
fuming and fermenting and smouldering since T. Rex and
with no vent. Second we punctures through with a drill bit—
be prepared, buddy, because there'll be one jeezes bad-ass bed
of gas bursting up through them pipes like a cyclone. And if
you can't hold her back, can't control her—she's gonna blow
and you're gonna blow, and every cocksucker snoozing behind
that mud tank is gonna blow. Just think of a whale coming up
for a blow beneath your punt," he added with a laugh. "Well,
that's a soap bubble compared to that gas bubble bursting up
through your floor."

He stopped laughing at the silence in the truck. "'Course,"
he added reassuringly, "that's why Push got to have Frederick!"
Ben cleared his throat, pronouncing the name with an
assumed dignity. "Frederick," he said again, with a deepening
of his tone, "is the engineer. He likes himself a lot—aside from
that, he keeps track of all what's happening underground—
rocks, fractures, salt piles—anything you comes across underground, Frederick knows from his seismic charts. So we always
know what we're drilling through, that we're not gonna
accidentally hit a bed of gas that's not on our charts and that
we're not prepared for."

"And if you do?" I asked. "I mean, she's not just going to
blow up—"

"Ohh, yeah—you drills into a bed of gas, she'll blow. But
we're not going to hit that bed of gas. So, you keep your
mind on peeling spuds for Cook. And you," he reached along
the back of the seat and grabbed Chris's nape as he would the

scruff of a dog, "you keep bringing Ben his coffee. Got that, bugger?"

"Got it, got it," yelped Chris. "Cripes." He rubbed the back of his neck gingerly. Fixing his cap straight, he rolled down his window, whistling towards the long prairie grass fringing the roadside. A dry wind flattened his hair to his forehead and he glanced towards me, grinning. I grinned back, smoothing down my hair from the wind tunnelling through the truck and flapping at our faces. Jamming his foot on the clutch, Ben wrenched into a lower gear as we laboured up a high grade, then slipped it into neutral as we mounted the ridge and looked out over a sweeping view of thick green forest. The steel grid of some kind of tower rose out of the woods to our right, another rising even higher to the left a bit farther on.

"Derricks," answered Ben as Chris pointed them out. "They're what rises up from a rig platform—have you never seen a picture? Cripes, not even a picture?" he asked as Chris shook his head.

"There's a fellow works on top, right?" I asked.

"That's right—listen to your sister, buddy, she got it. He's called the derrickman. That smaller tower over there—one to our right—is a service rig. The big one farther out is where we're going—drilling rig. Service rig services the holes already drilled by drilling rig—"

"There's another one," cut in Chris, "way over there—"

"Yeah, rigs everywhere around here," said Ben. "Popping up like gophers. Tomorrow's dinosaurs. Whoa …!" He hit the brakes. A gravelled access road was coming up to the right at the bottom of the grade with a shiny red truck off the road a few feet in, its front right wheel in the ditch.

"Trapp's," said Ben, pulling to a stop alongside. "Must've missed the turn."

"Is this the road to our rig?" asked Chris.

"No, road's another twenty miles down the highway. The boys hops over here to the service rig sometimes when they're out of smokes or booze—gets a lend, you know."

We drove a short distance over the bumpy road, which ended abruptly in a large clearing, the rig some distance away. It was too far back on the field to see anything clearly—a dark bulk of machinery sitting on what appeared to be the flatbed of a eighteen-wheeler, the steel-framed derrick rising above it about a hundred feet up. As Ben pulled to a stop beside a couple of dirt-grimed trailers, he stared over at a forty-foot tanker parked beside the rig.

"Nitrogen truck," he said, studying the canary yellow cab. "Tank's full of nitrogen—colder than a winter's night. Must be doing a frac job. Come on, get out, let's stretch our legs—see if Trapp's in the cookhouse."

"Does he—does Trapp know about Chris coming?"

"Yeah, he knows. You'll be a sweet surprise, though."

I piled out behind Chris, looking about the partly sodded clearing. Aside from the low moan of the generators running electricity through the trailers and the idling of the nitrogen truck, the air was quiet.

"Rig's shut down," said Ben. "Frac job, must be doing a frac job."

"What's a frac job?" asked Chris.

"Frac job is when you've got your well already drilled and you're looking to make it easy for the oil to flow into it, so you blasts shit down there—like nitrogen, or water—and creates small cracks or fissures in the formation. They mostly use water—this is a small well—you'll learn all this shit—hey, look over there." He shaded his eyes towards a couple of figures walking some ways past the truck. "There's Trapp—I think—

yeah, that's him, with Push." He started towards the two distant figures, Chris following.

Suddenly the air was shocked by a thunderous *BOOM!!!* Followed by a violent *HIISSSSSSSSSSS!* I stood rooted to the spot, watching in utter astonishment as the yellow tanker vanished within a belching white cloud. Bewildered, frightened cries of men sounded as the cloud mushroomed out, swallowing the rig, spreading silent as morning mist across the field towards where Ben and Chris stood immobilized.

Ben explained to me later what had happened, that the crew working the well-head accidentally sent a good-size chunk of metal flying through the air and punctured the side of the tanker—and *kaboom*, the compressed nitrogen collided against the warm spring air and blew the side out of the tanker, exploding into that frigid ball of London fog.

But there, in that moment, with everything being swallowed by a hissing wall of white, I bolted with a cry to Chris, grabbing his arm. Ben yelled at us to hang back and broke into a run towards the mist. Chris ran after him, with me holding on to his arm, trying to pull him back. Ben stopped, listening intently to a voice sounding through the mist—a harsh, wheezing voice: "Stun bastards, stun cocksuckin' bastards."

"Push!" said Ben. A greyish shape appeared and Ben lunged towards him, taking hold of his arm and half carrying, half dragging him towards where Chris and I stood staring. Push's thickset body fell heavily to his knees, his bull neck straining as he coughed and cursed. "Stun fuckin' bastards, stun fuckin' bastards, forgot the valve, forgot to open the gawd-damned valve—blew the pump off the rig—through the motherfuckin' tanker, stun fuckin' bastards." He broke into a harsh series of coughs, water squeezing out of his eyes and streaming down a hard, flat face.

"Oh," I blurted. I knew that face from the bar. He sat alone most times, grunting his orders and pawing back his change, even the occasional penny rolling off the table onto the floor. "Cheap as scuzz," Cork once said, "wouldn't tip a blind man he was sitting backwards for communion."

Push turned to the sound of my voice with the sharpness of a dog catching a scent. The quiver of recognition on his face was cut suddenly by a thin, terrified cry sounding from the fog.

"Where's everybody, where's everybody!"

Trapp. Push's bearlike hand clamped around Ben's, holding him back. "He's mine," he choked through his coughing, and staggered to his feet. He charged back into the fog, roaring, "Over here, over here, Trapp, buddy, over here."

"Where the fuck's everybody," cried Trapp as he tumbled through the white, his cries short, frightened mewls now as he made his way towards the sound of Push's roars.

"Over here, Trapp, man, over here."

"What the fuck you doing?" hollered Ben.

"Over here, Trapp, *run, run*," screamed Push. The mist swirled upward like a raised curtain, revealing Trapp's small face pinched with fear, his eyes bulging as he floundered towards us. Suddenly his body vanished as though he'd been sucked down through the earth, the fog closing around him like a coffin's satin lining.

Ben plunged in through the dense white, shouting his name. Chris stood looking about, dazed, then lunged in after him. I heard a frantic call from Ben, then Push's frenzied shouting: *"Gimme your hand, gimme your hand, Trapp, Trapp, man, gimme your hand!"* They sounded close, just a few yards away. Holding my breath, I ran in through the mist, singing out Chris's name. A fecal stench polluted the air and I covered my mouth. I heard Ben's shouts turn to a groan and a low cursing.

The mist thinned, becoming wispy, exposing Trapp on his gut, crawling, his body muddied and soaked, his face plastered with filthy wet toilet paper.

Push let out a loud, jeering laugh. Trapp staggered to his feet and lunged towards Push, who was now bolting into the mist.

"Get back, get back to the truck," Ben yelled upon seeing Chris and me standing there. "Go! Fucking go," he yelled again and ran after Trapp.

The mist was thinning fast. "He don't want Trapp to see us," said Chris. "Come on."

"What is it—what's making the stink?"

"Sump hole. Push lured Trapp into the sump hole."

"Sump hole?"

"Shit hole. Think septic—an open septic tank—three feet of water, shit, and piss. Like what they had in the hydro camp down Cat Arm last year."

Chris and I walked back to the truck as some of the rig crew crept carefully out of the woods, shouting out to each other, looking about in wonderment. The mist was mostly evaporated now. Push appeared from the direction of the tanker, his arms held off from his sides like a haughty commando as he marched to the rig.

I kept watch inside the truck till Ben came into sight. Trapp walked stiffly beside him, his head down. Hoisting himself onto the flatbed, he sat with his back to the cab. Ben climbed in beside me and Chris, the smell of feces stinking up the cab. Lowering the window, he gunned the motor, pulled a U-turn, and drove us back down the road.

"Was anybody hurt?" I ventured.

Ben shook his head.

"What happened?"

"Somebody pulled the wrong lever. Primary lesson, Bud," he said to Chris. "There's two levers on a rig. Lever A and lever B. If you don't fucking know which is lever A, you leave her be. You leave her fucking be."

"Did Trapp have anything to do with it—the explosion?" asked Chris.

"No, no—he was just looking for smokes. Him and Push both. Just happened to be there the same time." He snickered. "A dandy opportunity for Push to have a laugh. Asshole," he muttered, and braked beside Trapp's truck. "Hold on," he called out as Chris opened his door, "I'll do this, you stay put."

"Piss off," said Chris, and jumped outside.

Ben grunted and got out. Alone in the cab, I watched the three of them hooking Trapp's truck up to the wheel wench on the front of Ben's truck. They worked with their heads down, avoiding eye contact as though they were guilty of some crime against the other. Ben climbed back inside, snapping orders through the window, jerking and grinding gears, jolting us backwards and forwards as he revved and braked the motor.

Within minutes Trapp's truck was out of the ditch and we were back on the highway again, heading for the camp. Trapp was driving behind us, and with a show of impatience he gunned his motor, overtaking Ben, fishtailing from the sudden burst of speed as he raced ahead.

"Why did Push do that?" I asked.

"Because he's a stun prick," muttered Ben.

"No other reason?"

"Because they hates each other."

"But—yet they work together?"

"They're stuck with each other. Nobody sane will work with Push, and nobody sane will hire Trapp as a driller—he don't have enough experience going for him."

Ben's tone softened somewhat as he spoke of Trapp, then angered as he emitted another cuss, whether at Trapp, or Push, or the both of them was hard to determine. He drove in silence now, a sourness emanating from the grim set of his jaw that curdled the air and kept me from asking anything more. Chris patted my knee every few minutes, breaking the silence with an occasional comment meant to lighten the air.

It was late afternoon by now, and long shadows fell across the road. After another few miles Ben geared down once again, turning us onto a rutted access road. The woods were thicker here, darker, the truck vaulting over ruts deeper than Gran's turnip drills. Branches swiped at the side windows, skinning themselves of leaves and bark as they twisted around the side mirror and were wrenched along. Bogs appeared by the roadside, their low, ruddy surface like black mats beneath the walled woods whose western tips still burned with sun. The road became muddied, the tires biting and slipping up the side of a sharp-turning knoll.

"C'mon you bastard," cursed Ben, slapping the dash as the truck slid sideways. "How'd you like to walk in that mud," he shot past me to Chris, the softening of his tone offering recompense for his moodiness. "Sticks to your boots like cement and just as heavy."

Chris nodded, his eyes as intent on the road as Ben's. The knoll levelled off, the road gashing through the thicket ahead, oozing with mud until the woods opened onto a wide, open field patched with grass and bare earth. To the far left the last rays of the evening sun brightened the whitish siding of a group of trailers huddling the treeline. Several trucks were parked haphazardly before them, their dark greens and blues obscured by layers of dust. Tire tracks cut a road across the field from the trailers to another scattering of dust-coated trucks parked beside the rig. It was the rig that commanded my attention.

Looming thrice the size of the service rig we'd just left, its platform rose twenty feet above ground, its sides cleaned of dust and painted a cherry red. Other tanks and sheds—the same cherry red—crowded the rig floor and spread out beside it, along with diesel engines and generators that shuddered and rumbled and screamed over a jungle of machinery that swung and hoisted and spun beneath the tall column of the derrick rising a creamy white into the fading glow of sundown.

"So big," I said breathlessly, holding my nose against the stench of diesel and ground rot filtering through the truck as Chris lowered his window for a better look.

"She's Push's baby," said Ben. "Her bottom's a big stink, but as rigs go, he keeps her cleaner than Mother's floors. Can't stop its squalling, though—the screaming jimmies," he said as Chris raised his window again, softening the deafening whine, "four of them—motors—screaming and roaring all the time—they run the power to the generators, the pumps. And then you got the pumps, big piston pumps that are *bum-bum-bum-bum-bum* all the time, shaking and rattling everything—walls, ceiling, floor—everything shakes with the pumps, and the jimmies are shaking, and they're always screaming, can't hear a damn thing, can't hear your own teeth chattering."

"What're those men doing?" asked Chris.

Ben was quiet, his eyes ruminating over the four or five men wearing yellow hard hats, prowling through the jangled heap of metal making up the rig floor. "Running pipe," he finally said, "and going nuts." He shrugged, trying to make light with a laugh. "Easy to go nuts working the rigs—especially this rig. Nobody talks to nobody. Can't hear nothing but the jimmies. And your own head. Turns everybody into pricks after a while, hearing nothing but that. But it's all changing these days—they've got everything electric on the newer rigs. This is a relic."

"Can't you wear earplugs?" I asked.

"Can't shut down your head. Everybody gets stuck in their own head—days at a time sometimes. Gets to you after a while, all them stupid thoughts—thinking about this, thinking about that, the ones back home, what a prick buddy was last night and the night before and every fucking night—small, stupid stuff—getting more festering time than it deserves. Turns the mind to rot after a while."

"Gee, Ben, nice place you brought us."

He relaxed his shoulders, his tone softening. "Sorry. Thing with Push and Trapp back there—got me going. The boys are always at it, blows over in a day. How's she going over there, Bud?"

Chris was leaning towards the windshield, staring with trepidation at the rig, the machinery, tracking the movements of the men. He sensed me watching and nipped my fingers, grinning.

"Bucket of grease, good rag, and I'll have them jennies humming like lullabies."

"Jimmies, b'y, jimmies, not jennies, jeezes," said Ben.

"What's all that over there?" Chris pointed to a vertical stand of thirty-foot piping stacked by the side of the derrick, its black mass jutting into the faded blue of the sky.

"Pipes," said Ben. "Drill pipe. That's what she's all about, drilling holes in the ground, and that's the pipe we drill down the hole—all day long we're connecting pipe, drill one length down, connect another pipe, and then drill that sucker, thousands and thousands of feet underground. The fellow up the derrick—the tower—up there on the monkey bar—he pulls a length of pipe out of the stand whenever we need it, hovers it above the drill hole. Them fellows standing about on the floor, they're the roughnecks, they grab the pipe and connect it to the one we just finished drilling. And on and on and on, all day long, and that's running pipe. Then one day we hit the zone, and whooosssh! Up she comes! But you now, buddy," said Ben, wrenching the truck into gear, "don't gotta stick your head over a drill pipe, all you gotta do is keep everything greased—you carry a five-gallon bucket of dope on your arm like your mother wears her handbag shopping—"

"Dope?"

"Grease, b'y, grease, whatever."

"Ahh, I get it, pusher for a boss, gallon of dope, and thirty-foot joints," said Chris. "Yeah, starting to see why you like this job."

Ben wrenched the truck into park again. "That's older than Aunt Milly's bloomers. For fuck sakes, keep your jokes to yourself till you know what you're talking about—the boys love razzing. You got that?"

"I got that. And the derrick fellow—you never said what he does."

"Already told you—jeezes cripes, he forgot already, the derrickhand hauls pipe from the stack when we need it, hoists it over the hole we're drilling, and the fellows down below connect it and we drill that bastard down, and then another and another, and that's called making hole. Or tripping in. Call it whatever you want, it don't change till we starts hauling pipe outta the hole, and then we reverses everything I just told you. And if you thinks this is noisy, wait till we starts tripping outta the hole—getting it all, Sis?"

I turned to him, struck by the gusto flowing into his words, his eyes sharpening with excitement as he spoke.

"Why do you take the pipe out?" asked Chris.

"Lotsa reasons—lose something down the hole, the drill-bit wears down, anything can happen, and she all gotta be hauled back out."

"How does it get noisier?"

Ben snorted. "Think about it: every motor on that rig kicking in at the same time to lift that pipe out of the hole— that could be a hundred thousand pounds coming up that hole on cables—and when them motors kicks in— *Aaaoooorrrrrrrooonnnnnnnn!* Every motor there is singing, and they're all singing because we're running cables, throwing chain, whatever the hell. And everything's on winches, and the blocks are lifting, and everything on the floor's shaking and rattling with them motors shaking and rattling and singing. And, as I said, that's tripping outta the hole.

"Running pipe in is quieter. Don't need all them motors, gravity usually sinks the pipe down the hole. You got the blocks lowering the pipe, and the most you hears is the brakes *squeak squeak squeaking* as you're lowering the pipe down."

"You *like* all this stuff," I said with wonder.

He looked at me blankly.

"Jeezes, Sis, he's an engineer," said Chris. "How stuff works is what he's about."

"Still got me snorting coke on campus, eh?" said Ben. "Time I showed you something manly—like tucking you inside an apron." He wrenched the truck in gear, this time starting us across the clearing.

"Hold on a minute, slow down," protested Chris. "What's them big red tanks besides the rig?"

"Mud tanks—where we store the mud for drilling. I'll tell it to you later."

"Tell it to me now—will you stop—just fuckin' stop, what do mud got to do with anything?"

"Slow down, and let's get this grub in, Cook's drier than bone by now. Eh, look at him," he nudged me, "can't wait to get his new boots on."

Chris was wrenched around, his hands gripping his knees, staring back at the rig as Ben buckled the truck over the rutted clearing towards the trailers.

"You're gonna be fine," I said, patting his hand. "Greasing things, that's all you have to learn."

"Jeezes hell." Chris whipped his head around to face me. "I don't need you telling me my job, you keep your mouth shut—you says anything in front of the men, I'll heave you out the window."

"Look at him, foaming at the mouth," I chided.

"No fighting at camp," ordered Ben. "And you," he flashed me a look of warning, "wherever your brother's concerned, do as he says and Keep Your Mouth Shut!" He pulled alongside the first trailer, reamed the gearstick into park, cursed as the engine raced, booted her down and cursed again as it bucked and sputtered before shutting down. "Here we are, Miss Sylvie, your new quarters, the cookhouse. You'll sleep in there with Cook, the rest of us scumbags sleep in the bunkhouses. You'll love Cook, she's a doll."

I followed him inside the cookhouse. It smelled like coffee and fried bacon, and was small, rectangle shaped, with low ceilings. The walls were stained with dampness, no matter the smothering heat, and the floors squeaked beneath each step taken. A long, cafeteria-type table cluttered with dirty dishes stretched across one end of the trailer, with a sink and cupboards, stacked with dirty pots and pans, stretching across the other end. The wall space in between was tightly wedged with a deep freeze, refrigerator, and stove. The one thing of colour in the whole sparse place was a faded girlie calendar tacked to the wall. A door stood at each end of the rectangle. My bedroom, Ben pointed out, was off from the kitchen sink, and Cook's down a short hallway from where the table was sitting.

Cook was asleep in a chair by the table, her fat little neck cushioned by thickly padded shoulders. Her chins quivered with each snort of air she took in and gargled back out. A wheezing came from her lungs, something to do no doubt with the pack of smokes and ashtray sitting on the table near her.

"Emphysema," said Ben. "Hear them lungs clear across camp some days, rattling like cobras. Her medicine makes her a mite drowsy," he added, winking towards the brandy bottle partly tucked behind the breadbox. He bent towards the sleeping woman, examining her well-rounded face, knobby nose, and wet, bluish lips. "No, sir, she's no doll. Bit of weather beating at that face. Looks like she was moored off in some cove and forgot about for a week."

"Shikes, Ben."

"Sad truth," he said to me. "We don't exactly get the babes in a camp like this."

Cook's breathing stopped, her mouth gaped, and her head jolted forward, little green eyes flashing up at Ben and me. As if figuring us for a figment of dream, she closed her eyes, fading back into sleep.

"Wake up!" Ben clapped his hands.

The little green eyes snapped open with a cross look. "What do you want?" she asked in a gnarled voice, then broke into a series of dry coughs.

"What do I want!" Ben shook his head, tutting. "Wait till I gets her brandy from the truck, she'll land me a smile then. Meet your helper, Sylvie. Sylvie, meet Connie, the cook. Cook she likes to be called." He pinched my arm on his way back out the door. "She's a sweetheart. Have a chat with her. She'll be all over you."

Cook's face brightened after Ben. "Are you his girlfriend?" she asked, with a sudden suspicious look at me. Then relaxed into a smile as I shook my head. "Good. Not a place for shenanigans. You've met Pushie?"

"Pushie?"

"Push. Tool Push. It's his rig. Didn't he hire you?"

"Yes. Kind of."

"Kind of?"

"Yes, we've met."

"Pushie's my brother-in-law."

"Oh."

"He married my sister—Mare." Cook coughed. "She's gone now. Mare."

"Oh. That's too bad."

"She was a lot younger than me. Cancer. Do you smoke?"

"No, ma'am."

"That's good—that's what," more coughing, "gave me my bad lungs. Always bad when I first wake up. You cook?"

I hesitated.

"Better if you don't," said Cook.

"Guess I don't then."

Cook yawned, her eyes fading off as though a great sleep beckoned her. She pulled herself up with a start. "Good. That's good." She rapidly patted her chest. "Breathing's—always—bad after a rain. Your room's in there," she said, pointing to the door at the end of the kitchen. "I'll do the cooking. You'll do the prepping and cleaning." She gestured at the sink apologetically. "It's piled up a bit. Haven't had any help. Can't keep everything running without help."

I looked to the pile of dirtied pots and pans with a sinking heart. Something brown and glistening and curled into the corner beneath a side table caught my eye. Fur. It was a wet clump of fur. I drew back, bumping into Ben coming through the door with a sack of potatoes.

"There's something there," I said urgently. "There—under the table."

"What—where—?"

"The table—under the table. It's—it's sleeping—"

"That?" Ben pointed to the clump of fur and let out a laugh. "Jeezes, girl, that's my bear cap. Got wet in the rain the other night."

A hearty laugh from Cook. "Want to skin it for supper, Susie—or Sylvie, is it—Sylvie?"

Looking sheepish, I went outside, sinking onto the step, watching Chris up on the flatbed dragging about grocery bags. The rumbling, whinnying sounds of the rig overshadowed the quiet of the evening air. A white light suddenly flared over the rig floor and up the leg of the derrick, giving it a clinical, disorienting look. The stench of diesel tasted on my tongue and I closed my eyes, thinking despairingly of the soft green grass of la la land, as Chris disparagingly called it, and the late-evening quietude of guitars and song on the riverbank.

Ben came out on the step behind me, bear cap in his hand, gently stroking its fur. He held it before me as though in offering, but seeing my brooding look he tossed it inside the truck instead.

"Not impressed, huh—with the camp," he said. "That's fine. Shoot you if you were."

"Smaller than I thought."

"Minimal crew. Told you, rough camp. But hey," he dropped down onto the step, "what happened back there—with Trapp and Push—don't worry about that. They're always at it. It'll blow over—give it a day or two."

"Trapp's gonna be weird, seeing me here."

"Trapp's weird with everybody. Come on, grab some stuff."

"Told you not to come," said Chris. He hopped onto the ground, hauling a crate of milk off the truck. "Having second thoughts, aren't you? Told you not to come. Here, carry in some grub, earn your pay."

"Oh, shut up, Chrissy."

"Don't freakin' call me Chrissy."

"Swear like a man," I chided, and got off the step, ignoring the crate of milk he was pushing at me. Dragging my knapsack and sleeping bag off the flatbed, I headed back inside the cookhouse.

"I start in the morning," I said to Cook, who was dumping stuff directly from the bags into the deep freeze. Under her dubious look I dragged my gear to the room off from the kitchen sink.

It was little more than a rustic-smelling closet, consisting of a narrow bunk and a small, bare window. After checking beneath the thin mattress for anything that crawled, I unrolled my sleeping bag and sat down on it, drawing my knees up to my chin and staring morosely out the window. The skinned trunk of what was once a jack pine jutted up outside, a few limbs near the top sagging towards the forest. Ben's and Chris's voices sounded loudly through the room door, their words audible despite the continued opening and shutting of the fridge and cupboard doors, squeaking floors, and Cook's hacking cough.

"The mud, the mud," Chris kept on, "tell me about the mud part."

"Jeezes, he's gonna drive me nuts."

"I just wanna understand."

"You'll understand, give it a few days, Pabs, it'll all start coming to you, go check on your sister."

"She's pissed at herself for coming. Is it *mud*-mud, like outdoor mud?"

"Jeezes, it's how we checks for pressure—with mud. Treated mud. We pump mud down the pipe, we pack it down like cement. If she starts coming back up the pipe, something's driving it back up. What's driving it back up—that's your question—something's pressuring that mud back up your pipe—everything on the rig is about pressure. Maybe it's a nothing pressure, maybe it's something big—a gas bubble from a crack in the formation that the seismic's not showing. In which case you hope the fuck the mud blocks it—gives you time to cut off the pipe, keep that bubble from bursting up through and blowing your balls to smithereens.

"And that, buddy, is a major part of Trapp's job, of Push's job, the engineer's, the geologist, the mud-man, every fuckin' man—to always be looking, be reading them gauges, see what your mud's doing. If she's not flowing, if the mud's coming back up your pipe, something's pushing it back up. Shut her down. First thing you do is shut her down. Shut the whole fuckin' thing down till you finds out what's pushing that mud back up. Could be nothing, could be something. Could be U-tubing, meaning a little bit of an imbalance thing happening that'll right itself. Or it could be gas, pressure from an unknown gas pocket—"

"U-tubing? What's U-tubing?" asked Chris.

"Way to go, bud, that's a good question, that's a real smart question, that's a natural question because I never told you something integral about the whole mud thing, and you caught it—you never caught it, but you caught that you were missing something and you never bothered going on, letting it go, you questioned it. That's a good hand, that makes for a good rig hand, you're gonna be around for a long time, don't tell your sister—"

"So, what's U-tubing?"

"U-tubing is this. Imagine you got a big fucking straw, a McDonald's milkshake straw, and you puts it down the neck of your beer bottle—like this—now see, your straw is your pipe and we're drilling it down the hole—the neck of your beer bottle—now see here, all that space around your straw? Your straw don't completely fill the hole, do it—well, that space around your straw is called your annulus, and that's where your mud comes back up. The mud goes down your pipe, and back up your annulus—"

"Why?"

"Never mind your *whys*, I'll answer all your *whys*—just take your time and listen and you'll have all your *whys*—we pump mud down the straw, it filters out down at the bottom end— flows through your drill bit, got it? The mud flows down your straw, out through the drill bit, cools off your drill—gets pretty hot grinding through rock—and then as it's cooling off your drill bit, it's picking up all the rock and debris and shit that comes from your drilling, and then it floats it all back up your annulus to ground level. And then we drains it off into the shakers, shakes the shit out of it—your rock and stuff—and we circulates it right back down the hole again. Big cycle. And as long as everything is flowing smoothly down the hole and back up the hole, she's going fine. It's when the mud is not flowing fine—when she's backing up the straw—that you got to shut her down, figure out what the fuck's going on, what's pushing your mud back up your straw. And when you gets her figured, you starts her back up and gets on with your business. How's that, clear as mud?"

"So, how do you know when it's nothing?"

"Most times you don't know. Nobody knows what's going on thousands of feet below ground. You make educated guesses. That's why experience pays in this game. Roughnecks are paid to put the pipe down the hole. Push and Frederick are paid to keep it down. One bad-assed pocket of gas can send them pipes shooting through the air like spaghetti. And I already told you—foremost thing on a rig is pressure. Pressure of the mud flowing down the pipe, and the pressure of the formation pushing back up. If one pressure overcomes the other, you might have a kick. You think quick, you act quick. If something odd's happening, check it out, else risk losing your balls, your rig, your whole fuckin' crew."

"And a kick is—"

"A kick is when you got an almighty blast coming back up your straw—either we hit a gas pocket, or whatever—if we don't get her in time—see the pressure on our gauges—up she comes, and she's as unforgiving as the sea when she gets riled up. Probably the most important job on the rig is the driller, because he's the one staring at his gauges, always staring at his gauges to make sure they're balanced, always balanced."

"And Trapp's the driller."

"Trapp's the driller. Go check your sister, ask her if she'd like a drink."

"You all right in there, Sis?" Chris hammered my door, sending pain shooting through my head. Feeling more contrary than Mother on a dirty day, I slumped further into the sleeping bag, wondering what the hell I'd gotten myself into.

ALL BECAME QUIET in the kitchen after a spell, leaving just the muted roar of the rig for company. Believing the boys had turned in for the night, I peeled off my clothes and burrowed beneath my pillow. Sometime later I awakened to Chris and Ben clinking glasses on the table and arguing heatedly over a game of cribbage. I thought to get up but my limbs refused to move—jet lag, I thought, that's what's making me so tired and cranky, jet lag. I yawned and drifted betwixt sleep and awakenings. Someone, from somewhere outside the cookhouse, started strumming the sweetest of sounds from the heart of a guitar.

Chris poked his head inside my room once, whispering my name. I murmured something about joining them, and he went back to Ben and his cards, leaving the door ajar, their voices filtering through more clearly—Chris with his incessant questions about the workings of a rig, Ben's answers becoming more elaborate with each shuffling of cards and clink of whisky glasses.

"… Keep your eyes open, Pabs, and swivelling in your head. That, bud, is your safety training course, you'll get no more than that. So repeat what I just said every two seconds—got that, every two seconds—and ask questions, ask whatever question you want; the more you know, the more you watches out for. Problem with them roughnecks walking about town with missing fingers and lame legs is they didn't swivel their eyes, didn't ask questions. Most rig hands are just going along. They're mostly new and they're just going along. Only a few people on a rig really knows what's going on around them, and they don't really know—nobody *really* knows what's going on down the hole; you can only guess, you can only figure, you can only surmise.

"Your engineer, he's got to have academics. Tool push don't need academics, just a backload of experience working the rig. As with your driller—experience is what makes a good driller, and intuition. That doesn't come in books. And there's your geologist—he needs his academics. And then there's me and you, buddy, and a couple of others. Rig pigs. And rig pigs don't require academe or experience to be hired. The floor becomes our teacher. When you're working the floor you learns the floor—how to run pipe in or out of the hole, how to change motor parts, what to paint, what to grease, do this, do that, whatever the hell comes along.

"And after a few years you actually start learning some things about what's happening down the hole. You see things happen and after a while you start putting things together. You keep adding bits of knowledge every day and you start getting more than lumps in your head, you start to actually get some knowing about the way things work, you start adding two plus two, you start keeping the screaming jimmies from addling your brain—listen to them over there, screaming for days, one long jeezes scream …"

I tried not to listen to the jimmies screaming across the way as I lay there, focusing on Ben's and Chris's voices instead. Then the guitar found its way back in with another soft melody and I fell quietly into the dark hole of night.

NINE

I AWAKENED with a surge of panic and no notion of where I was. Something clattered against my window and I scrambled out of my sleeping bag with a cry.

"Hey, Sis. Wakey, wakey."

I near collapsed, my sense of relief as sharply felt as the fear had been. Crossing the room, I slid open the window. "Fool!" I hissed as Chris waved up at me. His face looked ghastly in the greyish, predawn light, but his shapeless, brand-new coveralls looked brighter than a chimney fire at night. "Fool!" I muttered again as he leaped back, doing a clumsy pirouette in his new steel-toed boots.

Creeping through the kitchen so's not to wake Cook, I unlocked the door to a cool rush of air. The treeline was black as smut against the brightening sky, the rig a ghoulish yellow. I quickly shut the door behind Chris, reducing the screaming jimmies to a distant whine. I looked at him easing himself into a chair now, a twist of orange in the cup of night.

"Got any tea?" he whispered, looking cautiously at Cook's door. "And bread, got any bread?"

I found the light switch and sat beside him. "Look, Chrissy—Chris—I know I done this," I began, speaking lowly. "But I can't help it, I don't like it here—no, listen to me," I pleaded as he started to protest, and I went into what I thought was a well laid-out argument about the dirtiness of the rig, the dangers, the racket, the bad tempers, the lousy beds.

"Tea, tea," Chris kept cutting in, "gimme a cup of tea."

I carried on some more about Cook, her coughing, her smoking, the crampy kitchen space.

"Knew you wouldn't like it, told you not to come—"

"Oh, stop it."

"No, you stop it, you just shush it," he exclaimed with a flash of temper. "Bloody la la land."

"Shush yourself." I pursed my mouth as the door popped open and in walked Ben, wearing yesterday's T-shirt and jeans, a yawn baring a full mouth of teeth, minus a molar.

"Just like back home," said Ben in hushed tones, "everything but grub cooking in the kitchen."

"She's picking on me, Ben."

"Feels sorry for you, bud."

I turned from them, staring at the package of bacon Cook had laid on the sink to thaw, torn between throwing it in the frying pan and throwing my knapsack aboard the back of Ben's truck.

"For the day at least, you're going nowhere," said Ben. "Can't leave the boys stuck."

I cut open the bacon, tossing it in the pan, cringing at the loud thump from Cook's room, followed by a rack of wet coughs.

"Her heart's big," said Ben.

I ignored him and set to making a pot of coffee, sliding bread into the toaster and fixing mugs none too gently before the boys. Cook's room door opened and she trod into the kitchen on little slippered feet. She tottered before Chris, then looked at me, her small eyes blinking with bafflement as though she didn't recognize us. At Ben's cheery good morning, her eyes cleared.

"You're an early rise," she said to my apology for waking her, and with a pleased look, she shuffled inside the bathroom.

The sound of the shower followed, and a few minutes later Cook reappeared, hair slicked wetly beneath a hairnet and underarms jiggling as she started whisking eggs for pancakes.

Some of my foreboding lifted as I spent the morning replenishing the men's coffee, serving them food in the same stealthy way I'd served the crowd in the bar. They were certainly a sullen-looking crew, aside from the big-boned, big-framed engineer, Frederick, who most certainly evoked the halls of academia with his black-framed glasses and cleanly pressed khakis.

He was a kinda likable guy, with a wide smile and a hearty voice that sounded loudly through the cookhouse as he boomed out good morning to Cook and me. No doubt he felt equally as big within himself as he took a seat, spreading out his elbows and taking up half the side of the table, and through long dips of coffee, engaged himself with an ongoing commentary about the weather, the muddied roads, and the latest *Rocky* movie crowding the theatres.

Hunched over a bowl of bran and cold milk was the geologist fellow, who kept looking around the table with the squinty eyes of one peering too long and too hard at something up close, and trying to determine what the thing was. Beside the geologist sat Dirty Dan the derrickman, a short, wiry fellow with a handsome face who seldom spoke. A couple of look-alike brothers sat next to him, thin and tense, small bright eyes zapping around the cookhouse as they gulped back coffee. Chris sat amongst them, chancing a few questions about the weather and the time. Aside from Frederick, who responded pleasantly enough, he was brushed aside by the others like a fly hovering around their necks.

Push blew in through the door, his thick, broad frame appearing to fill the cookhouse. Immediately his sights fell on me. A curt nod and he raised a hand of greeting to Chris.

"Which sandbox did you fall out of?" he asked roughly but with a hint of humour.

"Call me Rousty," said Chris.

"Rousty, is it?"

"Will that be coffee or tea?" I asked Push. Swiping off a place at the table with a rag, I pulled back a chair.

"Not before his whisky," said Frederick. He met Push's eyes with a deep, rumbling chuckle and went back to forking pancake into his mouth, still chuckling.

Push shot him a contemptuous look, his pale grey eyes glimmering like metal.

"Hang out in the doghouse till you're told otherwise," he instructed Chris and went to the refrigerator, one massive hand swinging open the door, the other scooping up a chunk of cheese and package of liver pâté. Frederick's chuckle switched to the heh heh heh-ing of a bemused parent as Push tucked a baguette beneath his free arm and marched out of the cookhouse.

Lifting aside a scrap of gauze filming one of the windows, I looked through the morning light at Push's bull neck as he strode towards a black pickup, one beefy hand fisting the cheese and liver to his chest, the other clutching the baguette to his side like a machete. He jerked sideways, then stood at ease before a crewman who was leaning against his pickup, hawking and spitting. I near busted my face through the window scrutinizing the crewman. With his flat face and silvery eyes he stood as a replica of Push, only skinny and gaunt, as though the air had been punctured out of him.

Ben had since returned to the cookhouse, wearing a faded, baggy sweatshirt that smelled like diesel and a hard hat clamped to his head. "Push's dumb-ass twin, Skin," he said, looking through the window beside me. "Starved in the womb. Push gluttoned all the grub. Oh, here we go." Ben let out a wearied sigh, leaning closer to the window, the cold plastic of his hard hat touching my cheek. Trapp, a brown sweatshirt tied around his neck like a fur collar, his lips baring small white teeth, was creeping furtively from his bunkhouse up behind Push.

Push twisted around, holding up his chunk of cheese like a live grenade. So quick were his movements that Trapp snatched back his step in surprise. Recovering, he held up his hands in mock surrender, rattling out his flat ha ha ha laugh.

Mouth twisting into a snarl, Push swung inside his truck. He raced the motor, jammed his foot to the accelerator, and burned towards the rig, the knobby cleats of his tires flinging back chunks of mud that splattered against the side of the cookhouse like turds of dogshit.

Trapp was silent now, his body stiffer than a week-old corpse as he watched after Push. A shudder went through him, and a smile of such eeriness that it felt its way through the cookhouse window to me. Ben watched, tighter than a strung bow, as Skin horked a big one in Trapp's direction and then hopped up the cookhouse steps.

"Just boys," Ben said, "got to have their playtime."

He went outside to have a word with Trapp, ignoring Skin, who was stepping in through the kitchen door. Draping a lanky arm around Cook's portly waist, Skin laughed at her chiding and waltzed her, with her platter of pancakes, to the table, whistling "Waltzing Matilda." With a thick lock of hair falling over his forehead, he fell upon the pancakes like the half-starved creature Ben had made him out to be.

And now Trapp walked in, his sharp features looking frail, his skin pallid with his shorn haircut. Without the sideburns and chin hair, his small, pinkish mouth quivered as though exposed to a sudden cold.

"Long way from home, ain't it?" he said to me in a distrustful tone.

"How you doing?" I asked politely, but his greeny eyes were already shifting past me. Chris, his cheeks stuffed with pancakes, his mouth shiny with syrup, raised a fork in greeting and slid his chair over as Trapp, touching a hand to his shoulder, sat down beside him. He mumbled a greeting to Frederick then set his eyes on Skin, who was ravishing the bacon and staring back at him through his overhanging lock. The rest of the crew carried on drinking their coffee and finishing off their pancakes, their bodies instinctively drawing away from Trapp as though he still carried the foul stench of the sump hole.

But Frederick spoke quite amiably to him, chatting up another film he'd recently seen and listening closely to the few sparse comments Trapp sent his way.

"Yeah, Trapp and Frederick—they like ganging up on Push," Ben would tell me later. "Plus Trapp's a sponge for learning the rig, and Frederick loves having someone listen to his spews."

Within ten minutes of Trapp's sitting down, all hands had cleared out and I was back to the window again, watching as Chris climbed into Ben's truck.

"He'll be fine," said Cook, clearing off a spot at the table. She sat, lighting a smoke, her lungs mewling like kittens. "Take them lunch. See for yourself."

I looked to her questioningly. "I thought we weren't allowed on the rig."

"I take it anyway—their lunch. Long as you leave again. Night crew make their own lunch."

The night crew were now pulling up outside. Getting tiredly out of their trucks, they headed to the bunkhouses—to shower before breakfast, said Cook. "Mix some batter, Suzie—Sylvie, is it—while I finish my smoke." She patted her chest. "I always take them lunch—can't this past while—no wind. Can't make the walk."

Turning up the heat beneath the bacon and mixing up batter, I listened attentively as she carried on talking about Ben and the boys going to town after work, drinking too much and gone all night—scarcely getting back in time for their morning shift.

"So I take them a big lunch. I'm their pal then—they like it when I take them a big lunch." She rattled out a laugh, her little green eyes dawdling over my face. "They don't want pretty girls then—they got Cook bringing them sandwiches." She stubbed out her butt. "So now you take it. Don't go out on the floor, go straight to the doghouse. See the red shed on the rig—by them stairs? That's the doghouse. Walk up them stairs, turn in the door. Put it on the table and come straight back. That's what you do. Put it on the table and come straight back. He won't say nothing he catches you—Pushie won't. Just come straight back—"

"Pushie. Don't quite suit him, somehow," I said, hoping for a bit of insight.

"Always takes care of me. Poor Mare. Been gone twenty years. Pushie never forgets I'm Mare's sister." Cook wiped at her nose with a bit of balled-up tissue. "Yes sir, always takes care of me. Batter started yet?—second shift's coming."

It was warmish and sunny when I struck across the clearing come noon with a hefty basket of fruit and sandwiches dangling from my arm. I was about thirty feet from the cookhouse when I started sinking in mud—thick, heavy mud that lay like wet cement beneath a scanty covering of grass and weed. Damn, not for the first time my feet were becoming entombed in Alberta mud. I backtracked to drier ground, feeling the wet seep through my sneakers.

The cookhouse door opened and Cook heaved out a pair of rubbers. "Won't get far that way," she called out. "They lost tractors in that."

Kicking aside my ruined sneakers, I donned Cook's boots and started out again, this time keeping closer to the tire tracks arcing around the clearing. The roaring steel mammoth both drew and repulsed me as I neared it. I stepped gingerly up the muddied, red-painted steps and then crept anxiously into its innards, the floors shaking and rumbling beneath my feet. The doghouse wasn't much bigger than a porch. Laying the food on a table as Cook had instructed, I huddled before its glass front, peering out at the men.

I saw how, as Ben said, the unrelenting roar of the wenches, the pumps, the screaming jimmies created a sphere of isolation around each man, keeping them from sharing a joke, a thought, or a comment, setting each man off to himself, prowling restlessly about his small corner. I could see how silly encounters or exchanges from the day before would get too much gnawing time, throwing faces into scorn whether the bone was with or without marrow. I watched them cringe before Push as he thrashed about, out-yelling the jimmies in his constant calls for their diligence in the working of his rig. All this for twelve hours straight, twelve days straight, being hailed, broiled, or rained upon beneath merciless skies, constantly dodging moving hunks of metal and iron and chain—I started understanding the men's glum faces and frayed nerves.

Standing centre in their misery, drawing their attention as a metal rod draws lightning, was the ill-concealed tension between Trapp and Push. Through the following days I watched as they held silent vigils, staring at each other across the screaming, shaking rig floor; across the short span of the cookhouse; across the steering wheels of their trucks as they passed each other to and from the bunkhouse. They pricked at each other like needles into a wound. And ensuring the daily flow of bad blood was Skin and his ceaseless scratchy snickers, pinching his nose behind Trapp's back each time he walked past, letting no man there forget his bath in the piss and shit of the sump hole.

Thankfully, Push never took supper with the boys—always waits till last, said Cook. Still, the tension he created through his frenzied, driven movements on the rig tracked the men back to the cookhouse during the evenings as they sat heavily around the table, their heads hung over their plates, too cross and wearied to talk. Trapp fed its presence with sharp glances that cut through the thoughts of each man present. He stalked each movement of their forks, their knives, from their plates to their mouths. He watched like someone hungry for some word or sign of ridicule. Even the chatty Frederick was looking a mite strained towards Trapp. Mostly, the only one talking was Ben.

"Long day, long day," he'd moan through absurdly long stretches and yawns, filling dead air with chatter: "How's your gravy, Pabs, gonna rain tomorrow, think it's gonna rain tomorrow, gawd-damned rain, how far down the hole are we, Frederick—hey bud, pass the gravy, man, pass the gravy, anything left in it—more gravy, Cook—damn, these are good spuds, anybody want the last of these spuds?"

Like a fisherman, I often thought, casting out chatter like a net, hoping to haul attention off Trapp and onto himself. *Always* that protectiveness towards Trapp. With his infectious smile and abrupt chuckles, he made a good diversion from the intense, silent Trapp, and oftentimes the despondent crew responded to his chatter with murmurs and nods, sometimes showing the whites of their teeth in a laugh over the rims of their bowls.

I too received a fair bit of attention from Ben—and Chris— during those first days. They'd keep glancing my way through the interminably long supper hours, tallying my smirks and grins, a little apprehensive, I often thought, that I might toss down my cloth at any second and beg a ride back to town. I wondered, too, whether or not I'd stay, given my persistent moodiness. It was enhanced by the constant strain of the crew, no doubt, but also by interrupted sleep—what with the distant roar of the rig, the trucks motoring back and forth from the rig to the camp, doors slamming, voices calling, thumps resounding in the kitchen from the night crew making sandwiches and sometimes pots of soup.

The phone call home changed all that.

It was a satellite phone, sitting in a wooden box in the engineer's quarters. There'd been a problem with the antenna since the day we arrived, and with no other phone at camp, Chris and I were frantic to call home. Father would be released from the hospital by now, and aside from our worries about his health, Chris was dreading Father's learning about the boat.

His face was drawn as he waited for the operator to put him through. I stood fidgeting beside him. No doubt every time the phone had rung the past few days they were all expecting it to be Chris. I could see them, Gran in her rocking chair, knitting in the dim light of her oil lamp, for it would be evening back home. I could see Kyle searching through the cookie jar for ginger snaps. And Mother fussing over Dad, who'd be brooding at the window. That first year in university they always made a fuss whenever I called home, the phone

being passed around, everybody taking a minute to talk, and
Gran being the last, talking loudly as though her voice must
carry itself the eight hundred miles to St. John's.

Chris leaned forward now, his face easing, calling out hellos
to Kyle, who had answered the phone. He was tapping his
foot, nervous and excited, telling about his rousty job, the
money, listening in turn and passing brotherly jollies to
the newsy bits Kyle was passing along. Then Gran was on the
phone, and I leaned over Chris's shoulder, the both of us
calling out greetings, sharing the earpiece and smiling at her
terse, quavering voice growing louder and louder as she kept
asking after us. We laughed outright when she passed the
phone back to Kyle impatiently, saying she couldn't hear a
thing.

Then Father's voice, loud and coarse. "Chris, Sylvie, who is
it—Chris?"

"Hey! Hey, Dad," said Chris, and I gave over the phone, a
comforting hand on his shoulder as his face tightened and he
drummed his fingers nervously on his knee, listening to
Father. Within the minute he was looking more self-assured,
his smile returning as he repeated some of Father's words back
to me,

"Feeling better—looking for his gun—Mother hid it, and
good she hid it," Chris exclaimed. "Sis said that—she said
you'd be on your feet in no time—didn't you say that, Sis?" He
looked at me and was instantly back to Father, his face looking
drawn again, and I bent my ear to the receiver, listening to
Father's voice, so much stronger, so much hardier than when
I'd last heard it. He was chiding Chris for all this talk about a
new boat, when he wouldn't be needing a new boat now, for
his brother, Jake, had given him his old one, which was good
as new with a coat of paint—

"Tell him to haul that rotting corpse away from the wharf," Chris cut in, and he rocked back on the legs of his chair, telling Father in overly loud tones that he was buying a new boat in the fall and driving it home in a new truck, "and big Sis will be sitting aboard with me," he announced with a wink my way, rocking in his chair and drumming his fingers, nodding to whatever was being said on the other end.

"And no arguing with Mother," he ordered, "do as she says, and Kyle can handle everything else till I gets back, couple of months I'll be back, take you for a cruise in the new boat, one with a cabin—"

I kicked Chris's foot, cautioning him against his bravado, and yet admiring the new confidence growing in his voice.

"... Yeah, it took some getting used to, the noise and all—but I'm there, I'm there," he said, glancing towards the roar of the rig. "Ben's been good, he's been real good showing me around—is that Mother? Put her on, put her on, and don't forget ..."

And then his voice fell soft. "Hey, Ma, it's your boy." He splayed back his shoulders in a good long stretch. "No, no, no, I'm not starving, I'm not eat up by flies—getting a few black-heads, is all—yeah, blackheads—on my forehead—from not scrubbing the grease off, Sis says—don't worry, it's good, it's good—noooo ..." He guffawed at her fretting, then squirmed, rolling his eyes impatiently at me as he listened, and yet his tone softened more as he assured her again, "I'm fine, just fine—no, no drinking, no dope—what's that—dope? How do you know about dope—are you—are you and Father—" He guffawed again, relaxing fully in his chair now, taunting Mother, scolding her. "Getting fat as a bear I am, Sis's a good cook, did you know that? Ye-es, she's got me and Ben stuffed with pancakes and spuds, I expect Ben's gonna propose to her any day—ooooff!"

He bent over with a grunt as I elbowed his gut, and after a few more assurances and jiving words about her nerves he passed me the phone, chuckling, "Here, tell her, Sis—tell her I'm not getting eat by bears or run over by trains."

"Sylvie? Sylvie." Mother's voice dropped as I greeted her, and I could see through the distance into the house, at her turning her back to Father, Gran, and Kyle and walking with the phone as far as she could into the kitchen so's to speak more privately.

"I haven't told your father—about the money—it's too much, too much, we don't need that much—" Her voice trembled with gratitude as she kept whispering, "We won't use it all, we'll keep some of it for when you comes home, my, Sylvie, you must've worked hard to save all that money, and now having to give it to us." And her voice trembled again, filling my heart, penetrating into deeper chambers where too much feeling had been pumped throughout the years and now surged upwards, clogging my throat.

Chris looked alarmed as I threatened Mother with hanging up, my voice starting to tremble along with hers. She made a tutting sound. "We won't use all of it then, we'll keep some for when you comes back—and so you're working on the rig too—but I thought you had a good job?"

"He's a bigger baby than I thought," I said lightly, "wouldn't go to work without me there—to scrub his underwear," I added with a laugh. "Seriously though, it's not where I wanna be, but I'll see it through till the fall. Probably drive home with Chris—in his new truck." I made a face at my brother, and Mother must've felt it for she gave a little laugh. "And Dad's good then, he's good?"

"He's good, but he's got the rest of us wore out trying to keep him off his feet." Her voice grew louder now, as though she'd turned back to the room and was talking more to Father than to me. "And he's fine then—Chris is fine?" she asked, then tutted at her own foolishness, her inability to keep from asking about Chris, even though she was trying so hard to keep her thoughts on me out of gratitude for the money, out of gratitude for the moment, the bigness of the moment, with Father getting well again, and that Chris was fine, he sounded just fine, and I, Sylvie, was right there, working alongside him on the rig—my, what a relief that was, and he was working alongside Ben too—

Her voice caught on a tremor as though she'd had a big cry. "Mom?"

"Ohh, I'm just being foolish. Hang up now and save your money, let me say goodbye to Chris, and then you say goodbye to your father—goodbye now, and you be good, you watch out now," and her voice strengthened as though whatever had set her crying was once again settling back down.

"HOT CUPPA TEA and thick buttered toast makes a strong heart for any kind of day" was Gran's morning mantra, and one I chanted repeatedly the following couple of mornings as I dragged myself out of bed, scuttled down the hall, ran cold tap water onto my face, bunching my hair into a ponytail. I'd never been early to rise. In my schooldays I'd been coaxed into morning by Gran gently scratching my back, luring me from bed into the kitchen with buttery smells, sitting me before the stove, feet on the oven door for warmth, loading up my lap with tarty jammed toast and mugs of tea. And in my four years of university I'd scarcely met with a morning class—I even switched once out of a cherished psychology course to an anthropological nightmare focusing on eighteenth-century land claims in the Andes just so's to escape cold floors and early, chatty risers. So the crowded, noisy camp mornings were a trial I hadn't considered when tossing my apron at Cork and chasing a muddied truck into the bush.

Yet, fuelled by the chat back home, I darted happily about the now-familiar kitchen. I had the kettle and dampers humming and Cook huffing to keep time as I cooked and cleaned twelve hours straight for the two work crews— thirteen hours, were I to count those swiped moments dawdling over tea and toast with Chris and Ben before the others arrived. For it had become a ritual, those early-morning mugs of tea and toast, bookended by their nightly cribbage games and shots of whisky before bed.

"C'mon, Sis, have a drink, have a drink," coaxed Chris as we started our second week into the job. He was bickering with Ben through their first game of the evening. Sitting with them was Cook, nursing a hot toddy. Her cough had been good this past while, but was starting up again. She complained in quick, winded sentences of the tickle in her throat, her lightheaded-ness from puffing so hard for breath.

As I was finishing the supper dishes I was drawn to the window, my attention caught by a light, jangly guitar tune coming from the bunkhouse. Pushing aside the screen, I looked out into the darkening evening. A reddish glow burned from the bunkhouse steps. Behind it Trapp's tawny head took shape. A light switched on over the doorway, sending Trapp to his feet, a mickey of whisky clutched by the neck, the cigarette flung from his mouth. Instantly the light went off and he stood for a second, then sank back into the shadow of the bunkhouse.

Aside from breakfast and supper, Trapp never entered the cookhouse. "Nothing to do with you," Ben assured me when

I'd asked about it. "He's always off to himself, just ignore him, is all."

"But he seems hostile towards me," I'd persisted, "like I've done something to him—or something—what's going on with him?"

"Nothing, nothing, slow down, don't think about him, just ignore him, got to do with me, not you," he ended with a finality that prevented any further questions.

Trapp's butt burned a brighter red and then arced through the air as he tossed it. I thought to say something to Ben, but was interrupted by the roar of Push's truck tearing across the clearing, the slamming of his truck door, the loud hork as he started up the cookhouse steps. He reamed in and tottered on his feet, his metallic eyes bleary with drink. They widened onto mine and instantly he lurched backwards as though he'd bungled into the girls' washroom.

"How you doing, hard-nuts," greeted Ben. He kicked out a chair, tossing a wink at me as Push staggered forward, reeking of booze, and clutched the back of the chair. "What's happenin, bud, want some grub—sit down, have some grub."

Push slumped onto the chair, leaning towards Cook as she rattled off a cough and lopped her hot toddy over the front of her blouse. "You sick?" he asked, trying for a softness he couldn't quite reach.

"Bit of a cough," said Cook, "bit of a cough."

"Take an early night," I coaxed, offering to mix her another toddy.

She gave me a grateful look, and shaking her head, said her good nights and ambled off to bed. Push slouched forward, looking to Ben, who was whistling a ditty and dealing out cards. Then he turned to Chris, his chin near grazing the table.

"How's your first week, Betty?" he asked, his speech thick.

"Betty!" Chris's eyes popped. "Sic him, Sis."

"You keeping her greased good?" rasped Push. He bobbed his head towards Ben. "You tell him that, eh—you tell him to keep her greased good—so parts move."

"Want some grub—have some grub," said Ben, and resumed his whistling.

"Rig pigs," grunted Push, abruptly, "all they do is eat." He turned back to Chris. "Parts don't move right—she burns. The rig burns. You keep her greased. First thing that burns is skin— thin skin, like this here"—he grabbed the bit of cartilage separating his nostrils, pinching it—"and eyelids. Ears. That's what goes first—when a rig blows. Cauliflower ears. Seen a few cauliflower ears working rigs."

"Yes, b'y, seen it all," said Ben with a dismissive air, scooping up his cards. "All right, buddy, your cut," he said to Chris. "How's your game, Push—try a game of crib?"

Push blinked. He shifted his attention to the cards, staring at them fixedly, like something foreign he might've enjoyed but had never learned. He made an imperious sweeping motion with his hand, and as if having done away with the question, he turned to Chris, his chest welling up, his neck thickening.

"Missing fingers," he grunted. "Seen lotsa missing fingers. Crawl away from that—crawl away from what takes a finger— nobody crawls from a fire—first thing goes—thin skin." He tugged at his earlobe. "No fat. Somebody screws up, something blows—patched with pig skin. Ever see a pretty pig—?"

Ben gave a huff of impatience.

"Hey." Chris knuckled the table for Push's attention and, just like those times he'd unwittingly galled Father, spoke in a yielding manner. "No need for worry—I'll have them jimmies trilling like larks. Sis over there—she likes waking to larks, don't you, Sis—want a game? Have a game with Ben, watch his cheating, he's a damn cheat."

Push's eyes had shrunken to slits. His head bobbed lower and lower at Chris's words, as though they were bits of a puzzle he had to put right. Shaking his head, he scraped back his chair and lurched to his feet. "Keep her greased, you young fuck," he growled. "Keep my rig greased." Shooting his hands off from his side for balance, he trod heavily towards the door and stumbled outside, leaving the door swinging in his wake.

I watched at the doorway as Push regained his balance and staggered towards his trailer. Then he stopped in his tracks, sighting Trapp sitting in the dark on the bunkhouse steps, flaring a match for a smoke he held in his mouth.

"Burn the fuckin' place down," muttered Push, and shoved off around the cookhouse. Trapp flicked his burning match to the ground, his cigarette glowing through the dark as he took a deep drag. I could feel him looking towards me. Closing the door against the dampish night air, I turned to Ben.

"Trapp's sitting by himself again."

"Not one for company." He pushed the cards towards Chris. "C'mon, Betty, deal her up."

"Drop the Betty, and I fuckin' mean it," said Chris. He'd spoken softly, yet his words were stiff.

Ben gave an appreciative grin. "You got it, bud. Now deal."

"They're *poisonous* towards each other—Push and Trapp," I said.

"Reared on poison, wouldn't they, Sylvie? The Trapp clan. Imagine suckling that tit all your life. From what I hear, Push and Skin weren't suckled any better."

"Well, time they weaned themselves, don't you think?"

Ben laughed. "The whisky bottle. That's as far as they got. That's their witch mother, the whisky bottle." He flicked

Chris's cards with the tips of his. "What have you got there, bud? What're you hiding—where'd you get them points? Hell you never pegged all them points. And look at his forehead— cripes, Sylvie, can't you fix it?"

Chris's forehead was blistering with zits. "Can't touch nothing without oiling up something," he complained as I rummaged through a corner cupboard, fishing out a first-aid kit and a bottle of rubbing alcohol.

"Here, keep still, I cleans it," I said to Chris.

"Yuh, they don't like each other much," said Chris. "Push, Trapp, Skin—seen stray cats get along better."

"Scaredies," said Ben. "That's all they are, scaredies. See themselves in the other's eyes—hates what they see, and tries to claw it out. Petty stuff. Petty stuff, is all. Like that on all the rigs, petty stuff—in banks and law offices, too—everybody looking to move up, trying to steal your job, whispering silly willies in somebody's ear, 'Hey Push, I seen Ben snoozing behind the mud tank, Hey Push, Ben's gone off early agin, Hey Push, Ben's jacking off down the mouse hole.'"

I gave him a dubious look. "Seen lots of bad-ass characters in the bars, but not all sitting at the same table. And I've never been inclined to join them. Sit back," I said to Chris, soaking a piece of cotton wool with alcohol. "Pull back your hair— aah, it's stiff with dirt, when did you last wash it?" He let out a yowl as I dabbed at his forehead and swiped at the liquid drooling down his cheek.

"For gawd's sakes," I said wearily.

"Just take it easy, will you, cripes."

"Hold still. Just what exactly is Trapp's job?" I asked, and sighed with impatience when Chris let out another yowl as the alcohol stung into his swollen pustules. "Don't touch it," I ordered.

"Get away with that—"

"Sit still."

"Will you get the hell away?"

I swabbed his mouth and he cursed again, bolting from the chair into the washroom. Laying down the swab, I sat next to Ben, trying to follow his words.

"He decides how fast or how slow we lower the pipe down the drill hole. He works the brakes holding it back. He watches his gauges—it's his gauges that guide him—is she losing pressure, or gaining pressure, or is she levelling off? That's the mud thing again—is the mud coming back up the hole, or going down and cycling back up through your annulus— which is what you want—what you pumps down the hole equals what's coming back up. He always got to be watching his gauges, figuring what's going on down the hole. He's Push's eyes. He's Push's eyes, nose, and ears. He got to be paying attention every second—especially when Push isn't on the floor. He reports to Push, he reports everything to Push."

"And to Frederick?" I said.

"No, no, Frederick is his own man. Told you before, Frederick's boss of the underground—which is a crew of one—himself. They consult—Frederick and Push and, well, the geologist, too—they consult about what's happening and how to go, but it's Push's rig, Push's crew. Frederick got nothing to do with the crew. Sometimes they get into arguing what certain pressures mean, and either one of them got the authority to shut down the rig if they thinks there's something happening that they're not sure of. But overall, it's Push who does the ordering. And perhaps it's based on what Frederick tells him, or based on his own knowing. But on this rig for sure it's Push who does the ordering, which makes me feel right at ease because Push got it all over that stun-fuck Frederick— greener than a spring pasture."

"Neither of them make me feel exactly secure," I offered.

"Imagine they feels the same about you," muttered Chris, shuffling out of the washroom. Dabbing a wet bit of tissue to his forehead, he took his seat, throwing me a petulant look. "Your deal," he said to Ben. "Any chance of a drink—witch mother?" he asked me.

I took another swab at his forehead, and exchanging a conspiratorial grin with Ben, made a round of drinks. I sat down to watch as Ben bullied Chris into a premature play and then assailed him with a double run on points. He egged Chris into another premature play and then pegged more points, knuckling Chris's shoulder with the affection of a big brother. He tossed me a wink as Chris nailed his next play for two points, and then let out a soft laugh, high-fiving me as he counted out a run and out-pegged Chris for game.

My belly tingled along with my fingertips. I feared mooning again. This cramped camp with its bullying scaredies was starting to feel warm and cozy beneath the pearly light of the moon. Myrah sauntered through my corridor of thought, ringing bells of alarm, of warning. I didn't care. I couldn't help it anyway. Love was a spring rain, and I stood thirsting from the long drought since I'd last been sprinkled upon by the attentions of Ben Rice. Adding to my growing sense of comfort in this unlikely place was the eagerness in Chris's eyes as he challenged Ben to another game of crib. One week. One week of living in this camp and working the rigs, and the guilt about Father had loosened its restraints from my brother's face.

I DOUBLED MY EFFORTS at cleaning and scrubbing the cookhouse floors. I double-dosed the scrubbing water with vinegar, detergents, and other lemony-scented cleansers. And yet I could never free it from the stench of diesel, of dankness, of ground rot. And no matter the savoury stews and soups Cook dished out, the hot bread and muffins, the juicy steaks and spuds, and no matter the fat, grey pussy willows I plucked from the roadside and sat on the table in a mayonnaise jar, an oppressive air jaded the cookhouse. Jaded the whole camp. Hung over it like the darkest of clouds.

I felt it each day as I trekked across the field to the rig and entered its rumbling belly. I felt it each time I laid my basket of sandwiches and fruit on the table inside the doghouse, huddling for a moment before its vibrating glass front, peering out at the men scarcely recognizable inside their shapeless, grease-blackened coveralls and hard hats, dancing and dodging around the swinging chain, the moving metal parts, Push's mouth warping to the side as he yelled into their faces, fisting his palm when it appeared none of them had either heard or cared to look, flashing his eyes up the steel tower, gesturing wildly at the derrickhand who stared back down, mouth pursed as though he might spit. I felt it each time Trapp's hands splayed like claws as he stared down the haughty length of his nose at Push, who was consistently wringing fists big as yams at him from across the rig floor, and at Skin, who was always sneaking glances at him through the greasy lock of hair escaping his helmet and pinching his nose as though staving off the stench of shit.

And I felt it the time I saw Frederick, the engineer, chuckling like a silly overgrown boy before Push's enraged face as they stood arguing before the array of gauges at the station where Trapp worked.

"Who's boss over who, agin?" I asked Ben later that evening.

"Frederick bosses the underground, Push bosses the rig floor. Formation, pressure, that's Frederick's stuff. Rig floor, rig hands, that's Push's stuff. Push wants to shut her down, he shuts her down. Freddie don't like what's happening under-ground, he shuts her down."

"So how come they argue all the time?"

"Cuz Freddy's the book-happy scholar, and he got the smarts and he got the papers, but he got dick-all according to Push because he don't have Ex-per-ience. And in this game if you don't have experience you got to trust others to guide you right—them with experience. But this Freddie Four-eyes, he just got his nose out of a book and hasn't learned yet what experience is, and Push hates him for that—hates his arrogance."

"And you trust Push—even though he works when he's drunk?"

"Bastard knows every squeak on that rig floor. Creeps about like a nervous mother, listening to gears, the pumps, the jimmies—most times he knows what's happening just from the sounds they're making, their grunting and groaning and whining—yeah, he's a good mother, Pushie is, I'll give him that. Speaking of mothers, how's yours?"

"Uh?" It was one of those rare moments when Chris had gone early to the bunkhouse and Ben was left sitting alone at the table, idly flipping through the cards in a game of patience, watching me standing at the sink dicing vegetables for a pot of soup for the night crew.

"I was talking to my mother," he said, "and she said that you and your mother had a spat at the hospital." He lunged forward, catching a turnip as it rolled off the sink. "Here you go." He bounced it from hand to hand like a ball. "Want me to peel it? Need some help there? Here, pass that knife, I peels your turnip."

I took the turnip from his hands and pointed at a bag of potatoes.

He was standing close, quite close; I could feel him. I fumbled with the carrot. He fetched a knife out of the block and started peeling spuds. My hair was sweaty from working all day and hung lank in a ponytail. I was wearing one of Cook's oversized aprons, permanently stained from years of splattering grease. I hadn't freshened my lipstick since right after supper, and my lips felt dry.

"We were arguing over ideals," I said, biting my lips to redden them, "the plight of the young and foolish—getting so caught in ideals and cleverness that we overlook common sense sometimes."

"And your mother says—?"

"She says some people need never leave home to learn."

"Like your brother."

I shrugged. "Yeah," I said quietly. "And that learning comes to some people, like my brother with his images. And in some cases—like with Chris—it's for the rest of us to bring learning to what he gives us."

"Your mother said that?"

"Kinda." I shrugged again. "I think she's right."

"I think I like your mother."

"Oh—and why's that?"

"Why's that—why's that, let's see—she thinks for herself?"

I laughed. "Yeah, she does that."

"That's a good thing, isn't it?" he asked, shouldering me. "People clutch on to other people's ideas because they've none of their own. Or they don't trust their own. Like you right now, eh, Sis?"

"Stop calling me Sis," I mumbled.

He threw a spud into the pot and scrubbed his grist-grained hands onto the sides of his jeans. He took the knife out of my hands and laid it on the sink and started kissing my mouth, wrapping one of his legs around mine like a snake, forcing me hard against him. I was caught unprepared, hadn't taken a breath of air, hadn't brushed my teeth after supper. He slid his hands beneath my T-shirt onto bared skin and I forgot about air and toothpaste. I wrapped my arms around his waist, pushing into him. "The night crew," I whispered against his mouth, "I've got to finish the soup."

"Fuck 'em."

"They'll soon be here."

He kissed my face and then pulled away. "You finish the soup, I'll clean," he said softly, and started to scrape peelings into a garbage bag. I finished dicing the potatoes, my hands shaky, and nicked a finger. I sucked on the cut, and was debating whether or not it needed a Band-Aid when I heard Chris calling, a tinge of alarm in his voice. I turned to Ben and we hurried out on the step. The pale white light of the moon showed up the blackness of the land, and of Chris's figure wavering towards the centre of the clearing.

"I lost me boot," he yelled. "I lost me freakin' boot, it's stuck in the mud, in the jeezly mud."

"What're you doing out there?" roared Ben.

"It suctioned off in the mud—I heard something—heard a cat—"

"A cat! You heard a cat—you're in the middle of the fucking wilderness—where you gonna get a cat in the middle of the fucking wilderness?"

"It was there, I heard—come help me, jeezes, I'm stuck."

A set of headlights was coming across the clearing. It was Push's truck.

"Jeezes, jeezes," muttered Ben. "Get back in the kitchen," he ordered as I started laughing.

"Sis—you there, Sis?" called Chris.

"No. Find your own boot."

I went back inside, hurrying through the cleaning up, leaving the door open so's to hear Ben cursing at Chris, and Chris cursing at the mud, and Push cursing at them both as he positioned the headlights of his truck onto Chris, who was wobbling on one foot, holding the other in his hand as he searched about for his boot.

The soup was bubbling on the stove, the cookhouse cleaned and the table readied for breakfast, and they were still out there—Ben laughing now, and Chris cursing, and Push sitting behind the wheel of his truck drinking whisky and snorting his own brand of laughter.

Another truck roared in bearing two of the night crew. I watched through the window as they joined the fracas—"He's got it, he's got his boot—the young fuck's got his boot," their loud guffaws following each shout. I looked at the clock. It was nearing midnight. Ben staggered into the glare of the headlights, scraping mud off his hands, his jeans, Chris limping behind him like a muddied hound.

The headlights went off and Push and the two men came noisily into the cookhouse, making coffee and pouring themselves bowls of soup, barfing out laughs at Chris and his boot. I stood in the doorway, shrugging helplessly as Ben looked at me, then at his muddied clothing, muddied hands, and the crew taking over the kitchen. He gave me a half-hearted good-night wave and started after Chris, clouting him on the back of his head for his fool thinking.

"Done it once myself," said Push, "lost a boot in the mud." He laughed. He caught me looking at him and looked torn for a second between a nod and a grin. He nodded, and I nodded and went to my room.

———

PERHAPS IT WAS THE ALMOST GRIN that I acted on the following day when I dragged two bags of garbage to the bin. Push's trailer was tucked just out of sight behind the cookhouse, the narrow walkway between leading to the bin. The past few shifts he had taken to working mostly nights because he wasn't trusting the night driller, Ben told me over tea that morning, and he was starting to fall asleep on his feet from working both night and day. His door was opened, and as I neared I heard the light, accomplished pickings of guitar strings. I listened. The occasional tunes the night wind brought me had been Push's.

The picking ended, then Push's voice started up with a hesitant singing of an old-time country song. He faltered on the words: *"Let's pretend—let's pretend ... we're together, you and me—we're together, all alone—we're together, you and I—"*

"... we're together, all alone," I finished with a flourish, then looked in through the doorway with a smile. Push was sitting at a small table, a guitar strapped around his neck. He stared out at me with the abrupt look of a youngster caught in an unmentionable act. Rearing to his feet, he kick-shut the door so hard the trailer shook. I jolted sideways, tripped over one of the garbage bags I was lugging, and fell. My forehead hit the side of the cookhouse and my hands squished through mud, one of them scratching across the sharp edge of a rock. I hastily got to my feet and dumped the garbage, hurrying back to the cookhouse.

"Slipped," I explained my muddied hands to Cook, and sat for a moment on the toilet seat, trembling. It felt as though I too had been caught in an unmentionable act, a wretched, unmentionable act. A truck roared towards the trailer, doors slamming, Ben's laughter sounding over Chris's. Another truck, more voices. My hand hurt. I ran cold water over it, over my face, noting a slight scratch from where I'd struck my forehead.

"Where's your helper?" Chris was demanding spiritedly of Cook. "Got her run off? No good, was she?"

"Ah, she was a lousy waitress too," chimed Ben. "Bring on the grub, by jeezes, I'm gut-founded. Slide your chair over, make room, Dirty Dan. Cook, what's happening, my lovely, and where's your help?"

I dried my hands and let myself out of the washroom, mechanically greeting Ben, who stood before me with a silly grin on his face, along with the rest of the crew, who were crowding noisily around the table, sharing jives with Chris about last night's escapade. Joining Cook at the sink, I helped scoop the last of the broiled bangers onto the mash, wincing as she drummed the spoon against the pot, signalling a buffet-style lineup for the rest of the food. The crew were unusually feisty, but I took no heart as they heaped their plates with peas and carrots and scoops of green salad. No different than if that boot had been aimed at my face, so unnerved was I by its crudity, its harshness.

Filling the sink with hot water and detergent, I left Cook to do the serving. A cry of mock fright sounded from Ben as Cook put a thick coiled sausage on a plate of mash before him.

"I'd rather keep yours—where it is," said Cook as he reamed his hands down the front of his pants. "I expect it works better there. I suppose," she added through a bout of snickers and laughs from the men.

Frederick tapped Trapp's plate with his fork. "Back east specialty, isn't it—bologna sausage," he asked loudly.

"Ye-es, my son," said Trapp, "good hunting too, hunting balonies, hey, Ben."

"Ye-es, my son," replied Ben, "hard to catch though, when they gets going."

"That why you Newfs are crowding us out—too stun to catch a baloney?" asked Skin.

"You got her," said Ben, "thought we'd do better hunting gophers, right Chris?"

"Naw, Ben's just teasing," said Chris, "not hard catching balonies, hey, Trapp?"

"Naw, stun as the gnat balonies are—like some rig pigs I know, ha ha."

"Pass the butter, Dan," said Ben. "Dirty Dan—helluva name, where'd you get that one, bud?"

"Called after me pa," said Dirty Dan. "So, how do you skin a baloney beast?"

"*Skim!*" said Ben. "You don't *skin* balonies, you *skims* them."

"How do you *skim* them, then?"

"Don't know, never watches. Squeamish when it comes to skimming. How about you, Pabs—ever skim a baloney?"

"Draws your blade across the belly and watches the skin skim back," said Chris.

Dirty Dan sniggered. "Favourite barb-b-q, is it—baloney steak?"

"Never eats it," said Chris. "Was born full of it—like Ben, there. You too, I'm thinking."

I lifted my eyes at the hoots of laughter and looked at Chris, his elbows sprawled across the table, his mannerisms slow and easy like Ben's, his T-shirt frayed at the neck and a thatch of hair, stiffened with dust, crowding his forehead. Aside from his boyish grin and the excitement glistening his eyes, he was looking no different than the seasoned rig workers he was sharing dinner with.

A heavy thud sounded on the cookhouse steps, and I stood riveted as the knob rattled, the catch unhooked, and the door opened. Push stepped inside, his flat face darkened with anger, the whites of his eyes reddened with either fatigue or booze, most likely both. The crew fell into a resigned silence as he bore down on them, snarling, "You gawd-damned pansies enjoying your tea? Where the fuck are we down that hole?" he hurled at the squinty-eyed geologist. "Them gawd-damn shakers are stinking of carbon, what the fuck have you been doing, powder-puffing that snout again?" This last he aimed at Frederick, the only man still eating.

"Nature of a borehole to stink of carbon," replied Frederick. Pushing his glasses up on his nose, he forked mashed potato into his mouth, chewing with exaggerated slowness. Push's face twisted contemptuously and for a second it appeared he would jam Frederick's face into his plate. Instead he threw a fiendish look at Trapp.

"Got the shit outta your eyes yet, shitface?" he growled. "You been getting any pressure on them gauges?"

"None I never told you about." Trapp leaned back on his chair legs, grinning stealthier than a mouse creeping alongside baseboards as Push looked at him blankly. "Wha'sa matter, Pushie, don't remember our chat? You need more sleep, my man."

Push faltered, his face taking on that pursed look of one trying to dredge forward last night's dream. Finding nothing to catch hold of, he rolled a fist towards Trapp. "Screw with me, you turd." He swerved the same massive fist towards Frederick who was assiduously examining a hunk of sausage before chomping a piece inside his mouth. With a snort of disgust Push turned away from the table. Frederick raised his head and I was jolted by the hatred in his eyes, by the hatred in Trapp's ha ha ha's pinging off Push's back as he stomped out of the cookhouse. Trapp and Frederick faced each other and then looked away, as though embarrassed by the intimacy of their combined hatred.

Swallowing hastily, the geologist scraped back his chair. "Better go keep the lid on," he muttered, hurrying after Push.

"Whose lid—the well, or Push's?" Frederick called after him, pushing at his glasses again. His shoulders shaking with mirth, he clamped his square white teeth through another bite of sausage.

Skin was looking through his greasy overhang at Trapp. "Did we or didn't we get a fuckin' kick in pressure?"

"The old boy's blood pressure," replied Frederick. "That's the only pressure kicking out there." He rose, dabbing at his mouth with a napkin. "Enjoy your desserts, good fellows. I'll go tuck cocky in."

"Ha ha ha. Bar the coopie door, man. Muffle that squawking." Trapp turned his humourless laugh onto Skin, who was holding a steak knife in one hand and a fork in the other, staring at him.

"Did we get a fucking kick?" demanded Skin.

"Ha ha, like cocky said, it's my balls hanging over that hole, sonny, and they don't like swinging."

"Your balls." Skin snorted. "Two fucking wet tea bags."

Trapp cupped his hands before his mouth, making a grotesque gesture with his tongue. Skin dropped his fork and sprang to his feet, holding his steak knife threateningly. Just as quickly Trapp was up on his feet, fisting a knife in one hand, his fork in the other.

"Hey! Sit down, sit the fuck down!" roared Ben. He was on his feet too now, his face contorting with disgust as Trapp and Skin faced each other like two hissing cats. Stabbing his knife into the table, Skin kicked back his chair and lunged for the door, shaking the cookhouse as he slammed it behind him.

"Sit down, for fuck's sake, sit down," Ben shouted at Trapp.

Trapp sat slowly, his eyes still slewed towards the door.

Ben let out a grunt of exasperation and dropped into his seat. "Did we get a kick?" he asked angrily.

"Naw, we didn't get a kick," said Trapp. He tried for an easy laugh, but Ben was madder than hell.

"I don't trust that four-eyed fuck of an engineer," he shot at Trapp. "You listen to Push, you don't listen to that stun, four-eyed fuck."

Trapp gave a dry laugh. He shot a glance at Cook, who was cleaning down the sink without any apparent concern. "Hey, Cookie—nettles in that soup? Rings burning our arses this evening."

Cook wheezed something unintelligible. I stood guardedly by the window, watching Ben drink deep from a glass of water Chris slid towards him. I watched the rest of the crew peck at their food and one by one filter out of the cookhouse. I watched as each of them paused for a moment outside the door, looking towards their truck, their bunkhouse, as though unsure of which way to go. Trapp was the last to leave. He too stood undecided before heading resignedly towards the bunkhouse. Men without comfort, I thought, dropping their unsettled heads onto whichever pillow would bear them and with nothing of themselves to unpack—no thoughts, no song, no commitment or loyalty—like the houses back in Cooney Arm, emptied shells, awaiting the souls that once were to come back and inhabit them. Small wonder they kept trekking into such unredeeming circumstances.

I looked from the window back to Ben, the same uncertain look playing itself over his face as he sat without moving, his eyes buried into the cold bangers and mash on his plate. Feeling my eyes turning onto him, Chris picked up his fork, feigning hunger over the cold grub. Begging off to bed with a throbbing head and her bottle of brandy, Cook closed her room door, leaving Chris and Ben staring dully at the table of dirty dishes and me standing by the window watching them.

"Come on, let's give Sis a break," said Ben.

I watched indifferently as they got to their feet, scraping plates, gathering cutlery, bungling their hands over the same spoons.

"I can't stay here," I said.

"Tomorrow I'll take you somewhere," said Ben. "Somewhere nice. Where I always go."

"When you're threatened by knives?"

He dropped the one he was holding and looked at me. "It was a bad show, Sylvie," he said humbly. He leaned against the table, his face taking on a stupefied look. "Dumb fuck," he muttered. "Stupid dumb fucks. It's not been this bad. Look, I wouldn't have brought you here—either of you," he said to Chris.

"So let's clear out," I said.

Ben fixed his attention on the cutlery, slowly gathering it into a pile. He opened his mouth to speak, then closed it.

"It's all right, buddy," said Chris. "Whatever the hell, we'll get past it."

"No. It's not all right," I said, my voice trembling. "There's nothing all right about this place—what the hell, Ben—what does Trapp have on you?"

"I owe him. I can't leave him here. And he's not ready to leave yet."

"Will he ever be? What do you owe him your life or something?"

Chris gave a blow of impatience. "You always jumps to the worst."

"And you're acting like there is no worst—"

"It's not that bad."

"Hell it's not, it's a fucking tinderbox. I can see covering for a friend," I said, turning to Ben, "but not to this degree."

"No. No, you don't see," said Ben stiffly. "You don't and I can't help you see it. Can't talk to you about it—either of you." He carried a stack of plates to the sink, fiddling with a pile of potato scraps, his back to me. I turned to Chris, who was noisily clustering a group of glass tumblers and casting resentful looks my way.

"What about you," I demanded. "Is this where our father would have you? He'd choke himself if he saw this place—and you working here *to buy him a boat*," I ended derisively.

"Let it go," muttered Chris.

"I won't, I won't let it go. He wouldn't have you here for ten trucks, for ten boats. You insult him if you think that. And your father too," I assailed Ben. "They'd both choke at this place."

Ben kept his back to me, fumbling with the plates. I turned to Chris. He lowered his eyes. My words had punctured him, but I couldn't stop. I clung to the back of a chair to keep from shaking. My breathing was quick and ragged and I felt driven, like something caged, needing to get out, needing for him to get out, too.

"Shamed, he'd be shamed of us," I drummed into my brother's silence, "and you know it—Chris, you know it. He'd burn every dollar you sent him. He'd throw it back in your face. No worthy man would put himself here. None."

Chris started away from me, the tumblers slipping from his hands and shattering at his feet. His face had been burnt by the sun but not yet darkened. It burned a deeper red now, spreading in splotches down his throat. Ben clattered a handful of forks and knives into the sink and crossed the cookhouse. "Your sister's right," he said to Chris, shoving chairs into the table with unnecessary force. "This place is getting bad. Me, I'm gonna be here for a while, gotta see some things through. But I'll drive you both to town—after work, tomorrow."

Chris let out a snort. "I'm not her youngster. Or yours either," he flung at Ben. "You can both go—but I'm staying till fall, like I said."

I stared at him anxiously. My hand stung from where I'd fallen and hot tears threatened to pour. I retreated into anger instead, and looking coolly at Chris, and then Ben, pointed to the door.

"Better still, the both of you go," I said, jutting out my chin. "Go. Get the hell outta my kitchen—this is what *I* signed on for."

We all three looked to the other. A tap on the cookhouse door jarred our attention, and Trapp stepped inside, an apprehensive look squinting his face as though it was a private home he was entering, not sure of his welcome.

"Gee, plumb out of nettle soup," I said sharply, placing myself before him.

He nodded, avoiding my eyes. He bent sideways, trying to see around me to where Ben was squatting before a cupboard, digging out his whisky. Chris started scuffing together the broken glass with the toe of his boot. I held my spot before Trapp, my chin jutted so hard it ached. He forced himself to look at me, his greeny eyes lustreless in the dulled light from the one bare lightbulb.

"I was looking for the tonic," he said, apologetically.

I stared at him without expression.

"For the burning," he added, his tone becoming nasal. I was starting to recognize it as one he used when looking to tease, whether in torment or jauntiness. For the smidgen of a second a hint of humour softened that sharp, pointy face.

Relenting, I stood back, allowing him to enter. Ben threw a garbage bag at Trapp, and with the belligerent tone of an irate father, ordered him to help Chris with the broken glass.

I went to the sink, twisted on the taps, and squeezed detergent into the water. I started scrubbing pots first, not trusting my quick, anxious movements with the fragility of glass tumblers and plates. Chris murmured some banal comment to Trapp and I looked to him, trying to catch it. My brother's face was pallid, and I felt deeply the slap of his rejection as he turned his back to me. I stared accusingly at Trapp, wanting to be angry with him for the terrible events of the night. But his awkwardness as he stood looking around with the garbage bag in one hand and holding on to the broom Chris had passed him drew a twinge of sympathy from me instead.

"Just sweep," I said, taking the bag from him and directing his attention to the floor.

He started sweeping, bumping into Ben, who was pouring a round of drinks. Then he stepped back, near tripping over Chris, who was crouched behind him, picking up pieces of broken glass. He started sweeping again, clicking his tongue in frustration as Ben, putting a drink on the counter beside me, trod through his swept pile of dirt. I wondered how he'd fared growing up amongst the Trapp kin, counting eight or ten to a household, plus cats and dogs. He kept looking towards me, towards Chris, towards his little pile of dirt on the floor. Ben taunted his sloppy sweeping and he gave a forced, uncomfortable laugh that showed him to be outside the moment, studying it, gauging it, as though lacking faith in the sincerity of the moment, and was courting it with suspicion.

Chris sat at the table, fidgeting in his seat as Ben dug out the cards. He gave the first game to Ben and Trapp and leaned back, watching their play, smiling but saying little to

Ben's attempts at banter throughout the strained evening. A few times he stole a quick glance at me with the petulant look of a youngster wanting to crawl off from a family dinner.

Working a round of ham out of the deep freeze, I laid it on the sink and cursed when it slipped onto the floor. Chris grabbed it, putting it carefully back. With that he gave an exaggerated yawn, and waving aside Ben's urging to wait, hold on, take on the winner, he bade good night to the room and headed for the door.

Ben's brow creased with growing irritation. He opened his mouth to call after Chris, but was checked by Trapp's wispy laugh as he pegged a run on Ben's last play. Ben played the next card, his forehead popping with sweat as Trapp snared another run. He looked expectantly to me, as though I might put an end to his moment of twisted loyalties. But I was already heading into my room.

I slid open the window and pressed my face against the coolness of the wire mesh, staring out into the dark. The muted sounds of Ben and Trapp's voices grew intense. I knew if I strained hard enough I might hear their words, but there was no room inside of me right then for their mystery. I looked with distrust to where Push's trailer was burrowed into the dark. I looked to his rig. I couldn't see it from where I stood, but in my mind's eye, I saw it lit up a ghastly yellow by flood lamps that scorched through the dark like fallen suns.

The sky opened to a sudden downpour that stung coldly through the mesh onto my face. I slept fitfully that night to quick squalls on my window and the distant screaming of the jimmies. Come morning I awoke with the same foul mood clinging to me like a bad smell.

TEN

A S PROMISED, right after work the next evening Ben
ushered me and Chris out of the cookhouse, assuring
Cook we'd be back for the cleanup. With bread, cheese,
smoked salmon, and a half dozen beer tucked behind the seat,
we climbed aboard the truck and set off. Chris sat staring out
his side window and Ben was wearing his graven image,
whipping the truck irritably between gears. Neither had
appeared for breakfast that morning, much less their early-
morning cuppa tea and toast. Yet there was nothing of last
night's anger among us, simply the hangover of weighted
thoughts and downcast eyes forbidding entry into territories
too tender yet for scrutiny.

Fifteen minutes of hard driving and Ben parked before a tall
hedging of jack pine, fringed beneath with grasses and golden
swaths of dandelions. I climbed out of the truck, dizzy with
relief in the absolute quiet, and drank back the sun-yellowed
air, tarty sweet from the balsam firs crowding behind the pine.

Ben pulled his knapsack and six-pack from behind the seat,
nudging me towards an opening through the woods. "Get the
other bag, I leads your sister through the wilderness," he called
out to Chris. "Come on, let's go meet Billy."

"Billy?"

"Head honcho around here." I followed him, stepping in the
wide tracks of his boots through a swampy patch of ground. A
slight incline and the path became drier, the overhang less

dense. The woods opened onto a meadow, as softly padded as anything matting the shores of Cooney Arm, and my camp-dreary eyes feasted on the purply blue sepals of the wild crocus springing up in clusters all about. I looked back. Chris was coming through the evergreens, shoulders more hunched beneath his knapsack than that great Titan's holding the weight of the heavens.

I turned dispiritedly back to the trail.

"Pardon me," said Chris, marching up from behind. He nudged me aside with a strong arm, walking past with the urgency of a ticket holder late for the first act. He broke into a run and I laughed, running after him. He skidded to a halt at the bottom of a slight dip, then cursed as I plowed into his back, the both of us sinking ankle deep into a muddied trough. Holding on to each other's arms, we levered ourselves onto drier ground, yelling out warnings to Ben, who was trailing behind. Then we scraped our boots across the gnarled root of an ancient pine and carried on walking, the leafy arches of the cottonwood giving way to a cobalt sky. Stretching out before us was a pond, still as glass.

"You could see a duck's balls on that," said Ben, coming upon us. "There's Bill." He pointed to a small brown head bobbing in the water near the shore and the greyish wooden clump of a beaver dam to the far side. "Best engineers around. Second only to women in changing things to their liking. And works only with their teeth—no claws, no bullying." He tossed me a wink but the heaviness of his tone belied any frivolities, and, as though knowing it, he clumped ahead through the grass. I followed him up to the top of a small hillock, fairly dry beneath the bared sun. "Catch a breeze up here, chase off flies," said Ben, and he threw down his knapsack, sitting with a loud *ahhhh!*

I looked back at Chris standing by the pond, shading his eyes towards the sky as might Father in his boat, searching for signs of weather. He kept standing there, gazing.

"He's feeling a bit twisted," said Ben.

"Thanks to me," I said.

"You spoke the truth."

Popping a can of beer, he took it to Chris, who was dropping his knapsack on top of a large, flat rock. A few words with Chris and Ben strolled back, leaving Chris sipping his beer and looking at the lake, rippling now from Billy's nose as he swam towards his lodge.

Shaking my head to Ben's offer of a beer, I found a place to myself by the side of the knoll and stretched out, using my coat for a pillow. The grass felt softer than Gran's pillow beneath my head, the scent of pine a laudanum for sleep. I gazed down past my feet, watching Chris sitting motionless, gazing at the pond. I thought to go to him, but a breeze wafted over me with the softness of duck down, stroking my cheek with a blade of grass. I closed my eyes to the rustle of the cottonwoods, the *tweedle eedee* of a robin, the chattering of a warbler. I drifted with a puff of cloud across the sky. I swam through the greens and pinks spiralling through the reddish dome beneath my closed eyelids. If not for the mosquito brrrr-ing in my ear, I would've slept—or perhaps I had, for when I opened my eyes Chris was no longer looking at the pond but hunched over a sketch pad, his knapsack in disarray around him.

With a languorous stretch, I left behind the comfy nest of grass and sat cross-legged beside him. His mouth was curled studiously, the fine hair on the back of his hand catching the sun as he sketched and shaded a meadow. He seemed oblivious to my presence, but tilted his drawing slightly as though hiding it from scrutiny.

"I'm sorry," I mumbled. "You were right, I shouldn't have come."

He grunted.

"Chris, I'm truly sorry—about last night, too."

"Freaking out over nothing," he muttered.

"Yup. Damn knife fights—gets me squeamish every time."

"That's what you call a knife fight?"

I gave him a sideways look. "What do you know about knife fights?"

"Knife fights, fist fights—seen a few brawls in the backwoods back home."

"Yeah, right."

"Jeezes, you're worse than the freakin' townies, thinking all we does in the outports is fish."

"All right, so I missed a few things. Don't remember you being so brave," I said, trying for humour, "all them times you bawled your head off wanting to go to Cooney Arm with me and Gran and yet clinging to Mother's skirts, too scared to leave."

He tossed his head with a snort. "Cuz Mother was pinching me shoulders, you nit, and pulling me back so's to stay with her."

"Yeah, right. Couldn't have gotten you in that boat with a bucket of candy."

"You only wanted me to come cuz you were scared of ghosts."

"Hey!"

"Hey, what! Remembers you now, huddling behind the house, frightened of your own shadow."

"And who was huddling behind me?" I asked, grateful for the grin chewing the corners of his mouth.

"Cripes, you had me freaked out—playing dead atop of graves all the freaking time. Half the reason I never left home sooner, scared I'd end up living with you."

It was a deeper fear than that, I thought to say, but curbed my tongue, for perhaps he hadn't recognized his fear. If I'd learned anything from this camp, it was that fear doesn't necessarily present itself in well-defined situations; more often it's that darker shade of red flowing through our veins, tinting our views and no doubt stripping us of the courage to make decisions along the way.

"Ghosts," Chris was muttering, shaking his head. "You bloody had me convinced."

"You mean it wasn't Grandfather Now that convinced you?"

"Foolishness."

"Foolishness, hell, I mopped up the water from his boots."

"Leak in the roof."

"Bloody hell."

"So, what do they want, then?"

"What do who want?"

"Your ghosts. What do they want?"

"How should I know what they want?"

"They're your ghosts, you made them up, you should know what they want. Jeezes, Sis, you don't think they were real, do you?"

"Swear to gawd I'm not making up Grandfather Now. I mopped up the water from his boots. Ask Gran, she don't lie."

"I will, I'll ask her, she'll laugh, can see her now, laughing." He twisted sideways, searching through some pencils in his bag, his sketch pad bopping on his knees. The patch of meadow had looped into a pond with a boat sitting on its surface and the lone figure of a man sitting in its centre, looking up at the sun.

"A dream I had last night," he said as I picked up the pad. "Strange dream. I was Father, sitting in his boat."

"You were Father?"

"Yeah."

"What were you doing?"

"Just sitting there, being Father."

"Well—what was it like then, being Father?"

He gave his quick little shrug. "Same as being me. The water was strange—darkish. Kinda strange darkish."

"Ah, the darkling sea—where dreams come from."

Laying his bag aside, he gave in to the lure of the grassy bed beneath him and stretched out, tucking his hands behind his head. "So," he said through a leisurely yawn, "what did your ghosts look like? And Grandfather Now, what did he look like?—lean back, you're shading me."

I leaned back on my elbows, drawing forward my one image of Grandfather Now. I'd never seen him, never even saw a picture of him, there weren't any. And yet clear as the hills on a sunny day I could see him in heavy, dark clothing, rowing across the arm in his boat, his sou'wester shading his face, his hands big and gnarled like Father's as he gripped his oars. It was because Gran couldn't let go of him, I heard her tell Mother once, that's why he kept haunting the shore, sitting in Gran's rocking chair at night, water dripping from his boots—because she, Gran, couldn't move on without him, needing him to watch over her on those stormy nights.

I thought back to when I was a kid, imagining pretty much the very same thing about the ghosts in the abandoned houses—that they weren't able to move on and were waiting for the folk who'd lived there to return and reclaim them. I looked to Chris to tell him as much, but his eyes were closed, his face all relaxed as though he were drifting with the clouds.

Leaving him there, I went back up the hill. Ben was sitting with his arms folded across his knees, a can of beer in one hand

and shading his eyes with the other as he stared westwards at
the distant ridge of the Rocky Mountains and their great
granite peaks, bluish in the evening sun. That tireless graven
image, which was starting to weary me, was still clinging to his
face, connecting him no doubt to whatever foul deed it was
that yoked his step to Trapp's with a loyalty that seemed more
weighted now with burden than devotion.

Twisting off an alder branch, I sat beside him, swiping
at flies.

Ben swatted at his neck. A dark curl around his ear quivered,
a mosquito toppled onto his shoulder.

I fingered the swollen catkins hanging in clusters from the
top shoot of the alder branch. "I want out of this camp," I said
quietly. "And I'm not leaving without Chris."

He took a mouthful of beer. "He won't leave," he said, his
tone resigned. "You won't get him to leave."

"Then fix it. Get him fired. Have Push run him off. Give it
a few more days—till pay day—so's he's got a good cheque to
send home. Then make it so's we have to leave. He'll be fine
then—once he has some money to send home, and he'll have
another job quick as anything."

"Sure," he replied dryly. "I'll just be somebody else deciding
his path—along with you and his mother … You don't get it,"
he said over my huff of impatience. "*He's* decided. He decided
it without any of us. And it's for him to figure when he wants
out. Not you. Not his mother. Not me—"

"I don't give a shit who decides it—long as it takes us outta
here." I sprouted to my feet, and brushing off my backside,
scurried like a Sunday picnicker away from an anthill. Picking
up a long, spindly stick, I sat at the water's edge, flicking at a
lily pad and staring into the protruding eyes of a frog partly
submerged behind a rock.

Chris came over beside me, muttering curses about red ants. He fell to his knees beside me, ducking his arms into the pond and splashing water about his neck.

"Size of them feet," said Ben, joining him and kicking sideways at Chris's feet. "Wonder they don't charge you land taxes."

"Good for paddling," said Chris.

"Paddling! Jeezes, bud, ever try oars?"

"Dog paddling, b'y. Across the pond."

Ben laughed, splashing pond water over his arms. "Yeah, dog paddling. That's about the size of it, born on a wharf and can't swim."

"Saved Sis once. Tell him—go on, tell him," Chris urged, flicking a handful of water at my face. "She walked out over her head. I dog-paddled to her, nudged her. She was saved. Tell him, Sis."

"Ohh, go get the food, Chrissy."

"Right, always giving orders. Should've left you drowning." He stood up, nudging Ben as he did so. "Like that," he said. "I nudged her like that. She managed to get her foot on a rock, and was saved. Should've left her there—snottin' and bawlin'. All right, all right, going, going, *cheez!*"

Bringing back the food, he began laying it out. "Can't believe you gave up drawing *totally*," he said to Ben. "You were good, man, I always thought you were good."

"Ahh, I only drew bricks," said Ben with a wry grin my way.

"Bricks are good, what's wrong with bricks?"

"I don't know—ask your sister."

"*Austere*," I said unhappily. "I don't like austerity."

I tried to smile at his attempt at lightness, but my heart was heavy.

"And that," said Ben, "is exactly why I'd draw *a* brick, *a* rock, *a* stick—to keep it separate. Freeing it from other things—like emotion," he added. His mouth curled as though he'd said a nasty word.

"Austerity creates its own emotion," I said. "Coldness. Detachment. You're not freeing anything."

"Immovable, then. Perhaps I like things immovable at times. Just sits there. Connected to nothing. Nothing touching it."

I shook my head confusedly. "Why? Why do you like things immovable—and all clearly defined?"

"Perhaps it's how I anchors myself," he said quietly, "when I'm too full of feeling." He shot a westward glance towards the Rockies. "Feel whatever you want when anchored to a mountain. Nothing touches a mountain. Ever touch a mountain? Colder than fuck, nothing but rock. Can't farm them, can't milk them, can't fish them—coldest fucking things out there, mountains—connected to nothing."

"That's foolish—mountains are more connected than anything—"

"That's how I see them."

"And that's why you'd draw mountains—because they're the coldest things out there?"

"Yeah—cold, hard. Don't sink, don't bob, don't flirt or burn. They're like the old man's boat anchor—good for one thing only, holding things steady. Holding things in place. Holding me in place while I bobs and curses with whichever wind comes along."

I shook my head, feeling truly bewildered. "I don't know what you're harbouring, Ben Rice," I said quietly, "but I'll tell you another thing about your mountain, you'll have more luck rolling boulders up its side than freeing yourself from whatever this thing is with you and Trapp. Leastways, long as you stay in this hell camp."

Tossing down the piece of bread I'd been nibbling on, I left
them there and started back to the truck with a sense of feeling
smothered, of feeling stuck—stuck in this camp, in my silly
mothering with Chris, and most frustrating of all, stuck in my
drawn-out adolescent relationship with Ben Rice. One thing
for sure, after Ben's strong words about holding fast to
mountains so's to anchor feeling, I was suddenly a whole lot
concerned for whatever ills or secrets he was carrying around
in his heart—for I was starting to see now just how strongly
they were holding him a prisoner unto himself.

———

THAT THOUGHT was to return to me with the greatest of ironies
later that evening. Long shadows darkened the road as we
pulled up to the trailers. Chris and Ben headed wearily for
their bunks, getting an early night. Cook was wavering by the
table inside the cookhouse with weepy eyes and a half tumbler
of whisky sloshed over the front of her blouse. "I sneezed and
wasted it," she offered by way of explanation, and gesturing
towards the half-finished supper dishes, she shook her head
sadly, chins quivering. "Couldn't finish—damn cough's back—
can you, *ach ach*, finish?"

Waving her off to bed, I tiredly shoved up my sleeves,
refilled the sink with hot water, and started in. I was halfways
through when Ben entered, swinging a jug of whisky, and took
himself a seat at the table, pouring himself a stout drink. From
his glazed eyes and sluggish movements, he'd evidently already
taken a few swigs. When it appeared Chris wasn't coming
behind him I kept on scrubbing dishes, too tired for more than
a scant nod of greeting yet keenly aware of his sitting there.
Cook had used practically every pot and pan in the cupboards,
and yet she'd still managed to smother the sink with wet

mounds of flour and splatter the stove with grease and gravy.

Ben had started talking, his words a trickle at first and then building into a solid flow. I don't remember how much he'd already said before I allowed his words entry—*betrayal*, he repeated the word *betrayal*, and I stopped clattering the cutlery into the drawer, listening. I gripped the sink, listening. I sat beside him at the table, poured a shot of whisky and nursed it like a glass of hot milk, listening. For well over an hour he talked.

"Did you think I'd forgotten our supper date that evening, did you think I had forgotten you?" His eyes sharpened onto mine but then fell away as he spoke in low, pained tones about his booked flight to Calgary with Trapp, the tickets already in his pocket as he was inviting me to supper, how he was meeting Ernie, his good friend Ernie, did I remember Ernie? The funny mainlander with the short, shaggy haircut, always balancing beer bottles or wine bottles on his head? Well, it was Ernie they were visiting—that *Ben* was visiting, for Trapp was only along for the ride; even though Ben warned him off, he insisted on coming because Trapp followed Ben everywhere, and to Trapp's figuring, a trip across the country was no different than a trip across town.

But it was his deal—Ben's. Ernie had the connection, and Ben had the cash for this great blow. Coke. Uncut cocaine. A fortune to be made, school loans paid off, trip to Europe planned, a doctorate in engineering waiting upon return. He'd share it with Trapp, not because Trapp was a part of it but because Trapp was his bud, and Trapp went along with him, and there were risks in simply being along for the ride.

He kept looking at me as he spoke those last words. There was an intensity about him, a strong need for me to believe him, to accept this truth of Trapp's that he didn't do drugs, that he was simply along for the ride and became more bent on going when he understood the risks Ben was taking, as though he were Ben's guardian. And he was nervous, Trapp was nervous: he didn't like flying, he didn't like drugs, he didn't like anything about this deal. But in true Trapp fashion he said very little and sat rigid for the five- to six-hour flight, face whiter than the clouds by the time they landed.

When they finally reached Ernie's small, sparsely furnished flat in downtown Calgary it turned into a hard night of drinking along with a heavy sampling of the coke. Come morning Ben was hungover bad, him and Ernie both. Trapp was nervous and quiet. He'd hardly drunk all evening, and was such a silent, brooding presence in the small room that Ben was wishing he'd left him back on the Rock. It was the next morning, their second in Calgary, that Ernie took them to the restaurant, the designated meeting place. They'd left the apartment an hour early so's to get some grub, coffee, straighten up a bit. They made plans for that night, their last night in town— a blues bar featuring George Thorogood, best blues-rock act to hit town in years. It would be a wild night; they'd leave the car at home and cab it. Hey, perhaps they'd start the party a bit early, Ernie figured. Soon as they scored they'd head back home, grab showers, more grub, blow a joint or two, pull off a nap, and then boogie. Yeah!

It was on this note that Ben headed out of the restaurant to get smokes at the shop next door. Ernie held up two fingers for two packages of Player's, and Trapp held up his package of Export As. Ben sauntered out the door, leaving his bag with the drug money on the chair beside Trapp.

Ben's speech quickened as he went through what happened next, as though spitting the distasteful words out of his mouth. The girl behind the counter was cute, with a flashy smile and full of chat. He lingered, he played himself up, she played back. A few minutes of bantering and he remembered why he was there, so he paid for the smokes and with a cheery wave left the shop. The guy bringing the coke had already arrived. Ben saw the back of his head through the restaurant window, sitting across from Trapp and beside Ernie. At that moment the cops moved in—four of them, two in uniform, two in plainclothes. He stood, riveted, watching the cops already entering the door. He saw Trapp get to his feet, then Ernie. Ernie bolted for the washroom; two cops chased him. Another two had Trapp spread over the table, cuffing his hands. The "connection," the guy who'd brought the coke, was leading Trapp outside. An undercover. A setup. Trapp caught Ben's eye, gave a slight shake of his head, warning him off. And so Ben stood, arms dangling helplessly by his side, still clutching the three packs of smokes, and watched Trapp and Ernie being led off. They found out later that the guy with the scraggly reddish ponytail back at the bar in St. John's was an undercover narc.

"Trapp and Ernie went down for two years in the federal pen."

Ben rested his forehead in his hands, rubbing his temples with his thumbs. He was quiet for some time, then looked to me for some words, some reaction. Getting none, he started talking again.

"You asked me once why Trapp was so disdainful towards you—after we ran into you in Grande Prairie. Well—" Ben paused. "He thought you might've talked. Remember the day in the corridor at university—we ran into you and Moya, or Myrah, whatever her name is. You accidentally seen my ticket, and Trapp freaked. He thought you might've talked, might've said something—the wrong person heard it—he knows differently now, of course. Was just something that stuck with him.

Just—thought I'd tell you that—why he was a bit derisive towards you."

He ran his fingers through his hair, scratching at the back of his head. "He swore me to secrecy—about the whole bust. I betrayed him once, I couldn't a second time. I stayed as close as I could, roughnecking. Kept bringing them smokes, cash. Mailed their letters. I tried to serve them. Will you talk?" he pleaded.

I tried to speak. My mouth was dry as chalk. I ran my tongue over my lips but could think of nothing to say. It felt so remote—those things he was saying. So remote. Like he was talking about some TV movie he'd seen. Such a simple story. So blatant, why hadn't I thought of it? A drug-related offence, the time already served—something of a relief in a sense. For deep inside I'd felt it was something more, much more, something real crazy, like Trapp had killed somebody or something and that it was still unknown, yet to be discovered.

"I'm sorry, Ben. I wish I'd known. Wish I'd known at least something of it."

"I promised him. Else I would've told you. You believe that, Sylvie? I would've called you," he said earnestly.

I opened my mouth to speak but couldn't, had no knowing of what to say, how to express the feeling of jealousy that was welling up inside of me. It felt as though the stream Ben, Chris, and I were swimming in had suddenly forked, with Ben swimming after Trapp in one, and me and Chris swimming up the other, the two becoming farther and farther apart as we swam.

"People get busted all the time," I said. "They get past it."

"He didn't do good time, Sylvie. He's not exactly Mr. Personality—not a fucking week he didn't get a shit knocking. Jeezes." He ran his hands through his hair again.

"Wish the fuck it had been me, I've wished the oceans dry it had been me."

"No doubt. You would've had your time done by now. I don't understand—not truly. I mean, why is this going so deep? Trapp's no youngster, he made the decision to fly with you—he made himself part of it—it's not all your fault, and yet you carry it so—so *deep*."

"Jeezes, Sylvie, I was responsible—"

"No, not entirely. And even if you were, we all do stupid things. So, get over it—like he's got to. I mean, how much do you owe him—isn't this a kind of prison?" I flashed my hand around the cookhouse, the camp. "You gonna imprison yourself to Trapp because he was unlucky enough to get busted, and you didn't?" I fell silent for a moment, thrown by the disbelieving look on his face. "I'm not without feeling here, Ben. I mean, I can imagine how you—and Trapp—must feel. But—I don't know, it all seems so extreme, somehow. And this camp—it just makes it seem—just keeps it extreme. You said you'd betrayed him once before. What do you mean, do you mean the shooting—the dog and the shooting? I saw it," I said to his look of sheer astonishment.

"If fucking Mother—"

"I told you, I was there—you didn't see me, I was visiting my grandfather, and I saw it—the whole thing."

He drew away from me, as though I were seeing inside his most hidden self. "That was so long ago," I said. "And you're still blaming yourself—you didn't shoot that dog."

His eyes flashed with anger. He turned from me as though attempting to hide whatever parts of him that might still lie secret.

"Why do you carry it all so deeply?" I asked again in a whisper. "I don't get it—why do you carry Trapp this way—"

"I don't know that I do," he said curtly, and started to rise.

"Why're you leaving—why're you mad? Tell it to me, tell me how you came to be friends with Trapp—after the shooting. Or, better still," I added, straining for a lightening of his mood, "how did you get Suze to keep that one a secret for all these years?"

His face looked immovable, just the way he liked things, uncluttered with emotion. And yet he was full of the deepest feelings, so deep they threatened to bury him. I thought back to university, the drugs, booze, bars. And even now, this thing with Trapp—all those things were a parade of sorts, a channelling of his emotions, like trained students during a fire drill, all flowing the one direction through the one corridor. I looked into his eyes, his sea-grey eyes, and saw their darkened pits, saw them quivering with light, with vulnerability.

"Why do you move away from me?" I whispered. "You always move away from me."

He lowered his eyes from mine, as though he couldn't bear the scrutiny. "I—is that how you see it, that I move away?"

"You do."

He was quiet for a moment, then shrugged. "Guess I just don't see things sometimes—how I do things."

"Tell me then. Tell me how you see things. How do you see Trapp? How did you become friends with him after the shooting? What did you do—did you go back and find him?"

He touched my hand, rubbing it for a moment, and then started rubbing at his chin, knuckling both hands through his hair in his old nervous manner.

"Yeah, I went back," he said roughly. "Thought I'd help him bury it—bury his dog. He'd carried it up the beach—and was sitting beside it, sobbing, when I found him. It was an hour past the shooting now, and he was still sitting beside his dog, sobbing. I never heard anyone cry so hard. Felt like *I* shot his dog, I felt so bad. He didn't even try to fight me when I went near him. He just kept on sobbing, like a river of tears were running through him, and I thought—swear to god—I thought he was gonna drown in them.

"I buried his dog. He followed behind as I carried it to this nice spot in the woods. He hardly spoke. He hardly speaks now. Can't imagine what shit went on in that house of his—that bastard old man. Got an inkling of it once."

I gently touched his hand. "How?" I asked.

He shook his head, reluctant to speak.

"Tell me. Ben, please tell me."

"Trapp's old man," he began quietly, "he never let no one in his house—but I chanced to see inside once—Trapp's mother was sitting in the rocking chair, coaxing Trapp to sit in her lap and be rocked. He looked shamed seeing me standing there, hearing his mother coaxing him into her lap to be rocked. She was skinny, not much bigger than Trapp himself. She had this crazy look in her eyes, like she was gonna start screaming if Trapp didn't go to her. He told me she was always sitting in her rocker, always calling out to him, always wanting to rock him. I think—I think he must've let her—let her rock him—lots of times." He faltered, leaning on his knees. No doubt he was too young for the outright memory of his mother forcing him to her breast well past the appropriate age. And yet, from the wincing on his face I well understood how the body remembers such things, and how it was remembering for him right now the smothering, hovering presence of his mother.

Neither of us spoke for a moment. "Do you—do you think she handled him too much?" I asked, resorting to Mother's word.

He said nothing. He nodded, and then rubbed at his face. "Yeah. I think. I dunno. She was crazy for sure."

"Was she crazy—I mean, like, really crazy?"

He nodded. "Yeah. She was something. Trapp's old man was crazy too, but a different crazy—he just kept everything going—food in the house, wood. Kept the house going, somehow—with help from the other Trapps. But he was a mean bastard, he just wouldn't let nobody around, paranoid of everybody—like all the fucking Trapps, they all got this thing about clanning together, as though they got to protect themselves from everybody out there."

Ben folded and unfolded his hands. He opened his mouth to speak further, but didn't.

"And so you kept taking him home with you. Were you, were you trying to spare him—his mother rocking him and stuff?"

He kept looking to the floor.

He started jiggling his foot. He sucked in a deep breath, his chest heaving as though it were too tight to breathe. "Perhaps," he said lowly, "perhaps. Jeezes. And then he felt like—like this thing I had inherited along the way, like a coat flung over my back that I couldn't get rid of."

"And you wanted to?"

Ben shrugged. "I dunno. He was—he was always looking to me—every time I went anywhere that summer he'd be standing there, looking towards me. He'd never go home unless I told him to. I ran off, sometimes, leaving him standing there. Started feeling like I was a fucking mother." He winced again, and I wasn't sure if his aversion was meant for Trapp or himself.

He drank deeply from his whisky, then he started talking again, his voice becoming more forceful as he told of how Trapp started following him around, going home with him—

and watching, always watching, how Ben chewed his food, how he chatted, laughed with the girls, hung easily with people, hummed a tune. He was like someone first out of the cave, said Ben, seeing everything clear for the first time.

There were times he felt Trapp coveting everything that he was; times he felt Trapp wanted to be him. And yet he took nothing. Whenever Ben asked him about his family, he'd take on that look, like a dissatisfied diner handing back a platter of untouched food. But he savoured every word of Ben's when Ben would tell him some story about himself and his old man out moose hunting, or fighting over the heart and liver from the Christmas turkey, or washing the windows in the house for his mother. Trapp reminded him of something untouched, innocent in the most bizarre way. He argued nothing, just nodded, even when he knew Ben to be wrong. The only thing he ever expressed an opinion on was drugs. He hated them. "Felt like he was my guardian those days at university," said Ben. "Used to get a bit much sometimes, when I had a girlfriend or something. He always spooked them off. I often wondered back then what would happen when we left university, went our separate ways."

He clasped his hands tightly around his glass of whisky, the white showing through his knuckles. He looked at me with a sad smile. Abruptly he put his glass down and got up, pulling me to him. His arms went around me and he held me tight, his face burrowing into my hair. The rest of him remained motionless. I kept myself quiet, my body, my thoughts. There was room only for him in that moment, and I knew he was simply holding me as he might've held himself, if he could, or that little, lost boy sobbing on the beach, the one who'd been handled so much by a needing mother that he kept cutting himself off from being loved.

"Seems we all have ghosts," I murmured against his shoulder. I drew back, looking up into his face. He looked so strained, his mouth tight as though he were holding himself in. "That little boy—he's more you than Trapp. Time you let him grow up, don't you think?"

Something of a chuckle sounded in Ben's throat. "Don't know how you and your brother survive," he said. "All those crooked lines by which you think, see things. I'm going to leave now. Night crew will be here soon, and—I'm beat."

He held me for a minute longer—this time I felt it was me he was holding, and the tender manner in which he kissed my brow, my cheek, my mouth, left no doubts about that.

———————

AT SOME POINT that night I woke up to rain drizzling against the window and voices outside. Trapp's. And Frederick's. I caught words. Mud. Pressure. Arsehole Push. I burrowed beneath the sleeping bag, the rig sounding unusually loud. Finally I fell back to sleep but the jimmies followed me, their screams sounding through the woods behind Father's house and me running up the path, searching for him, finding him standing before the screaming mouth of the old sawmill, shouting to me, his eyes filled with terror. I couldn't hear him over the jimmies, couldn't get closer, my legs barely moving as I struggled and struggled to run. And then I fell, waking up with a jolt to the rumbling metallic beast across the clearing.

ELEVEN

CHRIS CAME ALONE for breakfast. "Ben's a bit slow getting started," he said, his voice carrying that early-morning gruffness of a deep sleep. He sat back, cracking his knuckles, watching as I poured us both tea and slathered blobs of butter across the hot toast.

"You look tired," I said, passing him the bread and noting for the first time creases under his eyes. "Didn't you sleep?"

"Yeah. Damnedest night, though."

"Oh?" I backstepped, glancing out the window at the sound of a derisive laugh from Frederick, and saw Push's truck pulling up through the greyish morning light. He got out and rested against the door for a moment, his eyes puffy for want of sleep and his movements sluggish as he yawned heavily, pushing his hardhat to the back of his head. Seeing Frederick coming towards him, he showed more of a fist than a hand, and pushed off from his truck.

"Anything goes off, you come get me, scholar boy," he called out, his voice like charred oak. "You come rap on my door and get me."

Frederick, his heavy framed glasses splotchy with drizzle, was about ready to sink his teeth into an apple. "Have a nice morning now, Cocky," he said. "Nice easy day ahead."

"They're all easy till something goes off, you dumb fuck," muttered Push and walked off towards his trailer.

"What're they at out there?" asked Chris.

"The usual." I sat across from my brother. "What is it, what's wrong?—how come you couldn't sleep?"

He was cupping his mug, staring gloomily at the hot liquid inside. "Funny dreams," he said quietly.

"Ohh, good one. You and funny dreams."

"Dreamt about Father agin. Same dream as the other night. That I was him, sitting in his boat." He looked at me. "It was the exact same. Right down to the odd mitts on his hands."

"Odd mitts?"

"Yeah. He was wearing odd mitts—one green-checkered along the back, the other blue-checkered. It was the same freakin' dream."

"And—were you still just sitting there?"

He nodded.

"Him? Or you?" I asked.

"What?"

"Was it you being him, or him being you—?"

"Jeezes, how you split things. What the hell's the difference, me being Father, Father being me?"

"So, what did it feel like—I mean, were you nervous—like there was a storm coming—?"

"No. No, it was perfect. Totally content. More than content. Like this was everything—sitting in the boat. I dunno." He smiled. "Woke up feeling right calm, though."

"Well, that's Father there—always calm after a morning in boat."

"Know something, Sis—most of the time I was in boat with him, I felt him wishing I wasn't. He loves it, he do. Sitting in his boat all by himself, doing nothing, gone off somewhere in his head."

"No. That's you," I said, smiling, "going off in your head. Father's seeing every ripple in the water. Hearing every snap of the wind. He's as much outside of it as he's a part of it."

"Yeah. Suppose. Know something else though—lots of times I showed up ready to go with him, and he was already gone. Always felt like I was late or something. Mother was always hurrying me up—she didn't like him alone in boat. I wonders now—I wonders if he wouldn't sneaking off."

"Like the morning of his heart attack?"

He shrugged. "Don't know about that."

"We should go to town," I said impulsively. "This evening let's go to town. Ben will drive us—soon as the shift ends. We can buy a present or something for Father—and Kyle," I added as his eyes took on a glint of interest. "Been near on two weeks now—they must be missing you."

"Money," said Chris. "We'll send home money. I got about five hundred bucks clocked. You lend me that much and I'll stick it in the mail."

"Great, we'll take a few days off—"

"No, we won't."

"Then how you gonna send money, everything's closed by the time we get to town."

"Write a cheque, stick it in the mail."

"I just said, everything's closed."

"Right. So, back home when the post is closed, we shoves the envelope in through the mail slot, throws in the right change and—"

"—and the postmistress licks on a stamp and mails it," I ended for him. "Don't happen that way here. 'Course, we can always stay in town once we're there—find sensible work—"

"Jeezes, here she goes."

"Kidding, just kidding."

"Yeah, right, just kidding." He got up, slopping the rest of his tea down the sink. He stood there, watching the milky liquid run down the drain hole, then looked at me with a sad smile. "Don't think I'll ever sit in Father's boat agin." He shook his head. "Don't think I will." Draping his arms around my shoulders, he kissed the top of my head and went outside. When next I looked out the window he was sitting aboard the truck with Ben and Trapp, his arm dangling out the window, his flaxen head bobbing as they lurched over the ruts and potholes.

———————

I WAS AT THE WINDOW again ten minutes later when the night crew came roaring up to the cookhouse door.

"Cook! Come look, come look," I shrieked. Falling out of their trucks, the men looked like oversized boys just back from a mud fight on some riverbank. The whites of their eyes gleamed against their brown, muddied faces—their throats, hands, clothing—every part of them that hadn't been covered in coveralls was slathered in mud.

"Spillover," said Cook.

"Spillover?"

"Mud coming back up the pipe."

Spillover. I remembered Ben's big spiel that first evening at camp, sitting in the truck and telling Chris about the rig. Pressure. Everything's pressure, he'd said. Keeping it balanced. Same quantity of mud being pumped down the pipe comes back up the borehole outside the pipe. If the mud starts coming back up the pipe—you stop everything. There's something pushing it back up. And nobody moves till that something is known.

"Like a geyser. Broke the pipe to make a connection, and she flowed up like a geyser," said one of the irate men when I leaned out the cookhouse door to ask. He lingered behind the rest as they headed for the showers in the bunkhouse, his bald head the colour of chocolate, his round blue eyes like pools of spring water amidst his muddied face. "First time I seen such a thing," he said, and then followed after the others with a look of surprise still clinging to his face as though one of them might've smattered him with mud cakes when he wasn't looking.

I strained to understand their words as the men trickled into the cookhouse later for breakfast, faces scrubbed, hair wetted back. They weren't looking their usual tired selves, near falling asleep into their food as they ate. Their eyes were bright, their movements quick, and their talk loud and overrunning one another's.

"Can smell gas, can smell fucking gas in the mud—"

"Because it's down the hole, numbnuts, it's in the forma-tion—that's why we're drilling there—"

"Don't like it, don't fucking like it—"

The driller, nicknamed Eeyore for his high forehead, long ears, and slow, dragging speech, nodded as he spoke around a bite of toast. "U-tubing, boys. Small kick. She'll right herself, we're too far from the zone—"

"Can still blow, can always fucking blow, man—one highly pressurized crack, and she'll blow—"

"That's what drilling is, sonny," said a raunchy voice, "sitting on a mega bomb some stun bastard might trigger any minute. Can't handle knowing that, go to town."

"Can't hack 'er, pack 'er, sonny," said Eeyore, still nodding over his bit of toast. "This is just a phenomenal thing that happens in the course of drilling. We've pressured up—we're flowing a bit of mud—and now we'll see. She'll drop off in an hour. She's U-tubing—"

"Been smelling gas all night, and we got pressure, it's a kick," said a crewman.

"Shut her down, should be shutting her down, I say we call Push, get Push outta his bunk," said another.

"Thatta boy." A tall, bony man named Chop leaned forward with a snort, his shoulder blades lifting from his back like amputated wings. "You go wake *Pushie* if you want, I'd rather the blowout. Hey, boys, don't anyone trust ol' Eeyore, here— he's the one hired to see. That right, boss? Sees everything through them gauges, don't you?"

"What if he can't see anything, bonehead?"

"Then it's his fault if she blows—he's the driller—everything's the driller's fault—"

"That's good, numbnuts, that's just great—meanwhile we're flying through the air with DoDo and Toto—"

"Right on, bud—who the hell knows what's going on three miles underground; how the fuck does anybody know that?"

"Already told you what's going on," said Eeyore.

"Don't trust it, man—you're the driller, you should've shut her down. I think we're in the zone and you should've shut her down—it was your call, man, you're the driller."

"Opinions are like assholes, bucky; everybody got one." Eeyore's eyes hardened and a flush of anger reddened his ears, creeping up the length of his forehead. "I said we're nowhere near the zone, I made my call—you boys got that? You don't like it, take it up with Push. Take it up with Freddie the Engie— they're the ones calling the shots—I made my call, and now it's theirs. You boys got that?" He shot a surly look around the table then closed his eyes, rubbing the bridge of his nose as though the burst of anger had fatigued him. "But it's the driller's call to tell somebody if his gauges are showing pressure," he added. "I didn't see any pressure till she broke. That I can tell you."

"Sad to say it, Eeyore, but you ain't instilling a whole lotta confidence in me, man," said a quiet, steady voice.

I glanced towards the fellow talking. Kip. Hired on but a fortnight ago. He kind of looked like Chris with his blond hair blending into brows that ridged darkly over questioning eyes.

The confused, muddy-faced crewman from earlier, and two young cousins with black hair tightly clipped to their skulls, had been casting expectant looks around the table as though wanting this irregularity to be done with, to be soothed over so's they could fall into bed for an easy sleep. They'd looked dispiritedly towards Kip as he spoke, but their faces grew expectant again as the driller shook his head, saying, "Can't hack her, pack her, boys. Ride to town if you're looking." Eeyore shoved his plate aside and got up from the table as Frederick's truck drew up outside.

"Bonehead. Not a synapse in his fucking skull," muttered one of the crewmen, glowering at the door closing behind the driller.

"How'd they all find each other?" asked Kip. "Never seen so many boneheads on the one rig."

"She's not right out there—I warned the day driller—" said one of the cousins.

"What did he say?" asked the other.

"He didn't like it, could tell he didn't like it, but the engineer come up to him. Talked him over; I could see him being talked over, and I told him that too, that he was being talked over—"

"Fuck, what did he say to that—?"

"His face gnarled up like a knuckle, thought he was gonna spit at me—"

"What's going on out there—what's making them all so edgy?" asked Kip.

"That four-eyed fuck of an engineer is what's making them edgy—that's what she's all about, that four-eyed fuck hating the Push and calling his own shots. That's what's happening on that rig floor."

"They're laughing out there now," said the irate crewman from earlier, looking out the window at the driller and the engineer. "Must've figured out what was happening, else they wouldn't be laughing, would they?"

The cookhouse door opened and Frederick strolled inside, nodding towards the crew. "She was U-tubing, boys," he announced, with the satisfied look of a captain surviving a thunderous storm at sea. "I told everybody what was gonna happen. We'd pressure up, flow a bit of mud, and it was gonna die—pressure was gonna drop off in an hour." He looked at his watch. "Which is exactly what happened. She was U-tubing. We been drilling fast—too much weight in the annulus. Pushed the mud back up the pipe. She's evened out."

The men looked at each other as Frederick spoke, some nodding in agreement, others shaking their heads and grunting.

"I think we should be casing," said one of them with a heated look at Frederick. "I think we should call Push. I don't like that smell of gas."

"Small bit of gas in all these zones, Cocky, that's why we're drilling here," said Frederick. He looked at the rest of the men. "We're three hundred feet away from the reservoir. And three hundred feet could be another five, six days' drilling. Seismic's showing no changes. We're not gonna tippytoe, we're gonna make hole." He looked at Cook, who was draining a dipper of hardboiled eggs into the sink. "The boys are highly emotional this morning, Cookie," he said with a loud laugh. "Perhaps they can have their dessert before din dins." He flashed square

white teeth that looked like an attractive awning over an
empty storefront and backed out the door.

One of the crewmen cringed. "Dumb bastard." He tossed
back the rest of his coffee, glaring disgustedly at the cousins,
who were now snorting laughs his way.

"Hell with you all," muttered the crewman, and stalked out
of the cookhouse. A muffled thump sounded, followed by a
loud curse.

"Fell off the step, he fell off the step," said one of the cousins,
and they broke into a paroxysm of laughs.

The blond-haired Kip stood up with a look of disgust.
"Worked on a lot of scumholes, boys, but none this stinking
bad." He waved adios and walked out the door.

I watched through the window as he gunned his truck to
life and sped off down the road. I looked to the rig. I could see
its red-painted sides through the thickly saturated air, the
white of its derrick fading like an amputated limb into the
overcast sky.

I felt ill.

Cook was mixing a pound cake, the vanilla extract she was
pouring into the batter smelling like Gran, like home. Like
Mother. I felt like Mother. I wrung my hands. Then I busied
about the cramped kitchen, picking and poking at things,
tidying things already tidied and looking anxiously out the
window.

Frederick was leaving his trailer, chomping on an apple.

"I'm gonna go call home," I said to Cook, and donning her
rubber boots and bush jacket, ran out into the chilly, damp air,
meeting Frederick as he was about to climb aboard his truck.

"Door's open," he said, as I breathlessly asked for use of his
phone.

Wiping the damp off my brow, I dialed quickly. Mother's voice was light as she answered.

"Mom." Inexplicably, my mouth began to tremble.

"Sylvie—Sylvie, is that you—my, what a good thing you called, you'll never guess what's happened, we found the boat, we found your father's boat—Sylvie—you there, can you hear me—they found your father's boat—Gar Gillingham and Roger—it was run ashore on Big Island—carried by the ice, pushed right up on shore—not a scratch—Gran said that—she said to check Big Island, she told Chris to check Big Island— he should've thought to look, to go and look—what's that, I can't hear you—your father? My lord, the look on his face when he took a gander out the window and seen his boat—I thought he was seeing Jesus walking on the water. Poor fool, yes, yes he is a fool, a poor fool," she said to my quiet laugh, "and he's at the window now, still gawking—wait, wait now Sylvie, he wants to talk to you—is Chris there? He's working, is he—you be sure and tell him now, tell him his father found his boat, to not waste money buying a boat, they'll think we're starting our own fishing fleet—oh, my, here's your father—the patience of Job."

"Dolly, you hear me, Dolly—"

"Yes, Dad, hi, how're you doing—Dad—?"

"Back on my feet, Dolly, walking the river all week, with your mother—won't let me out of her sight—I looks at the boat and she throws a fit," he laughed a deep, raunchy laugh that sounded more pleased than irritated with the attention Mother was giving him. But then it became strained: "They're leaving in droves—all the young people, leaving in droves, tell him the fishery's all but dead—not just the inshore anymore, Dolly, it's the offshore too now, she's all but gone—"

"Dad?"

"That's your mother—at me agin—get him in school, Dolly, nothing here for the young—there's your mother agin, prying the phone from me fingers—"

"Sylvie—?"

"Yes, Mom—"

"Sylvie, you're all right then—you and Chris, you're both all right—perhaps you can come home for a good holiday with Chris when he comes? Gran would like that—and Kyle, he mentions you at the oddest times—and Gran—she hasn't been the same since you both left, swear to gawd she's aged ten years—she's having a nap now. She got sickish—just then, before you called, she got sickish—I had to help her to her room—" Mother's voice twisted worriedly. "Not often she gets sickish, I might call in the doctor. And Sylvie," her voice fell, as though shielding her ears from her own spoken words, "your father's right, about school. You're both right, I'm wrong there—but come home first—for a long visit, you and Chris, both—you both come home—you have a good day then, and yes, yes, I'll give Gran your love—bye, bye now, don't forget to tell him about the boat—you hear that, that's your father calling out bye, too—bye, Dolly, he's saying—Bye, now, you have a nice day, we're all fine."

COOK GREETED ME at the door with the lunch basket. It was already past noon. The rain was a steady drizzle streaming coldly down my face. I slugged across the field, turned swampy by the rain, grateful for Cook's rubber boots and lined bush jacket. Despite the heavy air, it sounded as though the rig was roaring louder this morning. I started up the garish steps, mindful of the slick, black mud coating them. Second step up I slipped and fell, grinding my knee across its grid. The basket buckled awkwardly around my arm, digging into my ribs. I cursed, rubbing first at my knee, then my ribs. Picking myself up, I grasped the handrail and limped up onto the rig floor.

I stepped carefully inside the doghouse, laying the basket on the table and walking over to the glass front. Everything, *everything*, was wet, slimy, and oozing mud. Skin was standing near the drill hole, his gaunt, flat face looking wearied and disgusted. He was holding the large-linked chain in his hands. Suddenly he threw it onto the rig floor as though it were a snake coming to life and went over to Ben. They shouted into each other's face for a second, then Ben spat and swerved over to the length of drill pipe sticking up from the borehole. As he bent over, fiddling with the slips on the rotary wheel, another crewman nudged his shoulder for attention. They both shouted back and forth for a moment, their shoulders hunched against the rain dribbling off their hard hats and streaming down their collar-chafed necks.

I spotted Chris partly hidden behind a tank, his shoulders hunched to the rain. He had his hard hat pulled low, his face pallid in the grim light. His squinted eyes were drifting around the squalid, vibrating rig floor as though he were allowing himself to see it in bits. Skin was making angry hand motions to Trapp, then clawed back the chain he'd thrown down earlier. Ben, the sleeves of his coveralls shoved up to his elbows, his forearms and hands slick with grease and mud, grasped the pipe hanging out of the derrick and stabbed the end of it onto the length sticking out of the drill hole. Now Chris was leaning against the side of the tank, motionless. He watched Skin swing the chain through the air towards the pipe. He watched the chain wrap itself around the pipes, and a roughneck moving in with jawlike tongs to torque them up.

Chris shivered. I could see that he shivered. There, I thought with sudden clarity, he's awakening to the beast. He's seeing it as I do. He's seeing the grease secreting through its pores. He's nauseated by the bad blood flowing through the crew as they feed like parasites upon each other.

I turned, not wanting to watch anymore, wanting this last thought of mine to be his truth. Hurrying from the doghouse, I crept carefully down the steps. I was but twenty, thirty feet from the rig when I heard a different sound—a huge whistling, roaring sound, like that of a jet about to land on the back of my head. I turned to see pipe—a straight line of pipe—spitting out through the side of the derrick and shooting like a black spear three hundred feet into the grey sky then breaking off in lengths—sixty-foot lengths, ninety-foot lengths—and falling back into the woods beyond. I watched the derrickhand, Dirty Dan, skim down the derrick like a cat on a greased pole. I watched Skin racing savagely across the rig floor, the other crewmen—all of them—racing to the opening—the vee-door—and diving down the slide. I saw Frederick on the ground, coming around the corner of some tank, a look of astonishment on his face as he saw the pipe vaulting into the air. He bolted for the woods. The geologist appeared on top of the rig floor and jumped without looking the fifteen, twenty feet to the ground and dove beneath the rig floor. Within the second Ben, too, appeared at the edge of the rig floor and jumped. And in that second—before Ben hit the ground—the rig started spluttering into silence, leaving only the clang, clang, clanging of the pipe as it ricocheted against the steel derrick.

Silence fell. Complete, utter silence.

I stared at the rig floor. I willed so hard I saw the orange of his coveralls, and then it was gone. I was onto my feet and

running to the rig. I grabbed hold of the handrails, my feet
scarcely touching the steps. He jumped. He must've jumped.
He saw Ben jump and he jumped too. I hadn't seen him
because he jumped from the back. He'd jumped from the back
so I hadn't seen him. I screamed his name in silence. I heard
someone shouting. It was Ben. Ben was shouting. Trapp was
shouting too. I slipped on the rig floor and fell heavily to my
knees. I scrabbled to my feet and bolted to the front of the
doghouse and slipped again. He was there, over there near
the borehole. He was lying on his back near the borehole, the
chain wrapped around his chest. I monkey-crawled to his side.
His hard hat was thrown from his head and tawny strands of
his hair lay in mud, his face averted from mine. I screamed his
name. I screamed it again, and again. I pulled his face towards
mine. His eyes were glistening as he looked at me. They were
glistening and bright, so bright I thought he was smiling. Then
they widened, his pupils narrowing. A sound. He was making
a sound. I stared into his eyes, his glistening brown eyes, I sank
into their softness, I heard him laugh, and I laughed too, wildly,
with relief, with joy. Then his pupils widened suddenly, and I
was caught in that fraught moment after lightning strikes and
the earth readies for the pending crash of thunder. "Wait!" I
screamed. "Wait! Chris, wait! Chriiiiiss!!!" and gripped his
shoulders as though it were time I was gripping onto—that
second of time before the heavens crashed and a dark fluid
frothed through his nose, through the corners of his mouth.
And the light emptied from his eyes.

I fell back. His silence reached after me, its coldness striking
my cheek like a chilled wind. I groped against his vacant eyes
like a lost child, frantically searching through a room suddenly
emptied of light. Ben stumbled beside me. He was making
hard sounds in his throat. I looked to him, into his eyes, the full

brightness of them. They were filling with horror as mine were already filling with sorrow, for I held no hope. Almost immediately I had known it—a part of me had known it all along. It had been born with me, it had shown me through his dreams, for they were never of the ordinary, but of Christ. Of moons without planets. Without time—as his art, his dreams too, were without time.

I whimpered in silence, unable to bring the sound through my throat. "I won't take him home," I whispered to Ben. My lips were frozen, yet I knew I had spoken, had seen my words register on his stone face. Then I crumpled like an autumn leaf onto Chris's shoulder, my face burrowing inside his dirtied orange coveralls, my hands clutching at his face, grasping his hair from the mud. I burrowed further inside his coveralls. I burrowed like a dog seeking warmth. I smelled his skin, his odour. How strange that his scent was alive when he wasn't. But the wind would take it soon enough. Oh Mother, what will you do now, and my heart leapt with fright.

I heard others piling onto the rig floor behind me, yelling, cursing, then falling silent as they came upon me, upon Chris. I heard Ben retching over the side of the rig floor. You left him behind, I said silently to Ben, it's not your fault, but you left him behind, it's your fault that you left him behind. I heard the cousins from the night crew speaking urgently as they rushed across the rig floor, then falling silent as they came upon me. I heard Push's truck roar to a stop, his snarl of outrage coming up the rig steps, then his silence, his words ambushed in his throat. Then the quiet of Dirty Dan's voice some distance behind, his hushed, urgent words falling like pebbles against the closed lid of a coffin as he told of what he'd seen from atop the derrick, the pipe shooting back up, snapping the chain from its mount on the rig floor and cat-assing around the rousty, who was just standing there, staring off. Must've crushed his ribs—the busted chain must've crushed his ribs, punctured his lungs, and his heart, too—must've, for it to have been so fast. Bled out, bled out on the inside. He'd read about it once, happening to some fellow in Louisiana, crushed his ribs, punctured his lungs and his heart, bled out in minutes. And he told, too, of another thing—of Trapp staring out at the rousty getting cat-assed, of Trapp staring at the pipe shooting up the derrick, of Trapp freezing at his station, and Ben charging to the panel and shutting her down—

Dirty Dan's voice faded and I heard nothing but silence, echoes of silence, the silence echoed by the ice field into the vastness above it, the silence of Father sitting motionless in his boat, the silence of his prayer before that proud virgin moon.

Grace, I once read, is an unearned gift of God, and sometimes given to those in great sorrow. I wondered at its power, like that of a narcotic, calming my insides as I watched the horror of the following moments pass before my eyes like that of a great drama, incorporating me into its most intimate scenes yet keeping me distant as the most unwitting spectator. I felt Ben lifting me. I saw Dirty Dan and the others gather around my brother. The most solemn of pallbearers, they lifted him and carried him past the rest of the men, who were standing single file, eyes down. The squinty-eyed geologist was standing at the bottom of the steps, blinking confusedly as he watched them carry Chris to Push's black truck and lay him on a mattress someone had dragged from the bunkhouse. Skin stood sideways, his eyes cast away from everyone, his foot jiggling nervously. Frederick stood beside him, his wide smile vanquished by a dropped mouth, his brows drawn in perplexity, his ears flattened back like a cowed dog's. Push charged back and forth between his truck and the rig, his arms jabbing off from his sides and falling in silence, his face wearing the wrath of a mother who had left her house intact and returned to chaos. He shot a look at Frederick, his flat face tighter than shrunken pigskin. And then I saw Trapp, staring out at me, half hidden behind his truck, and I was the girl again, crouching behind the woodpile by the sawmill, seeing those eyes for the first time, a part of me already knowing the imprinting of his footstep onto mine someday. This day.

My eyes hooked into his, their greeny brightness dulled now. "You did this," I croaked, drawing back as Ben tried to move me forward. My words were a whisper, heard only by Ben, but Trapp saw them on my lips, he saw them in my eyes, he saw them take shape through the drizzle and the fog and snake towards his neck like a noose. He bent his head, a ruff of hair falling forward, screening his eyes before mine as a curtain in a confessional.

"It wasn't his fault," Ben whispered.

Oh, yes it was, Ben. And you left him behind, Ben, it's not your fault but you left him behind.

"I won't take him home," I whispered.

He helped me into the back of the truck. I lay down again beside Chris, staving off looking at his face now, seeing only the heavily shrouded sun creating a dome of brightness behind the dark. I closed my eyes, resting against Chris's shoulder, his scent still there, same as yesterday, as this morning when I passed him his toast, thickly slathered with butter, the way Gran liked it. Gran. Mother. I filled with pity. And then with sympathy, and then with fright. A crushing weight cradled itself between my shoulders. I felt Ben covering me, stroking my hair. I nuzzled Chris's throat, willing him to speak as when he tired of playing dead before the tombstones of Cooney

Arm and suddenly sat upright, the leaves and cloth falling from his face. I whispered his name again and heard the horror in my voice. Something warm touched my cheek, soft, soft as air, a faint ray of the sun. My throat ached. I heard a small, nasal voice whimpering Ben's name. Trapp. Trapp's voice.

Ben's hands left my hair. I felt him lean away from me, heard Trapp's whimpers coming in snatches as Ben must've leaned towards him.

"Push would've shut her down," he was whispering vehemently, "Push would've shut her down—Frederick—Frederick should've reported the kick—he should've reported the kick to Push, he should've reported the spillover, should've gotten Push outta bed—that fucking bastard Push, I couldn't go to that fucking bastard Push, but Frederick should've, but he didn't, and he seemed sure, he'd seemed sure it was only U-tubing—" His whispers turned to a whine as he kept railing against Frederick, who should've known more, who should've shut her down, should've shut the rig down, but he hadn't shut her down, and he, Trapp, should've known, should've known, too—he'd seen the kick, he'd seen the pressure coming up the pipe, and the spill—all of it told him there'd be a blowout, and he should've reported to Push—but he reported to Frederick instead, he'd trusted Frederick, he trusted him, and now the rig had a blowout, the rousty was dead, and it was the engineer's fault, Frederick's fault.

All this Trapp was saying, his words accusatory. Yet I heard his own self-blame. As my hand cupped Chris's cheek, feeling its last moments of warmth, I heard the self-blame in Trapp's voice, that he had done it, he had killed Chris, would've killed them all if not for Ben shutting down the rig, if not for Ben hitting the kill switch and shutting down the rig. The truck started moving. Ever so slowly the truck started moving over the muddied, rutted road, and Ben's hand dropped limply onto my shoulder.

———————

LATER, MUCH LATER, Ben, holding tight to my arm as though I were a frightened bird at risk of flight, led me through the doors of a hotel suite. We'd been hours at the hospital. It was as Dirty Dan said, the snapped chain had wrapped around Chris's chest, crushing his ribs, puncturing his lung, his heart, and he'd bled out in minutes.

I crossed the compact living room, heading straight for one of the bedrooms. Ben was behind me, holding open the door as I tried to shut it. I let it stand ajar, unable to look into his eyes. I crossed the room to the window, looking down onto the grey street below, the storefronts, a small green square of grass with a park bench sitting on it. A girl stood throwing a stick to a dog who galloped, leaping into the air, catching the thing in its mouth.

I stood back from the window, closing the heavy night curtains, darkening the room, and wandered back to the door and the clothes closet next to it. I stood looking at the empty closet, its few hangers, and the two pillows on the shelf above. Pushing aside the hangers, I held on to the bar, leaned inside the small, dark space. I pulled a pillow from the top shelf and sank inside the closet. And, as when I was a girl crouching inside the closet in the haunted house in Cooney Arm, I drew my legs up to my chest and rested my chin on my knees. Chris had been frightened sometimes, crouching beside me inside that closet, watching for haunts. One time he started whimpering, wanting to leave, and I'd held on to him, hushing him to be quiet. Quite suddenly he busted into tears and, surprised, I let him go, listening to him scrambling out the door like a frightened mouse.

I felt frightened too now, hiding there in the dark. I heard a phone ring from a distance and dreaded the call I had to make. I could see them: Gran in her rocking chair, knitting in the dim light of her oil lamp; Kyle searching through the cookie jar for ginger snaps; Mother no doubt fussing over Dad, who'd be pawing at the window, anxious to be climbing aboard his boat.

I would call them soon. I would allow them one more night. One more night of Gran knitting contentedly beside her lamp. Of Mom, of Dad, sleeping soundly beside each other, and Kyle, curled up on the big, bright cushions on the sofa, munching his cookies. In this moment I would be their God, deciding when their lives, as they knew it, would end.

The brief sense of control I felt in making that decision soon ended, leaving me recoiling from that cold, white day I'd just traversed, where footholds that bore me one moment sank beneath me the next, leaving me scrambling for another and another, as did Father finding his way across a sea of pan ice. Bringing the pillow to my face, I quietly closed the closet door.

TWELVE

N TIME TO COME I would think back over the last hours of that night and the following. Each brought with it death to other parts of me, and yet the germinal seeds of promise for new life. The latter felt far removed, though, during those wretched first hours of sleeping and waking, sleeping and waking in that cramped closet, the horror of the day's events slicing its way through me upon each awakening. At some point I became conscious of Ben lying on the floor outside my closet door. The smell of whisky reached me, more medicinal than the sterile room across town in which Chris was laid out, with his flaxen hair flat back over his forehead, his eyes sealed, his lips faded to white.

I had wrenched away from his bedside. On the wall before me was a near replica of the darkly bearded Christ my mother had bartered with once for retribution from some past failing. He stared back at me, no longer the warm, comfortable figure of childhood fable and nighttime prayers but a frightening sorcerer chilling my heart with the stillness laid upon my brother. I shut my eyes to a rush of anguish, its intensity like that of a flesh wound ripping itself free from the rest of me and sprouting a life of its own in my entrails. A needle had been pricked in my arm—to calm her, they said—and I was led away from Chris, my arms clasped tightly around my belly so's to hold back that thing, that dark, new growth threatening to consume me.

I burrowed deeper inside the closet, pressing my face into the pillow. I raised it some time later to Ben's voice sounding faintly from the living room, his words bumbling amongst some broadcaster reporting the news on television. Later I awakened to his having jarred the closet door, sitting now with his back resting against it. I could see his profile through the greyish night: his fine, straight nose, his brow sloping back into his thatch of curls, his mouth pressed shut, his tightened jaw. I could see the dark around his eyes, all puffy and swollen.

I slept some more, then woke, finding him stretched out on the floor, his head partly inside the closet beside mine, his fingers stroking my hair, the smell of whisky souring around his words as he spoke in a low, throaty whisper, "Gotta do your own creating now, Sis ... don't matter if you can't draw, can't write ... gotta find something that's yours, a thought ... one unique thought ... only it has to be true, true to you ... and there you are, your own creator ... there, I read that somewhere ... don't know where, but I read it ... how's that for crooked lines, eh ... s'cuse me, my love ..." and he kissed the back of my head, and stumbling to his feet, lurched out of the room to the washroom.

He came back, crouching beside the closet door, reaching inside to touch my shoulder. He sensed I was awake and whispered for me to come out.

"I'll run you a bath," he coaxed, "it'll make you feel better. Sylvie? Will you please come out now? Please," he begged, as I shook my head. "Will you talk to your father, then—if I call your father, would you speak to him?"

"No, gawd, oh no," I whispered so harshly it hurt my throat.

"What then, what can I do?"

"Please—just close the door—I don't want the light."

"I will not," he whispered. "I will not close this door."

Chris appeared before me with his quick little shrug. I tight-ened my hold around my stomach. My face felt frozen, eyes dry as bone. Ben leaned inside the closet, taking my head to his shoulder. I felt like a stick person drawn by a child, my body stiff, my head forcefully bent to the side. I sat for a long time like that, feeling pain creeping up my neck, down my back. When some hours later I was forced to get up to use the washroom I walked bent, like an old woman. Ben argued when I crawled back inside the closet, begging to cover me on the bed, or the sofa, so's I could straighten my legs.

I couldn't bear the thought of comfort. Nothing feels more real to the living than death, I now knew. For happiness, anger, all other feelings sometimes lead to flights of fantasy where time is suspended, self forgotten. But death gripped me. It drew my knees up to my chest like a cord curling inward on itself. It drew me into a darkness without borders. It forced me into a pain more crippling than a broken wing. The small, cramped quarters of the closet contained me, kept my thoughts small and manageable, corralled that split-off thing inside of me.

Hours later I was forced to the washroom again, then started back towards my room. Amidst the rumble of television sounds Ben's words caught me, "Your play, Pabs, your fuckin' play, man."

I stepped back. I watched from around the corner. He was on the floor, his legs sprawled out in front of him, listlessly flicking cards from a deck into a small pile before him. The only light was the reds, blues, and yellows from an explosive battle scene on the television, flickering madly across his face as he rasped in a tired, broken voice, "... never listens, you young fuck, never listens ... got a skipper, do you ... got a skipper looking after your boat ... no need listening to Ben when you got a skipper watching your boat ... didn't I tell you to do your own looking ..." He stopped talking, his head falling forward, his chin resting on his chest. A shiver went through him. His body jolted as though something struck him. His head twisted back up, his words slurred, his tone filled with revulsion as he moaned, "... little shit ... too late now ... she's spitting pipe ... and that prick of a captain ..." he gave a nasty laugh, "... that prick of a captain's sleeping like a baby, bliss-fully unawares ... and where're you now, you little bastard ..." He swigged back whisky from the half-emptied bottle on the floor beside him, sneezed most of it back out. Rubbing at his face with his sleeve, he started flicking out more cards, froth gathering at the corners of his mouth as he started muttering thickly, "... you went off, little fuck. Didn't swivel them eyes. Didn't read them gauges, you little fuck ... the ones in your head, the one's screaming run, run ... and them stun bastards ... them stun bastards around you were singing lullabies ... *damn, gawd-damned!*" He fisted the carpeted floor. His face contorted and he knuckled his fists to his eyes, digging at them. He kept on flicking cards, he kept on talking, his words torn from his throat and raw with anguish, "... you went off, little fuck ... you went off ... been going off all day ... can't heave off here, Pabs ... kept telling you, can't heave off here, not sitting on the wharf here ..." His voice broke. He started blubbering into his shoulder, no more than a boy. And yet I saw within the grimness of his jaw the full dissolution of the lightness of youth, and wondered if he could ever again give himself over to a game of crib, the spontaneity of a laugh.

It was late evening when he next came and sat beside the closet door. He'd showered, yet the sour smell of whisky on his breath belied the freshness of his damp curls.

Mother was coming, he told me. Mother was coming. Now. There. To that hotel suite. She was landing right about now at

the airport. This is what he told me, that Mother was coming
to get me. That he'd called from the hospital, that he had to
call, that he couldn't allow too much time to pass without my
mother knowing, for he remembered when his mother's sister
had died in Toronto, and Suze hadn't been called till the next
day, and how Suze had been playing bingo at the community
hall that night, and how the greatest part of her grief was that
she'd been playing bingo at the community hall while her
sister lay dying. No, he couldn't wait for me to call Mother, for
he knew I would never be ready to call Mother, and then there
would be another guilt for me to take upon myself, my only
guilt, for thus far I hadn't made a wrong move in my life,
and this little deed here—well, this was the least he could do
for me.

I fought. When Ben told me, I fought hard, that thing inside
of me near busting free. I clawed at his face to get at the door,
to get away. I was surprised at how hard I fought, how heavily
he was breathing from holding me back in the closet now. I
wanted Gran, I wanted Gran, I told him, and he said he would
call Gran. And he did, he dragged the phone off the night table
to the closet door. One of Mother's sisters answered the
phone. She said Gran couldn't come to the phone just now,
nor could Father. They were both in bed, she said. They were
both in bed and unable to get up just yet.

"They're like you," Ben pleaded as I curled around myself
like a dog searching for comfort, "they're like you, they don't
have strength—they're feeling it, they're feeling it too."

I heard his words. They swirled outside of me like a foreign
alphabet, their meaning blocked by that split-off thing that was
weeping and weeping inside of me over what I had done that
had taken Gran and Father to their beds, that was keeping
them from talking to me.

"Your mother's come though," said Ben, "she's come all this way just to get you, she's come all this way—I told her you weren't coming home, and she's come all this way just to get you."

"She's coming for him."

"No, for you, she's come for you."

"I can't be here."

"You will be, she's come all this way."

"She's come for him." I nestled onto the floor, head buried beneath my arm, seeing Mother, seeing Chris, the both of them in the graveyard, Mother rocking him, brushing the dead leaves off his face, rocking him. Another cross now, two more pieces of wood notched together, for Mother hadn't wanted no fancy headstones for her three babies—nothing could be more dear than those three little crosses Father had cut and notched together and painted white, every year he painted them anew, painted them white against the greying rain and the greying, salty wind.

I shivered, drawing my knees up tighter to my chest. My mind latched onto Chris's drawings, trying to reap comfort, for I'd always believed they hinted of another place, a sense of safety from this world where everything shifted, where things rotted and died and then rotted again, leaving nothing behind, not a trace, except memories that died too with the mind. His drawings excited me as dreams excited me—more than dreams, for even they were but memories by the time they reached the tongue.

But he wasn't there, Chris wasn't there and I couldn't bring any of his drawings to mind. I grasped at the emptied air, feeling as though I truly had transformed into something phantom-like.

Mother's voice sounded from a distance, calling my name. The thing inside of me quivered. I crouched deeper into the closet, pressing my face into the pillow. I willed myself into silence. I held my breath. I could hear my heart hammering. My lungs pounded for air. Mother's voice drew closer and the thing quivered harder. It kicked and fought. I pressed harder into the pillow. My head became light. I felt dizzy. I felt myself fading, fusing into the wall, the singing started. The thing was screaming, screaming in terror, it heard Mother's voice drawing closer, it screamed and screamed, it sluiced through my veins like iced water—

"Sylvie!"

The pillow slackened. I gulped for air, harsh, racking gulps. A small band of yellowish light fell before me. It lit lightly upon my back. It crept around my shoulders, it tightened, then grazed the back of my neck like a whisper.

"Sylvie."

The thing was all through me now, leaping like fire through my veins, scorching my heart, burning through my throat like a breath of hell as I screamed to Mother's touch. I beheld with a flash of clarity the thought that surely those who have not felt death have not felt God, for only in grief can eternity be felt; that such depth of pain, unconnected to skin and bones, exists in such magnitude it renders time and the tearing of flesh into nothingness.

Many other thoughts were to come to me that night as I crouched in the closet with Mother holding me from behind—some were mine, some from that crazy mix of dreams and consciousness, but mostly they came from my mother as she spoke in bits and pieces about so much. A mesh of words Mother cried that night, a mesh of words that I would form someday into a picture but that were too tangled now, too embroiled with Mother's tears and torment as she spoke of things known only to her: how the second I was brought into the world and cut from the cord she had named me—so's to anchor me to the living, and to stave off the unmarked tombstone, the one unseen beside her bed, the one she always dreamed about since the burying of her third baby. She had taken me from the midwife's hands, full of blood and gurry, and passed me to Gran, commanding, Bless her—bless her with the waters and say her name out loud, real loud, as loud as the cross so's to mark her place amongst the living. Sylvia. Sylvia Now. Then she took me to her breast and cried some more because her nipples wouldn't milk.

"Come out now, come, we'll have some tea," Mother kept pleading. But I couldn't, I couldn't remove my arms from around my belly, couldn't look into my mother's eyes, was frightened of them, frightened of seeing that look of wariness, of trepidation. Mother pleaded some more, her hands all the time caressing my shoulders and stroking my hair as she lay soft against me from behind, talking in quiet tones about faith, about hope, about how she should've named me Hope, not Sylvie, for she had lost faith with her three dying babies, and then I was born and I lived, "and you brought me hope. Each day you grew, my faith grew with you; least, that's what I thought it was back then—faith. And when Chrissy was born, I trusted—trusted that he would live; that you, my girl, was my seal from God, that he'd forgiven my sins, and I was now freed to love, to be a mother like all others. Each time I saw you popping around a corner I was awed that you still lived. The silliness of it—that I always believed if another was taken from my breast, it would've been you. And so I let Gran keep you, and I was afraid to love you. And I poured my love into Chris, but no matter how tightly I held him, I never felt full. I was the mother who cleaved her baby in half; I sacrificed one half for the other, and prowled every living day since, pining for them both. No matter how much I loved you, how hard I hugged you, I could never feel your heart. And I know you've never felt mine. And I wonders now if I ever really had faith, or was it hope of faith. We'll be tested now then, won't we," she cried, "for it's not real in our hearts just yet, is it—our Chrissy—only the shock of it."

They weren't the words of a mother soothing a hurt, lost child, but of the hurt, lost mother groping for her child. They caught my heart. They circled around me like rafts in a sea of pain. They trilled like songbirds through the stuffy darkness of the closet. They held the same bitter sweetness as the nightingale singing her song of love, impaled upon the thorn of a rose.

"Come. Come out," Mother sobbed into my ear.

"I want to die."

"Then who would mourn him?" she cried. "If we all gave in to feeling and jumped off the wharf, who would mourn him? Fault," she scoffed with a touch of her old stridency as I whimpered something about fault, "we speak of fault, yet we speak of God. You think He leaves us to the other's will? What of His will? Perhaps His plan was aborted too, aborted by chance. Perhaps accidents are the way of life, and it's for us to bring them meaning—"

"I said that once," I broke in with a cry, "I said that to him once, that suffering helped us find meaning."

"Then it's for us to give him meaning, his life. It's a hard matter, but I've always felt it's what we do with things that's the most important. It'll be hard, my baby, it'll be hard," sobbed Mother, "but we must try—we'll do it together, all of us. So, come on now, come out. We'll pour a bath and have tea. And I'm tired. I need you to help me sleep. It was so long on that plane, I thought I was going to the moon—my, Sylvie, it was a frightening thing being on that plane—will you come out now, help me make some tea?"

"Were you afraid?" I whispered.

"Yes, yes, I was afraid. But fear falters like everything else now, before the love of one's own. You come out now, we'll have some tea, will you please come out?"

I bore the same fear as when I stepped inside Chris's hospital room after they'd laid him out. Uncurling my arms, my legs, I turned slightly towards my mother. I rose upon my knees, but then pulled back, holding down my head like a frightened child, one hand on the closet door, ready to pull it shut.

"Here, I'll stand back," said Mother. "See, I'll stand back here. I'm going to turn on the light, just this small one here. There, it's just a small light. Look up now, will you please look up."

I looked up. Mother was standing by the bedroom door. Her face was pale, so terribly, terribly pale. She looked small, and was holding her hands. And for all that, she looked the fabled queen with her hair pretty in combs, her chin regal, defying death, her eyes glittering with tears. She flung apart her hands, reaching for me, her voice strong as she called me to her. And in that moment she was the mother of my youth, ruling wherever she stood, her senses seeking out each of her youngsters from our hiding spots, commanding the boys to her side, Gran back inside the house to rest, Father out of his cursed boat and rubber boots, and me to the garden to help with the weeding. Once, as I hid behind the sheets flapping on the line, I watched in amazement as she even challenged the crows that had just snatched another seed from her soil and were lurking now in the nearby branches.

———

HOURS LATER, after we'd shared tea with Ben and I'd bathed and was curled onto the bed, facing the wall, Mother came in and curled behind me, speaking of other things—one of them being how she used to crawl inside the darkened hollow of the tuckamores upon the cliffs of Cooney Arm after her third baby had died. And how, after she curled there long enough, the dark overtook her—no sight, no hearing, no touching and thinking, rendering her no more than an unborn soul. And then, after many, many days of everything shut down around her, and her thoughts taking up no more of her, she started feeling again.

"For that's what happens," Mother whispered, "when something hits us too hard, we stop feeling. And then we get scared, because without feeling it's like we're nothing but air, and things flow through us without even a twitch, and how fair is that, for them babies to die, and it all to flow through me without even a twitch. Things must have meaning. We love that which brings us joy, and yet we wouldn't know joy without sorrow, would we? Perhaps meaning goes no deeper than that, finding love. I think I'm learning that—my babies taught me some of that, they had purpose through death. How anyone with a child in the ground can sleep without knowing there's a purpose to death is beyond me. Their stay was brief, but they created much; they created a different kind of life in me, and it was from that life you came, and then Chrissy, and Kyle. I would never have known love if not for you, for Chrissy. No, my girl, the second coming is no mystery to me when I've been dead and born agin myself. And perhaps this will take me again—I don't know just yet; but right now there's a hard pulse in my veins as I lie here with you. And I don't care, I don't care nothing for me; it's for you that I lie here, I've not done right by you. I'm a hard learner, but if it was you lying dead in that hospital there wouldn't have been a hole big enough to bury my sorrow, for I've not done right."

Long after Mother slept I lay there, hearing her words, feeling them, thick and soft and entangling around me like a skein of Gran's wool. I tried to think back over the years, to try and see them through different eyes. But, unlike my mother as she cradled amongst the tuckamores all those years ago, thought was coiled too tightly around me just yet, leaving me with no frayed ends to follow back through the past and separate the pettiness from the passion, the girl from the woman.

The soft murmurs of the TV started up from the living room.

Ben.

I rose carefully, so's not to wake Mother, and crept down the hall. He was sitting on the floor, as he'd been the night before—or day—I wasn't sure, anymore, of time. He was fully dressed, with his boots on, his knees drawn up to his chest. His jacket was hanging on the back of a chair alongside.

He didn't look up as I sat beside him. I whispered his name. I whispered it again, as he hadn't moved, hadn't blinked to the sound of my voice. I touched his arm. It felt as though it were me now, drawing him out of some closet, some locked-away place.

A muscle throbbed in his jaw. He swallowed hard, then nodded as though he'd been waiting for my arrival. "Push has everything arranged," he said, his voice hoarse like a rusty hinge. "You'll have a driver—he'll take you around in the morning. The hospital. Your mother will want to see him." He rubbed his eyes with the heels of his hands, then drove his fingers roughly through his hair. "He'll take you to the airport after. The driver. It's all arranged. Push arranged everything."

He fell silent, his eyes fastened onto a mound of baggage by the door—Chris's knapsack, his sleeping bag. My knapsack and sleeping bag were there as well, and a couple of other bags. One of them had a jacket laid atop of it, Trapp's jacket.

His shadow stained the blackest of nights.

"He didn't report the kick," I said coldly. "To Push. It was his job to report to Push."

Ben looked at me, his eyes bleary. He was still drinking, I could smell it. "If it's fault you're looking for, then make it mine—and I wish you could," he ended harshly. "I wish you could make it mine. Or Trapp's. I wish I could give you that. But you don't believe it. You rather the fault was yours.

"Guilt," he mumbled into my silence and lifted his head towards the room where Mother was sleeping. "More than you wanting the guilt for this one, Sylvie." He lapsed into silence then, his eyes falling inward onto himself. "Should've gotten you out," he mumbled. "Should've gotten you both out."

"I can hear Gran now," I whispered. "She'd say none of us can rightly claim it—for there's no knowing where one thing leaves off and another begins. Or if we can even look at things that way."

He rubbed his eyes again, rubbed his temples, pulling his hands down over his face. "You thought I jumped, didn't you. You thought I jumped. Left him behind."

I stared mutely at Chris's sleeping bag.

"You didn't say it, but I heard you think it. I didn't jump without looking for him, I'm a stun fuck, but I looked for him—thought he'd gone to the doghouse—thought I seen him heading for the doghouse, grab a sandwich—he must've been down, he must've been already down!" He gripped his knees with his hands and I leaned towards him, laying my forehead against his chilled fingers.

"You loved him," I said. "I know you loved him."

He pulled me against his chest, cradling me, cradling me hard. "Not just him, not just him that I love," he muffled into my hair. "When I told you about Trapp, it was the biggest thing—yesterday it was the biggest thing, I know it means nothing to you now, it means nothing to me now, but yesterday it was the biggest thing, I needed you to know me, to understand—"

"I do, I do understand, why do you say it means nothing?" I drew back, looking at his face, at the dark beneath his eyes, almost bruised from repeatedly burrowing his face into the heels of his hands.

"He's left the camp," he said. "He's took only his truck. He's took it on. You know the weight of that."

And then I understood. He was leaving. He was leaving again. He was going for Trapp.

I drew my knees to my breasts, covering myself.

"There's no one," he said listlessly. "He's got no one. He's only got me—and he's out there somewhere—he's out there lost somewhere. Sylvie!" He grasped my arm as I lowered my forehead onto my knees with a groan of dejection. "Sylvie, what would you have me do?"

I looked at him. I snorted. "You saved his ass, what more will he have you do? You saved the rig, too—it was his job, but you saved it, him—you saved all of them—" My voice choked, it choked on a quiver of fear. "You can't leave me," I whimpered. "He'll come home, he'll just come home after a while."

He didn't speak. He hadn't heard me. My words were tiny, he hadn't heard them, for I'd spoken them in a whisper; the little-girl whisper that I used talking to Mother once in the quiet of my bedroom after I'd near frightened her to death in the abandoned house, and was then afraid of what I'd done, was afraid of my mother's fear, that my mother would leave me, that my mother would go into the graveyard with her three little dears who were once little girls like me and sink into their graves alongside of them and never come back.

"I hate change," I whispered. "I hate how things are all the time shifting, like Chris's lines, going from one thing to another, to another. Ohh, my," I choked on a sob and it was just then, sitting there alongside of Ben, with my mother sleeping in the other room and Chrissy laid out in some morgue across town, I saw that as much as I revered Chris's lines I feared them too. I feared those waves curling into fish, into nets, into our father, into the stars. As much as I loved them, drew comfort from their foretelling of another place, a nicer place for those three little dears than a dark, ugly grave, I was frightened of how life can be here by morning, gone by evening, and as I sat there crumpled beside Ben, I desired to make things concrete around me, like one of his bricks, like one of Ben's damn stupid bricks.

"He'll come home, Ben. He'll just come home."

"No. He won't. He'll not feel worthy." He pulled back, tugging at my arm for me to face him. "He's running, what you would've done. Your mother came and got you. I've got to go get him. I'm not thought out like you—that little boy—I can't just turf him out—I've got to see him through, somehow—don't even know what I mean by that, please." He held me in place as I tried to pull away. "Wait, just wait—" He faltered. He let go of me, cradling his face into his hands, fingertips rubbing harshly at his temples as though erasing some stain, some spot of dirt grained into his skin. He took my arm again. "Don't go yet, just wait, just—sit beside me, I hate to go, I don't want to go, I love it when you talk, I love it when you sit beside me talking, I don't know how I'll do this without you there——" He paused for breath, and was talking again, "I've got to find him, and then I'm coming home. I'm coming home soon as I find him——here, this is yours, this is so yours," and he pressed a book into my hand, a sketch pad—— Chris's sketch pad. He pressed it into my hand, already opened, already folded back.

Tears bubbled out of his eyes. "It was on his bed, it was opened and on his bed, it's his last thing that he drew." He kissed my cheek, my mouth. He pressed his forehead against mine and grasped my hand, pressing it to his lips. "Don't hate me," he whispered, and then he was on his feet, pulling his coat so hard off the chair that the chair toppled over. Hooking Trapp's knapsack over his shoulder, he bolted for the door, taking a glance towards Mother's room before letting himself quietly outside.

I sat huddling into my knees, waiting, thinking perhaps he'd come back. After a moment I rose and went to the window. Darkness crowded the sparse light thrown off by the street lamps. The sidewalks were emptied of people, a few parked cars alongside the curb. I hurt from where I was clutching the wired spine of the sketch pad against my chest. Chris's sketch pad. His last sketch. I turned to the light and held it before me, tracing his lines with my eyes.

It was a night sketch of our father sitting in his boat. He was sitting with his back to me, his face held towards the huge expanse of darkened sky. But his hair was light in colour, and longish, curled around his collar——it was him, Chris. It was both Chris and Dad. It was his dream. The both of them sitting as one in the boat, the water rippling beneath them as they held up a paddle, looking expectantly towards that other, more ancient sea, darkling amidst its stars. And there, in the upper left-hand corner, was an exaggerated star. I knew it at once.

Proud evening star. And somewhere quite near, but invisible to see, its virgin moon.

My hands trembled. Did he know? Did he know it was his last day? My mind flashed back to the argument I'd had with him that time in the car, driving to the hospital to see our father, and I had demanded of him why he hadn't left home yet. I remembered how upset he became, and how I had felt fear in him, that same fear as when we were youngsters hiding behind the house from some unknown force of fate. Had it been built inside of him, somewhere, this knowing of his fate?

My hands shook as I flipped through his other, more recent drawings: Billy the beaver scrolling into a dam, into a forest; Billy scrolling into a pond and the pond into grass. I flipped to another page, another image, and caught my breath. It was a drawing of three head lice on the palm of a hand. The hand was without definition, simply the lines creasing its centre and three large lice sitting there, unshaded. White. I gave a cry. I clutched the book tight to my heart, leaning weakly against the window.

I'd forgotten about that dream of his. I'd never told him what Gran told me once about white lice in dreams. I'd been but a girl when I dreamt of them, and they weren't white, they were brown, tiny and brown, and had fallen from my hair onto my scribbler. "That's a good dream, Dolly," said Gran as she searched frantically through my hair the following morning, "for it's the white lice in dreams that foretells death."

Another memory seized me. It was before we left Cooney Arm, and he'd drawn a planet with three moons. Said he dreamt it. I saw pretty much the same picture later in a textbook after we left Cooney Arm. I remember this feeling of—of surprise, at first, that Chris could draw such a thing without first knowing it. And then awe. Because it pointed me towards something, those images that came without thought, that came out of nowhere, and yet somewhere, because, as the old thinkers said, nothing can come from nothing.

Clutching tighter to the sketch pad I laughed, tears wetting my face. I needn't have feared Chris standing gutted on a wharf like Father with his rotting boat and stage after the fish had gone. The thing Chris created lived in my hands, his breath upon my face. He had found that heavenly room, he'd never been without it. It had housed him in his flesh as I bungled unseeingly into walls of my own construct. It was housing him now as I stood there, understanding his lines. The thought came to me that undoubtedly we are but shadows, our thoughts shifting like clouds, never returning to what they once were, always searching for elsewhere. And yet some things are more solid than rock. He, my brother, was a one true love in my life. And his death, as was his birth, a wealth I would forever feed upon. Another thought struck me, that I need never fear how Chris's lines transmute from one thing to another, for we are too like them, we are never born and we never die, like the waters in a flooded riverbank, simply finding different channels along which to flow.

Ben appeared on the sidewalk below, Trapp's knapsack hanging limply from his hand, a slight shiver from the cool night air tensing his shoulders. He stood still as stone inside the light of a street lamp, the black of his curls glimmering like onyx. A cab cruised by, easing to a stop beside him. He raised his eyes to where I was watching him. I willed him to turn from the cab, to walk back in through the doors of the hotel, to come back to me. But I knew he wouldn't. He was wearing his resolute look again, his eyes piteous, pleading once again for understanding.

Without intent I slowly shook my head. His eyes fell. He opened the cab door and stood aside, as though expecting someone to hop in before him. Then he lowered himself onto the seat, a figure of such loneliness that my heart ached for him as it ached for my own loneliness. As it ached for my mother, who was surely lying awake in her room, lost in the quiet of her own thoughts. As no doubt Gran was ruminating through her own aged mind right now, perhaps rocking for comfort in her rocker, the soft yellow light from her lamp shrouding her shoulders. And Dad. Was he not hunching over his spot at the table, gripping a hot mug of tea whilst his eyes searched through the oncoming waves for reason? Kyle, I knew, would be in the woodshed, his elbows propped on his knees, chewing the sides of his thumbnail whilst his eyes chewed through bits of rind unfurling from the birch junks, struggling to see what Chris might see, but thwarted by his own unlearned self.

Without bidding, my thoughts went to Trapp. Took nothing but his truck. Most likely nose-deep in another ditch, with only his self to blame and his tortured thoughts for company. A twinge of pity stirred in the shrunken sphere of my heart, and I regretted shaking my head to Ben's imploring look begging for understanding, for sympathy for Trapp. For in the end we are all but solitary souls, seeking little more from the moment than the right to be in it, and the right to be understood.

The cab carrying Ben sped off down the road. I remembered back to a talk with Myrah, bemoaning the huge want I felt in my heart and was always trying to fill with romantic love. Watching Ben speed off in the cab, I waited for that feeling to again consume me. Curiously, my heart felt too full of other things now, and I wondered if it would ever feel want in quite the same way again. For I knew now that it was never a need for someone that I felt but simply a desire to return home, to that room Chris always felt in his heart, the one that fed him contentment, no matter which wharf or rock he sat upon.

A cough, or perhaps a cry, a soft cry sounded from my mother's room. Holding Chris's sketch to my heart, I hurried to her bedside.

EPILOGUE

THE SCREAMING OF THE SAWMILL falls blissfully quiet. I sit on the wharf, hunched against the side of the house, listening to the water lap around the pilings. The woods are black now, the sky dusted with stars, the moon silvery on the sea. Gran's voice sounds softly through the window as she asks Kyle to light her lamp and take it to her room. Since the accident she no longer sleeps without her lamp lit.

"No, no, I'm not scared of ghosts," she tutted as I teased her once, "it's just another blanket I wraps up in." And she drew down amidst her bedding, becoming little more than a ripple with a few greyish-white hairs spread across her pillow.

A light flares through the kitchen window, falling softly around my shoulders as Kyle strikes a match to the wick and fits on the chimney. I hear Mother calling out to him, cautioning him, "Be careful now, careful you don't drop the lamp, I'll come and comb your hair, Gran, you get in bed now, I'll be right there." More light pours through the kitchen window as Mother switches on the overhead light and calls out, "Sylvanus, go mix your tea, I've poured it for you, it's on the sink, go mix your tea now, I sees to Gran—Gran—" and her voice fades as she goes down the hall to Gran's room. She spends a lot of time in the room with Gran since the accident, the both of them talking in slow, steady murmurs, like a brook unimpeded by rock and softened with a thick edging of grass. I listened shamelessly once, on my way to the bathroom, caught by something Gran was saying to Mother, about a gun and a promise Mother made to her once, about burying Grandfather Now's gun with her in her coffin when she dies, for he was never given prayers or a burial, she rambled on to Mother—as she has taken to doing lately—he was never marked with the cross, and that's why he's never found peace for she could never let him go, and be sure and say prayers for them both, she begged Mother, and mark the graves with two crosses, one for each them, and to pay no heed to them gawking at the gun in her coffin, for it matters nothing to her what's said after she's dead, only that Grandfather finds peace after all this time, because for sure he must be wearied, poor soul, searching all these years for his grave.

The kitchen light switches off, leaving me comforted in darkness again. I hear the scraping of Father's chair. He's mixed his tea, and if I had leaned forward before he shut off the light I would've seen him through the window, his scruffy black hair uncombed as it always is about the house, his brows dark and heavy as he broods into his tea. Mostly, at night, he sits with the light off—so's he can see the water and not himself in the damn glass, he argues with Mother. But mostly it's because he likes sitting alone in the dark. He sits there for hours during most evenings, watching the water. Tonight his boat shimmers in the moonlight. His boat is white, he painted it white, for he says it, too, is a tombstone, a tombstone for fish.

Luckily, he doesn't spend much time on the water anymore, leastways, not the sea. He was offered a job on the river. His heart isn't strong, but his body is, and he can go for days without becoming winded. It's a small job, erecting a salmon fence, then counting the salmon to see how many are spawning each year, and plus, policing the river for poachers. It's a godsend, the job on the river. Not just for the food it puts on the table but for the long periods of time it gives him away from the house. Sometimes I walk with him for a short ways, up to the falls. It's not really a falls, just enough of a dip to churn the waters and dampen the air.

The other morning as we walked alongside the river he was notably quiet and glum. We sat for a bit near the little falls, and he told me his favoured brother, Uncle Manny, was laid off from the fish plant, and was leaving for Toronto.

"No fish in the offshore waters, now," he said sullenly. "All gone the way of the inshore—as we all said it would happen. Gawd-damned arse-up government. Soon there'll be nothing living in the water. Barren. Imagine that, the ocean barren." He fell silent, staring at the river rushing past our feet. I studied his face, wearying with time, weathered with salt. He lifted his dark eyes onto mine and I drew back, feeling sickish. All those times I'd seen him coming ashore in his boat with the water foaming like mad dogs beneath him, and setting off into the woods with the winds screaming through trees and blinding his path, and it was now, only now, sitting safe on the river, with the sun warming his face and his feet dry in his boots, that I saw fear in my father's eyes. Fear for his brother Manny, who had lived his life on the sea and was moving to a factory job in the city; Manny, who had lived his life amongst three dozen people, now moving to a city of three million. Jeezes, and Father shivered in his boots, dipping his hands into the river as though assuring himself it was there and not some illusion he might wake up from and then have to pack his bags like his brother and turn his back to his only salvation.

No wonder the houses of Cooney Arm are haunted, I thought. Fishermen like my father, his brothers, may have moved on, but, as with the linoleum on the floor, the hinges and locks on the doors they left behind, so too are their spirits still back there, hooked into the generations that lived on the land and in those houses before them. I was reminded of the day spent with Ben and Chris on the pond with the beaver dam, and Chris asking me about the ghosts in the walls of Cooney Arm, and asking me what they wanted, "For they're of your own making," he had said, "so you should know what they want."

I wondered many times about that, whether the ghosts were of my own making. And yes, yes, they are of my own making. And we all carry them, and we all create them. But, as with the sobbing little boy in Ben's heart, that didn't make them any less real. And it came to me that day as I sat facing the river with Father, and seeing his fear, that I suddenly knew what they wanted, those ghosts in the walls of Cooney Arm. They wanted to be freed from those walls, freed from the confusion and blindness of times since passed, and brought forward into the mindfulness of the living. Just as those parts of me, those marooned, stifled parts of me snagged on feelings of invisibility around my mother, had been brought forward into my awareness.

"You'll be happy here, working the river," I said to Father. "Factories aren't something you'll have to worry about."

He looked to the heavens with a prayer of thanks on his lips, and then ordered me back to the house so's he could carry out his work in peace. I left him as he'd asked. He had the river now. I remember Chris saying in the cookhouse that last morning how Father liked it best sitting in his boat by himself. A few times I thought to tell Father that, how Chris could see into his mind, for I thought he'd like it, Chris understanding how he felt about things.

But I didn't. He doesn't talk about Chris. He doesn't allow any of us to talk about Chris. Once when Kyle said his name at the supper table, Father threw down his fork and left the table and went to bed. He was drinking. He carried a small mickey in his inside coat pocket. It was his secret, and I didn't tell. We all have our opiates, and booze was becoming Father's.

The moon darkens behind a cloud, and I hear Father scraping his chair away from the table, saying something to Mother about bedtime. She must've been talking with Gran all this time, for her voice sounds tired as she speaks to Father, chiding him about the lights being out. They flare back on, as they are whenever Mother is about. She had always liked the lights on, flushing darkness along with dust balls out of corners. And as I listen to her voice sounding over the water lapping about the pilings, I am grateful for her need of light. I have learned that my great fear of things changing and rotting around me, my fear of death, came from a darkness that was constantly and poignantly signified by those three little white crosses. And I wonder, in looking back, how it was I'd never seen the fourth, marking the living grave where I had been burying my childhood feelings of invisibility.

I hear Father's chair scraping away from the table. I hear Kyle trodding back to the kitchen, creaking himself into Gran's rocker. He's had a growth spurt these past few months. But he still has those rounded, chubby cheeks, and his squinty eyes always carry a hue of smiles around them, no matter his brow buckling into frowns or his shoulders slumping with dejection. His shoulders look perky this evening as he munches on a ginger snap, they're always perky when he's munching cookies, like the cow with its cud, Mother says of the contented look on Kyle's face as he munches; if he had a tail, he'd be swishing it.

We always smile. Rather him munching cookies than chewing his fingers, a habit he keeps up with a vengeance since the accident. He, like Father, turns from me each time I try to talk, to bring our brother into the space between us. I wonder if he blames me, but I've seen him turning from Mother, too, and Gran. Still, I wonder.

A few weeks ago, about midnight, I'd been unable to sleep and had gone for a drive in Father's truck. I spotted him in my rearview mirror as I slowly drove past the club. It was a cold night, with an easterly wind driving hard. The bar had closed and Kyle was huddling against its back door, his hands jammed inside his pockets, looking lonely and cold. I backed up, and he eagerly climbed aboard.

"What were you waiting for, to be beamed home?" I asked gently.

He grinned, settling into a chew on the side of his thumbnail. We were near home when he said, "I had a dream."

It was the way he said it that drew me. His tone was soft, yet urgent, as though it held something precious. "I was in the shed," he went on, "stacking wood. And a voice spoke—kinda like it was speaking through me—I could feel it in my ribs. It was Chris. It was Chris's voice. And he said, 'You are a king.'" Kyle paused, looking at me. "It felt so real," he exclaimed. "It felt so real that I touched my head when I woke up, thinking I had a crown." Then he shrugged, as though it were a nothing dream.

"Did it leave you with something?" I asked him. "Like, when you woke up, did you feel—different?"

He nodded. "Felt good. Like this nicest feeling." He started back chewing his fingers, saying no more. I tried to think of something to say. I didn't need to, though; Chris's dream spoke louder than me at that moment, and carried more significance.

A night breeze ruffles the water. I huddle deeper into my sweater. Mother's in the kitchen again, chiding Kyle for being up so late, ushering him off to bed. "Sylvie!" she calls. "Kyle, is your sister in?"

"Think so." Kyle's door closes softly. I more feel than hear Mother coming across the kitchen and I hunch closer to the house, making myself small so's not to be seen should she look through the window. Her footsteps fade as she walks back down the hallway, closes her door. She's like that since the accident, wanting us all inside before she goes to bed, taking several walkabouts sometimes before finally settling into sleep.

Most times I like her fussing. But there are times when I wish to be alone. When I wish to think on dreams. For I dream too, now. Not often—and they're coming further and further apart. But for now, they are my cookie bag, my father's whisky. They leave me with something. Like Gran, I want the lights on at night, and lie for long hours on my bed some evenings, watching the quivering flame of Gran's lamp on the ceiling, unable to sleep yet sensing life ebb away from me on the outside and become two rivers of feeling within me, one flowing towards time and tomorrow, the other flowing backwards, seeking its source. It feels like those times I used to stand by the footbridge in Cooney Arm, looking towards Mother's house and looking back to Gran's, always feeling halfways home. Sometimes I have to stave off thought before lowering the wick and turning into my pillow, so's to clear an empty space in case he should come tonight. For like Grandfather Now, I am his stormy sea that he needs to sit and keep watch over during those nights I flounder amidst dreams of self-damnation, no matter my declarations of innocence during daylight thinking hours.

He doesn't awaken me. For he understands the way of dreams, that they speak in the language of the netherworld that exists beneath words and clouded thought; he understands that dreams are our truth beneath our language of lies, those lies that we will ourselves to believe but deep, deep down we don't believe at all. And when finally the waters abate, either from exhaustion or some disturbance, like Kyle coughing in the next room or Mother's door creaking as she takes another walk through the house, he comes. Like a beacon of light he is with me. The place always changes, but his heart is one with mine.

The first time he came we were in a green room, the colour of my room in Gran's house, and he was lying on the bed beside me; he was naked and his skin felt like crushed velvet as he held my sobbing body next to his, assuring me, It's not your fault, Sis, it's not your fault.

Another time he sat on the edge of the bathtub as I scrubbed my face over the sink, and he asked me how he'd died, that he had no knowing of how it happened, only that it had.

Another time he told me it was fine to grieve because he was grieving, too—it's like that here, he said, we grieve too, for a while.

Each time he comes I am his troubled sister, searching for peace. Each time he leaves I awaken to a warm heart and a stomach that feels like it's floating on a sea of love. For hours I walk or simply sit, revelling in such utter tranquility it feels as though I'm drugged, beautifully drugged. By midmorning I'm lying on my bed again, the pain in my belly so deep I'm unable to straighten my legs.

But he's becoming weary, now. And he's coming less and less, his precious gifts of tranquility becoming shorter and shorter. Once, I offered him a job, sweeping the school floors, a safe job. He looked at me sadly, no longer able to speak. He is fading, yet I hold on to him. I weigh him like an anchor. I am his ghost, no different from the haunts in Cooney Arm, anchoring him to a life he can no longer live. And in being his ghost, I have imprisoned parts of myself once more. Like Gran,

I must learn to let go. I must learn to relinquish him so's we can both be freed. Else, like Grandfather Now, he will become little more than a restless phantom, a haunt to himself and the life he once lived. And I, a slave once more to split-off parts of me, and perhaps this time with no caring Mother being able to deliver me from the darkness.

In time, I will let go. But not yet. Just not yet. And I already know that it will be Chris who releases me … but that is another story …

There is one last thing—I will speak quickly. Ben made it home for the funeral, but then left again. Not for Trapp this time. He'd brought Trapp home as he intended, left him fishing for shrimp and crab alongside his father and uncles in Ragged Rock. Ben's travelling for himself now. To find himself, he said. He looked sheepish in saying that, for it sounded clichéd.

As a gift, I gave him back his own words—those words he'd spoken to me that long, dark night when I had lain inside a closet and he stroked my hair, saying in a low, throaty whisper, "Gotta do your own creating now … don't matter if you can't draw, can't write … just gotta find something that's yours, a thought … one unique thought … only it has to be true, true to you … and there you are, your own creator."

And so he's out there somewhere, charting his own map. As I sit here, charting mine. Perhaps someday we will join trails again. But only for a while. In the end, we all travel alone.

I must go now, because Mother is calling—she checked my room, and now she's calling—it must be a restless night for her and she needs me safely inside. I look to the sky again. It stretches through the night like one warm blanket, covering me, covering Mother, covering Trapp, too, in his uneasy bed—covering all of us, the one slumbering child being guided through the dark corridors of sleep.

ACKNOWLEDGMENTS

THANK YOU to Mary Nutting, South Peace Regional Archives, Grande Prairie; right-wing, gun-toting redneck Barry Laporte; Karen Douglas, City of Grande Prairie; Michael O'Conner, prairie man of many hats; and spirited friends and neighbours Donald and Laurene Brown.

Thank you to my editors, Cynthia Good, Diane Turbide, David Weale, and Sandra Tooze, and to my agent, Beverley Slopen.

Thank you to that Big Iron Cavalier and tool push Rick Pelham; roughnecks David Collie and Dan Bignell; and for his remembrance of past journeys together, driller Lance Morrissey.

Thank you to Jane Buss at the N.S. Writers' Federation, the N.S. Council for the Arts, Dr. Lynn McAslan, and to John W. Doull's feel for the concrete.

Many blessings upon David Weale, Michael Chadwick, Roy Gould, Elaine Hann, Edward MacDonald, and Ron Lehr for their provocations and inspirations.

And for their countless cups of tea, glasses of wine, and pounds of chocolate, I thank Anita Dalton, Jackie Sunderland, Corrine Corbett, Mary Lynk, Mo Jo Anderson, Ismet Ugursal, Julia Hategan, and Cindy and Paul Douglas.

Most especially, I want to thank my fireside friend, Rick Ormston.

What They Wanted

A Penguin Readers Guide

ABOUT THE BOOK

What They Wanted, Donna Morrissey's fourth novel, is set in two very different yet similarly severe environments: the depleted, sea-battered outport of Hampden, Newfoundland, and the nightmarish atmosphere of an Alberta oil rig. While vividly revealing the hardship and beauty of these worlds, Morrissey explores how members of the Now family (first introduced in her award-winning book *Sylvanus Now*) grapple with notions of home, love, regret, and forgiveness.

Sylvie Now, the novel's narrator, returns to Newfoundland to visit her father, Sylvanus, in the hospital after he suffers a heart attack. Having left their small, struggling outport a few years before to study in St. John's and then to work as a waitress in oil-rich Alberta, Sylvie has no idea what to expect.

She's not sure how long she'll stay, and she doesn't know what it will feel like to be back in the house of her mother, Adelaide, a house that while Sylvie was growing up—despite being surrounded by her beloved brothers, Gran, and father—never quite felt like home.

In a story that spans two decades, Sylvie details life growing up in the Now household—her deep connection to her father, her mother's estrangement, a past haunted by the "three little dears" who died before Sylvie's birth, and her own childhood fascination with the dead and their spirits—as well as the emotionally complex adventure she undertakes with her brother Chris.

At the hospital in Corner Brook where Sylvanus is being treated, it quickly becomes clear that his physical condition will make it impossible for him to work and support his family. But Sylvie is paid handsomely by the men working in the booming oil industry, and she knows she can send enough money home to look after her family. The middle child, Chris, a dreamy, talented artist, also knows that fast money can be made on the oil rigs, and for reasons of pride and guilt, he secretly decides to accompany his sister when she heads back.

Sylvie has always encouraged Chris to leave Hampden to pursue his artistic career—much to the dismay of their mother, who dotes on her son—but even she questions his decision to travel west. Oil rigs are dangerous places, and Sylvie worries about her brother. This concern increases when they arrive in camp, and Sylvie's long-time love interest, Ben, a troubled man with his own secrets, has already secured Chris a job as a roustabout on a rig.

Quitting her bar job in Grande Prairie, Sylvie begins work as a cook on the oil rig where Chris, Ben, and another man from their childhood—the nefarious Trapp—are employed. It's an unearthly environment of unrelenting noise and tension, and the experience ends in a tragedy that ultimately offers opportunity for understanding and hope. As with all of Morrissey's books, this story is an emotional odyssey in which the characters struggle with unresolved conflicts and desires and the questions that arise from displacement. n

AN INTERVIEW WITH DONNA MORRISSEY

Q: You've mentioned that *What They Wanted* was supposed to have been a part of *Sylvanus Now*. What made you decide to tell the stories separately? How did you know that this narrative needed to be its own entity?

Sylvanus Now became a more in-depth story than I originally thought. I hadn't planned on delving so deeply into Addie's depression or the plight of the fishing industry. But as I got deeper into the book, I realized Addie needed her own story told from the inside out, and most certainly, Sylvanus and his struggle with the declining fishing industry demanded more than part of a book. Alas, we have to go where the story takes us. n

Q: One review of the book mentioned that you wrote the first draft in third person. What compelled you to change the point of view to first person? How is the story made stronger by telling it from Sylvie's perspective?

What They Wanted is based on the true-life experience of my brother and me. It was very difficult to stand outside the story and see it objectively. Writing it in the third person gave me the emotional distance I needed. Once I was able to see the story objectively, I went back to page one and told it from the first person.

Given that it is such a personal story for me, telling it through Sylvie's eyes was the best means by which I could get close to the bone, to really bring the reader into her psyche and understand her. Plus, given that it is largely my story, I couldn't imagine anyone else telling it besides Sylvie. ⁿ

Q: How did the process of writing this book compare with writing your others? Was telling the difficult story of your experience in Alberta more challenging? More meaningful?

This is certainly the most difficult book I've written, simply because of the emotional investment it demanded. I was very tight-chested writing it ... it resurrected emotion in me that I had long since buried. But I knew this would happen ... it's why I waited such a long time to write it. Certainly it is the most meaningful of my stories. Thus far ... ⁿ

Q: Did you ever consider writing a non-fiction book about your experiences on the oil rig? Is fiction always your vehicle for storytelling?

Naw, I could never write non-fiction. I like the creative energy ... I like the suspense of where fiction is going to take me. It is the only creative outlet for me. I can't do anything else, except weed gardens. Love doing that. ⁿ

Q: Sound plays an integral role in this book. For example, Sylvie seems to hear the sea in her father's chest when she first visits him in the hospital. The morning she leaves for Alberta, she recognizes the first sounds she must have heard: gulls, ocean waves, sounders. And in Alberta, the unremitting roar of the rig, Cook's rattling cough. Do you pay particular attention to sound when you're writing a scene?

I pay attention to all of the senses when I'm writing. I close my eyes, and I try to see, feel, hear, smell what a setting brings. It's critical for bringing a reader into the setting of a story. It's a critical tool for me—writing through the senses—for it helps me define the tone and mood of each scene; it helps me to present the personality of my characters, their mood. n

Q: At the end of the book, Adelaide says in conversation with Sylvie, "Perhaps accidents are the way of life, and it's for us to bring them meaning." Are your books ways of bringing meaning to the accidents?

Writing for me is a way of understanding life. It helps me delve deeper into character and learn the psychology of that character, to understand the archetypes reigning within us. It pushes me to learn from the old philosophers, history. There's much that I learn in looking for a character or setting or in psychological behaviours that never makes its way into the book. I love researching, but most of it never reaches the page or else it gets edited out before the book is printed. n

Q: Did you find it necessary to travel back to Alberta while writing the book? Were there parts of the story that required further research?

No, I didn't have to travel back to Alberta ... at least, not the rigs. I remember them as though it were yesterday. Those things I didn't know—the inner workings of the rig—I learned from several rough-necks who gave me their time. Google is also a writer's best friend—gawd, it was tedious learning the parts of a rig and how they all fitted together. And then in the end, as I already said, most everything I sweated over understanding got edited out. n

Q: Do you read for inspiration? What kinds of stories do you find yourself drawn to?

I read all the time. I read the classics, I read psychology, philosophy, ancient history, space stuff ... I go through stages where all I want to do is read, when I want for nothing but to be a student. But then my bank account signals, and I gotta go to work. n

Q: What are you working on now?

I've recently started a new novel. It opens in the town of Stevenville in Newfoundland (surprise, surprise) but then migrates to Halifax. And that's all I want to say about that ... Did I just quote Forrest Gump??? n

DISCUSSION QUESTIONS

1. Why do you think Morrissey chose the title *What They Wanted*? How does "want" play a pivotal role in the book?

2. How does Sylvie and Chris's relationship change throughout the novel? Does their interaction in Alberta differ from their interaction in Newfoundland?

3. If not for his father's heart attack and his guilt about losing the boat, do you think Chris would have left Newfoundland?

4. The night before Sylvie and Chris travel to Alberta, Sylvie asks Gran why everyone gets so upset when someone leaves the bay, and Gran answers, "From the way we used to live, I suppose. All by ourselves, getting what we wants from the other. When somebody leaves then, we feels crippled." Yet, in the same conversation Gran declares, "But you got to go." Why do you think Gran feels they must go?

5. How did you respond to Chris's drawings? What did they tell you about him?

6. The only time Sylvie sees fear in her father's eyes is when he imagines being forced to leave the bay. Where do you think this fear comes from? Do you think he felt fear when Chris and Sylvie left?

7. Why do ghosts, spirits, and shadows populate this book? What do you think Morrissey is saying about memory? About what it means to be haunted?

8. As a girl, Sylvie often hid in a closet near the porch hoping to see one of the ghosts in the walls. After Chris's fatal accident, Sylvie hides once more in a closet in her hotel room. Why do you think she does this? And what finally changes inside her to allow her to leave that dark hiding space?

9. We get to know Trapp only through other characters' perceptions of him. He is a character who haunts the book from beginning to end, but we never know exactly what he's thinking. Why do you think Morrissey decided to present Trapp in this way?

10. Do you think that Sylvie eventually comes to understand Ben's need to look after Trapp? Why do you think she initially rails against it so vehemently? What does it reveal about her own feelings regarding freedom and responsibility?

11. At one point in the novel Sylvie says, "No matter whose table I was sitting at, or how sweet the jam, it always felt like I was just halfways home." The book begins with the Now home being literally split in two. Does Morrissey offer a definition of home? What do you think home means to Sylvie? Does this change throughout the book?